SIR ARTHUR'S LEGACY  BOOK 3

CONQUERING WILLIAM

SARAH EDWARDS

Cover: Deranged Doctor Design
First Electronic Edition: October 2019
ISBN: 978-1-990731-07-5
ISBN: 978-1-990731-04-4

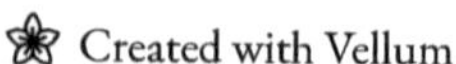 Created with Vellum

Chapter One

If she lived to be a hundred, Alice never wanted to attend another wedding, particularly not as the bride. The odor of roasting meats almost undid her, and she took a long draught from her water goblet. A bride did not vomit all over her wedding feast.

Her father, face ruddy with wine, sidled up and pinched her side. "God's teeth! Smile, you stupid wench. I have found you a good 'un this time. Far better than a whey-face like you could hope for." Goblet held high, he strode away, sprinkling wine across the heads of those he passed. His forced laughter grated on her ear.

To her right, her groom drank from his goblet. In a deep, smooth voice, he murmured to his mother on his other side. As he shifted, his muscular thigh pinned her skirt to the bench.

Loathe to draw his attention, Alice tugged the dull brown wool.

He inclined his head with a smile, moved his leg, and freed her skirt. "I beg your pardon."

God save her from her beautiful husband. "No matter."

"May I serve you more water?" Eyes deeper blue than the lake

1

beneath the castle twinkled at her. Candlelight gleamed off his dark hair and clung to his finely etched face.

"Thank you, but nay."

With another smile, he turned back to his mother.

She would prefer if he did not smile so much. Or did not smell so appealing. His subtle woodsy-sweet spice teased her every time he leaned nearer. He did quivering things to her innards. How could she hope to hold a man such as this? Atop the scarred table, their trencher sat between them, still full of mutton, gravy oozing into a brown puddle on the table. It couldn't be worse. Her father had outdone himself this time. Four husbands he'd chosen for her and this one, by far, the most daunting.

Aye, but William of Anglesea would make fine children. Tall, strong boys, broad and powerfully built like their sire, and girls to take after his mother and sisters. A child of her own. A downy head nestled against her breast, a tiny body cradled in her arms. She touched her palm to her flat, empty belly, and put her hand back on the table before anyone could notice. Even whey-faces had their dreams.

A jester before the dais capered about, ringing his bells and doing his best to enthuse the assembly with joviality. Poor man raised only titters of amusement. He must have come with her father for the wedding, for they had no resident jester at Tarnwych. A few determined souls cheered the jester on his way, and a band of minstrels took his place. The cheery pipes led the lutes into songs praising the bride's beauty and the groom's virility. Could they not spare her those? She'd wager the minstrels would change their songs when they left for the inn tonight.

The bawdy ballad of Alice of Tarnwych and William of Anglesea. She made up her own words to the cheerful wedding song the minstrel band warbled.

> *The peacock ruts with a dull, brown wren,*
> *A dull brown wren, a dull brown wren*

The peacock ruts with a dull, brown wren,
Fa-la-la-la-la.

William, the peacock, with his striking looks and finery had stood beside her in the chapel, and the top of her head had only reached his shoulder. How the ladies in attendance had sighed as he dipped his dark head and recited his vows to her—the dull little wren in her brown wool dress with her atrocious hair confined to a wimple. Both William's sisters boasted glorious flaxen hair the hue of summer wheat, not brazen red. Willowy and graceful they glided in rich, silk slippers like butterflies, whilst she stomped around in her sensible clogs.

Sister Julianna leaned in and kept her voice low. "This is a bad business. This family is sown with wild, spoiled seed."

Then there was that. Whispers of the taint on Sir Arthur's beautiful family carried even this far north.

"It is time." Gracious and lovely, Lady Mary of Anglesea rose with a sweet smile for Alice. "Shall we?"

"Aye, let us get to the meat of the matter." Smug grin eating his face, her father thumped the table.

Rising too, Sir William offered his hand to her. Grip warm and sure, he helped her climb over the bench, then straightened her skirts for her. No fault could she find with her groom's manners. As far as she could see, he had no faults at all. Men like William should marry their faultless equals. How different would this be if she looked like his mother and sisters? If she could enter his bed with her head held high, confident in her groom's delight in her beauty.

The other women stood with her. Lady Faye, flawless and serene in her pregnancy, golden hair framing her enchanting face. Her second new sister-in-law, Beatrice. Bea, they called her, and on occasion Sweet Bea. Not as fair as Faye, but her pretty countenance made more so by the lively march of humor across it.

God mocked her by surrounding her with all this overbearing comeliness.

"Come along, then." Beatrice's smile stretched false with forced good cheer. Nay, they no more welcomed this match for their brother than she did.

Another wedding night and she would endure.

* * *

Drained, her face stiff from forcing a smile, Alice tottered to the bed and perched on the edge.

Sister Julianna shut the door on the determinedly cheery faces of Sir William's womenfolk. "I would not have you suffer those women at such a time." Sister Julianna slid the bolt home. "It is bad enough your father ties you in marriage to such a family."

"Lady Mary seemed most gracious." William's mother had made a point of wishing her well and welcoming her to the family, pressing a kiss on her cheek after the ceremony.

"Poor woman." Sister Julianna smoothed the front of her pristine scapula. "Beset by such a husband. Your father may have forgotten Sir Arthur took his army and marched on King John, but those of us who value loyalty have not."

"They say the new king has forgiven him." Even this far north, King John's infamy had touched their lives. Long, hard winters had marked the late king's reign.

"King Henry is but a child. We must pray that the guidance of his guardian, the Holy Father, will prevail." Sister Julianna crossed herself and raised her eyes to the roof. "We must pray that...abomination never takes up residence beneath this roof."

"Amen," Alice whispered, because Sister would expect it. She hadn't yet seen the child Sister called the Abomination of Anglesea, but she knew no child should bear such a name. They had named him Mathew. Several years younger than his siblings, he must suffer a lonely existence with his brothers and sisters getting wed and moving away. If not for Sister Julianna's presence through her childhood, she would have wandered her father's keep for days without a soul bidding her good morrow, or even playing with her. Sister had not played, but she had provided company for a motherless little girl. Certainly, her father found no favor in his only child, a plain and quiet disappointment to him all these years.

"This is not your first wedding night." Sister Julianna folded her hands before her.

"Nay." It was her fourth, and she was as nervous as a first-time bride. Sir William unsettled her, left her stomach tangled. He would enter this chamber and find her not like the women he had known before. The ladies liked William of Anglesea. Her father had made sure to tell her so. All the loveliest ladies of the court flocked to him. Rubbing his huge hands together with glee, her father had informed her of her good fortune, congratulating himself on the rich prize he had landed.

"You know what to expect." Sister turned her about and worked on the lacings of her bliaut. "As is fitting, you must submit to your husband. It is the lot of women to suffer the bestial nature of men."

"Aye, Sister." Alice clasped her shaking hands together. She had done this before, her virginity long gone. What came next would be uncomfortable, a little painful, but her husband would satisfy his carnal urges and leave her.

"I am afraid he looks like a lustful one." Sister tugged her bliaut off. She brought Alice her nightrail and slipped it over her head.

Beneath the garment, Alice wriggled out of her chemise. Sister insisted on modesty at all times. "I see my wedding nightrail survived the moths."

"Indeed." Sister bent and snatched her chemise. "I laid it amongst layers of bay leaves, in case you would have need of it again. The devil employs wanton waste to his own ends. Our Lord frowns on excess."

Alice pushed her arms into the sleeves. Aye, she had worn it but once when her last husband had joined her on their wedding night. The linen retained its pristine white, the tiny blue flowers she had embroidered along the neck as perfect as when she had stitched them. She had not worn a new gown for her wedding, so it stood to reason she would not wear a new nightrail. Lady Faye had worn the most beautiful gown of deep blue samite, and Beatrice just as resplendent in emerald green. Alice would wager silk felt sinful and soft, like a constant caress on the skin.

She removed her wimple and handed it to Sister, who arranged it on the clothes tree beside her bliaut and chemise, ready for her to don in the morning.

With deft fingers, Sister braided Alice's unfortunate hair. In open defiance to its brazen red, her hair grew thick and wavy, almost touching the back of her thighs when unbound. She only freed it long enough for washing. Such a color hair spoke ill of the morals of its wearer. Devil's hair, Sister called it. Alice's burden and her shame. Secretly, when Sister was not about, Alice left her hair free. A tiny act of vanity that would bring Sister's wrath down on her head if she knew.

Icy flags chilled Alice's feet as she padded to the bed and eased beneath cold linens. She would grow warm soon enough. Straw poked through the thin pallet, and she wriggled to get comfortable.

"Get yourself with child." Sister stood at the foot of the bed. "The purpose of marriage is to bear children. This"—she waved a thin hand at the bed—"is an evil to be endured until the Lord blesses you."

Alice tucked her cold hands beneath her thighs. Teeth chattering, she managed no more than a nod. She should have braved the lecture and requested a fire. Only when her father made one of his rare visits did this rule get broken. Father preferred the comforts of Yarborough over Tarnwych.

"I will wait until he finishes with you." Sister shuddered as she studied Alice. "Remain steadfast, my child."

The door shut behind Sister with a muted thud. A small taper on the washstand flickered in the draft. Shadows clung to the corners of the chamber, making ghostly patterns on the unadorned walls.

Alice tucked the covers beneath her chin and waited.

The peacock ruts with a dull brown wren,
Fa-la-la-la-la.

* * *

William's bride, so tiny he could tuck her in his pocket, left the hall with a gaggle of women. Amidst the bright yellow, green, scarlet, and blue silks the others wore, the lifeless brown wool of Alice's gown stuck out like dog's ballocks. In the rearguard strode the nun who seemed never more than arm's length from his new wife. Emaciated, the nun's habit seemed to bind her twiggy appendages together.

Wed. Not yet bed, and the gnawing dread in his gut had him grabbing his wine goblet.

"Well." Roger drew the word out on an exhale. "It seems you're done for, brother o' mine."

"She seems mild tempered," he said. Alice had barely said a word above nay to wine and aye to water since they'd exchanged vows. Somewhere there existed a custom more agonizing than wedding a stranger, but he had not yet heard of it.

Roger adjusted his "good" tunic where it strained at the shoulder seams. "Meek even."

"Perhaps." William never assumed anything when it came to women.

"Not...that beautiful." Roger sipped his wine.

William almost laughed. His brother lacked a glib tongue in his arsenal. "Not quite plain, though."

"Aye." Roger nodded a touch too heartily. "And definitely not ugly."

"Indeed."

A dour serving girl refilled their wine goblets.

"Why in hell did you agree to this?" Roger lost his battle for further diplomacy, and yanked at his tunic until the stitches ripped.

William feigned a carefree shrug as if he hadn't asked himself that very question, for the last fortnight. "A man must marry. She will make as good a wife as any other. Indeed, better than most. She has land, and her father may have enough influence to restore our family's good name at court."

Roger pursed his lips and stared at their father.

Sir Arthur sat beside Lady Alice's father. A big, rough-boned man, Sir Ivo had the look of a wild boar. For certain, too hearty a man to have sired little Alice.

"God's bones but it's cold. Thank God we leave tonight." Roger huffed a cloud of white breath into the air. "You'll freeze your ballocks off getting your wedding tackle out."

In the gaping maws of all eight hall hearths, miserly flames eked out tepid heat against the bone chilling cold of a northern autumn. Barely three days into October, and already William smelled the bitter ice on the air.

"I would have a word with your lady about the fare." Roger poked his eating knife at the thin slithers of mutton on his trencher. Plain fare and in meager supply, suitable for an army on the move, but not for a wedding feast.

William drained his goblet. The wine had come from Anglesea, barrels and barrels of it from the depth of the Anglesea cellars where it had lain waiting to mark a celebration. Brought to Tarnwych by bullock train, it had provided the one bright point in his frigid wedding feast.

Cold, bleak, and as unrelentingly gray as the sky outside, his new hall resembled a tomb. Through the casement, blue water glittered from the lake beyond, the only color in a desolate view. God, what a depressing place. William snatched his goblet and found it empty.

Roger's nudge almost sent him to the floor. "You look like you might need this more than I."

William drained Roger's cup and put it on the table. He motioned for the serving wench and her wine jug. Soon, the women would finish preparing his bride, and he would be called upon to swive his way into conjugal contentment.

Chapter Two

William opened the door to his wedding chamber. Frigid air greeted him in a rush. Stark as a crypt, and with only one taper providing a flicker of warmth in the miserable dark. Bare of adornment, with a few basic pieces of furniture, the chamber lay free of the flowers and ribbons he would have expected for a wedding night. At the far end of the chamber, the bed hulked in shadow. A tiny mound in the center provided the only sign of life. "God's bones."

Alice stirred and then went still.

William didn't fancy frostbite of the ballocks. The chill of the miserable hall was bad enough. "Why is there no fire?"

"It is not yet December," she whispered.

Bugger that. William strode to the door and bellowed, "Cedric!" Getting the job done, and done well, deserved a scrap of comfort. "I'm bringing December a little early this year."

Alice made a soft noise.

Cedric barreled through the door, his cheeks flushed. "Sir William."

"Get some wood in here. Lots of wood." Let them have some semblance of good cheer between them tonight. He marked no honey cakes to sweeten the bride's disposition, no bridal broth to

10

stiffen the groom's resolve. "And wine." Neither he nor his wife had eaten much at the feast. "And fill a platter. Do it fast, Cedric."

"Aye, Sir William." Cedric spun about, crashed his shoulder into the doorjamb, and careened into the corridor. Nice lad, Cedric, willing and eager, but not the brightest squire he'd trained.

Silence filled the chamber. "That was Cedric. My squire." He chafed his palms together for warmth. "He means well, but you will have to overlook his clumsiness."

Alice might have moved, but who could tell in this fitful light. She had barely glanced at him through their parsimonious wedding feast. Every time he had shifted closer to her, his lady had shifted away. Part of him had wanted to see how far down the bench she would edge to put distance between them. As his efforts would have driven her straight into the lap of that sour-faced old nun, he'd resisted the urge and set himself to putting her at ease. Their wedding night would require renewed effort.

"Indeed." His voice rang. Had they no rugs to take the chill off the flags? Even the rats, it seemed, deserted Tarnwych for warmer welcome. "Cedric joined me recently. He is a cheerful sort, if you don't mind the chatter too much." He'd give his sword arm for a bit of Cedric's meaningless drivel right now. "He is a good lad."

He strode to the casement and peered into the night. On the far side of the lake, lights twinkled from the village. From the wisps of smoke ghosting on the night air, he guessed they had no December rule there. "Why December?"

She gave a small huff of breath. "It is cold in December."

"It is cold now." Sod the miserable North. Bad enough they played neighbor to those blasted Scots. Barren, gray, and cold. Very cold. He toyed with his breath, locking his jaw and sending white rings into the air. Half expecting a cracked tip, he crinkled his nose. He'd bedded more woman than he would admit to, unless Roger asked, and then he would even swell the number, because it irked his older brother no end. He could do this. Alice was a woman, much like any other, with all the parts he liked so well on others of her sex.

"Will you be much longer?" she said, startling him.

"Longer?"

"Aye."

At least he would be spared his wife chatting a hole in his head. "Longer about what?"

She stayed silent for so long, he prepared to repeat his question.

"The bedding," she whispered.

He spun from the window. Over the linens, two eyes glittered in the darkness. It might have been flattering if she hadn't sounded so pained about the idea. A new experience to be sure, and his smooth address deserted him. "I thought we might get comfortable first."

"I am comfortable."

William strolled closer to the bed. She lay on her back, linens tucked beneath her chin. The rest of her, barely reaching half the length of the huge bed, stretched straight as a dead fish on the block. "You do not look comfortable."

"I can assure you I am." She glared at the canopy.

They had not made a love match, and a seasoned woman would not expect any professions of devotion from their arrangement. In time, they would rub together like a pair of comfortable boots. If not, a man need not hover about his wife for much longer than the begetting of an heir or two. But this? William pressed his lips together, biting back his laugh. She looked like a bedamned corpse lying there. A grumpy corpse, at that. Did she expect him to leap on her, rut around a bit, and dismount?

Her rigid face gleamed pale, so tense, he would wager if he plucked a hair she would vibrate. He settled a hip on the edge of the bed.

Her eyes narrowed, and she pressed her lips together.

A shy, timid virgin bride he could gentle out of her fear, slowly put her at ease, caress her until she opened her petals like a flower before the sun. He almost snorted at his bad verse. Even a reluctant bride could be gentled like a skittish yearling. What to do with an experienced, ill-tempered one, who looked as if she would rather chew nails than share his bed? Did she even have a smile buried deep inside her? He loved a challenge. "I do not, as a rule, sleep like I am about to be laid to rest. But if you recommend it for comfort, I will give it a try."

She glanced at him and then frowned at the bed canopy.

"I wager you are warmer under there," he said.

The door swung open and banged into the wall.

"I am back." Cedric, laden with a large wooden board piled high with food, staggered into the room. Hair hung in his eyes. "And I brought help."

A handful of serfs slunk in. Wood, more wood and—thank you, God—wine. William welcomed a little fortification.

The tallest serf stacked wood in the fireplace.

"I found some more tapers." Balancing the heavy board with one hand, Cedric dug in his tunic front and produced a handful of tapers.

"Masterfully done, Cedric." William gave him a nod of approval. The lad had shown the first glimmers of initiative.

Cedric beamed at him and righted the canting platter.

A serf struck a flint, lit some kindling, and thrust it beneath the wood. Orange flames licked at the wood and caught with a soft whoosh.

"And then there was light," William said.

Alice gasped. Her frown deepened into a pinched expression of disapproval. Ah, a lady of faith, he presumed. Fitting, because the room resembled a monastic cell, and offered about as much welcome.

Cedric laid his platter down with only one loaf of bread dropped. He snatched it, wiped it on his tunic, and put it back on the platter. "Will that be all, Sir William?"

Leaning closer to his bride, William whispered out the side of his mouth, "Avoid the bread."

"I am not hungry." She shrunk further into the pillows as if afraid his breath might graze her skin. A lesser man would be feeling slighted about now. Unfortunately for Lady Alice, she had William of Anglesea in her chamber.

"But you must be." William ushered the last of the serfs and Cedric out of the chamber. He poured them both a goblet of wine and carried it back. "You barely touched your dinner."

She shook her head at his offer of a goblet. "I do not drink."

"I noticed that at dinner, too." Never one to miss an excellent wine, William sipped from his goblet and placed hers on the chest beside the bed. "Why is that?"

Her gaze flickered over him, light eyes, blue or green, he could not make out in the dark. "Drunkenness leads to lasciviousness."

And thank the Lord for that. William hid his smile behind his goblet.

Still bound in the bed linen, she scrutinized him.

He wandered back to the food board. The cheese looked edible, and he carved a slice for himself. Verily, she didn't look able to move. "Are you sure I cannot bring you aught?"

After a headshake, she went back to her study of the canopy.

William picked at the offerings on the tray. His lady did not drink, nor would she partake of any food, and she viewed him as an interloper in her chamber. To be fair, given that they had only met hours earlier, he could understand her reticence. For the most part, the ladies delighted in finding themselves in his company and took matters into their own hands. He drained his goblet, rejecting the idea of another. Any sort of victory here would require clear wits.

Bending, he unlaced his boots and slid them off. Next, he removed his embroidered wedding surcoat and laid it across a nearby clothes chest. Clad in his chemise and breeches, he padded to the bed. Thank God, the fire had taken the worst of the chill. Alice had left plenty of space on the other side of the bed, and he climbed up beside her.

A soft noise escaped her, and she went even more rigid.

Dear God, give him patience. Even his large conceit felt dented. He lay on his side, propping his head on his hand. She had a neat profile with a slight upward tilt at the end of her nose. Pale, thick lashes fluttered as she stared upwards. Not a pretty face, but her pleasant features bore a faerie-like charm. A gleaming, thick braid lay against the white pillow.

William took the braid between his thumb and forefinger. Glorious, rich copper and the weight of the braid in his hand told him of its length and thickness. The ends curled around the tie holding it confined. "Your hair is red."

"Aye." The delicate line of her jaw hardened.

"And very lovely, it would seem."

"Red hair is the devil's hair," she said.

The vehemence of her statement startled him. William knew many women who would lay down their lives for such beauty. "I beg your pardon."

She growled and, finally, looked at him. The anger on her face left him wrong footed. "Red hair is the mark of a foul temper. Foul temper is the playground of the devil."

God's Bones, who had he married? So meek and silent beside him at dinner, cold as death lying in wait for him in their bed, and now glaring at him as if he were a hound of hell. "I think it is beautiful."

She rolled her eyes on a huff. "My lord, there is no need for pretty words betwixt us. I am neither beautiful nor charming, but I am your wife. As such, we will lie together for the purpose of begetting a child. Can we please get to that part?"

Chapter Three

Alice kept her stare level on Sir William sprawled beside her. He threw back his head and laughed loud enough it rang about the room, and her cheeks burned.

"Indeed." He stilled, but his fine eyes still laughed at her.

Alice hadn't meant to blurt it out in such a manner, but he unnerved her with his offers of food and wine and his conversation. In her experience, a wedding night went differently. The husband entered, disrobed, and climbed in beside you. After he clambered atop you, he did the necessary, and left. Her first husband had slept beside her, but he had not consummated the marriage. Her second groom had discovered her chastity to his delight, but stayed only long enough to see her rid of it. After that, he had visited her chamber a bare handful of times before the village whores had lured him away. Number three followed almost exactly in number two's pattern. Strange, she never thought of them by name. Steven! Her last husband had been named Steven. John came before him, and the first, who could not bear to touch her, had been named William. Like this one. Two Williams, and both of them strange. This William lounged like a big cat beside her, head propped on his hand and amusement gleaming in his gaze.

"It is not that I do not appreciate your efforts to put me at my ease, but they are not necessary," she said. He had made more of an effort than the others.

"I see." He toyed with her hair, wrapping the curling ends around his forefinger. "Perhaps my efforts were for myself as well."

"Oh." She had not considered that. Men always seemed so much more comfortable in these situations. "Are they?"

"A little." He smiled at her.

She wished to God he hadn't. A beautiful man with his face in repose, but when he smiled—Lord above—it hit her as a small quiver in her belly and crept through her chest, snatching her breath.

"You see, my lady, having done this before, you have the advantage of experience."

He could not mean… "You are a vir—?"

"Nay, my lady." He tickled her brow with the ends of her hair. "Do not frown so fiercely. I do not claim chastity, merely new to the wedded state."

Well, of course, a man such as he would not be pure. A great favorite with the ladies. She would do well to remember that. Once he had gotten her with child, she could turn a blind eye to his activities outside of their wedding chamber.

He wrapped her braid around one large fist. "I meant what I said about your hair. It is beautiful."

"Thank you." She rather liked her hair, despite Sister's insistence it be bound.

"Now." Pursing his full lips, he laid her braid on her shoulder. "How best to carry on? Should we have some conversation?"

"It is not needed." Alice dragged her gaze away from his mouth. She had never seen a man with a mouth so finely wrought. Top lip firm and carved, resting above the much fuller pillow of his bottom lip. "I desire a child above all else. I know how they come about."

"And yet you have born no children?"

"Nay." They whispered of her barrenness through Tarnwych. If this husband could not give her a child, it would mean the worst. A dull pain throbbed below her breast. "I have not been so fortunate."

"Do not be sad, my lady." With soft fingers, he stroked her cheek. "I am entirely at your disposal."

Alice nearly laughed. His tone was kind, but his eyes invited her to share the joke. Best to get the unpleasantness over with. After, she would light a candle in the chapel every morning and evening, beg the blessed Madonna to grant her dearest wish. "You may proceed."

He laughed, a full-throated, deep rumble that shook the bed beneath her.

Alice knew not what to make of him. Did he not think her in earnest? "I made no jest."

"Nay, indeed." He sobered. "But I think we should get these out of their bindings first." He drew first one arm and then the other over the linens and lay them beside her. "In case you should feel the need to touch," he said. "This will prove far more useful."

"I have never felt the need before."

"I am quickly forming that opinion, my Alice." He winked at her and gave her another of his wondrous smiles. "Perhaps you could unclench your fists at the same time." He straightened her fingers and spread them on the furs. Leaning over her, he took the goblet from the chest beside her and drank before offering it to her. "This is thirsty work."

Strangely enough, she did feel like a drink. Once or twice, when Sister absented herself from dinner, she had tried wine and rather liked it. William certainly appeared to enjoy wine. "Perhaps just a small sip."

She raised herself on her elbows.

Evading her hands, William touched the cup to her lips, and she sipped. The rich, fruity flavor delighted her palate. "It does not taste like the wine I have tasted in the past."

"That is because I brought this with me from Anglesea. My

father has some of the finest wines in the land. Have another sip. Let it rest on your tongue for a moment. See if you can taste the blackberries.”

One sip was enough of a departure for her. Two seemed positively wanton. “I think not.”

“Not even for the blackberries?” He lifted a dark brow.

Two sips wouldn’t lead the way to hell. “For the blackberries, then.”

He put the goblet to her lips.

Alice sipped, resting the wine on her tongue. A little woody perhaps, with a hint of fruit, and then blackberries. “I taste them.”

His smile of approval made her glow warm inside. He put the goblet on the chest beside her and moved back to his side of the bed. Through her gown, he pressed warm against her side. She felt delicate, tiny beside him. Wood-hued skin, with a warmed spice scent teased her from the opening of his chemise. She had never seen any of her husbands naked. They had lifted her gown without removing more garments than necessary. Would William’s skin feel as hers, or rougher perhaps?

“You still do not look comfortable.” Pulling at the bedding, he tucked it about her waist. “Now I can see more of you.”

He mocked her, he must. “Why would you wish to do that?”

He studied her face. “Green.” He smoothed her eyebrow with his forefinger. “I could not see before, but I see now that your eyes are green. Like a pea.”

“A pea?” Alice had heard worse descriptions, but still, a pea.

“Pea-green.” He bent closer to her. “Or summer grass.” He seemed to consider her eyes for a long moment. “Nay, I have it. Your eyes are as green as a stagnant pond.”

Alice snorted. The man needed to work on his poetry. “And yours are blue.”

“As blue as?” He raised a dark brow.

“Blue.” Best get this nonsense done with. His constant study of her features made her squirm. The huge fire he'd built had made the room uncomfortably warm.

"You, my Alice, have no romance in your soul." He tapped the edge of her nose. "But you do have the dearest little nose. I would compare it to something fantastical, but you, I would wager, would prefer I call it a pig snout."

"Nay, I would not." She'd never been teased, and a tiny giggle escaped before she could control it.

He grinned as if she had handed him the moon. "That is much better. Now I shall move on to your cheeks."

"Please, spare me." The soft stroke of his fingers left a warm tingle in their wake. "I do not think I can bear any more of your sweet whispers."

"Let us discover if you can bear more." He brushed his nose against her cheek. "Cream."

Whispering over her skin, the caress took Alice's breath with it.

"Thick fresh cream for my pottage."

She should pull away, but her limbs melted into the bed. Cloves. She named the spice that clung to his skin.

"I must discover if it tastes as delicious as it looks." Hot lips branded her cheek.

For an instant she forgot how to breathe.

"And it does," he murmured. "Sweet and silky on my lips."

"My lord—"

"William." He nuzzled into her neck and trailed his lips along her jaw.

"William." Her skin blazed in the path of his wicked mouth. "What are you doing?"

"Inventory." He popped his head up. "Next we move to your mouth."

"It is just a mouth." Her lips seemed to swell and plump under his perusal. Dear Lord, what beset her? He had bewitched her with his glib words and soft touches. Wrapped her in the befuddling scent of warm skin and cloves, in the sultry length of his chest against her side.

"Never say so." His gaze heated. "Mouths are never just anything. They are made for smiling. For laughter and whispers between lovers." He dragged his thumb across her bottom lip. "For kissing."

His mouth drew closer, and Alice's belly tightened. He was going to kiss her. Her first kiss, and from a man so beautiful she had nearly wept when she first saw him. Yet, his intent expression spoke of desire, his desire to kiss her.

Large hands framed her cheeks, turning her toward his seeking lips.

Her fingers twitched against the bedding. She did want to touch, like he said she would, to discover if his dark hair felt as silky as it looked.

The first tentative press of his mouth on hers left her wanting more. She curled her hands about his forearms, hewn, hard muscle and so warm.

His mouth returned to hers and lingered a moment longer. Wanting more was unthinkably base. Alice tightened her grip on his forearms.

"Aye, my Alice," he whispered against her mouth. "Shall I kiss you or leave you?"

"I have never been kissed." The confession slipped from her, mortifying her.

"Nay." His face softened. "How is such a thing possible?"

She had not the courage to ask him to kiss her. The words clattered around in her mind, but if she voiced them, he might laugh. Or pull away from her in disgust.

"Let it be my honor to be the first to kiss you." He angled his head, slanting his mouth over hers.

Alice yielded beneath the firm demand of his mouth. The way he took control of the kiss robbed her of all thought and let her sink deep into the sensation. The touch of his tongue to her lip shocked her.

"Let me taste." His thumbs worked her jaw open, admitting his tongue into her mouth.

Alice froze. She had never heard of such a thing. His tongue slid slick against hers. The strange intimacy disconcerted her, but not enough to stop it. An odd thing, to be sure, but he tasted of wine and something else—musk and cinnamon.

His groan rumbled through her. He lay close over her, but not on top of her. She could move at any time and dislodge him.

Demanding more of her, he deepened the kiss.

Alice surrendered to his questing lips. Allowed him to explore her mouth with his tongue. Heat wound through her belly. It crept up her ribcage to the peak of her breasts. She was both unable to move and sparkling alive at the same time. Thus far, William provided her most enjoyable and intriguing consummation.

* * *

Finally, Alice responded to his kiss and triumph surged through William. Tentative at first, but growing in confidence almost as fast as his rod thickened. Her flavor flamed through him, rich, sweet, and a touch tart. Her full breasts pressed against his chest in a revelation he intended to explore with his hands and mouth. Lady Alice hid a lush little form beneath her armor of linens.

The chamber door swung open setting the taper flames flickering. The old nun stood in the doorway, the hallway light shadowing her face. "I brought water for you to cleanse yourself."

His voice to tell her to get out stuck in his throat. Too late. Beneath him, Alice stiffened, wriggling to escape him.

"You are still here," the nun said. "I shall return later."

Too stuffed full of lust to trust his voice, William flung himself onto his back. "Do not."

"I beg your pardon."

"You will not be required later." William clenched his fists. The need to shove them through a wall raced through him.

Beside him, Alice returned to a corpse. If it weren't so blasphemous, he would damn that nun to hell. So close to melting his icy bride and sinking into her wet heat. Another night then, and with no nun interrupting them.

His lady wanted him for stud, did she? Saw no other use for him but his seed. What a dreadful waste. He liked children, was very fond of them. More than children, though, he enjoyed women. Every woman presented a new mystery to be explored; the unique scent that clung to her, the stroke of his hand upon her skin, the taste of her. With one kiss, Alice had become his new favorite uncharted land.

Clearly, her last three husbands had failed to convince her of the pleasures of the marriage bed. Her first, William of Clarges, he could understand. Sir William had not leaned toward women at all. The subsequent two had only made his task harder.

William tucked his hands behind his head and smiled at the canopy. Challenge accepted.

Chapter Four

Alice opened her eyes to fitful sun painting the flags beneath the casement. She should get up and go about her day, but her warm bed whispered sloth in a tempting embrace of toasty linens and a hot, hard body beside her.

Her husband. Or not quite husband yet, considering that after Sister's departure he had lain beside her and chatted—aye, chatted—until Alice fell asleep.

Braced for the nip of early morning, Alice poked her nose over the edge of the covers. Warm air met her, and she edged her face out. Not as cozy as the bed but comfortable enough not to require her usual pained dash to the washing basin. God forgive her extravagant nature, but she loved the heat.

Dark hair tousled on the pillow, his face at rest, William breathed deep and even beside her. Together in the dark, he had told her of his family and his life at Anglesea. A very different life awaited him at Tarnwych, and one he might very well not enjoy. Would he find her wanting too? Well, he did not need to like her to fulfill his purpose. It might be nice, though.

Someone must have tended the fire in the night, because a cheerful blaze added light to the unenthusiastic sunshine. Careful not to wake William, she slid from the bed and crept across the chamber to her basin and ewer on the washstand.

Plunging her hands into the water, she gasped. At least there was no layer of ice to break before she could perform her morning ablutions.

"Good morrow, my lady." William sat knees splayed beneath the covers with his elbows resting on them. His warm smile caused a quiver low in her belly.

"G-good morrow." What did one say waking with a man in her chamber? Did one comment on the weather or speak of the coming day?

"Did you sleep well?" Thankfully, William seemed more knowledgeable in these matters. She refused to dwell on why that was.

"Aye, thank you." Stone chill burned her soles, and she rested one foot atop the other to relieve the discomfort. "Did you? Sleep well, I mean."

"Nay, my lady, I did not." He tossed the covers aside.

He rose and stood beside the bed in nothing but his braies. Heat flamed in her cheeks and she averted her gaze. Her new husband lacked modesty it would appear. Heavy shoulders crowned a wide muscular chest that tapered into his slim waist. Why, indeed would he hide such a form? A chaste woman did not think such things, even about their lawful husband. A modest woman, for certain, would not work this hard to keep herself from having a longer, closer look. Penance at morning prayers was required.

"That is not a comfortable bed," William said. "How do you manage to sleep on it?"

"I manage." Here a mere day and already he found fault with Tarnwych. However, the straw of the bed did poke through the old sacking as if one slept upon a hedgehog. Other parts of the palette had worn thinner than parchment. She had heard some places stuffed the bedding with down and feathers. She'd wager William had such a palette at Anglesea. He enjoyed his comforts too much to content himself with plain straw. Feather and down would be wondrously soft, like sinking into a happy cloud at night.

"Alice," he said from right behind her, and she started. A large, tanned hand appeared between her and the water basin. "William of Anglesea. Your groom."

Alice spun round and faced him, not at all sure what he was about now. "I know who you are."

He sketched a courtly bow. "I thought we might dispense with the awkwardness of the situation. Now you introduce yourself to me, and we shall proceed from there."

"But you know who I am." Perhaps his pretty face hid a fool. He stood too close to her with his broad, muscled chest the only place her gaze could go. She focused on the indent below his throat. "Are you mocking me?"

"Nay, Alice." He tilted her chin and his gaze met hers. "I am attempting to get to know you."

"Oh." She had no earthly idea why he would want such a thing, but it was nice. Considerate even. "I am Alice."

"There." He grinned at her. "That was not so very bad. Was it? Shall I send Cedric to the kitchen and we can break our fast right here?"

"Nay." He could not mean that. Taking your meals in your chamber like royalty—madness. "We must go to the hall."

"Very well." He pulled a wry face. "Allow me to assist you to dress."

He was addled. She'd already guessed it. "You cannot do that."

"Nay?" He titled his head. "Why is that?"

"It is not done." Alice was not very sure why it was not done. After all, a husband and wife lay together, but to assist each other in the mundane task of dressing seemed far too intimate. Did he have an army of squires to clothe him at Anglesea?

William moved to the fire, his back rippling with more intriguing muscle. Linen clung to the firm orbs of his...hindquarters. He added another log and flames roared into a hearty blaze.

Another thing not done until yesterday. But this one she rather approved of.

Alice snatched her chemise off the clothes tree. It lay limp in her hands. She could not very well dress with him standing right there.

"Allow me." He rose and approached her. Stopping before her, he reached behind her. "I believe we could begin here."

Alice stared at the length of hide in his hand. He had loosened her hair, and already the braid unraveled against her back.

Hands warm on her shoulders through the linen, William turned her about. "This, my lady, is a shame."

He loosened her braid until her hair lay heavy on her back and shoulders. Drawing his finger through the length of her hair in long, sensual sweeps that prickled her flesh into goosebumps.

"To keep such bounty hidden." William made a tutting sound. "Do you have a comb?"

"Aye."

His fingers roamed her scalp, loosening hair and easing the ache from the braid. He rubbed soothing circles over the ache. "May I have your comb?"

Alice snatched her comb off her washstand and handed it to him.

He growled, so close to her that the vibrations skittered up her spine. "This is a dismal affair. Do not move."

Cool air hit her back. His bare feet padded over stone, and a chest creaked opened. He muttered to himself as he rummaged. Words that no godly man would know, let alone use.

Bringing the curious warmth that emanated from his body, he returned. "This is a decent comb."

Between his long fingers he held a comb, but one so fine she would not have dared use it on her hair. Carved, intricate patterns marched along the spine, inlaid with mother of pearl. Such beauty in a prosaic implement, and yet she coveted it. The thick teeth would tug less at her hair than her old bone comb.

"Cedric combs my hair with this," he said. "A hundred strokes every night."

Alice lost her words. Verily?

He chuckled beside her ear. His breath brushed her neck. "I jest, my lady."

Even stronger sensations skittered down her neck. A funny picture formed in her mind of William settled before the fire with Cedric behind him, combing his hair.

"Is that a smile I see?" William smoothed his palm across her scalp and followed it with the gentle scrape of the comb.

"Perhaps." Touch firm but gentle, he pulled the comb through her hair from root to tip. He stopped when he encountered a tangle and worked the hair free with the smallest of tugs on her scalp. Sister wielded the comb with a rough hand, muttering about her hair as she went.

"So beautiful," William murmured as he combed the hair back from her forehead. "It is the most striking color."

"Brazen red?"

"Sunset red," he said. "Molten red. Copper."

"Is that another jest?"

"Nay, my Alice." He leaned over her and replaced the comb on the washstand. "Why do you bind it and hide it away?"

The waft of cloves weakened her knees. "Sister Julianna believes it to be immodest."

"Ah." He held a handful of her hair to the sunlight. "I would like to see you wear it without your wimple."

Alice spun and faced him. Sister would be horrified. "I could not."

"Nay?" He grimaced. "Let us make a bargain, you and I. You will wear it lose when you are here in this chamber with me. Until such time as you are comfortable to go about without your wimple."

It seemed a strange sort of bargain to her, but it would be nice to not always have her head grow hot and itchy beneath her wimple. "I will never go about without my wimple."

"We shall see." He raised his arms above his head and stretched. A long, sinuous ripple of muscle and sinew that took her thoughts with it. "Come sit by the fire with me."

"But the keep waits to break its fast."

"At this hour? Do you rise with the sun in the north?"

"Aye." When else did one rise?

"I see." Her strange new husband raised his face to the ceiling and blew out a long breath. He motioned the chair before the fire. "Shall we?"

There was only one chair before the fire, and he did not heed her that the keep waited.

William led her to the chair and sat. Then, he arranged her until she sat on his lap, like a child.

The heat of his bare thighs burned through her nightrail. The intimacy of their position discomforted her. Alice wriggled to break free, but he clamped his hands on her hips and held her in place. "Indulge me for a moment."

"My lord, the keep."

"William." His hand tightened about her hip. "Here, at least, you must call me William."

"I cannot."

"Why?"

Alice had no good answer for that, other than it would create a bond between them as man and wife. They were man and wife. An ache throbbed behind her eyes. This had her all turned about, and her thoughts grew clouded.

"If we are to have any sort of marriage, my Alice, you and I need to begin as friends." William tucked a strand of hair behind her ear. "I do not fancy the sort of union where we hide at opposite ends of Tarnwych from each other. And you?"

It sounded a lot like her other marriages. "I did before, with the..." Perhaps William wanted no reminder that other husbands had come before him. Steven had forbidden her from referring to his predecessors.

"With your former husbands?" William tucked her closer to him. "Tell me about them."

"Why?" That question came more and more from her lips this morning.

"I would like to know." He shrugged. "William of Clarges came first?"

"Aye."

"Was he kind to you?"

Alice nodded. Her first William had been kind, when he had been about. "He did not spend much time in my company. He had a friend, called Patrick, of whom he was very fond. They went everywhere together."

William nodded but a strange look, part amusement and part pity, flashed across his face. "Did he consummate your marriage?"

Alice near swallowed her tongue. The question caught her unguarded, and she answered before she could censor her tongue. "Nay. John did."

"As I thought." William's large hand spanned the breadth of her back.

"Wh—" She refused to use that word again. "William and Patrick were out riding when Patrick fell into the tarn. William jumped in to save him, and they both drowned. It was rather brave of him."

"Indeed." William tugged on his earlobe. "And the next."

"John." A bull of a man, of medium height, John she had favored the least. She had not loved any of them, and only the worst sort of wife would admit such a fault, but John she had not liked at all. John had a way of stomping around Tarnwych, bellowing orders and using his fists when they weren't obeyed fast enough. The relief after his death had her on her knees for weeks praying for forgiveness. "He fell from the walls in a storm. They say he went to check the guards on the battlements and slipped on the slick stone."

"And the last?"

"Steven." Alice had not minded Steven so much. Tall and

slim, he was rather a quiet man, but still insistent on having things his way. He and Sister Julianna had battled long and hard during his short lordship of Tarnwych. "He caught a chill when out hunting. He never recovered."

William laid his chin on her shoulder. "Were you sad, my Alice, when your husbands died?"

"Nay," she said. He stilled, and she glanced up to see if she had shocked him, but William smiled at her. "I was sad that I did not have a child, though."

"You want a child?"

"More than anything." Her chest ached with the confession.

"Then, my Alice," he said and pulled her against his handsome chest, "rest assured that I shall apply myself assiduously and make your wish come true. Morning, noon and night, I make myself available to you."

The laughter in his voice drew a giggle from her. "I appreciate your commitment to duty."

"Alice?" He jerked his head back, but grinned as he did so. "Was that a jest I heard?"

"Perhaps." Alice dropped her head, beset by sudden shyness.

The door flew open, and Sister Julianna strode into the room. "My lady." Sister's eyes narrowed, and she stopped short.

Alice's cheeks heated. Caught, and in such a position. She tried to get off William's lap.

He tightened his arms about her and held her in place.

"Sister." William tensed, but inclined his head cordially. "Good morrow to you."

"You are not dressed." Sister sneered at Alice.

"I was about—"

"The entire keep awaits your pleasure. And your hair!" Sister stalked toward her.

"Sister." William rose and put Alice on her feet beside him. "My lady and I will join the keep shortly. As you see, we are not attired."

"Nay." Sister flushed and dropped her gaze to the floor.

Tucking her hands beneath her scapula, she said, "We are not accustomed to courtly ways at Tarnwych."

"Nor, would it seem, are you accustomed to closed doors," William said.

Sister flinched as if he'd struck her.

Alice wanted to go to her, to comfort her. Sister always entered Alice's bedchamber unannounced.

William wrapped his arm about her waist and tugged her flush to his side. "I understand Tarnwych has had no lord for some time and you have grown accustomed to certain ways." A polite smiled crossed William's face but stopped short of reaching his eyes. "As such, I am sure your entering our chamber unannounced, twice, is an unfortunate oversight."

"I—"

"We will see you in the hall."

Sister took a deep breath, and squared her shoulders. "I will assist Lady Alice to dress."

"No need." William pressed a kiss to Alice's temple. "I am here now."

Chapter Five

William considered himself a reasonable man with rather ordinary needs. For certain, he enjoyed his creature comforts, but he could content himself with the simpler delights in life. Breaking his fast, however, was one of those needs he could not overlook. His mother assured him that even as a babe, he had woken hungry and squalling for his first meal of the day.

The mess in the bowl before him could not tempt even a morning appetite such as his. Alice he had left to dress herself. He'd shocked and shaken her enough for one morning. The woman puzzled him, challenged him to put together the pieces. During the long night he'd lain sleepless on that frightful bed, he'd decided to woo his wife.

This morning's surprise peek at her delicious curves had buttressed his decision. Oblivious, Alice had stood by her washstand, the firelight rendering her nightrail almost transparent. Barely tall enough to look over the sill of the casement, but shaped for the appreciation of a man's eyes and hands. And William aimed to appreciate.

God knows, she might kill him with her relentless prudish piety, but he had a plan to rid her of that. Behind her bristling exterior lay the intriguing parts of Alice. Her vulnerability plucked at him, made him want to protect and shelter her. The stark hunger on her face as she spoke of having a child. The wistfulness when she told him of her previous husbands. He would wager she remained unaware of those emotions within her. Aye, she hadn't loved the men, but she regretted their shortened lives. When his father first presented him with the match, it had occurred to him that Lady Alice had amassed and lost a suspicious number of husbands before him.

Unless she dissembled like a master, or his judgment of people had failed him, he could not suspect her of having taken matters into her own, delicate hands. That nun, on the other hand, chilled his blood, and she might snarl his plans of conjugal amiability. He doubted the woman had experienced a friendly moment in the last twenty years.

The lower level of the keep had been quieter than he would have expected. His boot heels rang on the bare flagstones and echoed through the abandoned hallways. At Anglesea people abounded at this time in the morning. His family had wished him well the night before, and left shortly thereafter. Alone, well and truly alone, and without his family for one of the few times in his life.

The chill in the hall snatched his breath away. Eight hearths and only two of them lit with a beggar's fire. By December they would have to scrape his frozen carcass off the floor. He caught the eye of the kitchen drudge who had brought him his bowl. "Bring more wood for the fires. And light the others while you're at it."

The woman blinked at him, tired eyes in her thin face. "Sir William?"

"Wood." William repeated the word slowly. "Bring wood and get the other fires burning before we all freeze to death."

"Aye, my lord." The woman shuffled off, head bent and muttering beneath her breath.

Trestle tables stood in stacked rows against the plain walls, leaving the lord's table alone on the dais. Not even a hall dog dozing before the fire. Leaving him to break his fast alone, or almost alone.

Sister Sunshine squatted at the table several places from him, spooning gruel as if someone would rob her of it. She might as well slow down. He wouldn't give this mess to the Anglesea beggars. Did the rake-thin nun live, or did they dig her out of the family crypt, dust her off, and put her in his path to irk him? After her second interruption this morning, he was disinclined to break the harsh silence with conversation, but his mother would box his ears for his poor manners, and he craved answers to his growing list of questions.

"Has the rest of the hall broken their fast?" William arranged his features into pleasant lines.

"We break our fast early at Tarnwych," she said.

William poked at the runny gray goop in his bowl. "With this?"

"Pottage." Sister Sunshine placed her spoon beside her empty bowl, frowned, and then made a small adjustment and straightened it.

"Pottage?" His empty belly growled, but he could think of many things he would eat before this. Straw perhaps. With meals like this, he understood the woman's waspish disposition. William had eaten better camped at siege. No honey or fruits to add flavor to the pottage lay on the bare wooden table before him. No meats, or even bread. Not even a mug of small beer to wash the mess down.

A man starts as he means to go on, and William stood. He had not come all the way north, married a woman whose children would inherit her father's lands, to freeze or starve to death. Thus far, his introduction to Tarnwych had his temper simmering low beneath his skin. He motioned the serving girl over. "Kitchens?"

Her gaze darted between him and Sister Sunshine before she pointed. "Back of the hall."

"My thanks." William nodded to Sister Sunshine and strode toward the kitchen.

The serving girl pattered along behind him.

"The men?" He spun about so suddenly she skidded to a halt and avoided plowing into his back. "Where are the men?"

"Men?" She blinked at him.

"Guards, men-at-arms, drudges." He enunciated his words. "Have they already broken their fast?"

Shuffling back, she shrugged. "I do not ken."

Was the girl the keep idiot? She did not wear a vacant expression, merely bit her lip and pleated her skirt between her fingers. "Did you not see them in the hall at their meal?"

She gaped at him. "The men do not take their meals in the hall."

"Why ever not?" Come to think of it, no males had moved through the keep this morn.

Crossing herself, she leaned closer. "Fornication."

"Eh?"

"The men do not eat in the hall because of fornication."

Mind empty, William knew he stared, but he had no response. "The kitchens?"

Sister Julianna left the hall, stopped and watched them for a moment, then hurried on. A pity she had decided against following them into the kitchens.

Heat from the cooking hearth hit him before he rounded a bend into the enormous kitchen. Three scrubbed wooden tables dominated the center. At the first, a lone woman sat with an earthen bowl before her. She rose, her apron spotless around her waist.

"You are the cook?" And the first cook he'd met with no spare flesh on her bones.

She nodded and placed herself between him and the hearth, where a flaxen-haired boy played on the floor with wooden blocks.

"Could I trouble you for some honey?" He gave her his most winning smile.

Cook tucked her thumbs into her apron, fanning her fingers above her sunken bosom. "No honey."

"Ah." Not the best of beginnings. He glanced behind him at the serving girl.

She shrugged. "No honey."

"Does that mean there is no honey, or you will not get it for me?"

"We have not had honey here since spring." Cook rocked on her heels, tapping her fingers against her apron. Her hands appeared as clean as her apron, nails cut short.

"Fruit?" His winning ways seemed to have no effect on the residents of Tarnwych. "Or cream?"

"Walter!" Cook shouted and an older boy, also flaxen, slid into view. "Get Sir William some cream."

A tiny chink in Cook's battlements, but a beginning nonetheless. William set his bowl on the table and slid onto the bench. "Have you been at Tarnwych long?"

"All my life." Cook sidled closer to the child by the hearth.

"Would you have some bread?"

"Only yesterday's." Cook's bellow bounced around the cavernous kitchen. "Walter, bring bread with that cream."

William shook his head and cleared the ringing in his ears. Cook had a powerful set of pipes on her. He had scant knowledge of running a household, so he took care with his next question. "Do you not bake every day?"

"We bake when the bread is all eaten."

The older boy appeared with a small basin of cream and set it before him. From under his arm, he produced a quarter loaf and placed it beside the cream.

"My thanks." William smiled at him.

The boy flushed and scuttled back into the pantry.

William poured the cream into his pottage. It went from steel to light gray, and his stomach clenched. Good God, he had to exert muscle to break the crust on the bread. It would bounce off the walls he'd wager.

"Cook." He rose. "The fare at Tarnwych is somewhat wanting." Bloody awful seemed a little strident, but closer to the truth.

Cook stiffened, her face growing a dull red. "I'nt my fault."

"I beg your pardon?"

"I cook what I gets given. You can't make a banquet from scraps." She sucked her cheeks.

Their conversation drifted into awkward territory. Running a household, something he knew next to nothing about, but even he knew that much about cooking. "Are you saying the larders are wanting?"

"Wanting?" Cook jammed her fists on her hips, and stuck her chin out at him. "Bare as a babe's ass is what they are."

"Cook?" Alice stood in the kitchen doorway, frowning. "Is there aught amiss?"

"His lordship do not like his meal," Cook said.

Alice's frown deepened. "But we always break our fast with pottage."

"That is not pottage." William pointed at his bowl.

Alice walked closer and peered at his bowl. "It looks like pottage to me."

"Pig swill." Cook threw her hands in the air. "That's what that is."

William couldn't have said it better. "Then why prepare it?"

"Told you," Cook said. "Do the best I can with what I have."

"We have harsh winters here." Alice picked up his spoon and stirred the pottage. "We do not like to force people to give food to the keep that they do not have."

William hadn't considered that.

"Crops." Cook jerked her head toward the casement. Her round cheeks flushed and shook. "Dunstan tells me the villagers hide their crops from the keep."

It was far too early in the morning for him to bend his brain to this, but with Alice looking confused and Cook looking bellicose, he didn't see any option. He faced Cook. "I think you should explain."

"Sister Julianna abhors waste and gluttony." Cook uttered the nun's name as if it tasted bitter on her tongue. "Therefore we only have enough to feed the mouths we have."

"Or not quite feed." A pattern formed and one William had no patience for. Incredulity prickled, that he—a man and knight—was having this conversation. "Have you enough stores for today's baking?"

"Aye." Some of the steel in Cook's posture softened. "But that will leave me short for the morrow."

"I tell you what." William tried another smile. "You bake and I will concern myself with tomorrow."

Alice gasped. "But Sister orders the provisions."

Sister kept herself busy it would appear. Why had Alice not stepped into her role as chatelaine? Lady Mary oversaw every part of her busy keep. "Not you?"

Alice blushed and dropped her gaze. "I..."

Answer enough. William asked Cook, "Do you have a bailiff I can speak with?"

"Aye." Cook averted her gaze and busied herself tucking a strand of flaxen hair beneath her kerchief. "Do you want him?"

"Please." William restrained his dwindling patience. "But before then, I would like to break my fast." He nudged the bowl across the table. "And not on that."

"I have some mutton from the wedding feast." Cook's eyes gleamed. "And a spot of cheese left, if that will do."

"That will do nicely." At least he had managed to choke down the mutton yesterday.

Cook crossed her sinewy arms. "What will we eat this evening?"

"What do we have?"

"Nothing."

God grant him strength. "Do the men not hunt for the table?"

"That lot." Cook snorted and rolled her eyes. "They collect

from the village and spend the rest of their days on their asses around their fire."

At least the men had a fire. Pain throbbed behind William's eyes. All he wanted was something to put in the aching maw of his belly. He held out his hand for Alice. "Will you join me?"

She slipped the tips of her fingers into his grasp and took a seat. She dropped her hand as soon as was polite. "I will eat the pottage."

"Nay." William snatched the bowl and handed it to Cook. "You will share my meal. I have an inkling we have a long day ahead of us. You will need your strength."

Cook ordered poor Walter off in twenty directions at once. His stomach took note with a happy rumble.

Alice perched at the table like a rabbit waiting to bolt.

William kept his tone gentle. "Has Sister Julianna always run the keep?"

A snort from Cook cut off any response Alice would make and she merely nodded. "My father brought me here when I was younger. Sister took care of me."

It would appear Sister still had the reins firmly in her grasp. "I will send to Anglesea to replenish the stores," he said.

Cook whirled about from carving mutton, knife still in hand, and charged at him. "You would never."

Alice shrunk back.

William stared at Cook—particularly the large knife in her right hand. Clearly, he had erred in some way.

"Take handouts from those southerners." Cook sucked in her cheeks. "We northerners fend for ourselves, not like them soft southerners."

William took a pinch of comfort from the implication that he was not one of 'them soft southerners.' "Just until we can restock our larders."

"We can stock our larders." Cook slapped both hands onto the table and leaned toward him. Her carving knife clattered against the wood.

It was a large knife, more cleaver than dagger, and Cook wielded it with some skill at the mutton. "It would appear not," he said.

"Perhaps if we spoke with the bailiff." Alice's soft voice broke in. "I am sure Gord has some ideas on what we can do."

"Right you are, my lady." Cook nodded and took herself and her carving knife back to the mutton. "Up north we get along without taking charity."

William applied himself to the meal Cook set before him. The stringy mutton caught in his teeth. The robust ale Cook unearthed helped ease the mutton down his gullet in a sharp bite of barley.

"Sir William." A thin, balding man slunk into the kitchen. He tugged at the ends of his neat tunic. "I am Gord, the bailiff. Walter said you asked for me."

"Took your time getting here." Cook slammed a platter of age-spotted apples onto the table. "Sir William did not fancy his pottage."

The throb behind William's eyes grew into a sharp ache, nearly as distracting as the steady pain in his ass. Men did not run keeps, become tangled in the small details of putting food on the table. Dear God, next he would find himself with a needle in his hand. "I am given to understand there are some challenges in keeping the castle supplied?"

"Challenges?" Cook hacked at a wheel of cheese. "Tight asses is the only challenge around here."

"Cook." Alice's voice carried a thin tone of steel. "That will do."

Cook wilted. "Beg your pardon, Lady Alice. No offense intended, but I'm a cook. Both my mam and dad were cooks before me, and they be turning in their graves to see the swill I serve here at Tarnwych. Turning, I tell you."

Alice opened her mouth to speak and William squeezed her hand to silence her. If you gave people enough time and silence, they would fill it with the truth.

"I have my pride." Tears welled in Cook's eyes. "Bitten my tongue all these years, swallowed my pride because nobody else would come and cook for this keep. Not with nothing to serve but yesterday's dog scraps and a handful of salt."

"I did not know." Alice's cheeks had gone quite pink. She picked at the table with her fingernail.

Another question around his bride, because Alice should have known. As much as William would like to acquit her of all blame, as a woman grown, the responsibility of Tarnwych fell to her. If matters were this bad in the kitchen, it augured badly for how the overall demesne fared. One problem at a time. The mutton helped ease some of his ire. "Tell me, Gord, how matters stand today at Tarnwych."

Chapter Six

William's sat through Gord's endless recitation and battled the growing fidgets. God, he wished he had not asked now, just eaten his mutton and gone about his day. However, he had asked and received his answer, and now he could not ignore the reality.

Leaving him and Gord in the kitchen, Alice slipped away several long hours later for prayers. To give Gord his due, the man knew the state of the keep in excruciating detail. Normally he gave his reports to Sister who—judging by the hints Gord dropped— barely took the time to listen.

With winter coming, William could hardly credit the state of the stores. They might not starve, but Tarnwych offered cold, dismal comfort through the snow-bound months.

Endless winter months, miserly fare, and freezing cold sat like a thorn in his ass. The deep cold of the north was enough for a body to tolerate. With harvest done for this year, he could supplement the table through hunting. The women might forage for some late nuts and tubers, but all the fruit from the extensive orchards had wasted. Gord reckoned the villagers had taken it, because it had not made its way into ciders, preserves, or been dried to provide variety to the keep meals when the hard freeze set in.

As a second son, William had not received instruction like Roger on the tasks of a liege lord. Yet, even he knew more than Alice. Frustrated by her lack of ability as chatelaine, in fairness he could see where lay the blame, and a future reckoning loomed.

"Sir William." Gord gathered his markers and tally sticks and tucked them into a sacking bag. He closed the ties with a double knot. "If I might offer a suggestion?"

Indeed, he needed all the help he could get. "Feel free, Gord."

Gord adjusted the folds on his bag. "I realize we are not on good terms with the...um...Scots."

"Aye." William restrained his desire to snap at the man. "This is generally the case when two kings are at war." Deep red flooded Gord's cheeks, and William felt the worst sort of lout. "I beg your pardon, Gord. Please continue."

"Well, we do things a mite different here in the north." Gord tied the bag to his belt, and smoothed it against his leg. "It does not seem to make much sense for neighbors to starve to death because our kings cannot see eye to eye."

Loyal to the king, perhaps not, but sensible, definitely. William motioned the man to continue.

"In lean times, I have been known to approach Aonghas the Red for help."

"Aonghas the Red?" Pictures of great, hairy Gingers cavorted through William's imagination.

"Verily." Gord shifted, but straightened his shoulders. "In exchange for the odd bushel and crate here and there, Aonghas helps himself to our animals."

"How many animals?"

"Umm...all of them."

Every muscle in William tightened in protest. Father did not tolerate poachers on Anglesea land. Then again, the well-provided-for Anglesea folk had no need to pilfer his father's herds. But Gord hinted at more than a bit of opportunistic poaching.

The bedamned Scott swarmed onto his land and stole the food from his table. "You mean he tosses us a bit of grain and steals our livestock?"

Gord adjusted his belt, then glanced up. "Would we call it stealing?"

"Aye, we would." William fixed Gord with a stare and drove the point home.

"He does send us some provisions to get us through the winter." Gord's voice grew softer and softer as William stared him down.

"Do you have a tally of what the thieving swine has taken?"

"Nay." Gord spoke rather too quickly, and then reddened to his hairline. "I judged it better to not keep too careful a tally."

"Indeed." William stepped closer to the man. "Or you might have to send our men to retrieve our losses."

Gord paled and stepped back. "The men...do not fight."

William must have misheard Gord. Men-at-arms fought. A keep succored men-at-arms for that primary purpose. "They do not hunt much, and they do not fight. What do they do then?"

"Umm." Gord took his time adjusting his cuffs. "They collect rents and our portion from the village. They guard, at times. Once, last winter they went hunting." He cleared his throat. "Only they did not have much luck."

"I imagine not." William scrubbed his hands through his hair. He should never have left his bed this morning. "Because your bloody neighbor has been replenishing his table from our lands."

Gord opened his mouth to argue.

"Do not." William stepped around him, done with this conversation for now. The list of inadequacies at Tarnwych grew with every conversation he attempted. "I am going to see the men. I presume they are in the barracks?"

"Of course, my lord." Gord frowned. "Where else would they be?"

Here at Tarnwych, William wouldn't hazard a guess. Swinging from the battlements perhaps.

He strode through the hall and took a grim, narrow staircase down to the bailey, encountering a few serving wenches on his way. Fornication? His earlier conversation came back to him and he shook his head. A keep rose or fell on unity between its residents. Tarnwych presented like a ripe peach for any ambitious young knight with no land and some men behind him.

He dodged the heavier puddles littering the inner bailey, but mud still sucked at his boots. Perhaps if the men swept the bailey instead of hiding their fornicating selves away, a pair of his boots might survive Tarnwych.

Built against the inner curtain wall, William mistook the barracks for animal pens at first and retraced his steps. Two men perched on upended crates, casting dice onto a makeshift table.

They stared at him.

"Good morrow." Sir Arthur would have thumped their heads together, but William preferred the polite approach at first.

The bigger of the two jerked his chin in response and hauled his bulk to his feet. Belly flesh pressed through the lacings of his tunic like a string of pasty sausages. Clearly, the men had found another way to supplement Cook's meals.

"Call up the men," William said.

"Eh?" The seated man rose. As fat as his friend, if a little shorter, and bald as a babe. These men hunted all right, only they kept the fruits of their labors to themselves. He had to wonder what else they kept, but that would save for another day.

"Call. Up. The. Men." William stepped closer. The reek of stale sweat and unwashed flesh had him fighting to hold his ground. "I need a hunting party and the strongest escort you can put together."

The men exchanged glances.

"I will call Dunstan," Sausage Belly said. He turned and bellowed into the darkened maw of the doorway. "Dunstan. Lady Alice's new man is here, wants to call up the men."

"Sir William." William held his breath and pressed his boot

toes to Sausage Belly's. "I am named Sir William. You may call me my lord. What should I call you?"

"Rufus," he said, and took a wary step back.

"And you?" William turned to his companion.

"That be Brown Aylard." An absolute bear of a man spoke from the doorway. Tall and wide, his shoulders brushed the door-frame on either side.

"Dunstan?" Dunstan wore the invisible mantle of power about his large shoulders. Rufus and Aylard shifted closer to him as Dunstan stepped into the bailey.

"Aye." Dunstan cracked his huge knuckles. A shock of dark hair tangled atop his wide head like a bird's nest. His sharp brown gaze swept William from boots to brows, cunning and assessing.

William let him look. Tarnwych could house only one lord. If Dunstan thought he filled the lord's boots, William would make it his special task to re-advise him. "Call up the men."

"May I ask why...my lord?" William tensed at the subtle taunt behind the words. Ending his morning in a brawl through the mud with a man-mountain made him weary to his bones.

"We hunt for the table."

"Ain't no game." Dunstan crossed trunk-like arms across his chest.

"Really?" William softened the air with the sting of derision. "Not one deer, boar or even rabbit in the entire demesne?"

Either Rufus or Aylard snickered, but William locked his gaze on Dunstan.

Flat eyes glowered back at him. Dunstan turned and yelled a string of names into the barracks.

From the speed with which the men appeared, they must have huddled just out of sight and listened.

William's heart sank. Tarnwych's men, filthy as pigs and clad in a motley collection of tunics and assorted bits of armor.

Only Dunstan wore the full hauberk over his tunic. "Get some horses and find something for the table."

"You will join the keep at meals," William said.

Rufus peered at him from behind Dunstan's shoulder. "We do not eat in the hall."

"You do now." William let his gaze meet each man in turn. "Clean yourselves up before you present yourselves at the hall." He let that sink in. "And now my escort."

"Where are we going?" Dunstan shifted his weight to one hip.

"To visit Aonghas the Red."

Aylard sucked in a breath, and a flicker of surprise crossed Dunstan's blunt features.

"Make sure the men understand: we cause no trouble, but prepare ourselves to meet it if it comes." William spun on his heel and tramped across the muddy ground separating the barracks from the stable. He held scant hope for the horses. At least he had brought his own horseflesh from Anglesea. Tarnwych would need more than his two destriers, however, if they planned to present an adequate mounted party. Sweet Jesu, like a hungry whore, Tarnwych would snatch up every shilling of the wealth he brought to this marriage. Sir Ivo had made himself a good bargain with this match.

Entering the stables, William got the first glimmer of hope from his miserable day. The horses were a swaybacked, raddled lot, to be sure, but whoever oversaw the stables kept them clean and the stable swept and tidy.

"Sir William." A short, wiry man almost bent double with age emerged from the gloom. "Are you needing your horse?"

"Shortly." Most of the stalls lay empty, but clean and clear of straw as if they stood ready for new occupants. He turned to the oldster. "Are you the stable master?"

"Aye." The man nodded his white head. "I be Gresby and I also keeps the hounds. Not that we have many of those. Sister do not care for dogs."

How to keep a fair head about a woman when every mention of her name meant a worsening of his day? "Indeed. How many horses do we have?"

"Eight, and your two."

God's, ever-loving, balls. Ten horses. Ten! "Why so few?"

"Sister—"

"Never mind." William would start hacking heads off shoulders if he heard one more thing about Sister Sunshine this day. "I will send to my brother by marriage for more." And bloody Gregory has best not rip the ass out the goose when he charged William for some of his precious nags.

Gresby nodded. He rubbed his gnarled hands together. "More steeds would be good. Perhaps some good breeding stock?"

"Aye. We can also bring a couple of sound bitches and some dogs with the horses."

Thus far, the easiest solution he'd delivered. He strode out the stables. Cedric had a hard ride for Anglesea ahead of him, after he informed Alice her husband was about to pay a friendly visit to Aonghas the Red.

* * *

Alice pulled the sides of her traveling cloak tighter about herself. Serviceable and hardy, it kept the worst of the evening chill off as she waited beside the horses for William to join them. She had rehearsed her argument in her chamber, and now she stood ready.

Cedric had given her the message that William left this night to meet with Aonghas the Red, or Canny Aonghas as he was also known. After the kitchens, she needed to do something to redeem herself. Exactly how had matters come to such a sorry pass? And how had she not noticed before now? Given this morning, she could not, in all good conscience, allow her new husband to journey to The Crags without her. Like a spider, Aonghas waited in his sumptuous manor for the juicy southern fly to drift into his web. Father refused to deal with Aonghas, as did most of the border barons, but Alice rather enjoyed him. His sharp brain and dry wit made any visit with him entertaining. Also, he called her a "pretty wee bird" and nobody but Aonghas had ever called her pretty.

Night fell early this far north, and already grim shadows cloaked the bailey. She drew closer to the comforting bulk of the covered cart, and out of the path of the two sturdy draft horses Gresby had harnessed to pull it. Placid and large, they did not frighten her as much as the enormous bay destrier awaiting his master. If she dared stand beside it, her head would not clear the horse's shoulder.

"Holy Hell! What is that?" William's voice cut through the muffled noises of shifting horses and waiting men.

"My lady's cart," Dunstan called from behind her.

William appeared before her. "Alice?"

"Aye." She bunched her hands into her cloak and steeled her spine. "When I heard you were going to The Crags, I thought I might come with you."

"Did you now?" The dark obscured his expression, but his eyes glinted at her.

"Aye." Sister Julianna had tried to talk her out of making the trip. For certain her tales of wild beasts and Scottish reavers had given Alice pause, but she had steeled herself and here she stood. "Aonghas knows me well," she said, before William could forbid her from accompanying them. "I could help. I know Aonghas's tricks, and I believe he trusts me."

"In that?" William jerked his head at the cart.

"I will not slow you down too much."

William studied the cart for a long moment and then turned back to her. "I should have asked Cedric to bring you a palfrey from Anglesea."

So far he had not uttered the words that would force her to remain. "It is no matter, for I do not ride."

"Pardon?" William bent and looked more closely at her. He shook his head and stepped back. "If you do not ride, my lady, then into the cart with you."

Alice stared at his outstretched hand. Braced for his refusal, he caught her wrong-footed.

"My lady?" He moved his hand closer. To assist her. Assist her into the cart so that she might go with him.

Alice grabbed his hand and clambered into the cart beside Gresby.

William mounted the great destrier with enviable ease, and they set off.

Alice clasped her hands together in her lap. What a strange one William was, but a trip out of Tarnwych always cheered her.

* * *

William kept Paladin to a walk. The destrier tugged at the reins, impatient with the crawling pace. What idiocy had compelled him to allow Alice along in her ponderous conveyance? He could tell himself he entered uncharted territory with Aonghas the Red, and that did form part of his reasoning. However, their current pace stretched their journey threefold. Not to mention he could not like the lack of a good escort when she accompanied him. Somehow, none of that had mattered in the face of her desperate need to come. Dwarfed by her ridiculous cart, fair trembling with suppressed emotion, her desire to accompany him had taken hold of his reasoning and muffled it. Bloody fool! He had helped her into the cart with nary an argument.

Sensing his mood, Paladin sidled and tossed his head.

William took a deep breath and corrected Paladin's path before he nudged the sorry nag beneath Dunstan. Alice could assist him, perhaps. Time spent away from Sister Sunshine might also give him an opportunity to unravel more of Alice.

It wouldn't have surprised him if the sour old besom had squatted in the back of the covered cart, her beady eyes burning into his back. But nay, she had sent him on his way with a stiff nod as he left the hall.

Around him, the men huddled like dark boulders atop their stringy beasts, heads lowered as they avoided the worst of the stinging wind. Sending men abroad without adequate clothing in this cold pricked his conscience. Anglesea's men were much better equipped, and they did not contend with this bitter chill.

Tarnwych and her people were in a bad state. The weight of his new responsibilities tempted him to dig his heels into Paladin and ride hard for home. Not even a full day as new lord and he had more snarls to untangle than a three-fingered yarn spinner.

It made no sense. Whilst not a wealthy lord, Sir Ivo's coffers remained adequate to care for his demesne. Father had used money as an incentive to this marriage, but more as an appeal to Sir Ivo's greed than to save him from poverty. Why had Alice let her keep drift into such a miserable pit? Yet, her people uttered no harsh words about her. Mostly, they spoke of her with fondness and pity.

Everything came down to Sister Julianna. What she did in Tarnwych baffled him. Nuns, for the most part, stayed inside their convents, sheltered from the world. Yet, here she bided, in a keep and apparently in command of it. Her influence over Alice concerned him the most. The woman had Alice, the keep, and all the residents in a death grip.

Well, he had dealt with difficult women before.

Ahead of them, the path wound through dark, oppressive spires of rock, close enough they brushed the sides of the cart. Hooves clopped on the hard ground, echoing against the unforgiving stone. Night closed around this barren, harsh land in an unrelenting grip of deep dark, and William could almost believe the tales of haunting and evil deeds northerners delighted in telling.

A man could imagine witches, fey folk, and demons peering down at him. If he was the sort of man who believed in such nonsense—which he wasn't. In the distance, a lone wolf sent its spine-chilling howl at the moon across the moors.

Beside Gresby on the cart, Alice looked like a child, and William drew his destrier as close as the narrow path would allow. "How do you fare?"

She turned her head toward him and grinned. "Is it not a fine night for travel?"

William chuckled, the sound pushing back the dark and the cold for a moment. He looked forward to solving the mystery of Alice.

Chapter Seven

Weak morning sun lit the rooftop of The Crags. William shifted in his saddle, his ass frozen solid to the leather. Despite his constant suggestions to call a halt, Alice had insisted they not stop on her account all through the interminable, bitter night. Right now, William felt every inch the soft southerner.

He wanted out of the nagging wind, off this bloody horse, a warm fire, and a full belly. Aonghas the Red had best not provide the sort of hospitality Sister Sunshine favored, or William might cry like a little girl. The bedamned northerners, none of them swathed in fur like him, looked as spry as if they had stepped out of the keep. Please God, let them hurt as well, or he would toss away his spurs and sword.

The lands around The Crags lay fallow. Rich, dark earth turned for the winter. Small thatched crofts nestled between stone walls that separated rolling grassy hills. Aonghas kept his demesne well. Tarnwych lands shared the same soil, and yet they suffered like a beggar beside a lord's table in comparison. A large herd of brown cattle cropped the grass beside the road. Travel improved across its well-maintained surface, for which his bruised ass throbbed in gratitude.

They passed through a tiny village and the road climbed toward a large, sprawling manor house. They stayed in the open, easy for watching sentries to spot. He creaked about in his saddle and faced Dunstan riding on his heels. "Do they mount no guards?"

"They have guards," Dunstan said on a grunt. "Only they know us well."

Or rather, they feared nothing from Tarnwych. A small party, alone on a broad expanse of land. Aye, Aonghas had no need for trepidation. The land about them offered no concealment for a force sneaking up on the manor, and as Englishmen he doubted they would find any help here.

As they approached, the manor's studded wooden door opened and a man stepped out. Dressed only in a chemise and chausses, he faced the cart with arms outspread. "It is a fine day when a pretty wee bird flies into Aonghas's hall."

Braced for a burly, ginger Scot, Aonghas the Red was a bitter disappointment. Thin and wiry, he would not even reach William's shoulder. Beneath dull brown hair, his winter pale complexion gave him a fragile air.

"I see our pretty bird has brought a visitor." Aonghas turned and greeted him. Keen intelligence gleamed in the light blue eyes of his adversary. William's nape tingled with anticipation.

William dismounted, gritting his teeth and forcing his numb legs to keep his ass out the mud. "Sir Aonghas."

Aonghas threw back his head and let out a boom of laughter completely at odds with his frame. "We have no place for sir this and sir that up here, lad. Just Aonghas."

Alice hopped from the cart. "Aonghas, allow me to present Sir William of Ang...Tarnwych."

"*Sir* William." Aonghas rubbed his hands together. "You have found yourself a pretty English lord here, Alice, my flower."

An invisible gauntlet whistled past William's ear. "When I am up north, it is merely William," he said. "I cannot have it said the new lord of Tarnwych puts his lady to the blush with his manners."

Aonghas narrowed his eyes. "You must be chilled," he said. "Not being accustomed to our cold. This is a hard land. It breeds hard men."

"With frozen asses." William threw Aonghas his most disarming smile. If the man chose to dismiss him as a soft southerner, he did so at his peril, and Aonghas would learn. Just as soon as William could feel his extremities again. William took Alice's hand and pulled it through his arm.

"Aye, well." Aonghas chuckled, his gaze lingering a moment on their twined arms. "I have fire enough to warm that for you."

William kept Alice tucked against his side as they followed Aonghas into the manor.

For a hard northerner, Aonghas enjoyed surrounding himself with the trappings of luxury. Large, sumptuous tapestries adorned the walls.

Aonghas motioned them to a set of fine, carved wooden chairs resting on furs before a roaring hearth.

Seating Alice closest to the fire, William perched on the arm of her chair. Beneath his fingers the intricately carved wood felt fine enough for a king.

Clapping his hands, Aonghas shouted orders to the large number of serving folk clustered about.

"My men?" Poor bastards had nothing near as fine as the raiment of Aonghas's people, but he would see them warm and fed.

"They are being well cared for." Sir Aonghas lounged on the seat across from Alice, one leg flung over the chair arm. "I will wager they already have a wench in one hand and a mug of something warm in the other."

William accepted a gleaming pewter goblet from a pretty serving wench.

The serving wench gave him a saucy grin, invitation glinting in her fine eyes.

Alice tensed.

William dropped his hand onto her shoulder. Whatever the future brought for them, his wife should know he would not accept every invitation cast his way. William sensed it would matter more to Alice than most. Even though her words on their wedding night would lead a man to believe she understood the way of things, even accepted them. Such a fool would grow frigid in his wedding bed. Behind her grass-green eyes lurked a fragility that tugged at William.

Rich notes of nutmeg and orange rose from the warmed wine in his goblet and almost brought him to tears of gratitude. Aonghas probably used Tarnwych's meager bounty to support his lifestyle, and William planned to enjoy it to the fullest.

"It was good of you to visit, with your wedding so recent." The old fox gathered details with each sweep of his gaze.

William's blood rose to the challenge. He'd spent years slithering his way around the venomous halls of King John's court. First rule of engagement: never underestimate your opponent. Men could appear weak and then develop a spine of hardened steal. Strong men could crumple at the first sign of opposition. Some might look at Aonghas and see a border Scot with no manners and refinements, but William knew better. He saw a man as canny as a ferret.

"Verily." William toyed with the edges of Alice's wimple. He'd like to damn the thing to hell for covering her glorious hair. "As nearest neighbors, I thought it wise for us to meet. Get the measure of each other."

"Ah, indeed." Aonghas sipped his spiced wine. He took a small sip, enough for politeness but not enough to risk muddling his senses.

"It is so easy in these troubled times for small annoyances to blossom into larger disagreements. Sir Arthur of Anglesea, my father, has earned a reputation as a man of war, but he has always taught his sons that war only happens when diplomacy and reason fail."

Aonghas's swinging leg paused, and then resumed. Aye, he got the message. William had powerful allies and a wealthy family.

"A wise man, indeed." Aonghas rested his chin on his palm. "Anglesea lies to the south, does it not? A goodly ways south."

"It does." William silently applauded Aonghas's parry. It's what he would have done. "We are a close family, and they write often."

A different serving maid refilled his goblet. This one even prettier than the last, with her generous bosom overflowing her bodice. So, Aonghas had made it his business to know all about William.

Aonghas sipped his wine, watching all the time over the goblet rim if William would take the delicious bait. "Tarnwych and The Crags have long been the most harmonious of neighbors."

"So Gord, my bailiff, informs me," William said.

"How is Gord?" Aonghas accepted a refill from the same girl. His gaze didn't stray near her bosom either.

"Gord is well." William grimaced. "Actually, Gord is not so well. He finds himself at a bit of a loss."

"Indeed." Aonghas cocked his head.

William slipped his hand beneath Alice's wimple and caressed her nape. "He finds himself unable to account for some missing beasts: cattle, goats, most of the deer. Enough for a man who keeps such excellent records as Gord to bring it to my notice."

Aonghas's shocked expression was wondrous, a thing of skilled dissembling. "I would like to tell you, Sir William, that such things do not happen in the north, but alas, I am unable to."

"Please call me William." William smoothed a charming grin over his features. He tightened his grip on Alice's nape. Please God, let the girl be sharp enough not to leap into this battle of wits. "Are you telling me theft is common in these lands?"

She sipped her wine. Twining the fingers of her free hand with his hand against her shoulder, she gave him a subtle squeeze.

Aonghas swung his leg faster. "I would not say common, so

much as not unexpected." He leaned forward. "Some of my countrymen are not always as honest as one would like."

"How disturbing for you," William said. "And you are sure it is Scotsmen responsible for these disappearances?"

"Aye." Aonghas cast his eyes down. "As much as it pains me to admit it. They come from the higher lands, where things are not as rich as they are here. It has become a sort of symbol of honor to steal from the English, and thereby the English king."

"Verily." William rubbed his chin as if giving the matter grave consideration. Aonghas lied, but with the sort of skill William admired. Not a man to ever play dice with. "I am guessing that you do not suffer such inconveniences as a fellow Scot?"

"Not that I have noticed." Aonghas looked genuinely regretful. William almost laughed out loud. This man would have wreaked havoc like a weasel in the dovecotes at court.

"Then, my path is clear." William heaved a sigh. "I must strengthen the men-at-arms at Tarnwych, run tighter patrols on my land, and treat with unfortunate brutality any transgressors. One can only hope that if one punishes swiftly and ruthlessly enough, the message will become clear to those who would view Tarnwych as a fat partridge." He too leaned forward. "Sir Arthur also taught me that it is often easier to make a preemptive strike than to engage in a long, drawn-out battle."

"That we should all have had such a wise and loving father." Aonghas's hard stare met his. Message conveyed and received. Aonghas would test his resolve, William would wager his life on it, but he had issued the warning.

Aonghas sat back in his seat. "But let us not disturb dear Lady Alice with this talk of fighting. Let us share a meal, and celebrate your good fortune."

"Was there ever a man so fortunate as I?" William said.

"I wish you long life and happiness." Aonghas raised his goblet. "Let us drink to your new land and your new marriage."

* * *

A masterful, thrilling battle of wits arced above Alice's head. Fascinating, and so much more satisfying than seeing two men hack away at each other with weapons. Here the weapons remained hidden. Thrusts made and parried with such speed a girl needed to pay attention to catch them.

She wasn't sure who had emerged the victor and had the sense these were merely opening feints, but William had matched Aonghas strike for strike, going into battle for Tarnwych. Alice shifted in her seat. Tarnwych's shame sat atop her shoulders. She had not understood much of William's discussion with Gord, but she had grasped the woeful state of the keep's stores. She had made this journey to make herself useful. Yet, William had not needed her at all, and still he let her come. If she knew him better, she might have asked why. Warmth spread from his hand on her nape, even through the linen. It was a gesture of claiming, possession. The sort of gesture a man made toward his bride. His wife. A delicious shiver danced down her spine.

Talk drifted to the weather, the history of The Crags. Light chatter of two men passing a pleasant time. Serving drudges carried in a meal bringing with them tummy-growling aromas of fresh bread, roasting meats, and pies. Platter after platter they laid on the trestle tables. Surely such excess constituted a sin, but it smelled and looked much closer to heaven.

At Aonghas's invitation, William rose and assisted her to table. He seated her on his right, according her the honor of his wife.

"Will you take meat?" His solicitude humbled her. Selecting for her the very finest cuts of meat, a loaf of nut bread still warm from the ovens. Using his napkin, he wiped the moisture from the fruit he placed beside her.

"My thanks." Alice wished for the poise to take his treatment as her due, but it touched a cold, lonely place within her, and rendered her near mute. He accorded her the respect of a new bride, and a treasured one. Without words, he shouted to the hall his pleasure in his marriage. *He does it for Aonghas's benefit*, whispered her practical nature. *But how lovely it feels,* simpered the girl buried deep within her. That girl's whimsical musings had stayed hidden deep within her for years.

William waited for her to begin her meal before he ate. He motioned a man over, eyes twinkling at her. "Wine?"

The rogue returned and brought her smile with him. "Aye, please."

Taking the jug from the serving man, William poured her wine for her and handed her the goblet. He watched her take a sip. "Any blackberries?"

Alice giggled. Verily she had giggled more since his arrival than in her entire lifetime. "Nary a berry to be found."

"For shame." He shook his head. "My Alice should always be showered in blackberries."

* * *

William's head hammered away like the devil used it for an anvil the next morning. Blasted Scot had a head for drink that had almost seen William sliding beneath the table. Had they drunk wine, William would have had the wily sod, but that bedamned "special mead" had nigh killed him off.

It still might as he blinked in the clear, bright morning light. Today, of all days, the north tossed out her loveliest mantle of blue sky. Clustered about on their nags, his men looked even more pitiful in the unforgiving light. He could bluster all he liked about taking a hard line with the thieving Scots, but not even he believed it when staring at his dismal force. Dear God, had the north no finer fighting men to offer? He may as well drive his herds into Aonghas's courtyard and spare himself the humiliation.

Aonghas, ruddy cheeked and bright eyed, beamed as if suffering none of the aftereffects of the night and offered him his hand. "Safe travels, Sir William."

"Call me William."

"Oh, aye." Aonghas batted the side of his head. "I keep forgetting."

Like bloody hell.

"Good morrow." Alice's sweet voice provided blessed relief. She entered the courtyard dressed little better than their men, but her shy smile dimmed the ache behind his eyes. He had sent her to find her rest hours before Aonghas and he had begun their rod-jousting over a jug.

Her cart stood ready with Gresby perched behind the horses. They wouldn't reach Tarnwych before the following day. That did not suit him, at all. Not if he had aught to say about it.

William hauled his bones onto Paladin, glad he managed a semblance of elegance, and nudged the horse to Alice.

She took a wary step back.

"Come, my lady." He leaned down and held out his hand. "Today you ride with me."

"What?" She eyed his destrier and pressed her hand to her throat. "I do not ride."

"But I do." He managed a reassuring smile. "I will not let you fall." If she demurred, he might toss her onto the horse anyway. He could not stomach a day of dragging his ass behind her ridiculous cart.

Alice shook her head. "I—"

William scooped her beneath her armpits. Light as a feather, he lifted her onto the mount before him. "There." He forced some good humor into his voice. "Now stop wriggling, or the horse might take fright."

She perched frozen before him, her nails digging into his wrists. "I would prefer the cart."

"That is because you have not yet tried the horse," he said. Motioning his men, he spurred Paladin out of the courtyard.

* * *

Alice clamped her lips together, swallowing the scream welling up in her throat. The ground flew past beneath them as the horse clattered over the cobbled yard and through the manor gates. A long, long way down, the blurring ground made her stomach lurch.

Father laughed at her fear of horses, but even he had not plonked her down on one. Only the fear of falling kept her still. They cleared the village and thundered out into the countryside. The motion of the horse would bruise her nethers black and blue. Behind William's shoulder, Gresby and her reliable cart grew smaller and smaller.

When they stopped she would set Sir William right about his actions. Her cheeks still burned from the embarrassment of him grabbing her up like a sack of grain.

"Breathe." William's voice rumbled through her back, his breath touched her ear. "It will go easier for you and the horse if you hold yourself less rigid."

Was he mad? "I will fall."

His arm tightened about her middle, pressing her closer to his hard strength. "I will not let you fall." He chuckled. "Although you might remove your nails from my arm before you draw blood."

He deserved having his blood drawn, but Alice eased her death grip on his arm.

"Feel the motion of the horse beneath you," William said.

How did a girl feel anything but all that man pressed against her side?

"Do as I do," he said. "Rock with the motion, do not fight it." William's thighs bunched and the horse lengthened his stride. They went even faster but jounced less than before. "My brother by marriage, Gregory, trained Paladin. He is the very best of his breed."

By that she assumed his horse was called Paladin. A fitting name for the huge beast. Powerful muscles played beneath

Paladin's gleaming coat as he carried them forward. Alice unbent her spine a mite.

"There," William murmured. "Work with the horse."

She allowed the rolling motion of the horse to move through her limbs. William was right. The dreadful jouncing eased. If she kept her eyes off the ground and fixed on the countryside flying past them, she might enjoy her ride.

"Alice." William's exasperated tone made her stiffen again. "Your wimple is flapping in my face. Would you remove it please?"

The starched ends of her wimple slapped his cheeks, and he had his head craned high and out of its way. He looked ridiculous craning his face clear of the stiff, snapping cloth, but to remove her wimple. The alternative of blinding William whilst she rode before him did not seem sensible. Finger by finger, she released his arm. Unfastening it with one hand took longer than she would have expected, but the ties gave eventually. Before she could catch it, the wind whipped it out of her hand. Alice turned as far as her awkward seat would allow. Her wimple fluttered down and disappeared beneath the horses following them.

Wind caught her hair and sent it streaming out behind them in a wave of bright copper.

"See, Alice." William laughed, the sound rumbling through her back. "You have your own war banner."

Reaching up she tried to contain the mess.

"Leave it." William tucked his head into her neck and out of the path of her enveloping hair. "Fly your flag proudly, my Alice."

My Alice? He called her that often, and she rather liked it. A special name he had for her, like how Aonghas called her "pretty wee bird," only better.

She was riding, on a great fearsome destrier. Her beautiful husband behind her, holding her steady. The day grew even brighter about her. A day on which she might believe herself his Alice.

Sister waited for them as their party entered Tarnwych's bailey late into the evening. She stood statue-like outside the keep doors, the white of her scapula catching the light of the torches.

Alice's body ached a bit from the riding. Fear had disappeared somewhere between here and The Crags, and she resolved to learn to ride. Horses were not so very fearsome after all. Alice straightened in the saddle before William.

William's hands held her steady as he lowered her to the bailey floor.

"You are returned," Sister said, smoothing her scapula front. "Did the cart have a mishap?"

"Nay." Alice ducked her head out of the glare of reproach. "William believed we would travel faster by horse."

"But you do not ride." Sister folded her hands beneath her scapula. "Your hair."

Her devil's hair snarled into a mass of curls down her back, and Alice tried to smooth it into a semblance of order. "I lost my wimple on the ride."

"You." Sister snapped her fingers at a nearby serving wench. "Go and fetch Lady Alice another wimple."

"My lady has no need of one." William stood beside her, his hand warm on the curve of her back.

"Your pardon, Sir William, but any lady has need of a wimple." Sister drew herself up. "No decent lady dares go about with her hair unbound. It is an affront in the eyes of our Lord."

William took a deep breath, the press of his fingers harder in her back. "An affront to our Lord?" His voice softened, silky with anger. "Our Lord is surely not so capricious as to create such beauty and then see it hid."

"No disrespect, Sir William." Sister raised her chin stretching her lips into a tight smile. "But I believe as a bride of the church, I am somewhat closer to the wants of our Heavenly Father."

Alice's skin prickled with the waves of anger seeping from William.

"Indeed, however—"

"I prefer my wimple." Stepping away from his light touch,

Alice moved closer to Sister. "I will repair my appearance and see you for the evening meal."

"The men and I will do the same and meet you in the hall," William said.

Sure she must have misheard, Alice stopped and whirled about.

Sister's chest rose and fell with her rapid breath. "The men do not eat in the hall."

"They do now." William strolled closer. The charming man who had ridden with her vanished beneath a calm, ominous stranger. "They will bathe and present themselves in the hall for meals from this point onwards."

"At Tarnwych we—"

"As a knight, Sister," William sketched a low bow, "I believe I am somewhat closer to the ruling of men."

* * *

William kept himself still as anger, indecision, and frustration all chased across Sister's harsh features. Riding with Alice before him had washed away the last of his sour mood, but it returned with a roar that left him wanting to punch something.

The way Alice had buckled and folded before Sister's condemnation roiled inside him. All day, he'd caught glimpses of a different Alice. A woman whose laughter rang, one who waited at the bars of her cage for someone to set her free. With one look, Sister Julianna had slammed the door shut on Alice.

He didn't trust himself around the malicious old crow. He needed to occupy himself elsewhere until he had a firm hold on his temper. "But for this night, the hall will sit down to its meal without us." He strode through the men to the barracks. "This night we work."

Crows cawed loud and raucous over the silence in the bailey. Heads whipped between him and Sister. "I want everything out of the barracks." Pinning the men nearest him with a hard stare, he raised his voice. "All the filth, all the beddings, everything. I want them out and burned. Rufus."

The man's head snapped up.

"Build a fire in the center of the bailey. The men of Tarnwych do not live like swine."

"Everything." Sister's voice rose from behind him. Sweet Jesu, this would not end well between him and this woman. She had enough love for her neck to remain on the steps leading into the keep. "Is such wanton destruction necessary?"

"Everything." William shifted his glare from man to man. "Right now. Burned."

"How will the men sleep?" Alice appeared at his elbow.

For her sake, William tugged hard on the reins of his temper. "They will not sleep until the barracks are cleansed of filth and vermin."

Dunstan cracked his knuckles and planted his feet akimbo. Aye, another reckoning came there too. William met his stare. He ached to take the big bastard on, right here and now. Disappointment soured his gut as Dunstan turned and shouted orders to the men around him. The man would make a good commander, if he could bend his bull neck to his new master.

"Will you not rest?" Alice touched his wrist. "They could clean the barracks in the morning."

Nay, he could not rest. He needed activity, something to keep his mind from the building anger within him. "I will rest when my men rest."

Alice took a soft breath, and nodded. "I will see that the serfs make up fresh pallets. The men will need them when they are done."

A small victory but it coiled within William and calmed the fire in his blood. His Alice would stand by him on this. From the keep entrance, Sister Julianna watched them through narrowed eyes.

* * *

Bone-weary, Alice returned to the hall after she had changed her gown and confined her hair. A new mood sparked the air as she entered. Faces full of questions turned her way as she murmured her greeting in passing.

Muted sounds drifted up the stairs from the bailey. Men's voices, raised and then lowered, the crack of wood, and the low buzz of activity. William worked out there, beside the men and if she judged it right, the work would take all night. She did not visit the barracks, as Sister judged it unwise, but she had noted the condition of the men as they rode. Seen how they compared with Aonghas's men, and if the barracks matched their residents, then she applauded William's wisdom.

Serving women carried out the meal and placed it on the tables, a testament to William's kitchen foray. Great platters of meat appeared, bringing with them the hearty scent of venison. Alice dared not meet Sister's eye, but she felt the rise of outrage battering against her as fresh breads and greens accompanied the meat. Where had Cook obtained fresh vegetables at this time of year? Later, she would ask Cook, but for now the tempting aromas set her tummy growling. Aspic jellies and blood puddings were added to the happy murmur of the hall. She had not eaten since they left The Crags. A quick bite of bread and cheese as they had rested the horses could hardly sustain a body.

"Have the men outside been fed?" Alice called to Gord where he sat at the table nearest the dais.

Gord cast a yearning gaze at the bounty set before him as he rose. "Nay, my lady."

"Would you see to it?" Commands coming from her mouth sounded odd. "Make sure they receive their share."

"They are working," Sister said. "They will not have time for eating. Your husband has seen to that."

"William would want them fed." Alice's head reeled a bit at her own daring. Seldom had she countermanded Sister, and never before a gaping hall full of people. "If Tarnwych is to have an effective army, they must be cared for." Nobody had told her this, but it stood to reason. "And on the morrow, Gord, would you put the seamstresses to work on new raiment for the men? We looked like beggars before Aonghas."

"Aye, my lady." A slow smile of approval spread over Gord's thin face.

Alice drew courage from it and returned his smile.

"They have raiment." Sister's dry tone pricked at her pleasure.

"They have rags," she said, forcing her voice to remain firm. "We cannot send them out into the cold without adequate covering. Our Lord would not condone such dreadful cruelty."

"Sir William sent his squire for new horses," Gord said. "But the men will need weapons, as well. I will call for the blacksmith when I go the village in the morn."

How had she not seen what a treasure she had in Gord? Perhaps because this was the first time she had actually commanded the man. "Perfect."

Chapter Eight

The next day passed in a blur of activity for Alice. Gord made good on his instructions, and the keep hummed with new activity. She stood at the center of the mayhem, issuing further instructions, answering questions, and filled with a sense of purpose that made her never-ending list of tasks seem lighter. Serving maids gathered linens, stuffed pallets and pillows, and cut rushes for the barrack floors. Seamstresses pulled bolts of cloth from the stores and spread it over the trestle tables in the hall. Their chatter as they worked filled the austere place with life and cheer.

Out in the bailey, the blacksmith got the old forge running, and his fires belched heat into the overcast day. Over the clang of hammer on anvil, work continued on the barracks. It gave her a thrill of excitement every time she glanced out the casement and saw the men-at-arms scurrying this way and that, their posture taut with purpose. William broke his fast outside with the men and worked alongside them throughout the day.

The hall that night fair buzzed with the number of voices. Scrubbed clean with damp hair and fresh faces, the men skulked into the hall and took their places at the newly set out trestles. Fires blazed in the hearths, dispelling the chill from the walls.

Cook blossomed under her new freedom, sending yet another excellent meal into the hall.

Beside Alice, Sister refused all offers of richer fare and worked her way through a bowl of thin beef broth. Alice rolled her eyes when Sister requested yesterday's bread, and near laughed aloud when the serving woman reported Cook had fed the pigs with it.

Sinful, perhaps, but Alice tucked into her dinner with relish. Her heart lifted as she looked about her at the contented faces in the hall. Despite Sister's dire warnings, the men did not get drunk, belch or pinch the serving women. Alice would wager their night and day of grueling work had exhausted them. It had thrilled her to do her part, and have the new pallets stuffed and smelling of heather delivered to the barracks. Today her keep functioned as a keep should, a place of refuge and respite.

William entered the hall and her breath gave a curious hitch. Hair still slicked to his head from bathing, he wore a simple linen tunic, still much finer than aught she owned. The deep blue fabric imperfectly mimicked his eyes as he looked at her and waved. As he moved through the hall, people returned his greeting. He stopped at the men's table, clapped a hand on the shoulder nearest him, bent and spoke with them. A deep, base guffaw rippled through the hall. Her husband had this way about him, as if he carried a pocketful of faery dust and scattered it about the heads of those he encountered.

She liked a lot less how the women blushed and simpered as he greeted them. Even old Maggie, eighty if she was a day, bridled and batted her eyes at him.

"Ah, my Alice." He took the seat beside her with a smile that twined inside her chest. "How I have missed your lovely eyes."

Sister's head snapped in their direction, her gaze burning the side of Alice's face. "My stagnant pond eyes?"

He grinned and motioned for wine. "Is it poetry you require of me now, my lady?"

"Thank you, nay." She could not resist the sparkle in his eye. "I have had an adequate sufficiency of your verse."

"Wise woman." He sipped his wine and gave a sigh of appreciation. Slumberous warmth filled his gaze. "Far better to glut yourself on my other skills."

Alice's throat dried. Not since he had kissed her had William gifted her with that look. It crept across her skin in a tingling rush of awareness, and she shivered. This man was her groom, not yet husband. A low thrum hummed in her belly, spreading its tendrils outwards.

"Wine?" William's voice startled her. A serving girl stood beside her, Lord knows for how long, waiting to know if she wanted her goblet filled.

Over his shoulder Sister's dark eyes met hers. Mouth twisted in a sneer, Sister turned her shoulder on her.

"Nay." Alice waved the girl away.

William dug into his meal and Alice let out her pent breath. Thank the Heavens he had decided against pressing the issue. She rather fancied a goblet of wine, but with Sister already wroth over her unbound hair when riding with William, followed by their disagreement in the hall yester eve, abstaining seemed wiser. The weight of Sister's voiceless anger pressed on Alice's shoulders. In her life, Sister had been the one constant, the person who stood by her when all others passed on. Only the most ungrateful of people would turn their back on such unselfish devotion.

* * *

His Alice looked pretty tonight, despite the hideous wimple concealing her glorious hair. The trip to The Crags had agreed with her, and a charming blush of color stained her wan cheeks. Her support of his efforts had pleased William immeasurably, and he meant to encourage her taking charge of her keep.

God's teeth, his tired limbs ached. A night drinking with Aonghas, followed by last night without sleep, and this day spent in hard labor had him bent like an aged crone. As much as he enjoyed Cook's renewed efforts in the kitchen, it did prolong the meal until his head threatened to drop into his trencher.

However tempting, he doubted he would be of much use to Alice in the bedchamber.

Sister Sunshine rose, casting an immediate pall over the hall. "I will now lead the keep in prayers."

Oh, dear God, nay. Dismay reflected on the faces in the hall sent his gut sinking into his boots. Sister Sunshine, he would wager his life, shunned any quick benediction sort of worship. Alice rose and followed in Sister's wake, dispelling his desperate hope of missing prayers and finding his bed.

Fortifying himself with a large sip of wine, William stood and offered Alice his arm.

She blinked at it, and then placed her hand on his sleeve. Small and delicate, with slim, elegant fingers capped with neat, trimmed nails. He had the sudden desire to see his jewels adorning her hand.

They entered the chapel at the far end of the hall. Taper smoke drifted in the flickering golden light, stinging his tired eyes. Tarnwych folk filed in and crammed the benches until a few hardier souls took positions against the wall. For a keep this size, the chapel was small and cramped with low stone arches pressing close to their heads. Behind the altar, the plain, mean casements glared at the congregation. He took his place beside Alice and tried to get comfortable on the hard wooden bench.

Sister Sunshine stood beside a rotund priest, who nodded as she whispered in his ear. So the goose led the gander here too. Despite the cold in the stone walls, the press of so many bodies warmed the chapel and sweat beaded on his forehead and slid down his cheeks. The smell turned his stomach. At Anglesea, Lady Mary insisted on weekly bathing for all residents of the keep. As boys, he and Roger had never managed to outfox their mother and escape their scrubbing, no matter how hard they tried. Lady Mary had the sharpest eyes at Anglesea, and whatever she missed, Nurse would catch.

Having grown to manhood in such a close and loving family, he had taken it for granted. Unfamiliar faces surrounded him in the chapel. In time they would become his family, but for now, he wished Roger sat beside him, fidgeting and cursing beneath his breath. Henry, the pious brother, would lean forward and glare at Roger to sit still. William had always sat between Faye and Beatrice. He used to make a game of seeing if he could get Faye to break her perfect poise, and Bea was always good for a giggle, even on the most somber of occasions.

Alice shifted on the bench beside him, her slight, heather-scented warmth a comfort against him.

The priest opened the singing of the mass with a deep, sonorous voice that swelled rich and lush through the chapel. Incense twined with swirling taper haze and heat. The priest sang on, a surprisingly beautiful voice that fell on the ear like a lullaby. William swallowed a yawn. He blinked against the weighted air, his eyelids growing heavier and heavier.

William's soft snore filled the gaps in Father Mark's mass.

Sister's head snapped in William's direction. Her eyes narrowed to mere slits.

Alice crinkled her face into a silent apology and nudged William.

He came awake with a jerk.

Alice dared not glance his way. The uncomfortable desire to giggle grew inside her and she jammed her nails into her palms. Still, silent laughter quivered in her belly and rose like bubbles in her chest. She was going straight to hell. Giggling in church, indeed.

Sister's expression dispelled the laughter. Sitting rigid, her set face fixed on Father Mark, Sister worked her rosary beads through her fingers in a blur. Would it be wrong for Alice to pray Father Mark got through mass quickly? For certain it would, and Father

Mark loved his singing voice too much to cut mass short. She should spend this time in careful contemplation of her sins, ready to make her confession. Did finding your husband beautiful constitute a sin? If aye, she risked eternal damnation.

William slumped against her shoulder in a hard, hot press of man. She gave him another nudge, but he murmured and his head lolled forward. He could not be comfortable falling asleep sitting on the hard benches. But William slept like a babe. During mass. With Sister, no doubt, praying with all her might, but whether she prayed for William's deliverance, or cursed his sacrilege, Alice remained uncertain.

Thankfully, he responded as Alice prodded him into kneeling and standing when required. The effort it took had her nerves jangling and she welcomed Father Mark singing out his final blessing and sending them all out into the world again.

"Your pardon, Alice." William strolled by her side out of the chapel. "It seems my nights have caught up with me." He must be exhausted, and Alice sympathized. Still, worship was a sacred time for reverent awe before their Creator.

"Alice." Sister hailed them outside the chapel.

Did William groan? His face remained mask smooth. Dark shadows beneath his eyes spoke of his fatigue, but he stood as tall and proud as ever. "I will see you in our chamber," he said, and with a nod good night for Sister, he left.

"Aye, Sister." Alice braced herself.

Sister motioned her into a small well at the base of the stairs. The same stairs William climbed to their bedchamber, his boots scuffing the stone as he went.

"Alice, I know not what to say." Only Sister did know what to say, and Alice knew she would hear it. "That man." She wrapped her rosary about her fist. "That man has no respect for the Lord."

"He was tired, Sister. He rode all day and then remained working with the men through last night and today."

"Did Christ our Savior rest when Satan tempted him in the desert? For forty days and nights, he remained vigilant."

Alice bit back her swift retort. Telling Sister Sir Arthur of Anglesea had sired William and not God would bring more condemnation down on her head. William climbed into bed as she stood here. For certain he would be asleep by the time she freed herself from Sister. "Nay, Sister, he did not."

"He did not." Sister unwrapped the beads and smoothed them against her skirts. "He comes from an un-Godly family, Alice. Never let his pretty face make you forget that."

Lady Mary had seemed such a nice lady. Alice would not call her un-Godly. Aye, but William did have a pretty face, and a glorious form to go with it.

"Are you paying heed to my words, Alice?"

"Aye, Sister."

"You must be on your guard, child. The devil comes in many forms, some of them fair enough to tempt the most pious, and you are not that, are you, Alice?"

Alice attempted to formulate her reply. In what way had she erred enough to earn such criticism? Except, some of her thoughts the past few days would have shocked Sister, for certain. "I do not think I have been sinful."

"Alice." Sister shook her head, and smoothed the ends of Alice's wimple over her shoulders. "Did I not see you ride into this bailey with your hair unbound like a wanton? A chaste woman does not display herself for the lusts of men."

Lust seemed a trifle strong for some unbound hair. "My wimple came off as we rode and was trampled in the mud."

Sister clicked her tongue. "A bemuddied wimple would not have prevented a woman of virtue from covering her head."

I am not a nun! The words rose hot and fierce onto her tongue. Alice clenched her jaw and stopped them from bursting out. Lady Faye wore her hair unbound, as did Lady Beatrice. However, Lady Faye had married a man who had turned his back on his calling to the church. And Beatrice had married a base-born bastard. She had always abided by Sister's teachings in the past. What had her asking all these questions now, and doubting Sister's wisdom?

"I do not blame you, child." Sister tucked her hands beneath her scapula. "I knew how it would go when I heard of your father's marriage plans for you. You obeyed your father, as is right. And you will always be subject to your husband, but that does not mean you must not guard yourself from the lures of Satan."

Very well for Sister to say thus, but the lures of Satan did not sleep in her bed, filling the air with the scent of cloves and warm skin, wrapping strong arms about her and holding her against a hard, male chest. There she went again. Perhaps Sister spoke true, and these unruly thoughts marked the first step on the path to damnation. Even as she thought it, part of her rejected the idea. William was not evil. She would not call him chaste or reverent but he treated with kindness those who served him. All of his actions in the past days aimed at improving life for Tarnwych folk. Best of all, he treated her as if she had value to him. He made her laugh, and it seemed a long time since she had laughed so much or so hard.

"See that you get yourself with child as soon as you can," Sister said. "Before the corrupting influence of evil can find its way into your heart and eat away at your faith."

"Best I return to my bedchamber then," Alice said.

Sister blinked at her.

"In order to...get myself with child."

Sister's face went wine-red, her eyes bulging out of her head. "Indeed."

"I will see you on the morrow, Sister. God be with you."

"And you." Color still stained Sister's cheeks as she gave a jerky nod.

Alice took the stairs a little faster. Her conscience prickled that Sister's discomfort amused her.

Chapter Nine

Alice attended prayers alone the next night. Just as she had sat alone at dinner. She hadn't spoken with William since he'd dragged his tired self up the stairs to bed and away from Sister.

He'd been asleep when she'd arrived in their bedchamber the night before, flat on his back, snoring softly. Alice had stood above him and watched him sleep. It still seemed strange that this beautiful man now occupied her bed.

The following morning, he had risen without waking her and spent the remainder of the day working with the men. When she had peeked out the casement around midday, William and the men cleared the old, abandoned beast pens beside the barracks. A serving wench told her they planned a practice yard. Alice had stopped a moment and admired the way the wind ruffled William's dark hair and played across the clean planes of his face. Thus far, her spying skills improved. Those keep trulls with eyes stuck on her husband best take note.

Opening her bedchamber door, she bid goodnight to Sister and entered.

William sat on the end of the bed, a huge grin on his face. "Good evening, my lady."

"Good evening." Alice stopped and stared at the large wooden chest open at William's feet. "We missed you at dinner. And at prayers."

Grin widening, he swept his arms over the chest. "I have a good reason for my absence."

Brilliant scarlet silk gleamed in the firelight, thanks to the large fire now always present in her bedchamber. Curiosity overcame politeness, and Alice stepped closer to the chest. "What is it?"

"This?" William shrugged. "Why, this is yours."

"Mine?" Alice reached out to touch the silk but snatched her hands back again. "Nay."

"Aye, my lady." William rose and approached her. "This is your bride gift."

"Bride gift?" Like a silly, wooden poppet, she repeated his words but could not fathom his mood or the chest. "Your father already sent a bride gift."

William shook his head. "Your bride gift from me to you."

"Oh." Little ripples of excitement quivered through her middle. A gift for her. Surely not. "I do not require a gift."

"Alice." William laughed and slid his arm about her waist. "If you required it, it would not be a gift. Come now. Are you not curious to see what I have brought you?"

Alice let him urge her closer to the sumptuous temptation of red spilling from the chest. Her father used to send her gifts for her birthing day, but he had not done so in years. Sister frowned on the custom of giving gifts over Christmas, so they offered alms to the poor instead. But a gift just for her. She nigh floated to the ground and knelt beside William.

"Touch it," he said. "There is no finer silk in the kingdom."

"I cannot." Alice clasped her hands behind her back. Would the silk feel as magical against her palms as it looked? Would it feel soft as down or cool like water?

"It is yours." William claimed her hand in his. "You can blow your nose on it if you like."

The idea made everything in her recoil. "Nay."

"Aye." William mimicked her tone. "Here." He took the silk from the chest. It spilled over his hand with a life of its own. "Feel."

Cool, smooth, soft, and delicate, the silk stroked her cheek. Alice pressed into the heat of William's palm beneath the fabric. He draped the silk over her shoulders.

"It is truly mine?"

"All yours." William drew it from the chest, the silk sliding over her nape and pooling in her lap. His expression softened, and he touched the back of his fingers to her cheek. "Look into the chest, Alice."

Beneath the silk lay more fabric in a green so lustrous it held life within it. A gasp escaped her. Surely, that could not be...

"Velvet," William murmured as he drew it from the chest. "My sister, Beatrice, tells me there are days when a woman feels for silk, light and airy." His voice deepened to a rich, bass rumble. "And then there are days when she wants the stroke of velvet over her skin."

Alice's fingers glided over the velvet in her lap. Queens and princesses wore such costly cloth. She'd heard of velvet, but to have it in her lap made her breath catch. Like the fur of a tiny kitten, the velvet felt alive and warm. The silk was lovely, but the velvet. Dear Lord, did anything rival this? "It is wondrous."

"Then you should wear velvet every day if you love it so much."

Wear velvet indeed! Alice snorted a small laugh.

"Why not?" William cocked his head and studied her. "I have the wealth to keep you swathed in velvet for the rest of your days." He leaned closer, a wicked gleam lit his eyes. "You could have your underclothes made of velvet if you fancied."

"Would that not be a fine thing." She laughed and stroked the velvet.

William rose and strode to a table beneath the casement. He carried a serving platter to where she knelt and set it beside her.

"What is this?" Alice had already dined.

"A wedding feast." Chuckling, he handed her a goblet of wine. "You will not drink it in the hall, but in here, I am afraid I must insist."

What else could she do? Airy bubbles of happiness rose inside her. Alice took the wine from him and sipped.

"Speaking of things I insist upon." A harshness entered William's voice. He frowned at her. "I thought we agreed no wimple in here."

"Aye, but—William!"

He'd whipped the wimple from her head faster than she could blink, and sent it sailing across the chamber. "I hate that thing."

Perhaps the wine muddled her thoughts, but she did not mind so very much. In truth, her head grew hot and itchy beneath it during the day, and it was a relief to have it off.

"Now." He reached into the chest. "What else have we here?"

Gold inset with shining gems hung in his fingers. A girdle made entirely of gold links and inset with precious stones. Alice clapped her hands over her mouth and stopped her gasp. "That is not real gold?"

"Would I give my lady painted steel?" William looked so affronted that she laughed. "A lady needs a girdle to wear over her velvet gown, would you not say?"

"I..." Words escaped her. Against the velvet, the girdle would look rich and fine, like the one Lady Mary had worn at her wedding. Lady Mary's girdle had swept her slipper tops. Silk slippers, Alice would guess.

"And what is a girdle without a matching necklace?" He placed the necklace around her neck.

"Oh." Alice had never beheld a thing so lovely. Glittering gems nestled in the centers of gold wrought flowers and swirls. Lady Mary had also worn jewels at Alice's wedding feast, but none as fine or delicate as this. Faery hands might have crafted it.

It was too much. Alice's chest tightened until her breath sawed through her mouth. A hard knot formed beneath her breastbone and lodged there. "I cannot."

"Alice." William took her face between his warm, calloused palms. "It is all for you, my bride. Along with everything else in the chest."

"Nay." More fabric lay beneath the velvet, and the Lord alone knew what else. She had done nothing to deserve such bounty. Where would she wear such lovely things? Beautiful women with silvery laughter who walked on tiny clouds wore things like this. Plain little Alice of Tarnwych had no use for them. Oh, but how she would love a gown of the green velvet, or the red silk. To sweep into the hall with the heavy links of a golden girdle resting on her hips. A tear escaped the corner of her eye and snaked across her cheek.

William caught it with his finger. "I did not give you this gift to make you cry, my Alice."

"I cannot accept them." Saying the words aloud released more tears until the room grew blurry around her.

"Sweet girl," William murmured as he touched his lips to her tears. "I wanted to give you joy, not tears. Do you not like the gift?"

"I love it." The words rode a sob that began in her chest and burst out of her mouth. "I do not know what to do with such things."

He tucked her hair behind her ear with a tender smile. "I am not a woman, but even I would wager that you would wear them."

His silliness brought a choked half sob, half laugh out of her. "Where?"

"Anywhere you liked, little Alice. To the midden heap if it pleases you."

Wouldn't that be a fine thing to see? Alice laughed.

"There now." He pressed at her nape, drawing closer, until the finely wrought lines of his lips seemed no further than a breath. "Now give me a kiss and say thank you William."

Warmth prickled beneath her skin. The last time he had kissed her still simmered within her. "Thank you, William."

Tightening his hands about her face he pressed his lips to hers.

Better than silk and velvet, even better than the jewels, was the firm caress of William's lips on hers. She tilted her head and pressed closer into his kiss.

On a groan, he slipped his tongue into her mouth.

Prepared this time, Alice sunk deep into the sensation. Ripples of excitement spread through her, growing stronger as the kiss deepened.

William claimed her mouth, possessed it.

His thrilling ownership blossomed into heat that began in her center and spread. Greed for more swept through her. More William, more kissing, more of everything else. Alice wrapped her arms about his neck and pressed closer. Her breasts swelled and ached, sensitive against the rough fabric of her chemise.

"Aye, Alice." He trailed his lips down her cheek and found the heavy throb of her blood at her neck. His hands at her hips urged her closer to him.

Alice went willingly to the reward of his hard, male chest.

Over her back, his hot palms roamed. His lips tortured her skin.

Her breath came in soft pants from her mouth. She felt tiny, delicate and feminine within his arms. Like a cat, she arched into his touch.

"So sweet." William's kiss grew hungry, as if he could devour her.

And, aye, she welcomed it, came alight under the stroke of his tongue. She hadn't known a man could taste of aught, and now it seemed as if she had lost years not knowing, and she could not waste another heartbeat. She burrowed her fingers in his hair, tightening her grip, keeping his mouth on hers.

"God, Alice." He pulled away from her, his harsh breathing filling the tiny gap between their mouths. "Let me get you onto that bed before we go any further."

Unease slithered down her spine, penetrating the blanket of lust he'd wrapped around her, and Alice drew back. He spoke of consummating the marriage. And suddenly she wanted to cry. She wanted him to keep kissing her, to keep making her feel like a live flame.

"Alice." He tilted her chin to meet his gaze. "Do not be afraid."

"I am not afraid." Not exactly, but she did not want what came next. It would tarnish all the wonderful he had just given her. "I know what must be done."

"Back to that are we?" William shocked her rigid with the nasty curse he uttered next. "Alice." He clasped her shoulders and gave her a small shake. "Nothing will happen here that you do not want."

Aye, so he said, but what she wanted did not matter between man and wife. "I want a child."

"Aye." William stood, and stared at her. "But the begetting of one does not have to be a fate worse than death." He tugged her to her feet. "You know, my Alice, I could speak until I turned blue in the face, and you would still look at me with that stubborn little chin stuck out. The best way to prove you wrong, wife, is to prove you wrong."

He hoisted her into his arms.

Alice barely had time to shriek before he lowered her onto the bed.

"Now." He stood back and tilted his head. "I see I have to start at the beginning. Never mind." He stretched on his side beside her. "I am a man who enjoys the lead into love, as much as the act itself. I also have the patience of a bedamned saint."

"William." Alice really needed to correct his blasphemy. "You should not—"

"Be still, Alice." He nipped at her bottom lip. "Forget about my language. Forget about what comes next. Keep your attention on this." His mouth covered hers, hot and hungry.

That she could do, and Alice let her thoughts flee to the corners of the room and beyond. As long as he kept kissing her, she could forget her own name.

She opened her mouth beneath his.

His answering groan thrilled her, gave her a sense of some ancient feminine power she held and could wield.

Hammering came from the door.

Alice bit back one of William's nasty curses.

"Sir William." Sister's brittle voice acted like spring water dousing Alice's mood. "There is trouble amongst the men."

"Back to the blasted nunnery." William growled and strode to the door. He opened the door with a yank. "What is it?"

Alice felt a moment's sympathy for Sister as William near bellowed the question.

"The men have a girl," Sister said. William blocked Sister from Alice's sight. "This is what comes of the men being familiar with the women of the keep. As you claim superior knowledge of the men in your charge, I brought this to you."

"Stay there." William left the chamber at a run.

Sister peered around the door at her, and smirked. "I warned you what comes of sin."

* * *

William drove his boot heels into the ground, his anger a living, breathing thing within. No habit would protect that nun if she launched another of her venomous insinuations between him and Alice.

"My lord." Gord dropped into place beside him. "Thank God, you are come. It is young Molly."

"Molly?" A bolt of alarm sparked through him, and William increased his pace.

Gord panted as he kept up. "She is young. One of the kitchen wenches."

"What in hell is she doing in the barracks?" William lengthened his stride across the bailey, his boots sliding through the cold, slick mud.

"I sent her," Gord said. "To take some washing cloths and soap to the men. One of the younger lads came to get me."

"Jesu." William drew closer to the barracks. From within came the shouts and jeers of men. Then, almost lost beneath their harsh guttural tones the murmur of a girl's voice, pleading.

Ivy's face flashed before him. Not the Ivy of now, calm and serene, almost angelic in her wisdom, but the Ivy Beatrice had first brought to Anglesea. Pale, her eyes haunted with the horror of what had happened to her. He would rip their bedamned heads off. Men who raised their hands to a woman, used their strength to hurt her, he would tear limb from limb.

Beyond the barrack doorway he met a solid wall of male backs. All their attention intent on the center of the room. The noise overwhelmed him, along with the sweaty stench of lust. William shouldered through them. Using his fist, he punched a path through those who didn't move immediately. As he shoved past the last line of watchers, silence descended behind him.

They had Molly pinned to the back wall. Two of them holding her arms back. Her torn bliaut revealed her young breasts bared and quivering with her rapid inhalation. Sweet Jesu, she could be no more than fourteen.

Dunstan's back confronted him. He should have guessed who he would find in the thick of this.

The girl watched him, big, brown eyes choked with terror, silently pleading with William for help.

His anger hardened into cold, impenetrable ice, sharper than any blade.

The men holding Molly caught sight of him. Rufus and Aylard, Dunstan's lackeys, always at his back.

Aylard dropped Molly's arm and stepped back. Rufus paled, his grip slackening.

"Hold her, you scum." Dunstan shoved Aylard at Molly. "Hold the little cunt."

A soft gasp at William's side made Dunstan whirl about.

Alice. Jesus Wept, she had followed William out into the barracks. Puking fear tore through William's gut. "Leave."

"Nay." She raised her chin, the top of her head equal with his shoulder. "These are my people. I would be here."

Men loomed over her, great hulking, crushing beasts. William had not the time to argue with her. "Keep her safe." He grabbed Gord by his tunic front. "Get her out of here if you need to."

Gord nodded.

A small group of men pressed closer to Alice. Two flanked her, pushing their shoulders in front of Alice to shield her. They nodded to William as well. The grim set of their features told him they wanted no part of Dunstan's malice, and they would protect their lady. Later, he would deal with them. He would have no leniency for any man who had witnessed this and not stopped it. But for now, he locked eyes with Dunstan.

His face flushed, blood high, Dunstan sneered at William. He threw one hand out and strutted before a terror-frozen Molly. "Look, our pretty lordling has come to save the whore."

Dunstan topped him by nearly a head. A massive lout with arms thicker than sides of beef. Despite the thick roll of lard hanging over his chausses, Dunstan had the confidence of a gutter rough and some speed with it.

"It takes three of you to subdue a little girl?" William raked his gaze over Rufus and Aylard.

Aylard flushed and dropped his head. "It were not my idea."

"Get your hands off her." Out of the corner of his eye, Dunstan pushed closer. Cocky and sure of his influence amongst the men, and his own strength, Dunstan had grown too comfortable in his position of power.

Molly crumpled to the ground. With shaking hands, she pulled the torn edges of her bodice over herself.

William approached her. Tension mounted behind his back.

Dunstan stood his ground, shoulders back, chest thrust out.

Arrogance would keep Dunstan from attacking his back, but

who else fancied his chances of ridding themselves of their new lord?

Alice remained in the barracks. He forced the fear back behind a rigid shield of purpose.

"Go." Angling his body to keep most of the room in view, he took Molly under the elbow and raised her to her feet. "Go to Lady Alice."

Rufus sidled along the wall, closer to Dunstan.

Aylard shifted from one foot to the other, his features pinched as his gaze darted between William and Dunstan.

William jerked his head at Aylard and Rufus. "Take them."

"I will cut the hand off any whoreson who touches them." Dunstan cracked his knuckles.

"Such a big man." William let his gaze travel Dunstan from tip to toe. "Raping little girls and threatening frightened dogs. Would you care to take your chances against someone who fights back?"

Chin fat jiggled as Dunstan threw back his head and guffawed. "You?"

"Aye, me." William's blood rose hot and angry. "But let us make this a fair fight." From the sheath at his waist he pulled his dagger and held it out. "Take this, you will need it."

* * *

William had gone mad, handing a dagger to a foe who towered half a head taller and carried considerably more bulk.

"Aye, I will take your dagger." Dunstan accepted the gleaming dagger. "And gut you like a pig with it."

Amid gasps and deep bass murmurs, the crowd slithered back.

"My lady." Gord tugged Alice's elbow. "You must step back. Return with me to the keep."

Alice shook her head. He was madder than William if he thought she would go now.

Palms up, William circled Dunstan. "Give it your best," he said. "Because you will get only one chance."

Dunstan lunged.

William danced back. The knife hissed through air where he'd stood an eye blink ago. Carved from granite, William's face gave no emotion. His glance flickered over Dunstan, calm and assessing, assured even.

Brazier light bathed men in amber. Absolute silence descended over the onlookers.

Molly pressed at her back, gripping Alice's skirts.

Swinging the dagger, Dunstan closed left, then spun and sprang to the right, blocking William's escape.

William ducked the knife and kicked. Boot connected knee with a sickening crack.

Dunstan bellowed and lumbered at William, thrusting the knife wildly.

Dodging, William hammered Dunstan's ribs.

Breath whooshed from Dunstan, his face a mask of pain as he roared and plunged the dagger through William's tunic.

William leaped straight into Dunstan's rising fist. It connected with a thud of bone against flesh.

Chest heaving, William recovered and leaped back. A red mark marred his chin, and he spit blood.

Closing on William, Dunstan grinned and raised the knife.

With both fists, William pounded Dunstan's knife hand, and the knife flew. Dunstan manacled both arms about William's ribs.

Face red, William kicked, catching Dunstan's thigh, then the injured knee.

With a sharp crack, Dunstan's knee buckled. He dropped William and stumbled.

William grabbed Dunstan's hair and drove his face into his knee until Dunstan's features melted into a mangled mess of blood and saliva. William roared. Feral. Enraged. Victorious.

The hair at Alice's nape lifted.

He snatched the dagger, yanked Dunstan's head back, and cut his throat.

As Dunstan crumpled to the barrack's floor, blood gushed over the pale rushes and stained the sandy earth.

Alice heaved and covered her eyes. William had cut Dunstan's throat like a diseased dog. Worse was the savage feeling of satisfaction that had whipped through her at the moment William killed the man.

"Anyone else?" William straightened his shoulders. His cold, furious scrutiny swept the men. "Whip those two." He gestured to Aylard and Rufus. "Whip them until they understand fear."

Men shrank back.

This was not the handsome, laughing stranger of her bedchamber, or the smooth, urbane diplomat who faced down Aonghas. A stranger, a wild, savage stranger whose calm unnerved her stood in front of them.

"This is how it will be." William wiped the dagger on his tunic before sheathing it. "You have this night to decide if you stay at Tarnwych or go. If you go, you leave with the clothes on your back and nothing more. If I find so much as a grain of dirt missing, I will hunt you down and kill you."

Men shifted, whispers rippling through them.

"If you stay, you stay under my rule and my terms. I will deal with anyone who breaks my rules. Do not doubt that for heartbeat."

Alice believed him and so did the shocked, nervous faces of the men about her.

"My rules are simple. You are here to serve the keep. Lay down your lives for those who find shelter here. No woman is to be harmed, ever. I'll kill you myself, like I did him." William toed Dunstan's body. "No child, elder, or any man weaker will feel your fist or your mockery. This is my demesne. Everything on it belongs to me. Your poaching stops now. Arms training begins when the sun rises. Make sure you are ready or get you from my keep."

William's ferocious gaze snapped to her, and Alice shivered. He stalked toward her, gripped her arm and all but dragged her out of the barracks. Halfway across the bailey he spun her to face him. "There are times, my lady, when you will obey me and do so without question."

Alice tried to firm her trembling knees.

"You are never to put yourself in danger like that again." He shook her, not hard enough to hurt, but a clear warning. "Do you understand me, my lady?"

Alice nodded. Danger crackled in the air around him. Dread purpose suffused his being, and she crumpled beneath the sheer force of his will. Deep inside, a weak protest rose to challenge his authority. To protest his rough treatment of her, but self-preservation shouted it down and she nodded a second time.

"Get her back to the keep." William spun back to the barracks.

"Come, child." Sister Julianna took her elbow. "This is no place for you."

Reaction set in as they entered the keep. Her shaking limbs stumbled and tripped as she climbed the stairs. The image of Dunstan's blood filled her mind, and her belly heaved. Red, red blood, oozing life with each precious drop.

"You poor child." Sister Julianna slipped her arm around her and supported her.

"He killed Dunstan." Was that thin, reedy sound her voice? The hammering of her heart near drowned it out. "I didn't think he could, or would, but he killed him."

"There now." Sister half carried her through the hall. "Men are nothing more than animals. This has been a harsh lesson for you, but one I trust you will remember and remember well."

"How is Molly?"

Sister Julianna clicked her tongue. "Silly wench is scared witless, but mostly unharmed. He got there before the men could do their worst."

William had saved Molly. Savage and vicious he may have

been, but he'd had good reason. Hadn't he? Right and wrong did not seem as defined in her mind anymore. Where lay the greater evil, in what Dunstan had done or the just taking of a life? Could one ever justify taking a life? A headache throbbed behind her eyes. None of her other husbands had caused her this much thinking.

* * *

William clung to the outer bailey wall as he heaved up his dinner. Away from keep eyes he dropped his mask. He had taken a life tonight. As a fighting man, born and raised, he'd encountered death before. Dealt it out more times than he cared to remember, but the senseless waste of life never grew easier.

He pressed a shaking hand to his screaming ribs and drew a careful breath. Strong as an ox, Dunstan had got a firm grip on his trunk before William got free. Now Dunstan lay dead. William took the washcloth Gord had handed him earlier and wiped Dunstan's blood from his hands. Would he could wipe it from his conscience.

He pushed away from the wall and strode into the inner bailey. Careful none of his thoughts showed on his face, he marched past the clusters of men huddled together as they spoke.

Dunstan had flown his "troublemaker" colors from William's first day. Still, William had wanted to be wrong, wanted to avoid the entire confrontation. In raising a weapon against his lord, Dunstan committed treason, a crime punishable by death. Had it gone unpunished, the next man to fancy himself a taste of power would rise in challenge of William's authority. And the next...

As a man of war, Father possessed very few finer graces, but he knew men. He had always told all three of his sons a hard, preemptive strike could mean the difference between a protracted, messy war and swift peace.

Lazy, undisciplined, and left like stray mongrels to develop bad habits, Tarnwych's men had wallowed in their squalor. Well, he'd sent a clear message tonight. By morning the malcontents would have slunk off into the night.

At rest for the night, the keep burned low tapers, lighting his walk through the hall. He'd stayed in the bailey long enough for the whipping of Aylard and Rufus. Another senseless act, avoidable if the dullards hadn't blindly followed the wrong leader. He'd had them cut loose and sent Father Mark to tend their wounds. Would Tarnwych have any men-at-arms left in the morning?

A boy passed him on the stairs, big eyes staring at William like he'd seen a ghost. The child bowed so low, his forelock brushed the ground. "My lord."

"Get to bed, boy. It is late." William tried to gentle his tone. He would wager tales ran rampant through the keep of his deeds this night.

"Aye, my lord. Right away, my lord." The boy backed away, missed his step, and would have gone tumbling down the staircase if William hadn't caught him.

"What are you doing up so late?"

The boy averted his gaze, and heavy breaths rasped through his mouth. "Rats."

"Rats."

"Aye, my lord. I am Will, the rat catcher."

"That's a fine name you have there, young William."

Will almost smiled and gripped his tunic. "My thanks, my lord."

"Do you always catch rats in the middle of the night?"

Will nodded. "That is when they are most busy."

Rats were not in William's collection of knowledge. What would his mother do? For certain, she would not support keeping young children from their beds. "Do you like dogs, Will?"

"Eh?" Will stiffened. "I mean, I do not know, my lord."

"Then we shall find out." William's bed whispered sweet nothings to his aching body. "We will get some ratters in here, and you shall have the care of them."

With a pat on the shoulder, he left Will and resumed climbing the stairs. Alice needed dealing with next. He'd spoken roughly to her tonight, and it sat ill with him. But, sweet Mother of God, when she entered the barracks after him, the fear had nigh choked him. If things had gone badly with Dunstan...

His flesh crawled. His Alice. Pocket-sized, flower-fragile, and innocent despite her three marriages.

She was also now frightened of him, and he might have undone all the progress he'd made with Alice. Of course, closer than a tick to a dog, the blasted nun had whispered in Alice's ear all the way back to the keep.

Here he'd thought marriage would be a simple thing. Find an appropriate bride, let his father make the match, and then get on with the business of being wed. Unfortunately, Tarnwych threw one snarl after another. His days of wedded bliss drifted further and further from his grasp.

He opened the door to his bedchamber.

Alice sat on a bathing stool beside a large bath. Her unbound hair shone to rival the large flames dancing in the fireplace. The tang of lemon filled the warm air.

"Sir William." She stood. Her little hands knotted in her apron. "I thought you might like to bathe, after..." She jerked her head toward outside the keep.

William stood in the doorway. Of all the receptions he might have expected...It almost brought him to his knees.

"Of course, if you would prefer not to bathe, I can—"

"Alice, you must be an angel." William strode across the chamber and stopped her mouth with a smacking kiss.

"I did right?" Her big green eyes undid him, packed full of uncertainty and the desire to please.

"You did perfectly."

Delicate pink stained her cheeks. "I could assist you."

"Alice." He took her face in his hands. "I can honestly say that given a choice between you and Cedric, I would take you every time."

"Cedric is riding for Anglesea," she said.

"Then it is indeed fortuitous that I picked you."

* * *

Alice busied herself as William disrobed. First his boots, and then his tunic. Fisting the collar, he hauled his chemise over his head. Finely wrought muscle covered his chest. A thin line of hair marched between the ridges of his belly and disappeared beneath his chausses. Aye, but he was finely put together. His skin was dark, as if he spent time in the sun without his clothing.

As he turned, she allowed herself the pleasure of studying his back in more detail. Wide shoulders tapered into his slim waist.

He removed his chausses.

Dear lord. She spun about and nearly collided with the bed post. This would never do for a woman married thrice before. None of her other husbands had looked like William, though. She couldn't resist another peek. His tight, muscular buttocks repaid the risk. With his hands on either side of the tub, he sunk into the warm water.

His deep sigh shivered though the air.

Alice gathered his discarded clothing and placed it by the door. The iron scent of dried blood curled her lip. Sister would have a method for removing the bloodstains. Alice would rather toss the clothes into the fire than ask Sister. Of course, she could sneak the clothes into the kitchen hearths without Sister knowing. It wouldn't be the first time she'd avoided hours of scrubbing in cold water.

Water swished behind her. "Alice?"

"Aye."

"Would you?" He pointed to the basin of bathing soap. William's wet hair was plastered to his head. Moisture gleamed from his skin. Her stupid head kept sticking on his nakedness beneath the water. What did the rest of him look like? The parts she hadn't seen. The parts no decent woman had any business speculating about. Belly fluttering, mouth parched, she approached the bathing tub.

"Shall I?" The soap basin teetered on her shaking palm, and she grasped it with both hands. Now she needed to spread the soap all over him, and then wash it off. Slowly. Her pulse hammered in her throat. Silly girl. Assisting someone with their bath did not mean an invitation to maul them.

"Please." His beautiful smile spread over his face.

Mauling it was then, and with a clear conscience. But first, she had one more little pleasure for him. She crossed to the casement table and poured him a goblet of wine, the special kind he had brought from Anglesea.

His look of delight as she handed it to him gave her the courage to pick up the soap basin and kneel beside the tub. Beneath her hand, his arm was warm and hard as she spread the soap from his wrist to his shoulder.

"You do not have to do that," he said and took a long sip of his wine.

"I know, but I thought you might be tired." She dug her fingers into the taut muscle of his shoulders and earned a heartfelt groan. A similar sound to the one he made when he kissed her. The too large fire heated her skin to discomfort. Nay, the warmth came from within her.

He dropped his head forward and she soaped his nape and shoulders. His skin was smooth, marred here and there by the odd scar. He must have earned the older scars as a boy. She imagined William as a sprightly lad, quick to mischief and keeping his nurse on her toes all day long.

Spreading her fingers wide, she ran the soap down either side of his spine.

William hissed and jerked beneath her fingers.

Alice snatched her hands back, not sure how she had erred. Perhaps she had been too enthusiastic in her attentions.

"Sorry." He exhaled. "My ribs are a bit tender."

"From the fight?" Red mottled skin covered his ribs, turning blue and purple in places. "You are hurt."

"You could kiss it better." He sent her a wicked glance over his shoulder.

Alice snorted and scooped more soap from the basin. Carefully she cleaned the injured parts and around to his other arm.

William shifted his goblet to the other hand and watched her. "I thought you would be...upset."

His steady gaze made Alice uncomfortable, and she rose and fetched the soap basin. "I do not like bloodshed. I have not had much occasion to witness it."

He clasped her hands around the basin. "But you understand why it was necessary."

A question so direct deserved a direct answer. "I am not sure that I do. I understand Dunstan did wrong and would have been worse had you not stopped him."

"But?"

The truth burned in Alice's throat, but Father did not like her to voice her opposition, and Sister often twisted her words until Alice wished she'd never uttered them. William was a near stranger to her. From the day he had walked into her keep—their wedding day—he twirled and turned like a gemstone on a string. Light reflected off first one facet and then another until she battled to see the stone for itself.

"Look at me." His tone compelled her to meet his gaze. "Never be afraid to speak your mind to me, Alice." He squeezed her hands. "Perhaps when we are amongst others, it will not do to be constantly challenging me. Here, in this room, I want your honesty, whether I enjoy hearing it or not."

"Did you have to kill him?" Faint and breathy, her words rushed from her. Alice froze. She hardly dared think where she had found the courage to utter them.

William grimaced and dropped her hands. "Aye, I asked myself that same question. I do not know for certain. At the time, my fighting blood was up and I obeyed my instinct." He scrubbed his face with his hands, leaving droplets of water spiked on his long lashes. "Now, I am not so certain. I keep thinking perhaps I should have shown mercy. But even as I say that, I know had our positions been reversed he would not have hesitated to kill me."

Alice absorbed the truth of his words. Dunstan would have killed him. She had read the man's brutal intent as he fought William.

"We men are a lot like dogs," he said. "Dogs need to establish who is the strongest amongst them from the first. Once that has been done, we get along rather well within our defined places."

"Indeed." She had no idea how to respond to that. Sister would have agreed whole-heartedly. Truth be told, Sister would have them all drowned as pups if she had her way. William had frightened her today, and not just with the fight. Did she dare test his claim to want her honesty? Aye, well there was only one way to find out. "You were wroth with me and I did not like it."

"Aye." He sank lower into the water and rested his head upon the tub lip. "I did not like it either, but I was furious to see you there. If something had happened to me, who would have protected you in amongst those men? Gord?"

"I do not enjoy being shouted at." She took his point, and he did not appear ready to bellow at her for daring to speak, so she aired the remainder of the grievance.

"In that you are not alone." A soft smile made him look endearingly boyish. "The women in my family would agree with you there."

"They would?"

"Lord, aye." He chuckled. "Faye would have given me a look to make my ball...blood freeze, and paid me back in some manner when I was least expecting it. Bea would have yelled right back at me."

"I do not yell," Alice said.

William's dark brow rose. "With that hair?" He snorted. "Alice, I have a feeling you have not begun to know the fire within you."

Chapter Ten

How did a girl find her 'fire' dressed in these? Alice's coarse linen bliauts, one brown and uninspiring as mud, and the other the shade of Cook's old pottage lay on the bed where she'd tossed them instead of getting dressed. A dull, brown wren wore bliauts such as these. Only she did not quite feel like a wren anymore. More of a robin, with a dash of color to her plain plumage. In the chest at the foot of her bed lay the glorious silks and velvets William had gifted her.

What gowns they would make. Beneath the green velvet lay more bolts of cloth. This morning she would like to wear the yellow samite. Bright and cheerful, it would surround her in silken sunshine all through the day. She picked up the pottage-colored dress. Not quite sunshine, but the closest thing to it she had.

The chest whispered to her of the treasures it held. *Yours, all yours.* Perhaps a quick peek. Like a thief, she snuck across her chamber and laid her hand on the chest's clasp. A waft of bay leaves, laid within the chest to keep the vermin from the fabrics, greeted her.

The jewels William had packed in the top of the chest winked up at her. Beside the gold-and-gem girdle lay another plainer girdle of silver links and yet another of silk shot with silver. A delicious shiver ran up her arm as she touched her fingertips to first one girdle then the other. So long, they would touch the ground as she walked, dipping and swaying with each step, drawing the eye to the roundness of her hips. Would William look at her with heat in his eyes if he saw her thus?

Silly thought. What did she care if he looked at her with desire? Her heart gave a dull thump. A man such as William would never look at plain Alice as if he found her beautiful. Alice slammed the chest shut. One could dress a hen up all one liked, but it remained poultry.

Still. There had been a small gold ring with a tiny gem in the center amongst the larger pieces. Not the sort of ring that would draw notice. William had given her these lavish gifts, and to ignore them might insult him.

She opened the chest again. Sifting through the sparkly temptation of the other jewels, she found the small ring. It slid onto her finger as if made for her. Nobody would even notice the small, pretty ring on her. Holding it up to the light, she let the sun play with the gem for a bit before she finished dressing and left her chamber.

She entered the hall as people broke their fast. At the men's table, a few places sat empty. So, not too many had left in the night. Aylard was not amongst the men, but Rufus sat apart from the others, hunched over his meal.

"Ah." William's voice carried across the busy hall. "The flower of the north has joined us."

Folk swung and stared at her. Alice's cheeks heated. It felt odd to be the subject of so much attention. A couple of good-natured grins made the heat flare brighter. He did like to tease, this man.

"Stop." She accepted his assistance onto the bench.

He looked well rested this morning. As well he might, after having excused himself from his marital duties the night before and fallen fast asleep within one blink of his head touching the pillow. Alice had not slept as well, and when she did, his naked, wet body followed her into her dreams.

William eyed her wimple and snorted.

"Not many of the men left?" She dodged the issue of the wimple. Why the man cared so much what she wore on her head baffled her.

"About ten in all," William said. "We could ill afford to lose them. The barracks are under strength as it is."

"And the rest?"

"Appear ready to work this morning."

Sister climbed the stairs to the dais. Voices hushed, people bent closer to their bowls upon her entrance. "Sir William." Sister took her seat. "Alice."

A serving girl put pottage before Alice and Sister.

"Here." William nudged her. "Try it with honey."

Before Alice could protest, he dripped golden honey into her pottage.

"Perhaps I do not like honey," Alice said.

"Everybody likes honey." William grabbed a pewter jug. "And cream." He added a healthy dollop of thick, rich cream to her bowl. "How will you spend the day?"

Alice's mouth watered as she dug her spoon into her bowl and mixed everything together.

"Alice and I will be making lye soap," said Sister.

"Good God." William shuddered. "The stench alone is enough to make me glad I am spending the day out of doors."

"Alice does not neglect her duties." Sister murmured grace over her bowl.

William stared at Sister for a long moment, before he said, "Alice seems to have a great many menial duties for a chatelaine."

With a tight smile, Sister inclined her head to William. "Alice does not hold herself above the other residents of Tarnwych."

"True. Indeed, one might say that Alice does such a fine job of it, that she misses her true place."

Alice sat right here. Wedged between the two of them like a

bone between two mastiffs. She needed to ease the tension. William seemed the easier prospect, and she turned to him. "What will you do today?"

William dropped his eye duel with Sister and nodded at the men. "I need to start as I mean to go on, and getting that lot to handle the right end of a weapon is my first task."

"Weapons." Sister refused any offers of honey or cream and ate her pottage with a sour face. "Too many times, reason is lost beneath the clash of steel."

"Indeed, Sister," William said. "But until our enemies do not use steel against us, I can see no other way to defend ourselves." William took a peach from the platter and paired it with his eating knife. He handed Alice the first slice. "I am all ears, Sister, if you can make a better suggestion."

"I would not dare to trespass on your superior knowledge." Sister pressed a hand to her chest.

"How kind." William cut himself a slither of peach and ate it.

Alice chewed her slice of peach. If they continued in this manner, it would ruin her breakfast, which would be a crying shame. The cream turned the pottage smooth and silky and the honey added enough sweetness to make it truly delicious. Verily if she had known pottage could taste this good, she would never have turned her nose up at it.

"Now, I must leave you to your soap-making, my Alice." William kissed her cheek and rose. As if obeying a silent command, the men rose with him.

His long-legged strides took him out of the hall, the men hurrying along in his wake. The hall seemed dimmer for his absence. More like the hall she had grown up in. Ridiculous! William was a man, not a ray of sunshine or some such nonsense.

When Sister had finished her meal, they rose together and left the hall. Great vats of fat oozed their acrid stench into the kitchen yard. About a dozen women, kerchiefs about their mouths and noses, worked at making soap ready for the keep.

Alice accepted a kerchief from Sister and tied it about her

nose and mouth. Of all the tasks of the keep, this was the most disgusting. The stench stuck to your skin and hair for days.

From beyond the corner where the kitchen yard joined the bailey came the clash of steel. Several women stopped working and looked that way.

William had the men at arm's practice. She'd once seen a traveling minstrel show with a swordsman they said came from beyond the seas in the far, icy North. Alice had clapped and gasped with the rest of the audience as the man twirled his huge sword about, bringing it down in a flash and stopping a hair short of a large, juicy apple.

She couldn't picture William doing all that swirling, and even less strutting about like a bantam rooster with his chest puffed out. For all he had a lovely chest.

"Get back to your work," Sister called.

"Now, Sister." Old Martha leaned into her paddle and stirred. "What is the harm in looking?"

Sister stiffened and rapped her paddle against the cauldron. "Idle hands are the devil's play things."

The two women beside Martha rolled their eyes but got back to their stirring.

The smith's three daughters huddled over their cauldron, casting longing gazes toward the bailey. Still young, the idea of so much male activity excited the girls. Alice saw nothing wrong in that.

"Back to your work, Aggie." Sister pointed at one of the girls.

Aggie dropped her head and murmured something to her sister that made Joan snicker. As soon as Sister turned her back to fetch more lye, Joan stuck her tongue out.

Alice ducked her head and hid her grin.

William's voice carried on a light breeze from the bailey. Heat from the cauldron fires burned through her clothing and perspiration ran down her back and sides. Large blocks of animal fat burped in her cauldron.

"I will fetch the rose oil." Sister laid down her paddle and strode toward the kitchen.

Aggie and Joan glanced at each other and dropped their paddles. They slunk to the corner and peeked around.

Alice smiled as they jerked their heads back, giggling.

"What are you doing?" Sister's voice startled the girls, and they jumped.

Dragging their heels and whispering all the way, they went back to their labors.

Aggie whispered to the third sister. Ruth, a few years older and already married, gave a small sigh and shook her head.

More steel clashed, and female heads swung toward the sound.

They had never had true men-at-arms at Tarnwych. Curiosity prickled beneath Alice's skin. What did William teach the men? Aggie and Joan spread their tale in whispers that travelled from one woman to another. They left her and Sister out of the gossip circle.

Enough. Alice did not want to be always on the outside staring in like a hungry fox.

Alice dropped her paddle into the cauldron and strode around the corner of the kitchen yard. In a titter of giggles and the rustle of clothing, the other woman followed her.

"Where are you going?" Sister shouted after them.

"To watch the men," Alice called back. The look Sister threw her promised a harsh lecture but Alice did not care. She wanted to see what men in arms practice looked like.

Women clustered around her, she stopped just in sight of the new practice yards.

"Ooh, Lady Alice." Young Tildy sighed. "Ain't it a grand sight?"

Grand, maybe not, but definitely stirring. William had the men arrayed in ranks behind him. He moved, more graceful than a dancer, sword flashing in the sunlight, calling out instructions as he went.

"Look at my Harry." Ruth jostled her shoulder. Pride shone in her face as Ruth watched her ungainly husband slash and stab his way through the thrust and parry William demonstrated. "He looks like a real knight, he does."

"Aye, Ruth." Alice smiled at her. If the woman saw her champion in the clumsy lad, who was she to say different?

The only real knight, William, belonged to her. Tall, broad, beautiful, and a tummy-clenching sight in his effortless skill.

William called out a command, the men responded in a deep bass rumble.

Around her the women collapsed into appreciative giggles and sighs. Alice kept her own sigh deep within. On second thought, Tildy had the right of it. It was a grand sight. Men doing what men did—manly things.

In the practice yard, William moved out of formation and the men continued through the forms. He approached a man, adjusted the angle of his sword. Stopped at another and adjusted his grip. Clapped a third on the back and earned a proud, sweaty grin in response, and so he went from man to man. Then he stood to the side and watched, his attention intent on the men before him.

Her father did not train with the men. He had a chief man-at-arms for that and a handful of younger household knights.

William glanced over and waved.

Tildy squeaked. "You have a handsome husband, my lady."

Alice smiled and waved back. "Aye, I do."

William spoke to the man beside him, then turned and strode to his horse. With a graceful leap he mounted.

The horse wheeled, hooves flashing, and cantered toward her and the women.

"He is riding over." Tildy clutched her sleeve.

Alice took a wary step back, but William stopped his horse short of the women and held his hand out. "Ride with me, my lady."

All she had to do was take his gauntleted hand. She had

enjoyed their ride from The Crags. The wind cold against her cheeks, running through her hair and whipping it out behind her.

"Oh do, my lady." Tildy poked her.

Ruth winked. "Go on, Lady Alice. It will put some color in your cheeks for sure."

"Quite right." William threw Ruth a charming smile. "Who wants to make soap on a day as fine as this?"

His horse tossed its head as if agreeing, big teeth chewing the bit between them.

It was a fine day. Chilly, but the sky soared above them in a blue arc, and a gentle wintery sun did its best to distill the worst of the cold. Alice placed her hand in William's.

A laugh ripped free as he lifted her over the saddle before him. "Today we ride to chase the wind," he said, and parted her legs so she rode astride like a man.

Straddling a horse with her legs on view from the knee down. Beyond shocking. "William." Frantically she tugged her skirts and covered as much as she could. "This is—"

"Hah!" William dug his knees into the horse, and they shot forward. His forearms pressed against her sides, his chest warm at her back.

So what if people glimpsed her knees. She had heard of plenty of women who rode thus. Everybody said it was far safer in any case.

Hooves clattered over the drawbridge and they cleared Tarn-wych. Beneath her thighs, the powerful shoulders of the horse carried them into the moors beyond.

They went so fast the ground blurred beneath them. Faster than their first ride together. Light and joy filled her chest. She flew. Free, glorious, and unfettered, and she never wanted to touch the earth again. Alice threw back her head and laughed.

William's laughter rumbled through her back, buzzing in her ear.

She grabbed her wimple ties and whipped it off. Wind ripped

it out of her hand and sent it sailing like a bird across the late blooming heather.

"Aye," William yelled. "Let the blasted thing go."

He pressed into her, hunching her body over the horse. The horse lengthened his stride until they galloped faster than the wind. Her hair streamed over them, flying across her face and William's. They rode the moor, following the lazy turns of the river.

When William sat straight in the saddle and slowed the horse, Alice's heart dropped. She never wanted their ride to end.

"I must have a care for my horse," he said. "He is a fine beast, but we do not want to tax him too much."

Alice stroked the proud arch of the horse's neck. "He is beautiful. And such a color."

"The color of my lady's hair," William said, tucking his arms tighter about her.

"You and your pretty words."

He chuckled and laid his head beside hers.

She had left her shyness and her reticence back at Tarnwych and galloped away without them. Out here with the moors stretching as far as the eye could see, a different Alice rode with William. An Alice who dared joke with her handsome husband, and an Alice who gloried in the wild, untamed bounty of her hair and her legs astride a powerful beast. Out here, she was light and air.

They crested a slight rise in the land and entered a small copse nestled into a crook in the river.

"This is a fine spot." William halted his horse. Hands beneath her armpits, he lowered her to the ground before sliding from the horse.

"It is indeed." Alice had never been here. She always left Tarnwych by closed cart. "Where are we?"

William put his hands on her shoulders and turned her. "Over there is the keep." His breath warmed her wind-chilled cheeks. "You can see the donjon just beyond that small crag." Crowding her around in the other direction, he said, "And over there is the village. See the smoke rising?"

"Aye." Alice had trouble attending anything but the feel of him pressed against her back, the cup of his large hands on her shoulders.

He slid his hands down her arms and wrapped his arms about her, pulling her tighter against him. The scent of him surrounded her, warm male flesh and a hint of cloves. At her back his heart drummed a steady beat, and his chest rose and fell. Still moors surrounded them. Wind ruffled the grass and low gorse bushes. The lone cry of a kestrel rode the silence as the bird circled high above them on widespread wings. It was as if they stood at the edge of the world, the only two people alive.

"Perfect." William nuzzled beneath her hair into her neck, his nose cold against her skin.

Alice kept still. She didn't want this moment to pass.

Hot lips replaced his nose sending warm shivers over her skin.

Alice closed her eyes and slid deeper into the blanket of her senses.

He explored her neck slowly, as if he committed it to memory. "So sweet." He nipped at her earlobe before drawing it into the heated damp of his mouth.

Heat blazed down the side of her neck and tightened the tips of her breasts. She stood in the midst of the moors while her husband seduced her with his beautiful mouth, and Alice did not care.

"I have been remiss in my duties," he murmured into the line of her jaw.

"Have you?" Her breath puffed through her lips as he built a heavy storm within her.

"Aye." He turned her in his arms. Blue eyes blazed at her for an instant before he lowered his head, nibbling her lips. "Wed nigh a sennight and still a bride."

Alice pressed onto her toes and slid her mouth along his. She welcomed his kiss as if starved for him. The familiar, thrilling taste of him called to an inner wanton in her who wanted to stretch and rub against him. Through their clothing, the hard press at the juncture of his thighs encouraged her wanton.

With a groan, he responded to the writhe of her hips, pulling her even closer.

When William broke the kiss they were both breathing hard. "One day soon, my Alice, I am going to make love to you out here with only the sun to see us."

Oh, she would like that. Alice laughed and wrapped her arms about his head. "Could we do so in summer?"

Chapter Eleven

"Do not move from this place." William settled young Will with a large blanket, a pillow, and enough food to see a hungry boy through the night. "Do not let anyone, and I mean anyone, past you."

"Nay, I mean aye, my lord." Will nodded with the earnestness of a boy given an important duty.

A more than important duty, a vital duty. Vital to the state of William's ballocks and his marriage. Any more of these near-misses with Alice and he might explode. Today, on the moor, almost had him lowering her to the ground and tossing her skirts up. The way she came alive in his arms, all passion and fire, filled him with a carnal anticipation that had his rod stirring in his braies like a lad Will's age.

Tonight he made her his. A well-planned campaign meant a smoother victory, and he had planned his campaign.

Will he positioned here at the base of the stairs to watch if anyone—namely the evil nun—decided on another nocturnal visitation.

With a final pat on Will's shoulder, he mounted the stairs.

At the top of the stairs, he passed Rufus with a nod. If Will failed to turn the miserable besom away, Rufus clamored to get back into William's good graces. Barricading the nun from his bedchamber would go a long way to accomplishing that.

The men slept like babes after he'd worked them hard all day. Happy that the conniving Scots kept to their side of the border, William stood ready. He almost rubbed his palms together in glee.

In the chamber, he built the fire to a roaring blaze, checked the wine, and rearranged the cheese on the platter. From the bath, the sweet scent of roses perfumed the air. He awaited his bride, presently laboring her way through evening prayers. A word with Father Mark and a few coins in the alms box had assured a shorter service than normal. The man had tears in his eyes as William released him from beneath the cat's paw.

The door opened and Alice entered.

* * *

Alice meant to speak with William about missing prayers. Last night had been understandable and the night before that, but tonight he had left her outside the hall with a wink and no explanation. She stopped inside the door and stared.

Lounging on the bed in his braies, William gave her a wicked grin. "Come in, my Alice."

My Alice? She rather thought not. "I would speak with you, William."

"Hmm." He propped his head on his hand. "I am afraid we will not spend our night talking."

The fire, the wine, the near-naked man on her bed. Admittedly, nobody had ever tried to seduce Alice before, but a girl had her secret yearnings. Her mouth dried, and she swallowed before finding her voice. "Not talking?"

He uncurled from the bed, big and sleek and male. Firelight caught the carved lines of his face and drew shadows over his heavy-lidded eyes. "My Alice." He cupped her face, his thumbs tracing her cheekbones. "I think we have waited long enough for tonight."

Her entire lifetime, a girlhood dreaming of a beautiful prince, three marriages which plummeted short of those dreams. Now she stood in this chamber with her beautiful husband. Alice swayed toward him, lost in the charm he wove about her.

Whisper-soft, his lips touched her forehead. Warm breath caressed her face as his lips moved over her brows to her cheeks. "So soft," he said. "Finer than the silks I gave you."

"William." His name caught on her soft gasp. The promise of his kiss simmered through her blood, heating her skin and melting her limbs. Levering herself onto her toes, she shifted and connected their mouths.

His lips softened beneath hers, giving her mastery of the kiss.

A heady rush of excitement roared through her. Opening her mouth, she teased his lips until he admitted her tongue. Just as he had taught her, she slid her tongue into his mouth.

He groaned, and his hands tightened on her face. Silently, he asked her for more, and Alice gave.

All the pent up waiting she poured into her kiss.

His response drove her further. She deepened the kiss. In command, the aggressor, and it went to her head in a rush of freedom. Free, like she had felt on horseback, Alice wrapped her arms around his waist. She needed the press of his warm chest against her. His body differed from hers in ways that thrilled and fascinated her. As he had done, she pressed her lips to the heated column of his neck and drew the salty male taste of him into her.

"Aye, Alice," he murmured.

At the base of his throat throbbed his pulse, strong beneath the sun-darkened skin, and she pressed her lips there. She explored the defined planes of his chest. Beneath his smooth, hot skin, his fascinating muscle tensed. Her touch hungry, she learned his stomach and lower.

His waist, trim and tight, slid under her palms. His hips, so narrow, gave way to the taut muscle of his thighs. And in between, the part of him she had only glimpsed. The need to see and explore that secret area had her hands at the ties to his braies.

He covered her hands with his. "We will get to that, my Alice, but first I thought you might care to bathe."

Nay, Alice did not care to bathe, she had other things on her mind, but he led her closer to the fire and the waiting bath tub.

Quicker than a maid, he divested her of her bliaut and chemise.

Suddenly shy, Alice covered herself with her hands.

"Nay." William drew her hands away from her flesh. "Let me see how beautiful you are."

She was not beautiful, she was plain Alice of Tarnwych, but the way William looked at her, the heat in his gaze as he dwelled on the roundness of her bosom, and the curls between her thighs made her feel like that Alice on the moors.

He helped her into the bath.

Silky water lapped her heated skin, stroked her nipples and her woman's flesh in a sinful embrace. She did not know what he was about. It seemed she spent much of her marriage in that state.

"My mother always complains the stench of making soap sticks to her skin." William stroked bathing soap up her arms and over her shoulders. Broad hands covered her shoulders and slid over her chest.

Her breasts ached for his touch, but William's hands moved up again and kneaded her shoulders and then back down her arms.

Alice stirred, restive and needy, in the water.

He moved to the end of the bathing tub and took her foot in his large hands. Strong fingers worked at the arch of her foot.

It felt marvelous, and Alice lay her head back on the rim of the tub.

"Aye, my Alice." His clever fingers dug into her foot. "Take your ease and let me please you."

Over her ankle he kneaded, and further along her leg. Then back to her foot again.

"William?"

"Aye." His dark head bent over his work.

"Are you...is this...?"

He nipped the pad of her foot. "Am I what?"

Alice yelped, more from surprise than aught else. "What are you doing?"

"If you need to ask that, my Alice"—he shot her a roguish grin—"then I am not doing it correctly."

He slid his hands past her knees and up.

Alice tensed.

William moved his hands down her legs. "What a pity these stay hidden beneath a skirt," he said.

Alice had never thought of her legs as objects of admiration. Under his sun-darkened hands, her skin glowed pale. "You like my legs?"

"Aye." Water gleamed on his wet arms before they disappeared beneath the water again. His hands travelling past her knees, a bit further this time.

Her thighs trembled. Her mind clamored to snap them shut, but the heat uncurling in her belly had her wanting to drop them open and encourage his touch where she throbbed.

"Come." William stood and tugged her up.

Water streamed over her body and splattered onto the floor.

He lifted her out of the tub as if she weighed nothing, and wrapped her in a drying cloth warmed from the fire. With tender care, he dried her. Fingers, wrists, shoulder, arm pits before moving to her breasts. Beneath the drying cloth the heat of his hands scorched her sensitive flesh.

He did not linger but moved over her belly and her hips.

Disappointment curdled within her. She wished she had the courage to grab his hands and put them where she wanted them.

William kneeled and dried her legs and then her feet, taking his time lifting each foot and working the cloth between each toe before putting her foot down again.

"William." She ached, and she throbbed. She wanted so many things and knew not how to ask for them. His name escaped her on a low, whisper of want.

He looked up at her and tilted his head. "What does my Alice want?"

Oh, the devious rogue. He knew what he did to her. She could see it reflected in his grin and his twinkling eyes. "I want..."

"Aye." He lifted a brow.

"I want to see you," Alice said it in a rush before her courage faltered. "Unclothed."

William stood. His braies dropped in a murmur of cloth, and he stilled before her, fully and gloriously naked. His male flesh jutted from a dark nest of hair.

Her woman's core pulsed in response. She had no virgin's fear holding her back. This would not be the same as before. Dark fumbling and grunts in a darkened room. Nay, William offered her a feast for her eyes and her curious touch.

As she fastened her hands about him, William dropped his head back on a hiss. "What are you doing to me, Alice?"

"Touching you." She explored his rod. Thick and hard, it pulsed in her clasp. Delicate skin covered his rod, softer with heavy veins barely covered. "Is it all right, if I do?" It seemed polite to ask, although the evidence of his enjoyment was stamped in high color across his cheeks, beamed at her from the intensity of his eyes. "I have never..."

He nodded, understanding what she could not voice. "Tonight is for you, sweeting. I want to share with you all the pleasure you have missed."

"What about you?"

He clasped her hand and stopped her. "We will both find much pleasure this night." He grimaced. "But not if you continue that for much longer."

He cupped her breast.

Heat shot from that point to her core. His thumb brushed her nipple to a tighter, harder point, and Alice moaned.

"Such pretty breasts." He bent his head and took her nipple into his mouth.

Hot and wet, his mouth at her breast built the ache between

her thighs. His hair inky against her skin. So carnal and erotic, she twined her fingers in his hair.

He moved to her other breast, lavishing his attention on it with his lips, his tongue, his teeth.

Moisture slid from between her legs, at first a little alarming and mortifying. She clenched her thighs together.

William raised his head, the devil gleaming in his eyes. "What is it, Alice?"

Her face heated, she could never tell him this.

He slid his hand over the curve of her belly and into the curls atop her thighs. His fingers parted her female flesh.

At last! Alice whimpered at the barrage of sensation his clever fingers unleashed. Mortification forgotten, she parted her thighs.

William gave her a low rumble of approval. He found a tight bundle of nerve endings and Alice's knees weakened. Right where she ached the worst, he caressed her. She grabbed onto his arms and held on. Every inch of her clamored for something, but where he touched held pure pleasure.

"My Alice." He slid his fingers inside her. "Do you know what this does to a man? To know that you desire him?"

She shook her head. Not the faintest idea, but she never wanted him to stop.

"Shall I show you more?" William pressed her back.

Dear God, Alice wanted the more as much as she wanted her next breath.

The bed hit the back of her knees, and William pressed her onto her back. With his hands on the inside of her thighs, he parted her knees.

His intent gaze fastened between her legs, shining with a hunger that matched hers.

"So pretty." He lowered his head. "I need to taste if you are as sweet as you look."

"Whaaa—"

Sweet Mother of God. His lips on her core sent a shaft of pleasure through her that arched her back. He suckled, nibbled, worked his tongue over her until she lost coherent thought. Something so good must be a sin of the flesh, but she did not care.

The sensation between her legs sharpened, drawing hard pants from her chest, curling her toes. It built within her, coiling tighter as William played his mouth over her. Bursts of pleasure shot through her muscles, ripping a cry from her.

"There, my Alice." William hovered above her, supporting his weight on his forearms beside her head. "Did you like that?"

"Aye." She melted into the bed.

Between her thighs, his hard rod pressed, a reminder of what they had not done.

William palmed his length, his weight braced on one arm.

His shaft stretched her, opening her until he slid within her. No pain, no discomfort as he filled and stretched her, stirring her blood again. She tilted her hips, taking him deeper.

William's breath rasped. "Aye, like that."

The muscles of his belly contracted as he withdrew and thrust again.

Alice fastened her thighs around his hips, drawing him deeper inside her. The pleasure built slower, concentrated on the place where he filled her. He drove into her, again and again, pushing the sensation higher with each thrust.

Alice writhed beneath him. Desperate for him never to stop, and even more desperate to reach that pinnacle again. Her completion swept over her in a devastating rush and held her there for long, beautiful moments.

William tensed above her, thrust deep, and shouted her name.

Sweat slicked their bodies as his weight rested on her. He was heavy, but she wanted to keep him there. She felt bound to him, connected and as one. One flesh, as her vows had promised.

After a while—perhaps moments, perhaps hours—Alice only knew the contentment in lying there, William moved to her side. The loss of his heat made her shiver.

He tucked her against his side, her head resting in the crook of his shoulder. Through her palm, his heart beat hard in his chest.

Alice's thoughts jumbled. Had they created a child? A being of light and love, born from something wondrous. Thrice married, twice bedded before him, and tonight William had shown her how innocent she had still remained. In one mind-altering act, he had opened a world of possibilities to her.

His voice rumbled low and quiet in the still room. "Alice."

"Aye."

"That was..." For once, her smooth-tongued husband had no words.

"Aye." Neither did she. Except..."William?"

"Aye."

"Do you think—would you mind if we did it again?"

His laughter rolled through the dark. "Right this instant?"

"Well, perhaps, not right this instant. But soon."

Chapter Twelve

Alice left her chamber without her wimple the next morning. Something within her had changed. In a greater sense of the word than she had ever understood before, she was a woman.

Twice more, William had awakened her in the night and taken her to even greater heights. Or depths.

Memories of their night crowded around her, and a blush heated her cheeks. She hugged them close, a delicious ache in her limbs a reminder she could hold throughout the day.

"Alice." Sister stalked the passage toward her. "You are not dressed."

"Aye, I am." Alice grasped the edges of her light mood and held on. "William prefers my hair uncovered."

"Does he?" Sister smoothed her scapula. "I trust you will draw the line at walking around naked, if William prefers that too."

"Oh, he does." Alice giggled. "But not before the entire keep."

She left before she could hear the blistering rebuke building on Sister's face.

"Lady Alice." Will rounded the stairwell at a run and ground to a halt in front her. It took him a moment to catch his breath. "My lord says to come right away. You have visitors."

"Visitors?" Alice tried to think of anyone who would visit them here. Her father perhaps. Her happy mood dimmed somewhat at the prospect.

"Aye." Will's thin chest swelled with the news he carried. "Aonghas the Red is here."

"I beg your pardon?"

"And he brings his sons." Will twirled his arms. "All of them"

Questions clattered about in her head. Well, she wouldn't get her answers standing here staring at Will like a moonstruck calfling. Alice picked up her skirts and rushed down the stairs. She stopped a moment outside the hall and smoothed her braided hair. She did feel a mite naked without her wimple.

"Ah, my pretty wee bird." Aonghas threw his arms wide and strode toward her. "See, I have come to visit you."

* * *

William kept his eye on the Scot as the man noisily bussed Alice on the cheek.

Alice! She'd surprised him last night. Beneath that prim exterior lurked a blaze that took very little to ignite. He had left their chamber this morning before she awoke, needing time to put his jumbled thoughts into order.

He had tupped his share of women. More than his share. Yet Alice had provided one revelation after another. Her frank, sensual curiosity and the delight she took in exploring it had swept him away. The passion between them rattled his complacency. Of course, Alice was too inexperienced to know this, but he did, and the knowledge swirled in his gut. It complicated his idea of keeping his wife at comfortable arm's length.

"Dear God, there is Scot in you, flower." Aonghas fisted Alice's braid.

Raw rage tightened William's limbs. If the man did not take his hands off his wife, William would remove them for him.

"I am sure not." Alice laughed and retrieved her hair.

"I am telling you there is." Aonghas waved his hand up and down her. "If your bonnie face did not speak the truth of your blood, then that fiery hair would do so for certain."

"I take it you are not here to discuss my wife's bloodlines." William's voice cracked across the large hall. God's teeth, he'd sounded like a bristling wolfhound.

Aonghas stuck his thumbs in his belt and raised a brow at him.

William slapped an affable smile on his face. Still, he ducked around the man and stood by Alice. She smelled of something light and floral, and he dipped his head and kissed her mouth. Cheeks were for strange Scots, but he owned her mouth. "Good morrow, my Alice."

Alice colored up and dropped her head with a shy smile.

"Now," Aonghas boomed. He slapped his hands on his stomach, his thin face wearing a grin that warned William negotiations came next. "I suppose you are wondering what I am doing here?"

"You are always welcome, Aonghas," Alice said.

As long as the cur kept his grubby paws off William's wife. He motioned Aonghas to take a seat.

"I will see to refreshment." Alice twisted out of William's grip and left the hall.

They both dropped their celebration faces. William took the opposite hearth bench from Aonghas. Next time Aonghas visited Tarnwych he intended to have two of the largest, finest carved wooden chairs he could find for Aonghas to rest his conniving ass on.

"Our talk the other day got me thinking." Aonghas pursed his lips, rubbing his forefinger beside his nose. "You see, William, we both have a wee problem or two."

A large problem indeed for Aonghas to have missed the opportunity to sneer a "sir" at him. "We do?"

"Tarnwych is a fair keep, to be sure, but she is undermanned, understocked, and it will be a long, cold winter. Up here in the north, we know the true meaning of winter."

There it came, the thrust the blasted man could not resist. "I have plans for Tarnwych."

"Aye, I am certain you do." Aonghas stirred. "You look to me to be a man always with a plan, but the winter is nigh on us, and you would need to be a bloody miracle worker to get your keep ready for winter."

There wasn't much point in arguing the obvious, so William kept his gaze leveled at the other man. "When do we get to your problem?"

Aonghas guffawed. Such a massive sound for the man's body. "I have sons."

"You are to be congratulated."

"Many, many sons."

"Ah." God help the man if they took after their sire.

"They be good lads. Strong, brawny, but a lusty lot. Always fornicating and fighting all about my lands."

Well, what did the man expect? William had heard stories about Aonghas from the men in the barracks. On his fifth wife, and twice as many lemans scattered about The Crags. "I imagine that could be uncomfortable."

"You have no idea." Aonghas let the mask slip a moment, and William felt a twinge of sympathy. "The lads are bad enough, but when their mothers get up me about them...this one taking up for her son, the other ready to rip her hair out for her son. It is enough to drive a man fair mad."

William fought his grin at the man's discomfort. "And how do our problems in any way relate?"

"I am glad you asked that." Aonghas patted his belly like it held a load of roasted beef. "You being a knight and all, and as I hear it, a strong hand at bringing a quarrelsome man into line, you could take some of my problem off my hands."

"You mean your sons. Take a son or two off your hands?" Holy hell, that didn't sound like a good deal at all.

"I was thinking more like nine or ten sons."

"How many do you have?"

"Fifteen at last count, but there be another belly swelling at The Crags and I will wager my right hand another boy is in there." Aonghas grimaced. "I do not breed daughters, you ken, just more bloody sons."

William silently commended Aonghas on his vigor.

Aonghas slapped his hands on his knees and grinned. "Each boy will come mounted and armed. No need to spend coin getting them set up. I will make sure of that before they leave. All you have to do is...shape all that lustiness."

"But Aonghas, as you have already pointed out, I barely have provisions to feed the mouths I have through the winter." The man's sons in his keep might ensure a little less raiding. God knew he needed the men.

Aonghas spread his arms wide. "William, lad, I would never leave a man to struggle. My nearest neighbor and all. I have thrown my larders wide, brought you a few gifts to welcome you to the north."

"What sort of gifts?" The edible kind, he hoped. Gord had almost ruined his fast breaking with an exhaustive list of all the shortages at Tarnwych.

"My man is with your Gord as we speak. We have brought a wagon or two with us, but we can be seeing to a couple of those other needs as well." Aonghas winked. "If you and I can reach a wee agreement."

Food he welcomed, and some stock beasts. A few creature comforts couldn't hurt to bring some smiles back to this miserable keep either. "I will take two sons."

"Nine."

"Three."

"Eight."

"Four."

"Seven, and it would not be worth my while to accept anything less." Aonghas held up his hand with a firm nod.

William could grow to like the man. Of course, he wouldn't trust him further than he could toss his scrawny carcass, but the man drove a fine bargain. "Seven, mounted and fully armed. That means weapons and full armor for the horse and the man."

"Done." Aonghas thrust out his hand.

"And"—William raised his finger—"for each son I take, an extra horse, and full weaponry for another man."

Rearing back, Aonghas gaped at him. "God's ballocks man, you will beggar me."

"I think not. Seven sons and their mothers can wreak a sizable amount of havoc."

Aonghas's frowned at the ground, as he weighed the offer. "An extra horse with each son."

"And weapons. I will supply the armor."

"From where?" Aonghas scoffed.

"From the extra breed stock you will send me."

"Jesu Wept!" Aonghas leaped to his feet. "You will starve us." He peered at William. "Are you sure your people are not Scots?"

"I also believe my Alice will look fetching in some of those fox furs your ladies sport. Not the white ones. They will make her look wan."

"You." Aonghas opened and shut his mouth, took a brief spin about the room and stomped back again. "You haggle like a Highlander."

"Seven sons, Aonghas, will take a lot of training. And no interference as I take it on."

"The least you can do is take eight of the sods."

"Seven, all my other conditions met. Take it or leave it. Tarnwych might be poor right now, but I brought money to this table. My father is a very wealthy man." He leaned forward. "A man who might also foster a likely boy or two."

Aonghas dropped back onto the bench with a huff. "You will be the death of me, for sure."

William stretched his legs out before him. "I wonder what is keeping the refreshments."

As if she lurked on the far side of the hall door, Alice appeared with a trail of serving women. "My apologies for your wait." She smiled at Aonghas. "We are not as well run as The Crags."

Her words appeared to soothe Aonghas's feathers, and he managed a tight smile in return.

William rose and offered her his seat. He poured wine, Anglesea's by the aroma, for the three of them and handed Alice her goblet and then Aonghas.

Aonghas quaffed his in one large gulp, his gaze darting around the hall.

William motioned a serving man to refill his goblet. They would have none of that savage Scots brew at Tarnwych. "Shall I tell my lady the news that she is to receive seven guests in the near future?"

"Blight on you, man." Aonghas shook his head. "But, aye."

Alice stared at him with wide eyes.

"My love." William put his hand on her slight shoulder. "I am sure you will share my delight in the news we are to foster seven of Aonghas's sons."

"We are?" Alice's voice grew weak. "When?"

"No time like this one." Aonghas sprang to his feet with a grin.

William's hackles rose at the sudden change in demeanor.

Puffing out his chest, Aonghas said, "I brought them all with me."

Of course he had. William could not prevent his smile. Aonghas had come here determined to win the day.

"Lads!" Aonghas bellowed loud enough to startle lice. "Get yourselves in here."

An unkempt gaggle of hulking Scots shuffled into the hall. Wild hair, bearded faces, and covered in furs, they resembled an army of barbarian marauders.

William guessed he'd probably gotten the worst end of a devil's bargain.

Aonghas's smug expression confirmed it. He pointed. "That

be Domnall, Dubhghall, Donnchadh, Domnall, Aonghas, Seamus, and Domnall. You need not concern yourselves with the rest of them."

Dear God, what an ugly lot, and massive. William did not care to speculate on the size of their mothers given their diminutive sire.

"Good morrow." Alice managed a weak smile.

"Greet Lady Alice," Aonghas thundered.

A deep rumble came from the lads. One made an attempt at a bow. William thought it might be the third Domnall, but who could tell beneath all that hair.

"Meet Sir William. He is to have the training of you lot." Aonghas strutted like a bantam cock before his towering sons. "Now he may look like a pretty southerner to you lot, but that man drives a bargain to make a Scots mother's heart sing. That sword he wears is not a nice bauble either, and he knows how to use it. If any one of you fancies your chances, remember Dunstan."

Alice peeked at him from the corner of her eyes. No doubt Aonghas had eyes and ears in their household.

God grant him strength. His bones ached from the idea of bashing this lot into order, and from the fire in their eyes, it would take a fair amount of bashing.

"Now." Aonghas spun about, rubbing his hands. "Let us break bread together, and seal our bargain. The rest of us leave at first light." He winked at William. "With that list from Gord."

William mentally added a bushel more items to Gord's list.

Alice sent the order to the kitchens that there would be many more mouths to feed.

"You there. Dubhghall." Aonghas snapped his fingers at a son with dark, tousled hair and light eyes.

"I am Donnchadh."

"I care not. Go and fetch those fox pelts for my pretty wee bird." He winked at William. "It pays to take a hard line and a harder hand with this lot. Happens I also thought Lady Alice would look right bonnie wrapped in fox."

William's laugh built in his belly. Aonghas had trussed him up like a Christmas goose.

Chapter Thirteen

With great difficulty, Alice modulated her tone. "We can tear these linens into strips for bandages."

Lord knew, not a day passed in the sennight Aonghas's sons had joined them that did not require the wrapping of one Scot or another. Having the lot of them bathed had almost ended in a nasty brawl. William drove them hard, and they fought back as hard, but her William had the better of them.

Nice boys, whose ages ranged from fourteen to twenty. Old for training as squires but they threw themselves into the task. They slept in the barracks with the men, and worked as hard as any man-at-arms. Alice had a soft spot for Seamus. Turned fourteen summer past, at least as tall as his oldest brother, he brought her little tributes at the end of the day. A late sprig of heather he discovered while out riding, a pretty stone from the stream where he bathed. He missed his mother, he had whispered to her in confidence. He liked nothing more than sitting beside her and listening to the stories told in the hall after dinner. Dubhghall, the budding charmer, newly shaved and trimmed, already plowed a swathe through the keep hearts at only seventeen. What he lacked for in looks, he more than compensated for with his silver tongue, and roguish humor.

"These linens are still good." Sister refolded the linens with sharp, jerky movements. "It is not our way to toss away good linens for naught."

Alice tried for patience, God's promise she did, but with more tasks mounting on her shoulders every day, Sister and her constant opposition wore thin. "We will replace the linens."

"I see." Sister sniffed. "I do not know why you seek my opinion if you dismiss it without a thought."

Alice had not asked her opinion. Sister had followed her and taken it upon herself to interfere. As she did when Alice visited the buttery to request herbs in the butter. Or when Alice planned the meals with Cook for the week. Whatever she did, Sister came with her. "I must take up my role as chatelaine."

"You are right." Sister hugged the folded linens to her chest. "Perhaps it is time I return to the convent. As I am no longer needed here."

William would curse her for saying this, but Sister had cared for Alice since childhood. She could not send her back like a horse that had outlived its usefulness. "Of course not, Sister. How would I manage without you?"

"You appear to manage quite well. Although these wasteful ways of yours will lead you astray, Alice."

"You have always been part of Tarnwych. This is your home." Alice touched her arm.

Sister shook her off. "My home is where the Lord needs me most."

"I need you," Alice said. Perhaps not as much as she used to, but Sister had been her rock for so many years, Alice could not think of a life without her.

The tower guard's voice came through the open casement, muted by the thick stone. Another result of William's training: mounted guards at all times. "Mounted party approaching!"

Visitors! Time past, Alice dreaded visitors, knowing it meant a visit from her father. But life seemed filled with endless discoveries since her marriage, and she strode toward the keep door.

William stood on the ramparts, his head facing Tarnwych's approach road. He pumped his fist in the air and yelled, "Open the gates."

Alice trotted into the bailey, keen to see who William welcomed so effusively. "Who is it?" she called as the gates creaked open.

"My family." William grinned at her and ran toward the gate. "Dragon's head proper on argent. They fly my father's banner."

William's family. Alice stopped in the middle of the bailey. His family had come to visit? She had barely spoken to them on her wedding day. Would they approve of her?

"Alice." Sister pinched her arm. "You cannot allow this."

"They are William's family." And now, her family.

"You know what they are like. He brings them into this castle, and they carry their sins with them. You must stop this." Sister's grip on her arm grew painful.

Through the open gates, the leading riders wove into view. It seemed a large party.

William waved to the lead knight.

The knight raised his fist and spurred his horse into a gallop. He reached William and flung himself from his horse. Throwing back his visor, he strode forward and clasped William's arm.

Sister hissed in a sharp breath. She had grown parchment pale, her eyes burning. "It is him."

"Who?"

The man removed his helm. He stood taller than William as they spoke. Built strong, with hair of deepest sable, Alice did not remember him from her wedding feast.

"The betrayer who denied our Blessed Son and entered into an unholy marriage."

Sir Gregory? He had not accompanied Lady Faye to the wedding. Lady Mary had told her his business, unfortunately, took him elsewhere. Alice took a small step closer. Sir Gregory had married Lady Faye, turning his back on his promise to enter the church.

"His soul is blacker than the hair on his head." Sister wrapped her rosary about her fist so tight it cut white flesh trails across her fingers. "If he enters this keep, God will rain down punishment on all who shelter him."

Sir Gregory did not look like a hardened sinner. His features were carved and graven, a handsome man in a quiet, earnest manner.

Another rider breached the gates and drew rein before William in a flourish of mud and hooves.

Lady Beatrice, dressed as no modest woman should in chausses and a tunic. Alice would never dare such raiment, but it would make for comfortable riding. Beatrice slid to the ground and William enfolded her in a hug.

"The immodest one." Sister sneered. "She married a common bastard, a blacksmith's apprentice."

Alice had heard it all before, in the weeks between her father informing her of her marriage and William's arrival at Tarnwych. Sister's ire had not lost one ounce of its venom. Indeed, Sister wound her rosary so tight her fingertips purpled. She would break the rosary if she persisted.

Following behind Beatrice came a woman on a quiet palfrey, riding amidst three children.

William hugged first one child and then the other.

Sister gave a strangled cry. She leaped back, hands clasped at her chest. "The abomination."

William assisted the last child from his mount.

A boy, his features flat, sloe eyes tilted upward, shambled toward William.

A low buzzing filled Alice's head. Her heart stuttered and then beat erratically. Fine sweat broke over her body. She stepped back and bumped into a frozen Sister.

"He cannot enter here." Sister clutched Alice's skirt and tugged. "Get it away from here. Alice, get it away."

Her voice had risen and carried across the bailey. The party by the gate turned and looked at them.

On a strangled cry, Sister ran back inside the keep.

Alice's world skewed before her eyes. Her vision blackened around the edges. Her breath sawed in her lungs. She needed to run, but her feet were nailed to the floor. The child had his arms about William's waist as he stared up at his older brother with obvious adoration. She wanted to yank William away from him. Pull him to safety. Her heart pounded in her ears as perspiration broke over her skin.

"Alice." William strode toward her, his face creased in a frown. "What is it?"

"Nay." The boy stayed back with the others, but she could not look away. Fear consumed her from within. It chased any reason from her mind. "They cannot."

"Alice?" William took her by the shoulders.

"You cannot let them in." Alice's fingers scrabbled for purchase on the hauberk William had donned this morning. Terror choked her, constricting her breathing. Her voice did not sound like hers. "William, they cannot come in here."

He stared at her as if she had lost her wits. "Alice, they are my family. Of course they will come in."

Words deserted her, even thought would not conform to order. She only knew that if that boy entered Tarnwych it would be bad, very bad. "Make them go away."

William's face hardened as his grasp on her shoulders tightened. "Stop it, Alice. My family has travelled from Anglesea to seeks succor here, and they will find it." He gave her a small shake. "Now, come and welcome my family, or go to your chamber, but they will enter Tarnwych."

She could not. She had to escape. The bad thing closed around her and she knew only that she had to run.

With a grating sound of anger, William turned about and stalked back to the waiting party at the gate.

* * *

William's hands shook with anger. He took them away from Alice before he gave in to the urge to shake her harder, shake some sense into the woman. What in God's name ailed her? Did she expect he would turn his family away?

She scurried back to the keep.

Good. Let her go. He could not stomach her at this time. The news from Anglesea filled him with the need to throw back his head and roar his denial to the heavens.

Illness had struck his family home, and rampaged through the occupants and the village beyond. Beatrice said many had succumbed to illness already, and more fell to the ailment hourly. Many familiar faces had left this world in the last fortnight. Lyman, the smith, was one of the first to die. And Lilly, sweet Lilly, who had initiated most of the lads at Anglesea into the ways of the flesh, was gone, along with her young son. So many it tore through him to listen further.

Beatrice and the children had travelled to Tarnwych for their own safety. As one of the few still able to defend the contagion-beset keep, Garrett could not accompany her.

And his mother, his beautiful, strong, gracious, adoring mother. William missed his step and stumbled. Lady Mary had fallen ill as the party for Tarnwych made ready to leave. She had exhausted herself nursing first their father, then Roger, and every other ailing soul at Anglesea. Father was on his feet once more, but Roger sickened still. He could not think of his large, powerful brother in anything but lusty good health.

Gregory had not given him the full extent. He did not need to. William read the grim truth carved into Gregory's face and reflected in the haunted look in Bea's eyes.

Hoping to contain the plague within, Sir Arthur had locked Anglesea. Faye remained at Calder with her sons, mere days away from delivering her first child by Gregory. With Gregory's family safe at Calder, Father had called on him to escort Beatrice, her children, and Mathew to Tarnwych and safety. Ivy had come along with them, despite her desire to stay and help. If any of their party carried the contagion with them, Ivy would recognize it and act.

Damn Alice if she thought he would send them away at any time, doubly so now.

Tired lines and shadows marred Ivy's beautiful face as she gathered Beatrice and the children together and shepherded them toward the keep. William would lay all his coin Ivy had worked as hard, nay harder, than anyone at Anglesea. Her tutelage under Nurse progressed well, and Ivy had an endless well of compassion for the sick and injured.

William pressed his eyes shut. Never more so than now did he curse the yawning distance betwixt himself and his family. Sir Arthur needed him, and here he sat in a remote northern keep, playing chatelaine and addressing whatever new basic lack Tarnwych tossed up. Father relied on him to succor this small family group, and so he would.

"Is Lady Alice well?" Ivy picked up Beatrice's youngest and propped him on her hip. At just shy of his second birthday, Adam had ridden with Ivy for most of the journey. Three-year old Richard had shared a mount with Mathew.

Mathew had a way with animals. He earned their instant trust, and he rode even before he could walk. On horseback he had a grace and ease of movement that defied the little lad on the ground.

"She is well." William burned to get to the bottom of Alice's unconscionable behavior. For certain, the evil nun lay at the root of whatever beset Alice. Undoubtedly the old besom had some rotten maggot eating at her head about his family taking shelter within Tarnwych. He would love to see her face when she learned of Ivy's past profession. Or perhaps she already knew and dripped her poison in Alice's ear.

"Is she displeased we are here?" Beatrice never danced around the point.

William forced a smile and slung his arm about her shoulders. "I am glad you are here. Even if it is under these circumstances."

Beatrice studied him though narrowed eyes. Garrett must have had a calming influence on his sister, because she kept her tongue between her teeth and followed his motion for her to enter the keep.

"It is cold enough to freeze your ballocks off here," Richard said and gave him a huge grin. "That is what Roger says."

"Roger is not far wrong." William buffeted his nephew gently atop the shoulder. "But if your mother hears you say that, you'll be spitting soap for a week."

"Nay." Richard cocked his head. "She is not so bad, and she says worse. But Nurse..." Richard rolled his eyes.

Nurse had escaped the illness at Anglesea according to Ivy. Not even disease had the effrontery to challenge Nurse. As his mother's most devoted supporter, Lady Mary had a stalwart warrior by her side in Nurse.

* * *

Alice's legs shook so hard she tripped up the stairs. As she drew closer to her chamber, the fear receded, and reality reasserted itself. What had beset her in the bailey? What had she done?

Pressing her back against the wall, she tried to stop the quivering in her limbs. This was not like her.

She dragged in a deep breath, and then another, and tried to reason through what had happened in the bailey. Panic had overtaken her, but why?

Sister had not spared her the grim details of William's family before, but she had felt no terror at them entering Tarnwych for her wedding feast.

The only difference was the boy. Mathew had not come with the wedding party. And her terror centered about the child. She could scarcely credit what she had done, how she had behaved. How ridiculous for a grown woman to fear a child so much she nigh ran away from him. In fairness, she could not blame William for his fury. She had implored him to bar his family the keep.

Where had those words come from? Only an awful wife would do such a thing. Only an awful person would behave so in front of an innocent child. Sister called him an abomination, but she didn't believe that. Then why? What had beset her? Nothing like that had ever happened to her.

She reached the landing above and tried to order her thoughts.

"Lady Alice." Gord marched down the corridor toward her. "We will need accommodations for his lordship's family. Have you any notion of how long they will stay?"

"Nay." She had run away before she could ask William anything. Why they were here, and only a few of them. How long they planned to stay. Why Lady Beatrice wore such a somber expression. "I would ask Sir William."

Tonight they would expect her to present herself at dinner and put a pleasant face on for her family by marriage. She owed them that much. She owed William that much and more. As she walked to her bedchamber, her sense of shame built. Along with it came the dread realization of William's anger. She deserved his censure. She did not think he would raise his hand to her, but had she destroyed the fragile, fledgling bond between them with her actions this morning?

Her chamber door stood open and she stepped inside.

"They are still here." Sister paced before the casement, her gaze locked on the bailey below.

"They are my family now." Alice kept her tone calm, but verily, Sister was not helping. She needed time and peace to try and make sense of what had just happened. "I will not turn them away."

"They brought the whore with them." Sister pressed her fingertips to her forehead, breathing deep. "I saw her with the children. A whore amongst the innocent. God weeps at such a travesty.

"The whore?" Alice recalled Sister mentioning a whore

before, but she had seen only Lady Beatrice and the beautiful dark-haired woman in the bailey. Surely she wasn't the whore?

"They spread their evil wherever they touch. Betrayers, whores, and immodest women. The abomination is God's judgment against their sins. Yet see how they flaunt him for all the world. They are shameless in their wickedness." Sister gripped the sides of the casement and leaned forward.

Alice stared at Sister's back. Even for Sister, that was a harsh mouthful. She could not stomach Sister's vitriol right now. "Stop it!"

Sister gasped and stepped back, clasping her hands at her chest. "I must pray."

"You are too harsh." Behind her eyes, Alice's head gave a dull throb. Any more of this and she might start screaming and never stop. "Judge not, Sister, lest you be judged."

Sister turned a wrathful face on Alice. "You would use the Lord's words to justify evil?"

"I am not justifying evil." Alice twitched with the need to shake some sense into Sister. "But they are my family now and it would behoove me to greet them with a polite smile and bid them welcome."

Alice might not understand what had happened to her in the bailey, but she was beginning to comprehend how much damage her actions had wrought. Her new family must despise her.

"I shall do no such thing." Sister folded her hands beneath her scapula.

"Then I suggest you take yourself somewhere where your rudeness will go unmarked."

Chapter Fourteen

A lice breathed deep, once, and then again, to still the nerves in her belly. She must seek to make amends for what she had done. Surely, what had occurred in the bailey was an aberration. It had certainly never happened to her before. First, she would mend fences with her new family, and later, with William.

After Sister left her, she had made an effort with her appearance. In an effort to appease William, and make him more receptive to her apology, she left her hair unbound and clasped the simplest of the girdles he had gifted her about her prettiest dress. When compared to William's gift silks and velvest, the dark blue linen presented as a poor relation, but it was the best she had.

In a further effort to soothe his ire and extend a silent apology to his family, she had run Gord and young Will ragged ensuring Tarnwych welcomed her visitors. Fresh linens, new pallets, refreshment—whatever William's kin required, she had seen it provided. All from the sanctuary of her bedchamber.

Her first peep into the hall had her slinking back beneath the concealing shadows either side of the door. "You can do this," she whispered to herself. "You must do this."

Beatrice sat beside William at table, the vibrant peacock tones of her bliaut providing a gleaming backdrop for her blond prettiness.

"There is nothing frightening about the Lady Beatrice." Saying the words aloud helped still the violent flutters in Alice's middle. Pretty enough, tall and willowy with a sweet smile, Beatrice's manner held a freedom that made Alice feel in the presence of a glorious, brilliant lark—made her feel dull and planted on the ground, ferreting through the undergrowth for grubs and worms while the other woman soared above her.

Alice snorted. Her verse had not improved since her wedding day. She took a breath. It didn't matter if Beatrice made her feel unworthy, she still owed the woman a sincere apology.

"My lady?" A deep, resonant voice cut into her meanderings. Sir Gregory emerged from the gloom of the corridor and stood by her side. His tall form cast long shadows that swallowed her whole. Offering her his arm, he nodded to the hall. "Shall we?"

Beneath her fingertips his simple linen tunic covered the rough-hewn strength of his arm. Sir Gregory appeared modest in his dress, rich but not showy, wearing dark fabrics that added to the mysterious air surrounding the man.

Taller even than William, Sir Gregory's shoulder cleared the crown of her head. She tried to picture him in a monk's habit and failed. Command hung in the air about him, a low buzz of bridled power clung to him in a manner ill-suited to a priest. Put a sword in his hand, aye. Set a hauberk about his shoulders and send him to the Holy Land to fight the non-believers—single-handedly— now that she could picture.

"Have you recovered?" People parted for her and Sir Gregory in a wave. For Sir Gregory, at least, and whoever had that still, compelling presence by their side.

"Eh?" Dear Lord, he had her tongue-tied. As for seeking forgiveness from William's family, she was not making a good start.

"William said you were not well this afternoon." Sir Gregory inclined his dark head. Eyes blacker than pitch, he stared at her.

The Archangel, Saint Michael, leader of God's armies, bringer of the deceased souls to heaven, guardian of the faithful. "Lady Alice?"

"Aye. I am much recovered." Her stupid head insisted on drawing great wings rising above his head. It must be her frayed nerves. "I do not know what came over me."

He nodded in the direction of the dais. "They have that effect on people, the Anglesea folk."

Not him though, Alice would wager, if she wagered, which she did not, because Sister would collapse at the mere suggestion. But if she wagered, she would place her last gold piece that he feared nothing.

Sir Gregory chuckled. "I can assure you, my lady, I am no stranger to fear."

Good Lord, had she said all that aloud? Her face flamed. Still, she didn't believe, for a second, Sir Gregory experienced a jot of fear. Alice made a point of keeping her lips shut before she allowed her last thought to escape as well.

"See the children are here." Sir Gregory's deep voice warmed like treacle over a fire. "You did not meet them in the bailey."

Nay, because she had run away as if the hounds of hell were on her heels.

"I look forward to meeting them." She forced her face into a smile.

Lady Beatrice had her boys about her at table. The smaller boy sat between William and his mother. Big eyes stared at her over the table as he shoved a chubby fistful of bread into his mouth. The older child, no more than three years, tugged on William's tunic, his little face crinkled in vehement entreaty.

Alice breathed a soft sigh of relief. She was fine. What had happened in the bailey was over, and now the time had come for apologies.

William rose as they approached, shoulders taut, his handsome face colder than the stones beneath her slippers. "My lady."

"My lord." Alice accepted his assistance over the bench and took her seat.

Beatrice leaned forward to see past William. "Hello, Alice."

"Good evening." Relief unfurled through Alice's chest, set into motion by the open smile gifted her by Beatrice. Beatrice did not appear to hate her.

Not as lovely as Faye, Beatrice had a charm all of her own, and it spread from her like the sun's rays warming everyone about her. "I must apologize for not greeting you earlier." Without a better explanation to offer for her unconscionable behavior, she grasped for William's excuse. "I found myself suddenly ill."

"Not at all." Beatrice's eyes warmed. "You must think us horribly rude to have descended on you like this." Beatrice's smile vanished, and her voice quavered. "But we have good reason. There is illness at Anglesea. It has struck the keep hard." She cleared her throat and tried to compose herself. "Our brother Roger is strong and young, but our mother..." Tears welled in the blue-green brightness of Beatrice's eyes.

"I am so sorry." Alice wanted to reach across William and take Beatrice's hand, but she didn't know if her gesture would be welcomed. The news Beatrice brought made her actions even more shameful. Illness threatened William's family. Alice wanted to say something comforting, but her tongue knotted. So, she said the only thing she could think of, "I will pray for Anglesea."

"Thank you," Beatrice whispered.

"Mother will recover, Sweet Bea." William put his arm about her shoulders. "You forget the strength of her will."

"You are right." Beatrice sniffed and took a napkin from the table. She dabbed her cheeks and drew in a breath. "Nurse will not allow it any other way."

"You have the right of it there." William chuckled, and a watery smile wavered about Beatrice's lips.

"You are welcome here," Alice said, and meant every word. Sweet Bea—it suited her new sister. A sister. What a wondrous notion. As a child, Alice had invented her own sister to follow her around the halls of Yarborough. "Stay as long as you need to. We are family now."

Beatrice gave her another sweet smile, but the one from William made Alice want to toss up her skirts and dance a jig atop the table. He loved his family, now her family. When they were alone, she would try and explain, but for now, peace had been restored.

"Gah!" The baby beside Beatrice opened and closed his chubby fist as he reached for the bread atop the table.

"This loud gentleman is Adam." Beatrice broke a small piece of bread and gave it to Adam. "You will have to forgive his manners, but like most men he is a bear when hungry."

"I am hungry too." The other boy wedged himself between Alice and William.

"Indeed, master Richard." William hauled the child up by the back of his tunic. Alice gasped at such rough treatment of a child, but Richard shrieked with delight. William tucked him in the narrow gap between them on the bench. "Now make your greeting to Lady Alice."

The tightness in Alice's chest loosened.

"Good evening." Richard had his mother's eyes.

Alice inclined her head gravely. "Good evening to you."

"I like your hair," said Richard. "It shines."

"Aye, it does." William wrapped her braid about his fist. "Like gold."

"Nay," said Richard. "Like fire."

"Like mead." William raised a brow at his nephew.

Richard's eyes narrowed. "Like...like honey."

"Like—"

"Enough." Alice fanned her hot cheeks. Any more of this nonsense would turn her head.

"Thank you." William kissed her cheek, and the dread within her belly dissipated. William did not despise her. "He had the best of me at honey."

Serving women brought the meal to the table, and Alice

allowed herself to relax. Beatrice's children remained amongst them, not confined to another table or even another part of the keep. Nothing dire happened with the children at table. Richard spilled a cup of water, but other than that, Alice enjoyed their presence. When she had children, she would make sure they sat like Beatrice's children amongst their family.

Richard's warmth pressed against her side, his small form alight with energy and life. One day her child might ask for more milk with his bread, and be chided by William not to stuff his mouth with meat.

At the hall entrance, a woman and boy appeared.

Alice's vision went wavy, and her throat tightened. Her heart drummed unevenly in her chest.

Nay, nay, nay. It was happening again.

She grappled for control. *Stop it, Alice.*

But she could not. Terror broke over her in waves. Sweat prickled over Alice's skin. Her belly threatened to disgorge her dinner as Alice dragged her eyes off the boy and back to the woman. Ivy. She looked like the sort of woman Alice could befriend. There was nothing to fear, and yet dread engulfed her.

Alice dug her fingers into the table as she tried to master the hideous fear sucking her under.

"There you are." Beatrice rose to her feet. "We had given up on you two."

"Mathew wanted to see the horses before he went to bed," Ivy said with a soft smile. Her gaze flitted to Alice and she bobbed a curtsy. "My lady."

Their voices reached her as if from down a long tunnel. Her fingers ached from the pressure of the unyielding wood, but the sensations would not subside.

Go away, go away, go away. She chanted wildly to herself, trying to shove the fear away, but her grasp on the scene before her slipped incxorably.

They were all looking at her.

Words to bid Ivy and the boy—*Mathew, he has a name*—

screamed in Alice's head but her tongue stuck, parchment dry, to the roof of her mouth. Her throat closed tight and refused to let words come.

William's gaze burned into her, but Mathew transfixed her like a rabbit caught in a fox's stare.

Silence pressed around her as Ivy and Mathew stood before the dais waiting for her to bid them welcome, invite them to join the table. Mathew fidgeted, pressing his head to Ivy's thigh.

Alice met Beatrice's gaze. Confusion, and then anger and condemnation written clear across Beatrice's features as Alice sat there, frozen to the spot. "I..."

She had to get away.

"You must be hungry." William's voice cut through the thick quiet. His joviality carried an edge. "Come and join us."

Go! Run!

Alice watched as if not part of the picture before her.

Ivy nodded and took Mathew's hand. She cocked her head at Alice, her gaze holding a wealth of understanding Alice did not deserve. Shame writhed inside her, but the menace was stronger, drowning out all else.

Mathew shuffled close to Ivy's side.

A bench scraped, jarring and loud. It was her. She was on her feet. Alice stumbled over the bench and righted herself. The hall entrance and safety rushed toward her as the sense of doom chased her from the hall.

Behind her, William's voice rose angry and demanding. Yelling her name but she couldn't stop. She needed to get out of the hall. Away.

Get away. Run away. Escape.

On the stairs, her skirts tangled with her legs and she came down hard on the edge of the sharp risers. Air sawed in and out of her lungs as she used the wall and righted herself. Beneath her fingers, hard stone pressed into the pads. Alice dug her fingers in, trying to grasp at something solid and still her mind. Darkness hovered on the edges of her vision, driving her limp legs to keep climbing.

She stopped at the top and retched. Her head pounded as her stomach heaved.

From below came the ordinary rise and fall of voices. The oppressive weight on her chest lifted enough that her breathing eased. Sticky sweat trickled down her sides. From this small distance she could battle her thoughts into order again. Force back the suffocating dread enough for her mind to work. Dear God, what ailed her? One glance at Mathew and she had lost all reason.

Sister called him the Abomination, but Alice recoiled from the idea. "He is just a boy. A small boy."

Pushing away from the wall, Alice stumbled into her chamber and shut the door behind her.

William's presence lay heavy on her refuge. A discarded tunic hung on the clothes tree beside her chemise. His chest of gifts skulked by the base of the bed. Gifts from a pleased groom to his bride. Cloves scented the fire-warmed air.

Heavy footfalls approached the door and Alice moved away just as William threw the door open.

He towered in the doorway, raw anger etched into the carved lines of his face. "You dare."

Alice backed away. She had no explanation. Again. "William, I—"

"You what?" William advanced as she had seen him against Dunstan, feral in his anger.

Her legs nudged the back of the bed, halting her retreat. She wanted to say something, anything, but confusion warred with her rioting emotions. "I do not know what happened."

William loomed above her, body tight with anger, fists clenched by his side. Peril lurked in each well-modulated, evenly delivered word. "You dare to treat my family in this manner."

"I did not mean to." Words spilled from her, but not the right words. She had no explanation for herself, let alone the very angry man before me. "I'm so sorry. I was frightened."

"Frightened?" His boots nudged her slippers.

Alice nodded. Still now, the terror beat through her blood.

"Of whom? Ivy?" William's head recoiled and he glared down his perfect nose at her. "Were you afraid she would taint your sanctified presence?"

"Nay, I have naught to fear from a whore." The moment she said them, Alice wanted to stuff the words back down her throat. She did not mean to use that word—Sister's word, not hers—but her roiling thoughts had her all turned about. She could not think. She could not explain, and she needed to explain.

William grabbed her shoulders. "That whore," he snarled the word. "Is worth a hundred of you."

His words pierced sharper than a dagger. Alice slid out from beneath his grasp and clambered onto the bed, aiming to put the large furnishing between her and her husband. If he would give her two minutes, she would try and make him understand. "I—"

"You don't get off that lightly." He caught her ankle and dragged her back to him. Her skirts rucked about her thighs. "If I ever hear you refer to Ivy in that manner again, I will have that poisonous nun locked away in a nunnery for the rest of her days. Give me one more reason and you will keep her company."

"Nay." Alice pushed her skirts down. William and his sweet ways had lulled her into believing he would not behave as her other husbands had, but in his anger he became like John. A new fear overtook her. "Please, if you would let me speak."

"Ivy is one of the wisest and most beautiful women I know," he said, twisting the knife through her heart. "You will learn, Alice, that a woman is not defined by what is between her thighs."

What he didn't say, that he found Ivy wiser and more beautiful than her, hammered like a gauntleted fist into her heart. She had behaved atrociously in the hall and the bailey, shamed him and insulted her new family. Her fear and hurt exploded into anger, and her emotions wrenched out of her control. "Is a woman then defined by who is between her thighs?"

"Only when that man is her lord and husband." His grip on

her ankle tightened. "The moment you said 'I will,' I became lord of Tarnwych, and you would do well to remember that."

"And that gives you the right to do as you please." Her voice rose until she was shouting. "This is my keep."

"Nay, my lady," he spat. "It is mine, and I can fill it with whores, gutter rats, thieves, murderers, and rapists if I choose." William pushed his face closer until their noses touched. "I can do what I like, because I am lord here. Dunstan learned that lesson at the ultimate cost. I suggest you learn faster than he did."

She shoved him away from her. "You threaten me?"

"I am telling you, my lady. Behave yourself, or you will not enjoy the consequences."

He dropped her ankle and spun about. The slam of the door reverberated through the chamber.

Alice collapsed onto her back on the bed. All the fight drained from her and she wanted to sob. "I am already not enjoying them."

* * *

William stormed down the stairs and through the hall.

Beatrice and Ivy clustered about the children whispering to each other.

He could well imagine what they said. Alice had shamed him in front of them, but that did not bother him as much as her reaction to Mathew. Aye, he had seen what drove his wife upstairs, and it had naught to do with Ivy.

Since the day of his birth, they had gathered about their youngest brother and protected him from the cruel tongues and derisive faces that followed the lad. Slower than other children, and at times only Ivy and Mother could manage Mathew, but when his world stayed ordered about him, no sweeter or more loving child could you find. Several people had tried to persuade their family to put Mathew away with the holy fathers or keep him on his own with a caretaker. Mother and Father had refused, and so they raised him with the rest of the Anglesea children.

The horror on Alice's face as she stared at Mathew was seared into William's mind. That his own wife could be one of the small-minded accursed fools who looked at Mathew and recoiled he could not tolerate. A woman he had lain with, one with whom he shared his life. He could not, would not, accept it.

He needed to hit something, hard, or he could not be accountable for his actions. His boot heels dug into the damp soil of the bailey as he strode toward the practice yards. There he would find an outlet for the fury gripping him by the balls.

Men stepped back, eyeing him warily as he entered the yards.

"You." He snatched a practice stave from a barrel beside the barracks. "Fight me."

"My lord?" The oldest Domnall dropped his stave tip to the soil and glanced at his fellows.

"Fight me." William closed on Domnall. He attacked. Stave met stave with a solid crack that sent shock waves up William's arm.

Stave still embedded in the soil, Domnall blinked at him.

"Fight someone more your weight," Gregory said.

William met Gregory's gaze over their crossed staves. Aye, Gregory would do.

Whispers broke out around them as William circled left.

Gregory twirled his stave. His dark gaze searched for the opening, his weight balanced on the balls of his feet.

William struck Gregory's stave hard enough to jar his hand. Pain numbed the anger to a low simmer.

Gregory danced, impossibly light on his feet for such a big man, and forced William to climb out of his thoughts and counter the rapid fire blows coming at him. Gregory fought at full strength, giving no quarter, not holding his blows back, and pressing William hard to counter.

Gregory fought with the ferocity of a Northman.

Sweat dripped from his face as Gregory locked him in the

bind before shoving him back. William caught his balance and circled.

He closed again.

Gregory met him.

Their blows tapped and cracked across the bailey faster than a bard could clap.

William fought until his lungs burned and his muscles trembled with exertion, until the angry burn sputtered and died. His only satisfaction lay in Gregory's sides heaving like bellows and sweat plastering his tunic to his chest. "Enough."

One of the men brought them both water as they stood, swaying with exhaustion in the practice yards. From the ramparts, the watch called the hour well advanced, and the keep casements had gone dark. They had fought well into the night.

His men had remained to watch, and now murmured amongst themselves.

Aches and pains from Gregory's well-aimed blows set a low throb from several points on his ribs and thighs. Legs turned to pudding beneath him, William pressed his back into the barrack wall and slid to the ground.

Gregory joined him with a groan. "You have improved."

William grunted. He suspected Gregory had landed more blows than he had taken. His ribs certainly concurred. "You are still the best I have ever seen."

"But not good enough when it counted." Gregory shook his head.

"Hugo played a dirty trick." William raised his aching arm and punched Gregory on the shoulder. It did not surprise him Gregory still carried the burden from his duel with Faye's late husband's brother. Gregory had killed the man, but not before Hugo's lackey had nearly gutted Gregory with a hidden knife blow. "My sister was well when you left?"

A rare smile crossed Gregory's face. "She is very close to her time now. I would like to return before she delivers our child. She did not fare well in the beginning. She was often ill. I thank God for it now because it kept her away from Anglesea."

"This is a worrisome business about Anglesea," William said. His mother, father, brother, so many people he loved and knew. Perhaps his worry for them had added to his anger toward Alice.

"It is in God's hands."

William pressed down the now familiar surge of irritation. "I have heard rather too much of God and His will since coming to Tarnwych. Between that blasted nun and Alice, it is all I ever hear."

"How fares Lady Alice?" Gregory upended the water gourd over his head.

"I threatened her." Shame snuck around his righteous anger and pricked at him. His father had raised him better than to thunder and rail at a woman, no matter how justified.

Gregory stared at him. "That is not like you."

"Nay." William had never lost his temper so spectacularly with a woman before. He had behaved badly, but Alice's reaction to Mathew had pushed him beyond reason. "Mathew is precious to all of us."

"I suspect there is more to this than first appears," Gregory said.

Always the watcher, Gregory kept his lips fastened and his eyes wide open. "What do you mean?"

"Her reaction." Gregory frowned and rested his head against the wall. "She was terrified. Beyond reason terrified."

"Of Mathew?" His ire gave a tired stir. "Who, in God's name, is terrified of Mathew? Unless they regard him as evil."

"Nay." Gregory shrugged. "It was not that sort of fear. It was something...else. I know not, but a wise man would find out."

William gave a rueful laugh. He did not judge himself a very wise man at this moment.

Chapter Fifteen

Skulking into her own hall to break her fast the next morning sat ill with Alice. Where William had spent the night, she knew not, but he had not spent it with her. Half afraid he would come back, and even more afraid he would not, she had lain awake and kept the fire fed until well past when the watch called midnight.

Yesterday's awful incidents had lost her William. As she counted the night hours, she had tortured herself with every flirtatious glance tossed William's way, every coy giggle that had greeted him since his arrival at Tarnwych.

"That whore is worth a hundred of you."

William's words taunted her. Aye, Ivy was worth a hundred of her, and she still had no good reason to offer for what had driven her from the hall like a crazed woman.

Lively noise rose from about her as she threaded her way through the tables. As if they knew of her chastisement, Tarnwych folk cast her sympathetic stares as she passed. She did not deserve them.

William's presence at Tarnwych had changed the hall. Not just the inclusion of the men adding a low bass murmur, but the general air of conviviality amongst those gathered for a meal.

Someone who had grown up in such a hall must find it common-place, but it gave her a kernel of courage.

Domnall rose from where he sat amidst his brothers. "Lady Alice."

"Good morrow, Domnall."

He thumped his chest. "We wanted you to know, the lads and I"—he swept his brothers with one large hand—"we stand beside you."

Aonghas's sons all nodded to her. What must they have heard of her altercation with William? Their support was sweet, but misguided. She had done nothing to earn it and she would not compound her sins by dividing the keep against itself. Trying to infuse some strength in her voice she said, "I am well."

On the dais, the Anglesea clan arrayed in strength this morning. William sat at table, with Beatrice to his left and Ivy beyond her. William leaned forward to speak to Ivy. Ivy colored and laughed.

William appeared very fond of Ivy. What man would not esteem Ivy with her dark hair, pale skin, and eyes the most arresting shade of green, nestled between thick, dark lashes? Only a stupid woman believed her husband did not notice lovelier women about him. Particularly when his wife had lost her wits.

Fa-la-la-la-la.

Beatrice's boys sat beside Gregory on William's right side, with a gap left in the middle for her. No Mathew. All four males rose as they caught sight of her. Clearly, his anger did not upset his manners because William assisted her as she took her place.

Alice's stomach clenched in rejection of the bowl of stewed fruit placed before her.

Stiff as wood, William sat beside her, his head turned to speak with his sister and Ivy.

"The weather looks dismal this morning," Gregory said.

Sure enough, broody pewter clouds disgorged a steady trickle from beyond the hall casement. Wind played willy-nilly with the heather plants and flattened the scrubby, brown grass to the soggy soil. Other than a miserable day, it meant the majority of people would be confined to the keep today.

Alice handed her untouched bowl to the serving woman. With winter fast approaching, one dreary day could stretch into a sennight or even more. An entire sennight trapped inside with her angry in-laws.

"It is fairly typical for this time of year," Alice managed to answer Sir Gregory.

Gregory pushed a cheese board closer to her. He cut her a slice and placed it on a hunk of bread before handing it to her. "I should leave soon. I want to reach Calder Castle before the worst of it arrives."

Alice shook her head at the food.

Gregory kept the bread and cheese out held.

"Your wife is there?" Alice took his offering and nibbled on it.

"Aye, and our two boys. Faye is due to deliver her child any day now." Love for his family filled Gregory's voice.

What young girl hadn't dreamed of finding a strong, handsome knight to dote on her? Alice put her meal down. Such silly dreams young girls had, and three bad marriages should have rid her of them by now. But with William—her heart twisted—with William, she had dared hope.

Until yesterday.

"The Anglesea folk are not like most," Gregory said.

Did Gregory offer her comfort or information?

A breathtaking smile transformed Gregory's face to graven beauty. "They do things a mite differently, and it can take some time to grow accustomed to them."

"Are you?" Alice leaned a little closer and lowered her voice. "Are you accustomed to them?"

"Aye." Gregory nodded. "They are very close and the love between them is clear to any who see them. They do not mean it as such, but it can often make one feel as if one sat on the outside."

She did sit on the outside, and she had earned her place there, along with their condemnation. If she could understand what had happened to her, she could apologize, but she had no reasonable explanation.

"It also makes them very protective of one another," Gregory said. "And Mathew is one who requires all of their protection."

Too afraid to ask where Mathew broke his fast this morning, she nodded.

"But they are good people." Gregory handed her a slice of ham. "Quick to anger and easy to forgive, and they embrace any who need them."

"Like Ivy?"

"Aye, like Ivy."

"Is she—" Alice could not ask what Ivy was or had been to William, no matter how hot the questions burned inside her.

Gregory chewed his own ham, and swallowed. "Ivy's story is her own to tell, but she has not had an easy time of it. She and Beatrice share a special bond, along with young Thomas, who was with Beatrice when she rescued Ivy. I believe the bond between Ivy and Thomas to be especially close, although neither of them have admitted as much."

Did Gregory reassure her about William? Or had he heard what she had said to William in her anger and turmoil?

"Will we go riding today?" Richard tugged on Gregory's sleeve.

"Nay, lad." William stood and climbed over the bench. "But I am sure we can find something else to do, right here in the hall."

"Inside." Richard's voice rose on an unhappy wail.

"Unless you want to get wetter than a duck," William said.

He led both boys to the hearth.

Beatrice rose and joined them, and then Ivy.

Gregory excused himself and left the hall.

Serving men dismantled the trestle tables and returned them with the benches to the side of the hall. Alice should rise and let them take this table away.

Before the hearth, the Anglesea family played a game together. It seemed to involve a lot of whispering and laughter. William raised his arms and roared. The boys shrieked and hid behind their mother, grins splitting their little faces. William stomped from foot to foot with his arms above his head.

Gregory had spoken true. As clear as ropes their loving bonds tied them together. And they offered her no rope to take up.

She did not deserve one after what had happened yesterday. For a short few weeks she had been part of them because of William. Now, she sat on the outside and watched. Not too different from her childhood. Sat beside her casement, she had stared out at the children playing in the bailey. A lord's daughter did not play with the keep children. Clearly, the same held for the lady of the lord.

Her self-pity turned her stomach. Alice stood and left the hall, her new duties sufficient to keep her from dwelling on the past.

* * *

Alice punched her pillow into a more comfortable shape. Nights stretched very long when you spent them wondering where your husband slept, or even if he slept, and if he would ever forgive you.

She missed so much about William sharing her chamber. Their marital relations, for certain, but also the quiet talks in the wee hours, and the way William would tease her about what she wore in the morning. The last two mornings had been dismal, lonely affairs.

Sister had not visited her either since their altercation the other day. Alice heaved onto her back. The canopy needed replacing, threadbare in places with the color dulled by age. She amassed enemies with every conversation she had. Or non-conversation. Beatrice looked right through her when they met. Ivy, in one of those twists that left Alice shaking her head, greeted her with a friendly smile and a few words. As for William...

She sat up and wrapped her arms around her legs. Flames flickered golden and orange across the logs in the hearth. William's infernal politeness stung the worst. He rose when she approached, assisted her to sit, opened doors for her, greeted her when he saw her. All with a cold, distant look in his beautiful eyes. Who knew a girl could want to scream at a man for his unflagging manners?

Alice wrapped her arms tighter and rested her cheek against her knees. With her other husbands she had been relieved when they sought other company and left her alone. How had William charmed his way into her life so fast? These two days removed from him had served as a bitter lesson in how far he had wriggled beneath her skin. With William, she could catch tantalizing glimpses of a future filled with laughter and happiness, snatches of a life fulfilled and joyous. They left her ravenous for more of the same.

She needed to fix this rift with William. Aye, he may reject her overtures, but the promise of a richer life merited the risk. On the morrow then, she would find a way to make this right. Even if she still did not understand what had beset her.

A knock at the door jerked her out of her heated imaginings. William? Although she had yet to hear him knock. It was more like him to fling the door open.

Heart thundering, she called out, "Who is there?"

"It is I, Cedric." Alice's heart sank. Not William. "I think you should come, my lady."

Alice slid out of bed. Her bare feet hit the cold floor and she walked faster. Cracking the door open she peered around it. "What is it?"

"It is Sister Julianna, my lady. Sir Gregory found her in the chapel and sent me for you." Cedric's brow puckered in a frown, his gaze uneasy.

"Sister?" Alice could not bring herself to voice the ultimate fear. "Is she ill?"

"Come, my lady." Cedric stepped back into the hallway and motioned her to follow. "You must come."

Alice snatched a cloak and a pair of slippers before joining him in the hallway.

Around them, the keep lay still. Few tapers burned in the narrow corridors as she followed Cedric down the stairs, through the hall, and into the chapel at the far end.

Sir Gregory appeared out of the gloom, setting Alice's heart pounding.

"Good lad." He clapped Cedric on the shoulder. "Now find your pallet for the night. Lady Alice and I will deal with this."

"Deal with what?" Alice trailed Gregory down the central aisle of the chapel.

"I came to the chapel to complete my evening devotions and found her," Sir Gregory said.

Supine before the altar lay a slim form. Bare feet poked out from beneath Sister's shapeless, linen shift.

Alice took a step closer. Sister often served a night thus in prayer, but the shift's shredded back bore dull, russet stains.

Alice froze and stared, her mind not able to make sense of what she saw.

Gregory stood beside her, his face grave. "I do not know how long she has lain thus, but I fear she may be feverish."

"Sister?" Alice sank to her knees beside Sister. "Sister Julianna?"

Sister raised her head. A bright flush of color gave Sister the appearance of good health, until you looked into the dull, listless sheen of her eyes. "My Lord has blessed me with my punishment."

"What?" Alice glanced at Gregory. Dear God, could someone help her make sense of this? "What have you done, Sister?"

"Penance." Sister dropped her forehead back to the floor.

Gregory crouched beside Alice. "I think she has been mortifying her flesh." He pointed at Sister's back. Deep, crusted lines crisscrossed her skin. "Those look like whip marks to me."

"But why?" Alice could barely stand to look at the damage Sister had wrought on herself. She laid her fingers against Sister's nape. Hot, damp skin confirmed Gregory's fears.

"Only she knows why," Gregory said. "I attempted to help her, but she insists on remaining here. That is why I sent Cedric for you." His concerned gaze met hers. "She needs to be treated, Lady Alice. At her age, she cannot be left here in this condition."

Alice knew nothing of tending the sick. Sister attended to that. She did not know what to do. Surely any touch would be agonizing to Sister. Encrusted with dried blood, the wounds on her back stuck her linen shift to their edges. Cleaning those wounds would cause untold pain.

Clean the wounds. She had the first step. And to clean them, she needed to get Sister to a bed. "Sister." She brushed an unmarred part of Sister's shoulder. "Can you rise?"

"I must not. I cannot." The position of her head muffled Sister's voice. "Penance. For the abomination."

"Sister." Alice gave her a tiny shake, careful of her wounds. "You are ill, and we need to see you tended."

"The Lord has visited his judgment on me for my sins."

Alice hoped against hope Gregory would have some suggestion. They could not leave her here in this condition.

Gregory shrugged.

"Sister." Alice applied a bit more force to her voice. "You are ill. We need to take you to your chamber and attend to you."

"Holy Father, forgive me." Sister's entire form shook with wracking sobs. "Forgive me. Forgive this unworthy sinner."

Alice was drowning. She knew not what to do. Inspiration

struck and she sent a prayer of forgiveness for herself. "God has already forgiven you, Sister."

Gregory's head snapped around, and he stared at her.

Alice made an apologetic face at him. Sister needed to be seen to, by any means possible.

"I will await my sign." Sister's voice grew muffled again as she recited in sing-song Latin.

"We have already had a sign," Alice said. She tried to compel Gregory with a look. She would welcome a bit of help here.

"Um...indeed." Gregory grimaced at her. "I have seen it."

"No sign to a sinner," muttered Sister.

"In...the sky," Alice said. "At sunset. I saw the clouds form the face of our Blessed Madonna."

Gregory raised a dark brow at her and mouthed "clouds."

He could very well make that face. Fine help he was being.

"You did?" Sister raised her head.

"Clear as the eyes on my face," Alice said. She would confess later. Later, when she had Sister out of this freezing chapel and her wounds cleaned and bound.

"I saw it too." Gregory stepped in.

Sister shifted her head and glared at him. "Judas," she hissed. "Peter. The one who denies our Lord."

Perhaps Alice did not need Gregory's help after all. "I did not know you were here praying," Alice said. "I could not know at the time, but now I see it was the sign you searched for."

Sister frowned as if considering her words.

Alice held her breath. This had to work, or Sir Gregory would have to resort to force.

"Nay." Sister lowered her forehead back to the ground. "It is not the sign for which I seek. It was a sign for you, warning you from turning your head away from the Lord."

Sister launched back into her muttered prayers.

Enough! Sister needed to get out of the chapel and into a bed. If she would not come willingly..."Can you lift her?"

Gregory looked taken aback. "It will hurt her."

"It will kill her if we leave her here. Is that not what you said?"

"Aye." Gregory shifted back with a frown. "But she does not want to be taken from here."

"Well, she can hardly stay here." At her feet, Sister recited the Hail Mary. "I will ask her forgiveness once she is better."

"Very well." Gregory gave her a wry smile. "She will not thank you for this. Or me."

Gregory fisted the back of his tunic and dragged it off, then his chemise. He flushed dark red and averted his eyes. "My apologies, Lady Alice. I need to provide some padding for her back."

Alice waved his apology off. Her cheeks heated. William was put together nicely, but Sir Gregory...Well, all that carved and bulging muscle made Lady Faye a very lucky woman. God forgive her for her adulterous thoughts, but surely God did not shape men like this and then condemn a woman for looking.

He laid his clothing on Sister's back and lifted her into his arms.

Sister shrieked and lashed out, catching him a blow on the jaw.

Gregory grunted and positioned Sister in such a way as he could pin her arms to her sides.

Sister shrieked louder, her legs kicking out and raising her shift past her knees.

Alice rearranged her shift more modestly.

Sister abruptly slumped against Gregory's chest.

So be it. Alice led the way out of the chapel.

Eyes pinched closed, Sister muttered bible verse after bible verse.

Gregory bore her along as if she weighed no more than a thistle.

Thank the Lord, her voice grew fainter and fainter.

Sleepy faces beneath tousled heads appeared along their journey. Eventually they reached Sister's small chamber just down the hall from Alice's.

Alice stripped the linens and Gregory laid down his burden.

As he released her, Sister raked his forearm with her nails, leaving three long grooves. She sat up, her face contorted in rage, and hissed at him.

Sister dropped like a stone onto her back.

Alice flinched at the pain that must have caused, but Sister lay insensate.

"I am sorry about that." Alice gestured at Gregory's injured arm.

He shrugged and turned Sister on her belly. Some of her lash marks had opened in her struggle, and fresh blood oozed through Gregory's tunic.

Sister's eyes opened and locked on Gregory. "Betrayer. The Lord will visit his condemnation on you."

"Do you think you can send Cedric for water?" Alice peeled Gregory's clothing from Sister.

Sir Gregory nodded. He took his clothing from her and balled it into his fist. "She will need a healer."

"I do not understand," Alice said. "What sins can she possible have to atone for? Especially her. And to do this to herself."

"Ah, Lady Alice." Shaking his head, Gregory gave a sad smile "There breathes not one amongst us who can cast the first stone. We all battle our own demons."

Still waters ran deep through this tall knight. More than Alice could have suspected, knowing the stories she'd heard of him. Then again, those stories had come from Sister, and Sister did a lot of railing about the word of God. Sir Gregory seemed to live it.

A slim figure slipped into the room. Ivy cast a glance at Sister and then looked at Alice. "How can I help?"

"Get you from me, whore." Sister's voice faded into a rasp, and her lids fluttered closed.

Alice did not want to upset Sister further. "I am not certain..."

Ivy grinned and winked at her. "Perhaps we should speak outside."

Alice followed her into the passage, certain she would not look so cheerful after being called a whore.

"I have some knowledge of healing." Ivy stood with her hands folded before her. "She will not allow me to tend her, without making herself worse. You tend her, and I can provide you with what you need."

Alice recanted every horrible thought she'd had and every nasty word she'd uttered about Ivy. The woman was a saint.

Chapter Sixteen

Too tired for much else, Alice sat and stared at the kitchen hearth fire. Tarnwych had long since settled for the night, and Cook and her boys snored from their pallets close to the warmth. Above stairs, Sister needed Alice to return with Ivy's poultice for her wounds. Over the hearth, Ivy steeped yarrow in a large pot with Ivy alone knew what else. All day Ivy had battled by her side to bring Sister's fever down, but the lashes on Sister's back had become fouled, and the fever ate at her frail form.

The old scars beneath the fresh lashes disturbed Alice more. Sister's back bore the scars of a lifetime of whippings. Why? What sin did Sister seek to flay from her flesh?

"Here"—Ivy put an earthen mug before her—"drink this. You must be tired."

She must be tired? Alice nearly laughed aloud. Aye, she was done in, but Ivy worked just as tirelessly. Alice accepted the mug with a smile of thanks.

Ivy sat on the bench on the far side of the table, her hands clasped around a similar mug. "We need to wait for the yarrow."

Alice nodded. Yarrow would draw the infection from Sister's

body and halt the bleeding, Ivy had told her. "How did you learn about healing?"

Ivy sipped her warm milk and placed the mug on the table. "When I came to Anglesea, Nurse took me under her wing. Some of this I learned from my mother when I showed I had a knack for it. When I was younger, I always tended the animals about the farm or the other children."

Ivy's dark hair lay braided down her back, her bliaut unadorned dun linen. If she had met her on the street, Alice would have judged her a farmer or craftsman's wife.

"You can ask," Ivy said.

Alice's face heated. She had been staring, and both of them knew it. Weariness rid her of any idea of dissembling. "You do not look like...what you were. What they say you were."

"A whore?" Ivy tucked a stray strand of hair behind her ear.

"That is a horrible word."

A delicate snort escaped Ivy. "It is a horrible profession."

Alice giggled. Indeed, a horrible profession, and Ivy joined in her laughter. Ivy's smile transformed her face into breathtaking. No wonder William forever made Ivy laugh.

Their laughter cleared the air. "Is it true?"

"Aye." Ivy rolled the base of her mug on the table. "My father sold me to a man named Rudd when I was fourteen."

There was naught funny about that, and Alice sat straighter on the bench. What an awful thing for a father to do. Except...had her father not sold her too.

"I was a little older when my father married me to my first husband," she said. "Although it is not the same, as he was but one man."

Ivy propped her chin on her palm. "One man. Many men. Women are sold as chattel to further a man's ends."

True enough. What a depressing thought. Alice sipped the warmed milk and honey Ivy had prepared for her. "How did you come to live at Anglesea?"

A look of distaste crossed Ivy's face. "Rudd believed I was his to pass about as he liked, and he liked to pass me out a lot. I did not agree. Lady Beatrice came upon one of my disagreements with Rudd and rescued me."

"Lady Beatrice did?"

"Oh, aye." Ivy chuckled. "With no thought for her own safety, she attacked three men."

Sweet Bea, indeed! She would like to know a woman with such boldness. Except Beatrice barely acknowledged her, and Sister's illness had delayed her plans for making amends. The thing that had happened when Mathew had appeared nagged at the back of her mind. It was not normal, nor was it right, but she had failed to stop it in the hall, and was anxious it might happen again.

Ivy rose and tended her yarrow. "It is ready." Movements neat and efficient, Ivy drained water from the yarrow and tipped the root into a clean basin. Ivy stood between Sister and her Maker, and Alice would have struggled without her.

"It was not you," Alice said.

Ivy looked at her.

"The other day in the hall. When I ran out. It was not you."

Ivy paused in grinding the yarrow. Potent, sweet herb scent filled the narrow space of the table between them. "Who was it then?"

"It was the boy. Mathew. But I cannot explain it. I saw him and I was overcome with the worst kind of fear. As if my life was in danger. I ran before I could stop myself." Saying the words out loud sounded ridiculous.

With a frown, Ivy fetched a clean square of linen and laid it on the table. "Mathew cannot help the way he is. He was born that way."

"How is he?" Alice would rather ask Ivy than William, or God forbid, Beatrice. Perhaps if she could understand Mathew more, it would provide a clue to her lunacy.

"He is...slower to learn than other children." Ivy straightened and stretched her back. "He is easily confused and upset by change. But for all that, he has the sweetest nature of any person I have met."

Alice's heart sank. There was nothing to fear in Mathew. The size of her mistake swelled until it threatened to engulf her. "William is wroth with me."

"William loves Mathew very much. He cannot tolerate any cruelty toward his brother." Ivy spread a thick layer of slime-green paste over the linen. "What is it about Mathew that makes you fearful?"

"I do not know." And therein lay the thorn. She did not fear the boy himself. She feared...Alice groaned her frustration. "I do not understand it."

"Well." Ivy pressed the poultice into the basin. "Have you tried telling William so?"

"I have not seen William since Sister fell ill." And their last private conversation had gone badly.

"He is a reasonable man," Ivy said. "But his love for his family comes first." She handed Alice the basin with the poultice. "Take this up and lay it across her back."

Alice took the poultice from her.

"Make sure she drinks that tisane as well," Ivy called after her.

Alice dragged her bones upstairs and into Sister's airless chamber. Putrefaction hung heavy and cloying in the air.

On the palette, Sister tossed about. Alice had tied cloth constraints to Sister's wrists to keep her from turning onto her abused back. More good advice from Ivy.

She carried a basin of fresh water to the bed. Alice cleansed the wounds as gently as she could. Sister had flayed her flesh raw. At first, Alice's gorge had risen at the sight, but she had grown accustomed to it now. Still, the pain Sister had inflicted on herself defied Alice's comprehension. She could not believe God would demand such cruelty from his flock.

Alice cleansed around the wounds before laying the poultice across Sister's back.

All the time, Sister mumbled and muttered about her sins and the abomination. Alice gave up trying to make sense of Sister's feverish meanderings, but a vicious taskmaster haunted the old woman. No person deserved the torment Sister suffered.

Sister had sacrificed her life at the nunnery to stay and care for Alice. Alice could do no more than repay her in this small way. Still, Sister's reaction to the Anglesea party seemed unreasonable, strange even.

Then again, no stranger than what had happened to her.

Getting Sister to swallow the tisane lying on her stomach presented a double challenge. Alice dipped a cloth in the tisane and pressed it to the upward corner of Sister's mouth. She stroked her throat until Sister swallowed. It took time and more tisane ended on the linen beneath Sister than in her mouth, but Alice persisted until she had emptied the basin. If this room boasted a casement, Alice would throw it open and let the cold night air in. But Sister has insisted on occupying this tiny, comfortless cell.

Bare, unadorned stone covered the walls and floor, the sparse furniture rough and worn, like a sort of penance all of its own.

Alice added more wood to the fire and sat on the bench beside it. Ivy said the fever should break at some point, so now she waited. A prayer for Sister's healing might help, but Alice had no prayers in her, so she sat and listened to the quiet sounds of the sleeping keep.

* * *

William stood outside the chamber door and cursed himself for his cowardice. He dreaded the look of trepidation on Alice's face when she saw him.

He had threatened her, spoken to her so roughly Father would have kicked his ass. While he bore the shame of his actions, she bore the fear. He knew a thousand ways to wheedle a woman out of a pet, or tease her out of a temper. Not one, however, to replace destroyed trust. Aye, Alice had erred in her treatment of his family, and they would still speak of that. But as his reason returned, he kept reliving the look on her face as she ran from the hall.

People often turned from Mathew in disgust, but Alice had worn a face of pure terror.

He had stopped Ivy as she made her way to bed. Ivy told him Alice wore herself out caring for the nun. As much as he disliked the woman, he would not see her dying untended like an injured dog—however tempting the idea.

His answers lay beyond a door he hesitated to open.

William took a deep breath and pushed open the door. He recoiled a step into the passage as the stench belted him in the face. God's alive! How could anyone bear this for more than a breath?

The nun murmured and shifted about on the pallet.

Drawing fresh air deep into his chest, William stepped into the room.

Alice lay crumpled like a bundle of rags on a rough bench before the fire. She could tuck her entire form on the narrow bench. Such a delicate creature he had bellowed at and bullied. He would welcome Father's ass-kicking. Shadows lurked beneath her closed eyes, and she frowned in her sleep. Glorious red hair tumbled onto the bare stone flags.

A queer constriction happened in his chest, much like it did when he watched one of his nephews at play.

So loyal, his Alice. She must have remained here and watched over Sister until weariness overcame her. Loyalty he understood. His loyalty to his family had led to this chasm between them.

He crouched beside her. Strange how he had thought her a trifle plain when he first saw her. Of course, he had not said as much to Roger, but he had harbored the thought. How could he not have appreciated the delicacy of her features, the sweet tilt of her nose, the lushness of her mouth? Spending the past nights wrapped in a blanket in the hall, he had missed her curvy little body pressed against him. Several times a night, he woke and reached for her to find himself alone. A married man had no reason to deny his desire for his wife, especially not when he had a lusty bundle like Alice in his bed.

His Alice. His to honor, keep, and guard, for richer, for poorer, in sickness and in health, as ordained by the Holy Church till death parted them. A lifetime seemed a long time to nurture a grievance between them.

Gregory had remarked on what he had seen—the unadulterated terror and anguish as she ran from the hall. He needed to temper his family loyalty with his need for answers. Did Alice not also deserve, at least, a fair hearing?

* * *

Alice floated warm and safe on her own cloud.

She snuggled into her deliciously warm cloud and drew the faint smell of cloves in deep. Her cloud moved. Her eyes protested her opening them.

"Hush." William's voice lowered and silky. "Go back to sleep."

Oh, she would love that. Alice closed her eyes again. *Nay!* She could not sleep. "Sister! I must care for Sister."

William's fine features hovered above her. "Sleep. Someone will watch her while you rest and come for you if you are needed."

"She does not like anybody else near her." Her dreamy fog cleared enough for her to realize William carried her in his arms.

"I know, and Ivy gave her something to help her rest while you do." His face softened into an expression almost tender. "Sleep, my Alice. Martha will watch over her while you do."

She should remain awake, but her heavy eyelids drew toward each other. Against her ear, the steady sure drum of William's heart lulled her.

They reached their chamber and William lowered her onto the bed. Bending, he unlaced her shoes and slid them off.

"Arms up," he said.

Alice obeyed, and he unlaced her bliaut and slipped it off.

Next, he pulled down the bedlinens and helped her scoot under them. Beneath her aching back, the soft pallet folded about her like an embrace. William must have had it replaced.

His footsteps grew fainter, and the door creaked open.

Alice raised her head. "Stay."

William stopped, his hand on the door latch.

"Stay." Alice did not want to spend another lonely night in this bed. She held her breath as he stood by the door for a long moment.

Finally, he approached the bed, shed his boots and clothes, and slid naked in beside her.

Tears pricked Alice's eyes. She scooted closer to his warmth. When his arm came about her shoulders and drew her head onto his shoulder, she nearly lost the battle with her tears.

He pressed a soft kiss to the top of her head. "Sleep."

* * *

Alice screwed her eyes shut against the forceful sunlight insisting she wake. She stretched out her arms and encountered empty bed. Her body protesting each movement, she sat up. Wintery sunlight caught dust motes in the air. At least the infernal rain had stopped.

William had left the chamber.

Twice she had woken in the night, just to confirm William had carried her to their bed and joined her there. His pillow still bore the imprint from his head.

A gentle tap came from the door.

"Come in."

Ivy poked her dark head around the door. "I see you are awake. William said to let you sleep, but I thought you might be hungry."

"How is Sister?" The food Ivy bore made her stomach growl. She had barely taken time to eat whilst tending Sister.

Ivy smiled. "She is more peaceful this morning. The fever broke in the early hours and she sleeps now."

"Thank God." A weight lifted from Alice's chest. "And thank you."

"It is what I do." Ivy shrugged. She placed the food on the table beneath the casement. "Come and eat."

"She will not be grateful." Alice took the pottage. Bless Ivy! She'd put honey, cream, and apples into the pottage.

"William prepared it." Ivy gave her a mischievous grin. "He said he knew exactly what you liked best."

Alice nearly snorted her mouthful of pottage. Her face heated. Such a bad one, William. Even sweeter than Sister recovering was William opening a small chink in the door between them. Aye, Alice would skip through. "Is he about?"

"Nay." Ivy busied herself fetching Alice's garments. "He rode out with the men earlier."

"Oh." She would have liked to find him right away and set matters straight.

"But he will return." Ivy fetched her boots and placed them near Alice. "He gave the command that you were not to spend the day in the sick room. One of the serving women will sit with Sister, and you are to join me for a walk in the fresh air."

"William said that?"

"Indeed." Ivy shook a clean chemise out. "Now, come and dress. Clouds are already building to the north. I fear we will not have much sunlight left."

Alice checked on Sister before she and Ivy left. Martha sat beside Sister and tended to some darning. "I will keep a sharp eye on her, my lady."

"Call me if there is any change."

"Right away." Martha waved Alice out. The elderly serving woman had lived at Tarnwych as long as Alice, before her arrival even.

Weak winter sun had never felt so glorious as it did on her face as Alice stepped into the bailey. Ivy's threatened clouds boiled about Tarn Crag, driven forward by the stiff breeze. For now, Alice reveled in the freshness of the wind, the warmth on her back.

Ivy led the way through the inner bailey and into the outer. Around them, people stepped lighter as they too enjoyed the respite from the driving rain and cold. Ice rode the wind in a sharp bite holding the threat of snow.

Sir Gregory would need to leave soon or risk the weather trapping him at Tarnwych. "Snow is coming. We must warn Sir Gregory."

"He left at dawn." Ivy raised her skirts and picked her way around the puddles. "He hates to be separated too long from Lady Faye."

What a grand thing, to have a man who loved you as much as Gregory loved his Faye. She might settle for a man who prepared her pottage for her, or carried her to bed and undressed her like a babe. He may not love her, and Alice's heart gave a small twinge, but she preferred it to the cold, lonely silence. She hoped William's unbending meant he would, at least, hear her out. Although her explanation would consist of so much that was inexplicable.

Their boots rapped on the wood of the drawbridge as she and Ivy strode across. Outside the shelter of the keep walls, the wind picked up and tugged at their skirts.

"Where are we going?" Alice raised her voice over the wind.

"There." Ivy pointed.

From where she stood, the land sloped to a meadow sheltered by low scrub on one side and tucked against the side of a long rock outcropping. In the meadow, Lady Beatrice's golden head gleamed in the sunlight. Three children clustered about her. Alice missed a step. The fear returned. She dared not risk it happening again.

Ivy stopped and watched her, head cocked.

She could do this. She must do this. Alice clenched her fists. She would do this. Mathew. Just a young boy. Her heart thundered and she drew a long breath. She could meet him without giving in to her fear. She was forewarned this time. Sweat beaded her palms and she wiped them on her dress. "It is a fine day for playing outside."

"That it is." Ivy nodded, and threading her arm through Alice's, tugged her down to the meadow.

Alice's legs shook as she stumbled beside Ivy.

Her fear of a small, harmless boy shamed her.

Beatrice raised her head at their approach.

Alice swore the woman's eyes burned a hole in her bliaut.

"What a lovely day," Ivy called and waved at the boys.

Richard came running toward her. "Ivy. We found a rabbit hole."

"How wonderful," Ivy said. "Are there any rabbits in it, for the pot tonight?"

"Ivy." Richard scrunched his face. "These are not the eating sort of rabbits."

Alice used their chatter to edge closer to Beatrice. "Good morrow."

"Good morrow." Beatrice could give a person frost-bite with her gaze, the same as William could.

Alice tugged her cloak tighter about herself. "It is lovely to see the sun."

"Aye." Beatrice folded her arms. "Is there anything I can do for you?"

Mathew sidled closer to Beatrice and wrapped an arm about her legs.

Beatrice put a reassuring hand on his head.

Run! Alice forced the growing clamor down and took a breath. Her heart thundered, her palms grew slick. She could not let it happen again. Her voice shook as she said, "I thought I might come outside and play."

"Did you now?" Beatrice raised her brow.

"Aye." *Get away. Get away now!* The dark threatened the edges of her vision and she forced herself to take a deep breath.

"What are we playing?" Ivy cut into the growing silence.

"We are not playing anything," Richard said. "We are just looking. It is not like home."

"Aye," said Ivy. "Then we should ask Alice to show us all the wonders to be found. She grew up here."

All stares turned to Alice. Her mind went dead.

"Heather," she said. "We get a lot of heather. It is not in bloom now, but it is very pretty. When it does bloom."

Richard crossed his arms and sighed.

"I would like to see that." Ivy ruffled Richard's hair. "It must be like a tapestry of flowers."

Her limbs quaked as she forced herself to remain in place. "Aye. A tapestry of flowers."

"Flowers?" Richard kicked a rock away.

"Ponies!" Alice nigh shrieked the word. The children perked up a bit. "We have wild ponies."

"Ponies," whispered Mathew, shifting away from his grip on Beatrice.

"I do not see any ponies." Richard looked about him with a sniff. The lad threw up a tough wall to breach.

"Oh, they are here." Alice made herself look at Mathew, to take note of each of his features. His tentative smile, his sturdy limbs, his wind-flushed cheeks. Just a child, a harmless, sweet child. She would master this. Her heart still pounded but her breathing came more even now. "But they hide from us because some people catch them."

Richard deigned to show a little more interest. "Why?"

"Because they are the strongest little ponies in the kingdom." She had loved the wild ponies as a child. She still did, when she could catch sight of them. "They have short legs and great big chests and heads."

Adam bounced in Beatrice's arms and chattered, his face alight with joy.

"We should look for them," Ivy said.

Richard narrowed his eyes at Alice. "Are you sure they are

really here?"

"I am sure." Alice nodded. She wanted to hold out her hand, but it shook so badly, that she clenched her skirts instead. The terror shifted like a restless viper in the back of her mind. She catalogued what she could see about her. Crags, straggly grass, sky, and heather. "Come, we will see if we can find the signs that mean the herd is close by."

"That sounds like fun," Beatrice said, and gave Alice the tiniest of smiles. "How fares Sister Julianna?"

"She is recovering." Alice kept her gaze trained on the ground. The damp peat beneath her would show the ponies' hoof prints. "Have you news from Anglesea?"

Beatrice nodded. "A runner arrived earlier. My brother Roger is much better. But my mother..."

"Mama?" Mathew peered at Beatrice.

"She is not doing well. They fear for her."

"Mama." Mathew grew louder. He grabbed onto Beatrice's skirt and yelled, "Mama."

Mama! Mama! Run, Alice, run! Alice leaped away from him. The terror ripped free, and she took flight. Her foot caught on a tuft and she landed hard on her hands and knees.

Behind her, Mathew's pitch got louder and more demanding. *Alice! Alice! Run, now!*

Beatrice murmured to him, words Alice could not decipher.

Alice had to get away. *Danger.* She scrabbled to her feet.

"Alice," Ivy called.

A hand fastened on her arm.

"I must run," Alice fought the hand that held her. "Run, I..."

"Stop it." A sharp blow to her cheek stopped Alice. Beatrice stood before her, her face tight and angry. "Stop it. You are frightening Mathew, and he is already upset over our mother."

Alice shook her head. Beatrice had to understand. She must let her go so she could run.

"Nay." Beatrice shook her shoulders. "Do not dare to do this again. I will not have you treating my brother in this manner. Mathew deserves better." Beatrice gave her a hard shake.

Alice's head wobbled, and the moors swirled before her.

"William deserves better than this from you. I have kept my peace because he and Ivy asked it of me, but you are behaving worse than a child. William is a wonderful, decent man. He does not need a cold-hearted, cruel sow as a wife."

"Beatrice." Ivy's voice came from a long, black tunnel. "She is not hearing you."

Beatrice's face drew closer as the other woman peered at her.

Alice couldn't meet her eyes. She wanted to explain, but the words lodged behind the fear and wouldn't come.

The children huddled beside Ivy. Richard looked puzzled, whilst Mathew sucked on his thumb and stared at her. Little Adam squatted at Ivy's feet, more interested in the tough, stringy grasses.

"Then I shall speak louder." Beatrice's grip on her shoulders tightened. "I will slap you if you make me."

Alice shook her head. She did not want another slap. Her cheek still smarted from the last one.

"Ugh." Beatrice released her with a look of disgust. "I cannot even speak to you."

Alice's knees sagged, and she thumped onto the ground. She sucked great gasps of air into her lungs.

Beatrice's hemline wove into view. "What is wrong with her?"

"I do not know," Ivy said. "But surely you can see this is no ordinary reaction."

"To Mathew?" Beatrice's derision weighted the words. "How could anyone fear our gentle Mathew?"

"And yet she does," Ivy again. "See, she can barely move. She is like a trapped rabbit."

Beatrice crouched and came face to face with her. "What is it with you, Alice?"

Alice shook her head. Hysterical laughter bubbled free. God's mercy, what she would give to able to answer that question. She had believed her fear gone, and then Mathew had become agitated, and it had returned in full force. With a cool hand, Beatrice touched her brow. "She is clammy."

"And see how pale she is," Ivy said.

"I am not carrying her back to the keep," Beatrice said. "Until she masters whatever this is, she can stay out here."

Alice dug her fingers into the ground. From somewhere she summoned the strength and stood. "I do not require your help."

Chapter Seventeen

William studied the down, cross-body strike Aonghas made. "Watch your weight," he yelled. "You stick your ass out like that and somebody's going to ring your bell for you."

Aonghas swiped at his sweaty brow with his forearm, but William caught the resentful jut of his jaw. He pushed the lad hard, but Aonghas's fighting skills grew in leaps. The lad had a knack for the blade, and an almost unholy sense for where the next strike would come from. William would make a superb knight of him yet.

"Try it again." He motioned for Rufus to lead with the thrust. Pampering did not make for good knights. Skill took time, effort, and constant repetition until it melded with a fighter's very sinews, beat with each pound of his heart. Fighters who hesitated in battle died before they'd finished thinking about their next move.

"William!" Frowning, Beatrice stalked across the bailey toward them. She smoothed her expression into a smile for the Scot.

Aonghas went bright pink and slunk back with a mumbled greeting.

"I was just out on the moors with the children and your wife." Beatrice made "wife" sound like a dread disease.

"Did you kill them all and bury them out there?"

Beatrice snorted and tried not to laugh. "It happened again, William."

His sisters' propensity for believing he knew what they spoke of all the time could drive a man to rip hanks of hair out. "What happened again?"

"With her and Mathew."

He should have pressed the issue sooner. "I will deal with it."

"Stay." Beatrice caught his arm as he tried to leave her. "Ivy and I have been speaking. We do not think it is as simple as we first believed."

Her words mirrored his own thoughts, and he stopped.

"It is as if she is taken over by her fear," Beatrice said. "We have seen many people react ill around Mathew, but this is not the same."

"Do you or Ivy know what it could be?"

"Nay." Beatrice stuck her fists on her hips. "But it must stop."

"Dubhghall," Aonghas yelled. He ducked his head, tried to sheathe his blade, missed, and got it on the second try.

Could Aonghas, the elder, not have taught his sons to put a string of words together? "He is in the barracks," William snapped. "Instead of bellowing for him, go and find him."

"Nay! Dubhghall." Aonghas took a deep breath. "About him. When he were lad." Aonghas toed the ground in front of him. "Saw a dog. Tears and snot."

"By this I deduce that young Dubhghall demonstrated a fear of dogs as a boy," William said. Good lads, the Scots, keen and powerful fighters in the making, but they had a mouth full of teeth and brains slower than a plow beast.

"Aye." Aonghas nodded. "Da thought would do him good to lock him in the stables with the dogs."

Beatrice made a soft noise of disgust.

"Worse." Aonghas gripped his sword pommel. "After went barmy."

Beatrice cocked her head and approached Aonghas. "Are you saying your brother was worse after being made to spend the night with the dogs?"

Poor lout went the color of beetroot and retreated. "Barmy. No sense."

"Beatrice?" William did not have the time to stand here and play follow-the-word-clue with the hulking brute. He had a conversation to have with his wife, and he dreaded it.

"Nay." Beatrice shushed him with a wave. "Is he still afraid of dogs?"

"Do not like 'em," Aonghas said. "But better."

"How comforting." William could not see what Bea found so fascinating in all this.

She made her quieting motion again. Why did women always do that and expect obedience? Still, he clamped his lips shut and got armed for a wait.

"How did he get better?" Beatrice said.

"Bit him." Aonghas glowed so red he might explode.

"Wonderful." William glared at Bea. "We will find a dog and get it to bite Alice."

"Nay." Aonghas's eyes bugged. "Before. Dog bit him before."

Bea clapped her hands and gave William a look of wonder. "Do you not see?"

"Nay." Because he did not see aught other than Bea's skirts lying in a mud puddle.

She rolled her eyes and growled her irritation at him. "Dubhghall was afraid of dogs because one bit him."

"Aye." Aonghas beamed.

"And that is why he went...er...barmy when he was little." Beatrice patted Aonghas's arm. "You are so clever to have thought of it."

Now Bea needed her head looking at. "This is all very fascinating, but how does it pertain to Alice?"

"William, you are so dense sometimes."

He was dense and Aonghas was clever? Oh, what sublime joy!

"Aonghas is telling us Dubhghall was frightened of dogs because of something he experienced as a child."

"He is not telling us anything." William needed to get that clear.

"Perhaps there is something in Alice's past that makes her so afraid. Something nobody knows about."

It made sense. Blast his hide, but Aonghas and Beatrice had something here. Years ago when he had been on siege with father, they had rescued a wretch from the dungeons to find he could not abide rats. Apparently, rats had chewed on him in the dungeon. God's ballocks, he hated saying these words, but honor demanded it. "You could be right, Bea."

"Aonghas." Her smirk made him grind his teeth. The evil minx knew him too well. "You should thank Aonghas."

"I will." When the fires of hell flamed through the ground. "If we discover he is right about this."

"It is worth discovering if he might be," Beatrice said.

William nodded. Alice showed many of the signs of Ratty, as they'd dubbed him. "Aye, I will look into it."

* * *

Alice stared at her bedchamber door for so long that when it opened it took her a moment to register.

William stood in the doorway, one hand holding the door open

She had been waiting for him since she spied Beatrice talking to him in the bailey.

"I am sorry," she said before he could rail at her again. "I do not understand why it happens."

"Aye." William nodded and crossed the room to where she stood by the casement. "I just had an interesting conversation with Bea and Aonghas."

Braced for him to bellow and rant at her, Alice took a moment to catch up. "Aonghas spoke to you?"

"In his way." He leaned one hand on the wall above her head. "This thing with Mathew." He tilted her face up. "It is a sort of overwhelming fear, is it not?"

"Aye." He did not look angry, or sound it. Tears of relief flooded her eyes. "I wish I knew why I become so stupid when he is about, but something takes me over."

"Something you remember?"

"It is not clear. There is this emptiness in my mind, and it terrifies me."

"What if you tried to see what was in the...emptiness?" William frowned at her, as if he wanted to understand but could not.

"The fear stops me. I cannot fight my way past it."

"Come, Alice." He drew her against his chest. "We will do our best to unravel this. Together."

* * *

Alice began nursing duties shortly after her conversation with William. An uneasy peace lay between them, but it could shatter at any moment.

She found Sister awake and unbound when Alice entered the chamber. "So, you have come?"

Color improved, but still pale, Sister appeared on the mend. "Are you faring better?"

"Where were you?" Sister plucked at the bed furs.

"Outside, getting some fresh air."

Martha rose from her seat by Sister's bedside. "And it looks to have done you a power of good, my lady." She patted Sister's hand. "Sat by you day and night did our Lady Alice. Sir William sent her outside today, that worn out was she."

"Of course he did." Sister sneered and ripped her hand out from beneath Martha's. "Stupid woman."

Martha sucked in a breath, snatching her hands back as if stung.

Now Sister had gone too far and her rudeness jolted Alice. "Sister."

"Go away." Sister turned her head from Martha. "You will kill me with your stupid fumbling."

Martha was a good woman, one of the best at Tarnwych. She drew herself up and blinked at Sister. Her mouth opened and shut.

"I apologize for her." Alice rushed to Martha's side. Martha did not deserve such rudeness. "She speaks without knowing what she says."

Martha folded her arms.

Alice wanted to use one of William's foul curses as Martha's lips pinched.

"You cared for her wonderfully." Alice squeezed Martha's arm. "You have my gratitude."

"At least someone is grateful." Martha sniffed and stalked out of Sister's chamber.

Alice waited until the door slammed behind Martha. Alice had not always agreed with Sister, sometimes she had even wanted to shout at her, and a sharp, cool anger washed over her. "You had no right to speak that way to Martha."

Sister grunted and rolled her back to Alice.

"I needed some fresh air, and she kindly took my place while I was out."

"With him."

"I beg your pardon." Alice stepped closer to hear Sister better.

"You were not here because you were with him."

"William?" Sister sounded jealous of William? What a ridiculous notion. William was her lawful husband. He did not replace Sister in her life.

Sister shut her eyes. "I am tired."

Alice stood undecided. All the things she would like to say stewed inside her. Sister was ill. Her health must affect her humor.

Granted, Sister never had a sunny disposition, but for the most part, she kept herself civil. A cold civility, but not outright rudeness.

Except she had been awfully curt to William on occasion, and Sister's behavior around William's family rivaled even Alice's. She needed something to do with her hands, or she might wake Sister and speak her mind. She dropped another log on the fire and stirred the glowing embers into hearty flames.

When the Anglesea folk had arrived here, Sister had whispered harsh words to Alice. She had not yet met her new family, and already she had made up her mind to dislike them. What could Sister gain by pitting Alice against her new family? Could she be jealous? Worried perhaps that Alice would have no more use for her once she married again?

What a strange day. Alice took a seat by the hearth. The thing with Mathew had her quite wrung out. Then William's unexpected reaction had set her head spinning. Since her wedding day, naught seemed the same.

Prepared for another husband like the others, William kept her on edge and uneasy in his treatment of her. Lord knew she had had no inkling of how much she would enjoy intimacy with a man, and pine for it once she lost it. William had sunk himself into her being, and lodged there like a stubborn burr. Her body cleaved to him. Before William, she had only an idea of what that could mean.

Too restless to remain seated, she tidied the water basin and rags Martha must have used to tend Sister. More disturbing was the dizzy relief that had swept over her when William had come to her earlier without anger or judgment. Nestled against his chest, Alice had felt a calm and peace unknown to her. Safe. And she craved that more than anything.

Chapter Eighteen

Sister's presence made the hall feel like a funeral procession marched through it. Wan and cross-faced in her black habit, like a death-portending crow, Sister crouched in her seat and robbed the hall of any laughter or good cheer.

People huddled, murmuring to each other and casting guilty glances at Sister.

Alice wished she could take a broom and sweep the stifling atmosphere out of the hall. For five days, whilst Sister regained her strength, Alice had drifted in an odd sort of in between state.

William spent his nights with her, but other than holding her while she slept, he did not touch her. Any more of this and she would take matters into her own hands. William's matter.

Sister's keen gaze fastened on her, and Alice choked back her nervous titter. She would call Holy wrath down on her head if Sister divined her thoughts.

"Good evening." Beatrice floated into the hall, resplendent in red with Adam in her arms and Richard leading the way.

No Mathew or Ivy.

"Aonghas?" Beatrice stopped by the table with the Scotsman. "Is that a new tunic I spy? How will the ladies of the keep resist you?"

Aonghas reddened, whilst his brothers broke into guffaws.

"Easily enough, Lady Bea." Dubhghall gave her his skirt-lifting smile. "He is an ugly brute."

Light and joy entered the hall with Beatrice, and Alice could have cheered. A wave of smiles crossed faces as Beatrice and her children wound through the residents. Beatrice paused every now and again to exchange a word and a laugh with someone. She and the children approached the dais like a royal procession.

Alice knew not how Beatrice did it, but she would dearly like to learn the trick.

"Faithless," Sister muttered. "Soiled by her baseborn bastard of a husband."

"Do not." Alice leaned closer to Sister. "Be civil."

Really, she wanted to smack Sister like she would a naughty child. Despite Beatrice's anger with her, Alice could not help but like her.

"Bastard-get, all those children." Was Sister hard of hearing or merely impossible?

"They are fine boys." Alice struggled to keep her voice from reaching others when her anger threatened to rip a shrieking torrent from her. "I will not have you speak of them in that manner."

"Good evening, Lady Alice." Beatrice gathered her children onto the bench. A slight chill entered her voice. "Sister Julianna."

The distance between Sister and the boys could not be an accident. Alice would not have her children near such a frightening figure either.

Her children. Alice would tuck them close to her. Fuss with them as Beatrice did, until Richard batted at his mother's hands.

"Whore!" Sister's voice pierced the hall chatter.

The hall hushed.

In the doorway, Ivy stopped, color drained from her cheeks.

Beatrice sprang to her feet.

"You dare." William entered the hall on Ivy's heels. His anger throbbed from him in waves that had people ducking and dodging out of his way.

Sister shrank into herself as William stalked closer. "You dare sit in my hall and insult one of my family."

Sister huddled into her habit, head down, glancing at Alice.

Nobody would defend her. Not one person in this hall loved Sister. But when Alice had been a young, unloved child, Sister had stood for her.

"She is ill." Alice tried to fill her voice with conviction. Her heart faltered in her defense of Sister. God, she wanted to box Sister's ears herself. But just as Ivy was family to William, so Sister was family to her. "She does not know what she is saying."

William drew himself up. "She knows exactly what she is saying." He loomed above Sister, hands bunched into tight fists. "Hear me, old woman, and hear me well. If you wish to remain here, you will watch your tongue. This is my keep, my hall. We will do things my way. Your meal is done."

Sister clambered to her feet and, with a final look of condemnation at Alice, skittered from the hall.

Her meal lay on the table uneaten. She should eat to recover her strength.

Alice took up Sister's abandoned trencher. Someone needed to ensure she ate at least. And the task, clearly, fell to her, because not another soul in this hall would dare William's anger for Sister.

William's hand clamped around her wrist. "Sit down, Alice."

"She did not eat."

"She does not deserve to." William stared her down, and Alice dropped her gaze first.

God, she did not want to fight with him, not with things so tentative between them. And not over this, when she condemned Sister's behavior as much as he did. But she could not ignore Sister's need. The tussle inside her threatened to burst out of her chest. She tugged her wrist from his grasp. "I cannot ignore her."

* * *

William stayed in the hall much later than he should and worked his way through another flagon of wine. Aye, the old woman revolted him, but he had sent a sick woman to bed without food.

Alice was loyal. He would give her that. Loyal to a sodding fault, unfortunately.

He could not back down about this. Alice and her shadow of death needed to understand how matters lay at Tarnwych. He would not bear the attacks on his kin. So, he drank his wine and fortified himself against the inevitable confrontation.

Five nights, he had kept his paws to himself. Lain beside Alice, so hard he thought his ballocks might burst, and left her alone. Some foolish notion of chivalry had kept him from foisting himself on a tired, worried woman.

He had actually welcomed the evil nun back into the hall. With the old shrew well enough to rise, his wife would have her freedom again. Which meant...

Sod it. It meant nothing. Because now, instead of responding to him with that passion barely contained in her ripe, delicious curves, Alice and he took up cudgels again.

His parents made this marriage thing look so effortless. Indeed, they had words occasionally, and he recalled times his mother had refused to speak to Father for weeks over something Father had done, but they never appeared caught in the storm buffeting him and Alice.

He placed his goblet beside the chair. No sense in hiding here all night. Best to storm a keep early before they had all their defenses in place.

"Do you need me, Sir William?" Cedric had grown half a foot since returning from Anglesea. Unfortunately for Cedric, and on occasion William, the lad still tangled his inches together.

Since coming to Tarnwych, Cedric had applied himself to his weapons training. His young shoulders drooped from exhaustion. "Nay, Cedric, find your pallet for the night."

"Aye, my lord." Cedric spun about, tripped over a hall dog,

and managed to right himself before plowing headfirst into the wall.

William climbed the stairs like an oldster, dragging his feet from one rise to the next. He slipped into his and Alice's bedchamber.

Alice sat up in bed, her long hair loose about her back and her gaze on the door. She eyed him warily.

Avoiding her gaze, he took extra time disrobing. She appeared a little concerned but not angry. Using water gone tepid but still smelling of fresh herbs, he washed under her watchful gaze.

"Can I assist you?"

"Nay." William played for time as he washed himself. "I have this."

"You are angry with me?"

With her? Although furious with that nun, he understood loyalty. He had been raised on it. William rubbed himself with a drying cloth. "Angry?"

"About me leaving the hall with Sister."

A swift offensive strike often gave the biggest battle advantage. Except, he really did not want to battle. Not with Alice sitting in his bed, sweet and tempting, her pretty face gentle. "I understand you feel loyal to her."

"And you are loyal to Ivy," she said.

Did he detect a slight edge in her voice? William shucked his chausses. "Ivy is like a sister to me."

"She is a very lovely sister."

"Is she?"

Alice raised a brow at him.

William flushed. Aye, his Alice saw straight through his dissembling. "When Ivy first came to Anglesea, I was like every other man there. We all chased her from one end of the keep to the other."

Alice stiffened, and her fingers curled into the furs atop her.

"But," William said. He sat on the end of the bed and took

her hand. "That was some time ago. Ivy is only interested in Tom, and I do not see her that way anymore."

The smile Alice gave him warmed his chest.

"Tell me about Anglesea." She threaded her fingers through his. "Tell me about your family."

So much better than waging war, and William settled his back against the wall beside her. Snuggled at his side, she listened, her face alight with interest, as he talked of how he and Roger could never do anything without it becoming a competition. He spoke to her of Bea and how she had met her husband, Garrett. Alice laughed at his Bea stories. His youngest sister had a way of getting into trouble with her big heart and unfettered spirit. Alice went quiet and contemplative when he told her of Faye, and the torment she had suffered at her first husband's hands. A stray tear snaked down her chin as William went on to tell the story of how Faye and Gregory found their way together.

Sharing with Alice had a rightness about it. "I am concerned for my mother," he said. "You would not know it to look at her, but she was not well after bearing Mathew, and her strength is not as it should be."

Alice slid her arm about his middle and cuddled closer. "I will keep her in my prayers."

The hearth flames danced orange, yellow, and blue, sending shadows playing about the chamber. Alice smelled fresh and sweet, like a spring breeze. Her breasts pressed full and soft against his side.

"William?"

"Aye."

Alice sat up and peered at him. "If you are not wroth with me...and I am not tired..."

Lazy heat in his blood quickened. He cupped her sweet face and drew her toward him. "Is there something I can do for you, my lady?"

"Aye, William," she whispered against his mouth. "You could stop talking."

She took his breath away with the fierceness of her kiss. Hot, hungry lips devoured his as if she could not get close enough.

William let her take the lead. Like heady wine, her uninhibited passion swept him along with it. She had him hard and aching within mere moments.

He cupped her breasts, loving the way it made her moan when he toyed with her nipples. So passionate, his Alice, and so responsive. She liked his hands firm on her. Writhed when he applied a small pinch to her nipples.

Sweeping aside the linens, she straddled him. Her core pressed warm and wet against him.

Right here, in the spot where her neck joined her shoulder, she welcomed his mouth. He drew deep breaths of her into him.

Beneath the covers she moved against his shaft, rocking her heat on his hardness.

"William?"

"Aye?" Words grew harder to manage. It had been too long since he had lost himself in Alice, and her writhing atop him nigh killed him. He wanted to sink into her and feel her fasten about him like a wet, hot fist. Sink into her and pretend that all was well between them.

"When you put your mouth on me, I like it," she murmured.

Dear God, if she talked gutter to him he would come off just like this. "Aye?" He raised her hips an inch away from him. "As do I?"

He needed the taste of her. William shifted her to his side and attempted to press her down.

"Nay." Alice took hold of his hands. "I wanted to know if you liked it."

"More than anything. The taste of you drives me wild."

"Nay." Fever bright color stained her cheeks. "What I mean is, do you like it done to you?"

His ballocks fisted tight and pumped more blood into his shaft. "Eh?"

"Is it possible...for me...to do the same to you?"

The fierce demand for her to take him in her mouth rose inside him, but he tamped it down. He did not want to offend her. "It is possible."

"Will you tell me how?"

Torment, sweet hellish torment. William struggled through the haze of lust as he instructed her. He did not know which made him ache more, the telling her how, or the caress of her tongue on his shaft. When she took him into her mouth, his back bowed off the bed. God in Heaven!

"Alice." He panted like a dog after a bitch on heat. "God, that feels so good."

She sucked and he dug his hands into the bedding to stop his completion. She needed to stop before he lost his control, but stopping her would kill him for sure.

She swirled her tongue over his sensitive tip as she hollowed her cheeks and sucked him harder.

"Alice!" William knifed up and grabbed her shoulders.

"Did I do it wrong?" Her face glowed, pure naughty temptress. She knew what she did to him, and she loved it.

William flipped her onto her back and came down atop her. "You are entirely too good at that."

Wrapping her thighs around his hips, she giggled and wriggled until her heat brushed his sensitized tip. "Shall I swear never to do it again?"

"Enough, wench." He tore her night rail from her.

Alice laughed, a full-throated, deep chuckle as she reveled in her female power over him.

He had to have her, own her, possess her. William took her in one deep thrust.

She arched and cried out, her legs wrapping around his hips and drawing him deeper.

Needing to see her, William raised himself on his arms. God, what a stirring sight. Her hair a copper tangle on the white linens. Face flushed, eyes bright, she moaned his name.

Around his shaft, she tightened in a heated, slick grip that nearly pushed him over the edge.

William drove into her, relishing the sounds she made, the digging of her nails into his forearms.

Harder he thrust, and she met him with a tilt of her head and a wild cry of encouragement.

He could not get deep enough inside her. Fever coursed through him, to join himself to her and stay there. By sheer will he held off, craving completion and wanting to make this last. Sweat coated both of them as they moved and ground against each other.

Her climax came on in a tightening grip about his shaft. It spread across her in a fascinating flush that beaded her nipples and threw her head back.

William went over the edge with her. Tumbled headlong into a dark, honeyed place crammed with the taste, the feel, the smell of them.

He knew his weight crushed her, but he took his time separating from her. Even then, it hit like a blow, and he tucked her tight against his side.

"William?"

"Aye."

"I like that so much better than fighting."

* * *

Something wrenched her hair, making her scalp throb.

"Pretty," said a voice she knew but could not place.

Alice screamed and clawed at the thing causing pain.

"Pretty." Her limbs banged together as it shook her.

Beneath her dangling feet water rushed past in frothing, boiling white foam. God, she would die if she went in there. She could not swim.

"Alice."

She fought the hold on her. She had to get free.

"Alice!"

She woke with a cry, her heart pounding in her ears.

"Alice." William's voice, deep and soothing. William's hands, stroking her back and drawing her close to the comfort of his chest. "You were having a nightmare."

It had been so real. The smell of the river, the blurred faces staring on in horror. Alice burrowed into William's chest.

"Can you tell me what is was about?" William tightened his hold on her.

Alice shook head. In his arms, the shadows of the dream place receded.

Chapter Nineteen

William would rather impale himself on a gatepost than do this, but he needed answers, and the rotten nun seemed to keep the secrets at Tarnwych. At least, she kept Alice's secrets.

That must have been one damnable dream Alice had the night before. She might not want to speak of it, but she'd called over and over again to Sister, pleading with her not to do something. It had taken a long while for her to ease back into slumber.

Thus, he set off to find the evil nun because of a conversation he and Beatrice had had with thick-skulled Aonghas.

Thin shoulders hunched over, the crone crouched before the fire in the hall. Condemn them as wasteful for the larger fires, did she? If she got any closer to the heat, she'd catch flame.

"Sister Julianna." He eased into the upcoming chat with a charming smile and a friendly tone. "I am very glad to see you so much recovered."

She snatched her rosary beads and wrapped them around her fist. "Are you?"

So much for the pleasantries. "Of course, Sister. I would hate to see anyone suffer."

With a sniff, she turned back to the fire.

At this rate, they would be thicker than ticks by the end of the day. Perhaps brush each other's hair. He took the chair opposite her and motioned a serf for wine. "I wanted to speak to you about Alice."

Her dark eyes glittered as she stared at him.

"Did anything happen to Alice as a small girl?" His impaling gatepost might very well provide more information than the evil nun.

"Lots of things happened to her." Sister tightened her grip on the rosary, her knuckles whitening.

"Indeed." The late King John in a temper had more charm than Sister Sunshine. "I was more referring to an incident that would have upset her enough to follow her into adulthood."

"Why?"

"She had a nightmare last night," he said.

"Her conscience is troubled." Sister hunched her shoulders and stared into the fire.

William grabbed onto the fraying ends of his temper. "Has she had nightmares before?"

"Why do you not ask her?" Sister worked the beads through her stick-thin fingers.

"Because it upsets her to speak of it."

"Then do not speak of it."

He rather fancied giving her a shove into the hearth to see if she remained untouched by flame. "You have been with her a long time, have you not?"

The subject change might have caught her off guard, because she swung her head back to him. "Since Alice was an infant."

"And how came that about?" In his experience, Holy Sisters remained cloistered for most of their lives. Two days hence lay a convent. He had seen it when he rode this way for his wedding.

"She was a babe. Her mother died after delivering her."

"You were here for a birth?"

"Alice was born at Yarborough," she said in a tone that indicated he should have known as much.

"Indeed." He showed his teeth in a mockery of a smile. "Then, you were at Yarborough for Alice's birth."

Sister nodded. The hag knew she got beneath his skin and loved it. "Her mother had a difficult time giving birth. Sir Ivo sent for me."

"Because you were good with healing?"

Sister heaved a harsh sigh. "Nay. I was the woman's nearest relative. She was my cousin."

"Ah." Convents often sent a close female relative to help in times of trouble. "So, why did you not return to the convent?"

"You would like that, would you not?" Her eyes raked him from head to toe. "You would like to have a free run here at Tarnwych."

William reached the end of his tether. "Indeed." He rose. Five more minutes in her company and he would forget he did not hurt women. "Your presence here creates ill will, and I dislike your influence on Alice. But Alice loves you and feels loyalty to you, and for those reasons you have a home here. However, my tolerance wears thin."

She flushed and then paled. "You threaten me?"

"Not a threat, Sister, more of a promise. Watch yourself in my keep."

"I see you." Sister jabbed a bony finger at him. "I see you, Satan, behind your pretty mask. You will not prevail here."

"Oh, for the love of God—"

"You speak the Lord's name?" Her eyes started out of her head. "You utter the name of the most high from your tainted lips?"

She was working herself into a lather. "Sister, I suggest you calm yourself."

"You fill this keep with whores and blasphemers. I am all that stands in your way and you would see me removed."

If she lost her reason, he could justify slapping her. William winced at his own thought. He knew better. "Be calm, Sister. I—"

"The Lord will rain down his vengeance on your head." She

jerked to standing and stood before him swaying like a sapling in a storm. "He will visit his wrath on the unrighteous and the un-Godly. He will...."

She ranted on in that vein, but William ceased listening. He searched for a likely serving woman. "You. Go and fetch Lady Alice. Tell her Sister is unwell."

Eyes round as trenchers, the woman gaped at him before nodding and scampering away.

Sister had gone so pale now her skin appeared translucent. She had lost her mind, her reason addled, and worked herself into a steaming froth. Every time he opened his mouth, he made it worse. William clamped his lips shut as her reedy voice bounced off the walls. Even Sister had to run out of imprecations to God at some point.

Alice entered the hall at a run. She glanced from him to Sister.

William shrugged. "I was asking her about the convent."

"Asking her what?" Alice approached Sister. "There now, Sister." She caught Sister's flailing hand. "It is Alice. You will make yourself ill if you continue in this manner."

Sister's feral gaze found Alice. Spittle spattered her chin. "He would see me removed from here. The Evil One dwells within him and forces him to send me away."

Alice frowned. "William would never do that."

William shifted. Actually, he might well send her away. "Not without discussing it with you first," he said to Alice.

Alice drew Sister away from the hearth step by step. The woman looked ready to collapse, but still stopped every few feet to call down hell upon his head.

Back to the convent she would go. He now had to convince Alice of it.

* * *

Alice added one of Ivy's concoctions to the warmed milk for Sister. Perhaps her recent illness made Sister more fervent, because it grew harder to calm her after each incident with William.

Supporting her shoulders, Alice encouraged Sister to take a sip of the milk.

"You must be vigilant, Alice." Sister clasped Alice's hands around the mug. "Temptation rises like a noxious weed to choke this keep."

"I will be, Sister. Here, take another sip. I prepared it for you myself."

Sister took another small sip. "I curse the day he came to this place."

Alice blessed that day. The day light had entered her life, and colors grew bolder and sharper. "Have another sip. It will calm you."

"What is in it?"

"Milk." God forgive her the lie. But her head hurt from Sister's near-endless shrieking. Finally, Alice had escaped to the kitchen and warmed some milk for her.

Ivy had slipped in and wordlessly handed her a powder.

Sister took a longer sip and lay back against her pillows. "Do not let him send me away, Alice."

Snap. The trap jaws fastened around Alice. Sister stared at her, waiting for her promise. And she could not. "Rest now, Sister. You have had an upsetting day."

"I have cared for you when nobody else would," Sister said. "A motherless child, unloved by any, scorned by your father."

"Drink your milk, Sister." Alice tipped the mug and forced Sister into a bigger sip. Aye, Sister had cared for her, and her father did scorn her. She still did not like hearing it, though. Not as much as Sister enjoyed repeating it.

"He will wheedle his way into your heart. He will make you send me away," Sister said.

"William has never spoken of sending you away." She spoke true, although their situation could not continue this way for much longer. Ungrateful child that she was, Alice might not stop William if he did send Sister away. And what did that make her? What sort of person repaid another with treachery?

Except, it felt right for Sister to return to the convent. When Alice and William grew closer, Sister stepped into the gap and widened it again. Alice had three people in her marriage, and that meant one person too many. Ironically, Sister had persuaded Alice to accept the match without argument, and now Sister wriggled between husband and wife and it did none of them any good.

As for Sister's assessment of William's family, Alice did not agree with it. Not even the smallest bit. How anyone could look at Ivy and call her whore baffled Alice. Aye, Beatrice marched to her own drummer, but the woman was kind and loving, and filled those around her with joy. As for Gregory, Alice had never met a Godlier person. He did not lecture and sigh like Father Mark, or rant and rail like Sister. From him in calm waves of certainty came Gregory's faith, as much a part of him as his strength and his size.

Quite simply, Alice did not see the world through Sister's eyes anymore. Her world grew into a bigger, brighter place, full of scents and tastes and sensations, each new one a delightful revelation.

Perhaps Sister should leave Tarnwych.

Sister snuffled in her sleep, and Alice snuck out of the room. Beyond the casement a dull, gray day greeted her. Not perfect weather for a walk, but it would help work the fidgets from her head.

Light drizzle misted the air as she crossed the bailey out onto the moors. Daylight faded, and the air held a chill that crept beneath clothing and settled in bones.

Alice trudged away from the castle and crested a small rise. From here she could see as far as the village to the south and to the north make out the smudged outline of the crags from which Aonghas's manor drew its name. As a child she had imagined the fae folk dwelled in those crags. Sharing her imaginings with Sister had earned her a week's worth of sore knees as she had sought forgiveness for false idolatry.

Like her mood, the weather pressed heavy and glum. Her dream of the night before had stayed with her throughout her day. The scene had been so real, familiar, as if it were a memory. She had tried to make sense of it, to wheedle out some tiny thread of remembrance. Dark nothingness met her attempts, but laced with the terror she experienced when Mathew drew near. Her damp skirts clung to her ankles and slowed her progress. Out here on the moors, she could always clear her head and think. Many called them ugly and barren, but Alice found beauty in their harsh solitude.

Possibly, Sister's constant carping on Mathew as "the abomination" had wormed into her mind and festered. Certainly, Sister did not help, but the trouble ran deeper than that. It lurked on the periphery of her waking mind and refused her attempts to delve deeper. Her boots sunk into the peaty, rain-soaked ground. Rain fell thicker around her, seeping through her cloak and chilling her skin. She trudged back to the castle.

Muffled hoofbeats sounded behind her.

Beatrice rode a large, chestnut horse, her seat so natural it appeared horse and rider were one being. Like Alice, the rain had soaked her to the skin.

"What are you doing out here?" Beatrice drew level with her.

"I came for a walk to clear my head." Alice had walked farther than she intended and faced a long tromp through the rain to the keep and dry clothes.

"Come along." Beatrice held out her hand. "Put your foot on mine and I will take you back with me."

With Beatrice pulling and a good bit of clumsy clambering, Alice settled behind Beatrice. Funny, how her fear of riding seemed to have disappeared.

"Strange day for a walk," Beatrice said and heeled the horse into motion.

"It was not raining this hard when I left."

Beatrice nodded and urged the horse into a fast walk. "As much as I would like to run for cover, this rain makes the ground slick, and I could not bear it if Breeze slipped and broke a leg."

"Your horse is called Breeze?"

"Aye." Beatrice covered her head with her hood. "We have been on a few adventures together, my girl and I."

Alice slid her arms about Beatrice's waist. With the woman so cold with her, she did not want to impose, but falling off the horse would hurt more than her pride. "Is this the horse you rode to London?"

Beatrice stiffened. "I see William told you about that."

"I asked him about his family." Alice ducked behind the shelter of Beatrice's shoulder. Much-taller Beatrice acted as a welcome weather break.

"I am surprised you were interested," Beatrice said.

She might never have another opportunity like this one. Wet and miserable though they both were, she had Beatrice's attention. "I was interested...am interested. William adores you and your sister. And Ivy."

Beatrice snorted. "So he says when we are not about. But there you have brothers."

She envied Beatrice that sort of statement, exasperation laced with fondness and familiarity. "I do not have a brother, or a sister."

"Indeed." Breeze sidestepped a waving clump of heather and Beatrice clucked to the horse. "As much as my brothers vex me, I am glad for them."

"William tells me Henry has gone on a pilgrimage to the Holy Land?"

"That was quite some conversation you had with William," Beatrice said. "Indeed, Henry has always been a pious ache in the ass."

Alice gasped before she could stop it. Never had she heard a woman say "ass." She rather liked it, and she giggled.

Beatrice peered around at her and made a wry face. "I know.

My language is shocking. Garrett's is worse, and it only encourages me."

"Ass." Alice tried the word out, rolling it around her mouth. "Ass."

Beatrice laughed, full, rich, and pushing back the day's gloom. "Do not be telling William I am responsible for your swearing."

"It is the first time I have said it," Alice said.

"Ah." Beatrice grinned over her shoulder. "Then you should say it again."

"I think I will." Using the word brought with it a delicious thrill. "Your pardon, my lady, but could you move your ass?"

"My lord you are naught more than a horse's ass," said Beatrice.

Alice collapsed against her back in giggles. Even the rain did not seem so bad.

"Ah, Alice." Beatrice chuckled. "We will make an Anglesea of you yet."

What a lovely thought. "I would like that."

Beatrice reined Breeze in. "Would you?"

"Aye." She could think of few things she wanted more than to be a part of this loud, loving, chaotic family. To roll her eyes at Henry's pomposity, or have Roger tease her and tug her braid. "It is why I was walking in this miserable rain."

Beatrice snorted. "The idea of being an Anglesea had you determined to catch a chill in the rain?"

"Nay." Beatrice's dry expression made Alice giggle. "I was thinking about Sister and William. They do not get along."

"Ah." Beatrice got Breeze moving again. "Does anybody get along with Sister?"

Beatrice posed a fair question. "I suppose there is only me."

"And you did not really have a choice in the matter," Beatrice said.

"She did take care of me." It would not be fair to have Beatrice think of Sister as a monster.

Beatrice grunted. "And now William and your Sister are stretching you between them?"

"Something like that."

"I have that a bit," Beatrice said.

Alice found that hard to believe.

"Between my father and Garrett. Actually between Roger and Garrett, too. William manages a little more tolerance, but not much."

Alice had grown used to thinking of Garrett as "the bastard" or the "accursed villain," as Sister referred to him. He took on form when Beatrice spoke of him. "Your father does not like your husband?"

Beatrice flapped her hand. "Oh, Father likes him well enough, but they have a complicated past, and both of them are too stubborn to admit that it is over."

Alice would ask William to tell her the story. Listening to him speak of his family in his soothing, deep voice was a special treat. "So, what do you do? When your husband and father make you feel tugged in different directions."

"I side with Garrett," Beatrice said, then chuckled. "For the most part and in front of other people." She shrugged. "He is the man I chose, but then I have been in love with him since the moment I first saw him."

Perhaps they had that in common.

* * *

A mud beast stood in the bailey, and Alice could not drag her eyes away. It had William's height and form, but covered in filth and muck from head to toe.

Beatrice drew Breeze to a halt outside the stable.

William's horse capered past them, pursued by a red-faced Cedric. He caught Alice's eye and pressed his lips together, but the laughter still reached his eyes.

"What is going on?" Beatrice pushed her hood back.

William swiped mud from his face and flung it at the floor. "I fell off my horse."

"You what?" Alice and Beatrice said together.

William sighed. "I fell off my horse into the mud."

A group of men standing outside the stables watched him. They did a poor job of hiding their amusement. Aonghas's boys in the midst of them, wearing the widest grins.

"Is that some of your knightly training we need to learn?" Middle Domnall propped his elbow against the stable wall. His brothers dissolved into laughter.

"Aye," said oldest Domnall. "His lordship was just instructing us how to mount without use of the stirrups."

"You fell off." Beatrice's voice carried to the shadowed corners of the bailey.

"My thanks, Bea. Rub it in and make sure everyone knows." William stood beside Breeze and held his arms up for Alice.

Alice did not care about the dirt and mud encrusting his arms as she slid into them.

William's sweet smile made the mud worth it. "I was coming to look for you."

"I went for a walk."

"In this?" William frowned at the sky.

"That is what I said when I came upon her." Beatrice joined them. "Apparently, our Alice had some deep thoughts that required plenty of rain to untangle them."

"Deep thoughts, hmm?" William cupped her chin and studied her face.

"For God's sake, William, you are getting mud all over her," Beatrice said. "Not that her bliaut's color is much different."

"Exactly. It does not matter." Alice could drown in the endless blue of his eyes. Especially when they looked at her as if she were the only woman on earth.

"Tell me your deep thoughts." William caressed her cheek with his finger.

Alice wanted to hold onto this moment. "They were silly thoughts."

"Nay, they were not." Beatrice jammed her fists on her hips. "Alice was telling me she feels like a bone being fought over by two dogs."

William glanced at his sister and frowned.

"And in case you missed it, dear William"—Beatrice pushed her face closer to William's—"you are one of the dogs in the piece."

William tugged her closer to him. "Alice?"

Alice could have clapped her hand over Beatrice's mouth. Lesson learned there. Never share anything with Beatrice you wanted kept between you. Or had the woman done it to drive a wedge between Alice and William? Beatrice had never struck her as devious, but Alice had learned to see all sorts of things in different ways now. "That was a confidence," she said to Beatrice.

Beatrice tossed her hands into the air. "You never said that."

"Not that it would help," William said. "Bea is incapable of keeping a secret."

"That is not true," Beatrice said, chin stuck out, arms akimbo.

"It is so." William matched her chin jut. "Everybody at Anglesea knows not to tell you anything they want kept secret."

"It is not so much a secret." Alice stepped between them before their disagreement grew.

"This tussle with Sister Julianna and I, it worries you." William's warm hand cupped her chin.

"Of course it bothers her," Beatrice said. "She feels like she is caught between you."

William glared at Beatrice, and then his face turned thoughtful. "I suppose it does. You are a loyal one, my Alice."

"Ergh!" Beatrice stomped her foot. "My Alice? Is that the best you can come up with?"

"I like it." Alice tried to read William's expression. He did not seem angry, more rueful and contemplative.

Beatrice snorted and trudged off toward the stable. "Come along, Breeze. We know when we are not wanted."

"I have a bargain for you," William said.

"A bargain?"

"Aye." William drew her against his chest. Mud mixed with her wet bliaut and made a sucking sound between them. "I know how much you feel you owe Sister Julianna."

"I do owe her."

William lowered his head and whispered in her ear, "On the other hand, I am your husband, and we are not doing so very badly. Are we, my Alice?"

"Nay." Nothing like she had expected, but still not bad.

"But we need time to build on what we have. Time alone from the influence of others, particularly your Sister Julianna."

Sister did always seem to wedge herself between them. Alice nodded.

"So here is my suggestion," William said. "Let Sister return to the convent for the winter. Give us some time without her, and if you like, we can send for her again come spring."

Most men would have sent Sister away for her meddling and her viper tongue. "You will let her return in the spring?"

"If you desire it." William cupped her cheeks in his palms. "It shall be done."

She still had to get Sister to agree, but Alice liked the plan. The idea of time with William without Sister lurking in the hall sent a tingle through her. "I will speak with her."

"In the meantime, we are both wet and dirty." William slung an arm about her shoulder and walked them toward the keep. "What say you to bathing?" He leaned to her ear. "Together."

As if she needed to think on that for more than a moment. "Aye," she said. "Aye, thrice over."

Chapter Twenty

Alice broke her fast before going to see Sister.

Dressed and seated beside the hearth with her rosary draped across her lap, Sister appeared much more rested than the day before.

"Good morrow." Alice searched for a clue to her mood. "Are you feeling better this morning?"

"Indeed, Alice." Sister looked up and gave her a thin smile. "I believe I was not myself yesterday."

It both relieved and concerned Alice. Although it boded well for Sister's mood, it made the coming conversation harder to have. Alice dragged up a stool and took a seat across from Sister. "You look better."

Sister pinned her with a stare. "I feel better."

"And you look it."

"Alice." Sister slapped her palms onto her lap. "I have known you for too long for you to sit there with your mouth full of teeth. Whatever you came here to say, say it and be done with it."

Alice scooted her...ass...back on the stool. "I spoke with William yesterday."

"He is your husband. I imagine you have much to say to each other."

"Indeed." A strangled giggle escaped Alice. Lord, she wished she had let William speak with Sister, but that would be cowardly and unfair to Sister. "We were speaking of you."

"Go on." Sister stilled, her rosary between her fingers.

"You at Tarnwych."

"Ah." Sister sighed and stared into the flames. "I thought this might come." She cocked her head and gave a rueful smile. "You want me gone from Tarnwych."

"Nay." Alice took Sister's hands. "Tarnwych is your home and you are welcome here for as long as I am here." Now, why had she said that? Because she desired to comfort Sister. William had agreed to no such thing. "At least, Tarnwych has been your home for many years and William knows that."

Sister pulled her hands away. "When do I leave?"

"William has sent Cedric to the convent."

"Is that what you came here to say?" Sister's face grew colder than the walls in mid-winter. "Then you may leave. I seem to have some packing to do."

"Nay." Helpless frustration clogged her words, and Alice clenched her hands in her lap. "It is not forever. Just for the winter."

"Indeed." Sister limped to her clothes chest and opened it. "I am to go away for the winter and come back when?"

"In the spring." Alice rushed to help. She pulled out a few worn chemises and two habits. "William felt it would be good for us to have a little time for he and I to get to know one another better."

"I am sure he did." Sister snatched the clothing from Alice's hands and laid it on her pallet. "And I am sure I will see Sir William at the convent doors as soon as the snow has thawed."

"Perhaps not that soon." Alice stood there feeling useless as Sister unpacked her chest. Some pots of herbs, a few vials of different colored liquid, a tub of soap, a comb, and some bath linens. Other than her Bible, Sister seemed to have no little keepsakes or remembrances of her over twenty years amongst them. "But I will send for you."

"Alice, Alice, Alice." Sister's chuckle sounded hollow as she gathered her meager belongings from the floor beside the chest. "I honestly think you believe that."

"I do, because it is true." Words in her defense rushed to the fore. "William promised me it would be so, and I believe him."

"Of course you believe him." Sister slammed the empty chest and positioned her pots and things in a straight line beside the clothing.

"William does not lie."

"Of course he does not." Sister grabbed her cloak and two wimples from the clothes tree. "He always tells you enough truth to make the accusation of a lie ridiculous."

Did William do that? He had said Sister could return if she desired it. And she would desire it. So, not entirely an evasion. "I give you my word."

"Your word." Sister shook her head. With a snap she shook out her cloak before folding it. "Your word is not what it once was, Alice."

Sister accused her of falsehood? Alice blinked back the sting. "I keep my word."

"Oh, Alice." Her arms blurring in a series of jerks, Sister folded her wimples into tiny squares of cloth and laid them atop her cloak. "You are so blinded that you no longer see. Your head has been completely turned by his fair form and his honeyed words. He calls you 'my Alice' and you melt beneath his charm. I have seen it with my own eyes."

Melt? Now Sister bordered on insulting. Aye, William did have a certain effect on her, but to hear Sister tell it, she stood powerless beneath his mesmerizing presence. He did have a way of making her thoughts run awry. Particularly when he took it upon himself to bathe every inch of her. A delicious little shiver raced through Alice.

"Even now." Sister heaved an enormous sigh. "He sneaks into this room and robs your thoughts."

Her thoughts were not helping. The images skulked to the back of her mind. "You and William do not get on. The entire keep has noted it."

"We do not." Sister put her shoulders back. "I have made my disapproval clear for all to see."

"And whilst you are fighting, William and I cannot forge a strong union."

"These are William's words." Sister stomped over to the wash-stand. "You have never uttered a desire to forge a strong union with any of your previous husbands."

"William is different."

"In this we are in agreement." Sister cradled her plain wooden cross. She laid it atop the small pile of folded garments, then rearranged it so the Christ figure lay perfectly in the center. All Sister's worldly possessions would only half-fill a travel sack. "I do not blame you, Alice."

"Oh?" Sister had changed direction again, and Alice scrambled to keep up.

"You have been enslaved, bewitched. Nay, I blame myself."

Alice had no idea what Sister meant, and she put a questioning expression on her face.

"The Lord set me to stand against evil and I have failed. I have been too vehement, too outspoken in my righteousness. It is mete that I return to the convent and pray and reflect on my failings."

"Sister, I do not believe William is evil." William had far too many noble traits to fit the mold into which Sister would shove him.

"Evil does not always show its face to the world," Sister said. "Nay, Alice. This is the best way. I will return to the convent. If God judges me worthy to resume my duties, I will see you in the spring." Sister folded her hands beneath her scapula. "This is the end for us, Alice. God be with you."

God be with you. Just like that. All these years with Sister by her side, over with a simple God be with you and a nod.

* * *

Alice took her seat in the hall the next morning. Beatrice's children sat at the table, and it saddened her that they still kept Mathew from her. Even as it gave her a wicked relief. She did not trust herself around him, but that was not Mathew's fault, it was hers.

She needed to discover the cause of this upset with Mathew. When she thought about it calmly, she could see no reason for her fear. Then the dream of the other night would pop into her head, and the fear would threaten to overcome her.

"William has broken his fast and is with the men," Beatrice said.

"In this weather?" Wind from the north streamed dull, heavy clouds. That wind would cut straight through the thickest cloak.

"Aye. William does not let much stop him." A wicked grin took over Beatrice's face. "He said to give you his special regards."

"What does that mean?" Richard peered at his mother. "And why is Lady Alice all red?"

Beatrice winked at her.

Ducking her head to her meal, Alice tried to hide her hot cheeks.

Adam smacked the table with the flat of his palm, demanding his mother feed him.

"Aye, Sir Adam." Beatrice nuzzled her son. "I will get to filling that belly of yours. Just like your father, are you not?"

"Gah!" Adam bobbed on his mother's lap and grasped at air with his chubby fingers. Little fingers made for nibbling on.

At Anglesesa, William and Beatrice must have broken their fast every morning with the happy sounds of chatter and life all about them. Alice would have her children grow up the same way.

"You should keep the children inside, this day." Alice accepted her bread and meat from the serving woman. "The wind comes from the north and will be icy."

"I am not afraid of the cold." Richard stuck his little chest out.

"Maybe not," Beatrice said. "But I am, and you cannot go outside on your own."

Poor lads. With winter closing in, the weather would try their patience by keeping them indoors. She hoped Mathew did not chafe at his isolation. "We could get one of the serving women or the squires to—"

"Ah, nay." Beatrice glanced at her. "There was some trouble a little while back with Faye's children. I always watch them myself."

She should have thought before she opened her mouth. "I beg your pardon." William had told her the story of how Faye's late husband's family had kidnapped her oldest son from just beyond Anglesea's walls. "I did not think."

Beatrice waved her off with a shrug. "Of course not, and I know I am being a bit foolish. Garrett twits me about it all the time. There is no reason for me to be so careful, but..." She ruffled Richard's hair.

He ducked away with a growl.

If those boys had been hers, Alice would have guarded them like a wolf bitch. Motioning Richard to her, she said, "Those of us who grew up in the North know all about having to stay in. I am sure we can come up with a good game for inside."

Richard sidled closer, scowling and chewing his apple. "William is allowed outside."

"William is a big boy," Beatrice said.

"My lady." Seamus entered the hall, his cheeks chapped bright red from the wind. "There is a messenger from the south."

Beatrice rose as a squire entered the hall behind Seamus. His clothes stained with hard travel, the man wore a grim expression. "Lady Beatrice," he said. "I bring news from Anglesea."

"What is it, Oliver?"

Ivy entered the hall at a run. "I saw Oliver arrive. Do you have news?"

"I do." Oliver looked at the floor before lifting his head.

Beatrice paled and grabbed the table edge. "It is bad, is it not?"

Alice rose and put a steadying hand beneath her elbow.

"Is my mother...?"

"Nay, my lady." Oliver hurried forward. "There is no change with the Lady Mary, but Nurse is still very concerned for her. She urges you to remain here until this is passed. Sir Roger is fully recovered, as is your father. The message I carry is for Mistress Ivy."

Ivy folded her hands before her, twisting her fingers together. "What is it?"

"It is Tom, mistress." Oliver wrung the edges of his cloak. "He fell ill whilst on his farm. It was days before we discovered him, and he is very bad."

Beatrice clasped Ivy's hands.

Ivy stood still as the dead, barely breathing.

Beatrice found her voice first. "Is he...does Nurse believe he might...?"

"She said to tell you to prepare for the worst," Oliver said.

With a whimper Ivy collapsed on the bench behind her. Her hands shook as she took up her water goblet. "I must go to him."

"Nay, mistress." Oliver stepped up to the dais table. "Nurse said you would say that, and she told me to tell you, in the strongest terms, that you must not come. She said to say you will do Tom no good if you come home merely to die."

Beatrice dropped beside Ivy and wrapped an arm about her shoulders. "He is strong, Ivy. Tom is healthy as an ox. He will get better."

Ivy stared at the table. She shot to her feet, bumping the table and upending a water goblet. The bench screeched across the flags. "Thank you, Oliver. If you will excuse me."

Beatrice stood and ran after her. "Ivy, wait."

The women disappeared up the stairs.

Oliver stood before the dais, twisting his cloak.

"Thank you." William had mentioned Tom when telling her of Beatrice's adventures. Clearly, he meant a lot to both Beatrice and Ivy. She smiled at Oliver. "You must be tired. Can I get you something to eat before you seek your rest?"

"Thank you, my lady." Oliver managed a wan smile. "It is a long way from Anglesea."

"Indeed." Alice motioned a serving woman closer. "Please see Oliver fed, and make sure he has a place to rest after his ride."

Tildy eyed Oliver up and down and grinned. He was a nice-looking lad. Alice would give Tildy that.

"Come along," Tildy said and swished her skirts out of the hall with Oliver following.

Richard turned and stared at her.

Adam banged the table for more food.

"Martha," she called the woman who sat amongst a small group sewing.

Martha rose. "Aye, my lady."

"Would you see to Master Mathew." Ivy looked in no condition to be caring for a child. "Make sure he is well and has everything he needs." It was her fault, after all, that Mathew did not join the hall with the other children. "Make sure he is entertained."

Martha bobbed a curtsy and left.

"Now we finish our meal." Alice scooped Adam onto her lap. "And then I will teach you a good game."

"Not like the ponies." Richard eyed her suspiciously. "There were no ponies."

Snorting, Alice passed Adam a hunk of bread to squeeze. "That is how much you know. The ponies were there. We just did not find them."

"Huh." Richard stuffed a slice of ham into his mouth.

"You will choke," Alice said. "And then I will not be able to teach you my game."

Richard chewed and swallowed, eyes huge.

Alice waited for Adam to stop smacking the table for more food and then she rose. The two boys followed her deeper into the hall. Kitchen drudges cleared the trestle tables against the wall and left a large, clear area, enough space to work off the energy of two young boys.

Only, what to do with two children? She wished she were not so beset by the strange terrors that prevented Mathew from joining them.

In a chest near the wall, Alice located a pile of soft linen sacks filled with dried beans. Under Richard's stare, she dropped the small sacks before the boys and went back for the wooden block.

"Now." She placed the block a good three strides from the boys. "We see who can toss the bags closest to the block."

Richard toed the bags. "This is a silly game. Adam cannot throw. He is too little."

Seen that way, it was a silly game. During the long, winter confinement, the keep occupants used the bags and block almost daily. Now that she thought on it, they did not seem to enjoy it all that much.

"What would you like to play then?" She looked at Richard.

"I know." Richard's face lit.

Adam hummed and stacked bean sacks at her feet. Then pounded them into shape.

"What will we play?" She wondered if she dared send for Mathew to join them. If she had another of her attacks, however, she risked doing more damage than good.

"Dragons," Richard said. "I would like to play dragons."

Her childhood had lacked many useful skills it seemed. "I am not sure I know how to play dragons."

Richard gaped at her. "You are the dragon, and you chase us."

"And?"

Richard rolled his eyes. "You breathe fire."

He stared at her, poised and ready to play.

Alice had never had playmates. She had no idea how to play an imaginary game.

Richard leaned forward, and whispered, "You need to roar."

"Raaawr?" Alice felt ridiculous.

He blinked at her. Adam sucked on the edge of a sack, and she bent and took it out of his mouth. He immediately wailed a protest, and she handed it back to him.

"RAH." She tried again.

Richard crossed his arms. "You are not scary."

Nay, she was only scary when she was losing herself to the terrors. Her dragon, unfortunately, was as frightening as day-old bread. A drudge swept the rushes, the swish of his broom rising above the fire's crackle. A serving woman dusted around the casement.

Screwing up her courage, Alice leaped at Richard with a mighty yell.

Richard screamed and bolted, his high-pitched voice clattering around the hall.

"I am going to eat you." Alice raised her arms above her head and lumbered toward Richard.

Face alight with glee, he ducked around her. "I am too fast for you. You will not get me."

"I will grind your bones to make my bread." It sounded like a fine threat to Alice. "I shall use your hair to pick my teeth."

Round-eyed, Adam sucked on his bean sack and grinned at them.

"Here I come." Richard did not move that fast, and Alice stuck to her slow, side-swaying gait. Now that she played the game, it did not seem at all silly, and she kept up her flow of grisly threats. The grislier, the more Richard grinned and shrieked with delight.

Richard took to ducking behind her and plucking at her skirts.

"Who goes there?" Alice swung around.

"Me." Richard danced away.

Adam sat with his bean sacks and giggled.

Alice made a business of sniffing the air. "I smell little boy bones."

Richard's eyes widened and he clapped both hands over his mouth.

"And I smell dragon," William said.

With a shriek, Alice spun about. Caught playing dragon, and she wanted to run away and hide.

William grinned at her, and her cheeks burned. "What shall I do with this dragon, boys?"

"Slay her," yelled Richard.

"I think I shall." William lunged, grabbed her by the hips and upended her over his shoulder.

Richard cheered and capered about.

"I have my battle prize." William toted her around the hall.

The drudge leaned on his broom, laughing. The serving woman had stopped sweeping ashes and stood by her bucket, cheering William on and waving her brush in the air.

Alice flopped about on his shoulder like a sack of grain. She laughed so hard tears streamed as William paraded her about. Behind him came Richard and Adam, marching and clapping.

"Put me down." Alice tapped William's back. All the blood had rushed to her head.

William lowered her to her feet. "Do you submit?"

His eyes bore a different, more thrilling message, and Alice grinned back at him. "I submit."

"I am hungry," Richard said.

"Me too." William ruffled his hair. "This dragon-slaying is a hungry business."

"Abomination." Sister appeared out of nowhere. She had a frightened Mathew by the arm. His eyes huge in his pale face, silent tears crept down his cheeks. "Martha tried to conceal him from me. But I found him. Abomination."

Closer than William, Alice leaped for Mathew. His look of terror overrode anything she felt, and she tugged him free of Sister's grip and put herself between him and Sister.

Small hands fastened in her skirt as he pressed his face into her back.

"Nay!" Sister lunged for Mathew.

William ran at Sister. He grabbed her about the waist before she could reach Alice.

"Get the abomination away from here." Sister thrashed against his hold, clawing at his restraining hands.

"Stop it." William shook Sister.

The edges of Alice's vision darkened. Sister's shrieks came from a long way off, echoing around her mind. A boy with features like Mathew, but not Mathew. His face grinning at her, slack jawed with spittle on his chin. The earth shifted beneath her, and she dangled above the water.

"Alice," William's bellow clattered around her brain as her stomach lurched and everything went black.

* * *

William dropped Sister as he lunged for Alice.

She crumpled onto the floor in a rustle of skirts.

He caught Alice just before her head smacked onto the hard stones.

Donnchadh and Domnall rounded into the hall at a run.

"Hold her." William jerked his head at the crone closing on Mathew.

Jesu, Mathew stood rigid, his mouth working as his breath rasped in and out.

Rage unlike any he had every felt coursed through William.

Domnall reached Sister first. Impervious to her screams, he snagged her flailing hands and pinned them behind her back.

Sister struggled against Domnall's hold, arching her back and butting her head into his chest.

Donnchadh crouched before a sobbing Mathew. "There now, lad," he said. "All is well. See, my big ugly brother has hold of her."

Adam wailed, and Richard went to him.

Richard had gone pale as parchment. His lips trembled as tears streamed down his face. Still, he hugged his little brother close to him.

Dear God, he could rip her head from her neck for doing this to the boys. And Alice.

She stirred in his arms.

"Sweeting." He clasped her against his chest. In his arms she felt feather light, too tiny and fragile. *Mine.* The roar built inside him. For Alice and the children, he contained it. "Alice, sweeting."

Her lids fluttered open. She frowned and blinked at him. "What happened?"

"You fainted."

She tensed. "Mathew?"

"Donnchadh has him."

Mathew leaned against Donnchadh's leg. Richard had drawn closer to Donnchadh. The big Scot now held Adam in his arms.

Sister lay spent in Domnall's hold.

"What shall I do with her?" Domnall shook Sister. He looked ready enough to do William's bidding if he told the man to toss her from the battlements.

"Confine her." William stood and hoisted Alice into his arms. "Find some place we can keep her until the Holy Sisters come for her. Somewhere she cannot escape."

Domnall looked disappointed. He tugged Sister away. "It is a crying shame for me that my Da would whip me if I harmed a woman and a nun."

Alice stared after them, tears in her beautiful green eyes. "Why?"

"I know not, sweeting." William pressed his cheek to her head. "Do not worry about her now. Send for Ivy," he said to Seamus who had wandered into the hall in his brothers' wake. "Tell her Lady Alice is ill."

"Ivy is—" Alice did not want to bother Ivy when she was so upset.

"Can you find Beatrice and take the boys to her?" William

rolled over her protest and she did not feel well enough to fight him.

Donnchadh nodded. "Come along, my brave lads. Let us find Lady Bea. I am sure she has something tasty for a man who has had such a scare." He motioned for Richard and Mathew to join him. "We have it all in hand now. No need for fear."

Aonghas had raised fine men beneath the bluster and brawn. William carried Alice to their chamber.

"I have never fainted," Alice said as he laid her on their bed.

"Well, you did today." William would make sure Ivy got to the bottom of why. Perhaps the shock had overset Alice. He might have jostled her on his shoulder for too long. Either way, he would ensure Ivy discovered why.

* * *

Alice wanted to comfort Ivy. Her puffy eyes and red nose said much, but she was otherwise distant and preoccupied. If Alice knew her better, she would pry.

"Are the boys all right?" The look on Mathew's face stirred that dark memory again, but not the terror. "Is Mathew recovered?"

"Beatrice has them." Ivy checked her with firm, gentle hands. "She will ensure they are well." She glanced at William. "Tell me what happened with Alice."

She listened as William told her and then nodded. "Right. Time for you to leave."

"But I—" William protested as Ivy closed the door in his still sputtering face.

Ivy settled on the edge of the bed. "When was your monthly?"

Alice squirmed inside. Never had she discussed the curse of Eve with another woman. When her time first came, Sister had shut her in a room. Martha had explained why she bled and what it meant, but only much later. For all of that long afternoon after

Sister had locked her into her chamber, Alice had fretted about what ailed her. "I..."

Alice counted back, and then back a bit further. "Before my wedding." An almost unbearably sweet hope bloomed inside her. Tears sprang to her eyes. "You do not think?"

Ivy squeezed her knee through her bliaut. "I think it is a definite possibility."

Too scared to hope, Alice clenched her nails into her palms. "I have not felt ill."

"Not all women do," Ivy said. "And it may even be too early for that." She shrugged. "However, with all that has happened, and those episodes of yours, we cannot dismiss shock."

Alice could not contain all the emotion welling up inside her and she grabbed Ivy's hands. "How would I know for sure?"

"I am not the best at midwifery." Ivy pulled a rueful face. "If Nurse were here, she would be able to make certain for you, but I only know about the other end of the process. The delivery."

"What should I do?" Alice covered her belly with her hand. Dear God, she would make sure she protected the possible life inside her with all she had.

"Much as you are doing." Ivy chuckled. "Eat well, go about your life as you do now. There is no need to lock yourself away from your husband unless you cannot bear him near you. Other than that, do not take any chances that you might fall and hurt the child."

"I wish I knew for sure. Can you not...try?" Her flat belly mocked her. "I need to know."

"Well, you must have missed at least one monthly if you have not had your time since before your marriage. I would say that bodes well. You say you have never fainted before?"

"I have not." Then again, she'd never experience mind-altering terror before either.

"And that could be another sign. If you are with child, you should start to feel changes in your body."

"Like what?" Alice wanted to peer past the skin on her belly and see inside.

"Perhaps you should ask Bea," Ivy said. "She has had two children and knows far more than I. And"—Ivy leaned closer—"she is not saying anything, but I suspect she has another on the way."

"Why would she not tell?"

Ivy shrugged. "Garrett would worry more about her if he knew she was pregnant. And…" Ivy's expression grew serious. "Many babies are lost in these early stages. I do not want to frighten you, but it is wise to wait until you are more certain."

How would William feel when he got the news? She got ahead of herself. She did not even know for certain she carried a child. A nasty thought snaked into her mind. If William knew, would he leave her bed, see his job as done, and seek out other women?

"Why that face?" Ivy studied her.

"I am afraid," Alice said, but she could not admit her real fear. Only a woman hopelessly lost in sin would admit that she feared losing her husband in her bed. "I do not know what to do."

"Ask Bea." Ivy stood and smoothed her skirts. "I could ask her for you."

"Nay." What Bea knew, William would know soon enough. She needed to tell him in her own time and way. She cherished each moment of wonderful William had gifted her, hoarded them to herself. She wanted to cling to her happiness for a while longer. At least until she knew for sure she carried a child.

Alice touched her belly. A child of her own. *Please, Lord…*

* * *

Alice stood in the hallway outside Sister's chamber and dithered. At this rate the dinner hour would come before she made a decision, and she irked herself. It had all been so simple before. She would have marched right to this chamber and shared her news with Sister.

Little Domnall—little referring more to his age than his hulking shoulders—stood guard outside the chamber. He leaned against the wall and watched her pace the corridor. Fortunately, he did not urge her to speak. She felt foolish enough.

Everything had changed, with Sister a twisted, dark stranger. Well, Sister had always leaned to the bleak and joyless. Had she not seen it herself, Alice would not have believed Sister's actions in the hall.

Guards had spotted the party from the convent this morning. Alice's time with Sister grew short. Perhaps Sister would share her joy, and her possible pregnancy could restore the tattered strands of their bond.

Alice nodded to Domnall. "I am ready."

Martha answered Domnall's fist on the door. "Oh, it is you, Lady Alice. Sir William said I am to stay with her."

"Is she overwrought?"

"Not anymore." Martha rearranged her apron with a smirk. "I gave her some tea brewed by Mistress Ivy and she has slept like a babe ever since. She does a power of good with those plants of hers does Mistress Ivy."

"She certainly knows them well." Alice slipped deeper into the chamber.

"Sister Julianna was that upset when Big Domnall carted her in here." Martha pursed her lips. "Mistress Ivy had to do some ministering to the poor lad, too. That scratched up he were, and Sister with her claws out giving it all she had."

"Thank you, Martha." Alice stood beside the pallet. "Could I have a moment, Martha, to say goodbye on our own?"

Martha snorted and jammed her hands on her hips. "I am going to tell you a thing or two, Lady Alice. And I never would have done so in the past, what with you here and Sister stuck to you like a burr. She may have raised you, my lady, but she did you no kindness."

"Thank you, I—"

"Always railing on you about God and sin. Never a kind word or a cuddle for a lonely little girl. We saw it all, we Tarnwych folk, and it fair to made a body sick to see the way she treated a young girl like you. Squashed." Martha mashed her fist into her palm. "Like chaff beneath her heel you were. All the life pounded out of you."

"Mart—"

"And then that handsome Sir William comes here, and the sun comes out for our Lady Alice. Does a body a power of good to see your pretty smile when he is about." Martha puffed her chest.

Alice stood and let her say her piece. Martha had suffered enough censure from Sister through the years to earn her right to speak.

"A blessing from God that man is. For all she calls him and his kin names and does those awful things. I saw her filling your head with her vicious nonsense and my heart fairly failed." Martha sucked in a deep breath, and tears glittered in her eyes. "I thought your new man would go the same way as the others, but he's a wily one. I told my boy, the moment I clapped eyes on Sir William, 'He's a wily one, that one. He will see Sister coming from a league off, he will.'"

Sister lay on her back, her breathing deep and even, her face relaxed. She looked peaceful, a harmless old woman.

"Then she started with her twistings and turnings afore Sir William had his knees under his table. Whispering to you. Trying to make Sir William look like a bad one." Martha chuckled, evil enough to lift the hair on Alice's nape. "But he saw her then, too. Kept his lip buttoned. Watched and waited and she wandered right into the fox's den, she did."

Sister had not made many friends in her years at Tarnwych. Here she lay, rendered senseless by Ivy's herbs and only Martha, who disliked her, would sit with her. What a terrible, lonely existence. In a keep the size of Tarnwych, Sister had not one soul who would bid her God be with you and shed a tear. All these years

Alice believed only Sister stood by her. But perhaps, she was the only person for Sister.

"You are a kind one, Lady Alice." Martha peered down her nose at Sister. "And she does not deserve a heart like yours to ache for her going, but you are the way you are. God bless you for it. I will wait outside until you are done." Giving her a nudge hard enough to push Alice to the side, Martha chuckled. "That young Domnall will make a pleasure of the waiting."

The door closed behind Martha.

Sister's chin rested on the smoothed linens. Did it make her a bad person that she felt relieved that she no longer needed to decide whether or not to share her news with Sister?

"You could have given me a hug," Alice said to the sleeping woman. "Or pinched my cheek and told me I had done well."

Nay, Sister's always instructed and corrected. Today, with the boys in the hall, Alice had played the first children's game of her life. Sister did not approve of the keep children as companions.

Alice bent and kissed her dry cheek. "I may be with child. I shall love them, and cuddle them, and tell them every day how wonderful they are."

* * *

"There you are." William strode down the passage.

Alice shut the door to Sister's chamber behind her.

He nodded to Domnall and Martha. "I came to find my wife, cosset and spoil her in her illness, only to find her rampaging about the keep."

Martha sighed and clasped her hands to her bosom.

"Hardly rampaging." Alice worked up a wan smile for his benefit. She would not miss Sister, and that saddened her most of all.

William slid his arms about her waist. "Are you well?"

"I am." And she was. In the chamber behind her lay the past, and before her, the future, which grew brighter every day. "I came to bid her God be with you, but she was asleep."

"It is for the best." William kissed her cheek. "I know you will be saddened to see her go."

Alice could not accept his sympathy. "I do not think I will, and that makes me sadder than anything."

"My Alice." He drew her with him down the passageway. "You are so loyal. Beware of where you bestow that precious gift. Make sure the person you give it to is worthy of it."

"Have you and Martha been speaking?"

William chuckled. "Nay, but I have been here long enough to see how things lie."

They reached their bedchamber and William guided her inside. "Now, I believe Ivy said you needed rest. I came up here determined to give my lady company during her tedious confinement."

"Confinement?" Alice's heart skipped a beat. What had Ivy told him?

"After the hall." William pressed her to lie on the bed. "I will not be gainsaid in this, and I have had Cook prepare all your favorites."

Alice removed her shoes and lay against the pillows he propped for her.

"I have noticed you have a taste for sweet things, my lady."

He went to the table, his back to her.

How strange life could be. It took and it gave, and left a woman reeling to catch up. "William?"

"Aye?"

"I can think of something I like better than sweet things."

William spun, an answering gleam in his eyes. "My lady, you are ill."

"Not that ill."

Chapter Twenty-One

William refilled Sister Margaret's goblet. For a woman of the cloth, the Prioress could tuck away the wine. Short, stout, and with pleasingly round features, Sister Margaret the Prioress of St. Stephen's Abbey had arrived amid a flurry of nuns.

He would send a couple of Aonghas's boys with them on their way home. He could not like the idea of women traveling on their own. It couldn't hurt to bolster the Lord's protection with a bit of steel.

"The Abbess sends her apologies. She means no insult, but she is not in the best of health." With a wrist toss, Sister Margaret drained her goblet. Perhaps he should see if any of those Scots had their infernal brew with them.

"She is ill?" He gave her more wine and topped his half-full goblet.

Sister Margaret snorted a laugh. "Nay, Sir William, merely older than dust. She can barely make it to her bench in the sun, never mind two days travel from Old Stoney to here."

"Old Stoney?"

Sister Margaret guffawed and slapped her thigh. Her cheeks jiggled around her wimple. "It is my name for St. Stephen's.

Abbeys are built of stone. Stephen was stoned to death. Old Stoney."

"Indeed." Not quite what he had expected of a nun. What with Sister Sunshine's amiable disposition, his enlightenment regarding Holy Sisters continued.

"Any more wine in that flagon you are clutching, Sir William?"

"Plenty." It was as if he entertained a tavern wench in a nun's habit. William motioned Cedric for more wine.

Cedric put one careful foot in front of the other, eyes locked on the flagon as he poured. The lad had returned with the nuns, whole and hale. The lad had grown another inch in his absence. Task completed, Cedric straightened, his cheeks flushed.

"Now then." Sister Margaret rested her elbows on her knees and gave William a penetrating stare with keen brown eyes. "Let us hear what has been going on with Sister Julianna."

He would wager not much got past this woman. "She has a rather vehement attachment to my wife. Understandable, given that she raised Lady Alice. The problem is her reaction to the rest of my family."

"Oh, aye."

Cedric obeyed the silent command of the outstretched goblet.

"She has taken to calling a certain member of my household a whor—a woman of low morals. Just yesterday, she attacked my brother, Mathew, calling him an abomination," William said.

Sister Margaret shook her head. She leaned back in her seat, and her expression grew contemplative as she swished wine from one cheek to the other. "When your lad arrived, I took it upon myself to do a bit of digging."

"Did you?"

"Indeed." Sister Margaret's gaze sharpened. "Your Sister Julianna came from our Abbey. Seems she was related to your wife's family in some way, a bit distant but enough for the Abbess to send her to oversee the birth of Lady Alice."

William already knew all this, but he had been raised not to interrupt a lady, especially not a Bride of the Church.

"But that is not the interesting part." Sister Margaret tapped the side of her head. "I kept wondering why the Abbess had not called for her to return to the Abbey."

"Aye." William had thought that enough times himself. "Could you discover why?"

"There is some...murkiness in the records." Sister Margaret took a long draught from her goblet. "The Abbey then was a different place, and they were not inclined to record their...indiscretions. The Prioress then, now no longer with us, did not like to have the Abbey's troubles available for scrutiny."

How much trouble could an Abbey full of nuns get into? William kept his polite listening face in place.

"I am not such a woman." William would wager his horse she was not. "I like to see trouble out in the open, where one can deal with it." She stared at him for a long moment, and then grinned. "You are wondering what sort of trouble nuns get into."

William's face heated.

"The Abbey shelters all types of women, my lord. I would never dismiss another woman's calling to serve the Lord, but let me say that there are times when the calling is rather convenient. Nobody looks for a woman who has taken up the veil. Her actions are no longer subject to such keen scrutiny."

It made sense and William nodded. "And Sister Julianna?"

"Hard to say." Sister Margaret held out her goblet. "By the by, this is an excellent grape you serve, Sir William."

"Thank you, Sister." William chuckled. The woman had her own brand of charm. "I will see a few barrels find their way onto the cart and return with you."

"I was hoping you would say that." Sister Margaret winked. "Your Sister Julianna joined the Abbey a little later in her life. The records show she had already been married, but they do not say to whom."

"Do they usually?"

"Oh, aye." Sister Margaret waved a hand. "The Abbey likes to know whose daughters and sisters we have beneath our roof. It can be very useful during leaner months to have some outside support."

Everybody needed a crust of bread. William motioned for her to continue.

"If the husband is not listed in the records, my predecessor sometimes had a good reason for the omission. It took me forever to divine her system of recording, but I know my way around it now. To hide where a woman came from often meant the woman wanted to stay hidden."

"But why?"

"Sir William." Sister Margaret pursed her lips and stroked the armrest with her free hand. "This world we live in is not kind to women. There are as many reasons as hairs on your head for a woman to want to disappear. Bad fathers, worse husbands, cruel brothers, the list goes on and on."

Sir Arthur had raised his sons to mind their strength, but all men bore the shame of those who would not control their baser natures. "And Sister Julianna was one of these women? A woman escaping her lot in life?"

"Perhaps." Sister Margaret waggled her head. "Or perhaps it was just a day on which the late Prioress did not make a proper entry. There are enough of those in the records, too."

"Ah." No closer to learning the truth. Not that it mattered at this stage. He aimed to do all he could to ensure Alice did not miss her nasty mentor.

"I took my questions to the Abbess." Sister Margaret snorted into her goblet. "Mind emptier than King John's coffers. She barely remembers her name on most days, but she did show some recollection of Sister Julianna." She leaned forward and pierced him with a stare. "Seems Sister Julianna has a secret she wants kept that way. She was definitely married when she came to the Abbey, and her husband was not propping up a headstone."

William found it fascinating that any man would have chosen

to marry the old hag. Of course, even Sister Julianna must have been young at some point.

"And, I cannot be sure, but the Abbess did talk about a child."

That shook him. "Sister Julianna had a child?"

"I cannot be sure. Like I said, the Abbess is not all there, but I suspect that to be the truth."

"What happened to the child?"

Sister Margaret tossed up a hand and sat back in her chair. "Most likely the same thing that happens to any child born at the Abbey. They join the band of mouths we feed and are cared for by the good Sisters."

"Are you saying that not all the children in Abbeys are orphans?"

"Nay. A hundred times nay." Sister Margaret winked at him. "A Prioress would never hint that the good sisters are anything less than pure as a fresh snowfall. Brides of Christ are above worldly temptation, Sir William. Everybody knows this."

William had to laugh. Gregory had dispelled his innocent belief in monasteries being filled with pious men. Why then would nunneries and convents be any different? He had a strong sense that Sister Margaret had a long and interesting story of her own.

"So." Sister Margaret slapped her knee. "We will bundle up our sister and take her with us in the morning. She will have less mischief available to her at Old Stoney."

"I will send some men with you."

"I appreciate that." Sister Margaret stood and adjusted her skirts. "Although I heard a rumor that Aonghas's rabble are less often seen this side of the border. Imagine my surprise when I saw his sons here at Tarnwych."

"I believe Aonghas and I have reached a sort of truce."

"Aye." Sister Margaret pinched his cheek. "For all your pretty face, Sir William, you are a clever man. I am glad you are here."

She left him gaping like an idiot and strode out of the hall.

* * *

Alice had to keep reminding herself not to stare at the party from St. Stephen's.

They laughed, as loud as any of the men, drank wine, and enjoyed Cook's largesse. One of them had taken Martha's place beside Sister Julianna in her chamber.

It helped alleviate the gnawing guilt about sending Sister away. These women looked happy and content with their place. Alice prayed Sister would find a good home amongst them and learn to enjoy their companionship.

"Are you well?" William whispered.

Alice nodded. He had asked her several times, aware that Sister's leaving weighed on her. Her relief she could barely admit to herself, saying it aloud would constitute the worst kind of betrayal of a woman who had raised her. "It is for the best."

William nuzzled her neck. "We will make a fine winter here, my Alice. You shall see."

"Aye." What would winter at Tarnwych be like this year? Cold outside, for certain, but perhaps warmer within the walls. Filled with people and life and laughter pressing back the worst of the lingering icy misery. In a fortnight they would celebrate Martinmas, and the advent following promised sweeter than ever before. Cook already had the geese picked out and fattening up.

William would not allow any stringy beast for Martinmas beef she would guess.

"I have a surprise for you," William said.

"What is it?" Last time he had surprised her with a trunk full of jewels and glorious fabrics. Fabrics she still lacked the courage to have made into a dress. Still, with Sister leaving, perhaps she would get Martha to help her fashion a gown. Perhaps in that golden-yellow, or the green that matched her eyes.

William winked at her. "You shall have to wait until morning to find out."

"Will I now." Alice so enjoyed bantering with him. "Or perhaps I shall use my wiles to get the secret out of you."

William's voice lowered to a thrilling, husky bass. "If anybody could, my lady, it would be you."

* * *

Alice reached out her hand to touch and snatched it back. "She is not mine."

"She most certainly is." William took her hand and placed it on the mare's silky neck. "When I asked Gregory to send me destriers, I asked him for his sweetest palfrey as well."

"For me?" Alice's voice wobbled, as she tried not to cry. Such a creature could not belong to her, a beautiful mare with her glossy coat nearly matching Alice's hair. Huge, patient brown eyes blinked at Alice. "What is she called?"

"Whatever you name her." William covered her hand with his and stroked the taut muscle on the horse's neck. "Young Will has kept her exercised while I waited to give her to you. Now that Sister Julianna is gone, I could not wait any longer."

"Mine." Alice stepped closer. Rich, horsey aroma filled her nostrils, and she drew in a deep breath. The mare stood shorter than William's destrier. Long-legged and delicate, she was the perfect ride for a lady. "But I cannot ride."

"That is my next surprise." William grinned at her. "I am going to teach you to ride."

Ride? Who would ever have thought such a thing? For certain not her. "Nay."

"Aye." William copied her breathy whisper. "Although I shall miss your ass pressed against me while we ride together."

Alice shivered in delight. William's wickedness did the most delicious things to her innards. "What if I fall?"

"All riders fall at some point," William said. "But I aim to teach you not to."

Ivy had advised caution, but also to live her life. Then again,

Beatrice rode every day, and Ivy suspected she was pregnant as well. If she rode very, very carefully...

Her conscience hissed at her to tell him. First she must make certain she carried a child.

"Are you ready?" William cupped his hands for her foot.

"Aye." Alice stepped into his hands, and he hoisted her onto the mare's back. The mare shifted beneath her weight and settled.

William strode to Cedric holding Paladin. "She is bred for a lady. You will find her mouth soft and responsive and her nature biddable."

Biddable, maybe, but the mare's back rose a long, long way from the ground.

Paladin tossed his head. One big eye rolled around and glared at her from beneath his forelock.

Her palfrey shifted her weight and paid no mind to the great, pawing lout beside her.

"Your reins, Alice." William battled the great beast to stillness. "Pick up your reins and let us begin. The reins are one of the ways you talk to your mount." He cast a sharp eye over her. "And sit up straight. The way you sit on your horse will also send messages to her."

Alice jerked up straight.

William chuckled and edged his big-toothed beast closer. "Be calm, my Alice. She can sense your agitation and it will agitate her."

"I am afraid." Riding alone differed from sharing the saddle with William.

"Of course you are." He smiled at her, warm and reassuring. "But once the pair of you learn who is master and who is beast, you will see there is nothing to fear."

Alice spent the morning watching and listening to William. As a teacher he remained patient, chiding at times, but for the most part filling her lesson with fun. By the time he assisted her from the mare, her fear had subsided to a low belly niggle.

"Have you thought of a name for her yet?" William handed the mare's reins to Cedric.

Alice squirmed on the inside. She had never named a horse before. It seemed a serious undertaking. "I shall call her Rhiannon."

William nodded. "A great mythical queen to be sure. Make sure you cool Rhiannon down, Cedric, and give our new queen a proper rub down."

"Do you think we might ride out of the bailey next time?" William had her riding circles around the practice yards again and again. Repeatedly, he had gone through her halting and then getting Rhiannon moving again. As her lesson progressed, the idea of taking to the moors with her Rhiannon had taken root in Alice.

William raised his brow at her. "First, I need to know you have control of her. Then we can see about leaving the bailey."

"You did well," Beatrice called from where she perched on a stool beside the barracks. Her blue gown made a splash of color against the stone.

Ivy stood by her side.

"Thank you." Alice still wanted to fidget when she encountered Beatrice. Perhaps in time they could grow comfortable with each other, like sisters. "William is a patient teacher."

Beatrice snorted. "Not when he taught me, he was not. Tossed me up on a destrier he did."

"Bea." William shook his head at his sister. "Remind me who refused to ride the pony father bought to teach her."

"That is neither here nor there." Beatrice gave a nonchalant shrug.

They argued happily, moving on from horse riding to other childhood slights.

"Have you told William?" Ivy sidled up beside her.

"Nay. Not yet." William and Beatrice progressed to some argument about a Midsummer's bonfire and Beatrice's poppet. "I want to be sure."

"You need to be wary of riding," Ivy said. "If you fall off, you could lose the babe."

"I will tell him," Alice said. She had no clear idea when or how, but she would. It stood to reason William needed telling before she grew a great belly.

"Tell him soon, Alice." Ivy sighed. Grief carved into the depths of her eyes. "It is a terrible thing not to tell somebody what they need to know when you have the chance. Fate steps in and takes that chance from you."

Before Alice could question her further, Ivy made her way back to the keep.

Beatrice shook her head as she watched her friend go. "I hate seeing her this sad."

"Why is she sad?"

Beatrice's expression grew closed. "That is not my story to tell. You will have to ask her that. I heard you had a spell in the hall the other day. Are you well now?"

"I am."

"And that Mathew was there when it happened." Beatrice's eyes narrowed on her suspiciously.

"There was a bit more to it than that, Bea." William slung his arm about Alice's shoulder.

Alice drew courage from the gesture of support.

"What more?" Beatrice stuck her chin out.

Alice strolled with William back to the keep. "That is a story for another day."

$$Chapter\ Twenty\text{-}Two$$

William crouched over Paladin's neck as the horse widened his stride in a burst of speed. Through the sparse moorland vegetation, the hart bounded for the safety of the crags. It had taken all day to find this single quarry, and now he hesitated to kill such a magnificent creature, a hart of twelve points at least, and in his prime.

Hunting mastiffs surged forward in their pack, staying clear of the horses.

As much as his blood rose to the thrill of the hunt, William always left the kill to another. He did not relish the fade of life from a creature's eyes. This hart would make a fine trophy for the barracks and feed the hall in the feast cook prepared for them.

Martinmas, the beginning of the festivities leading to Christmas. Tonight they would eat well of goose, beef, and if the hunter's luck held, venison. William had a mind to celebrate. Tarnwych flourished in the weeks since the weight of Sister Julianna had lifted from her back.

His conversation with the Prioress stayed with him. When spring came, he would set out and discover more of Sister Julianna's origins. A woman that bitter must have good reason, and he liked knowing with whom he dealt.

A fresh delight every day, he watched Alice blossom and discover the world around her, free from her tether. Especially at night, when he had her all to himself. Alice took to bed sport with an eagerness that quickened his blood more than the hunt. The things he could, and would, show her. William shifted in the saddle to get more comfortable. Thoughts of Alice in bed hampered his seat.

A twang, almost lost in the baying of the hounds and the thunder of hooves, then the flash of an arrow. William threw his weight left. The breeze of the arrow's passage ruffled his hair. His heart drummed in his chest. If he had ducked a heartbeat later, the arrow would have found its mark. In his eye.

"My lord!" A shouting, stomping, milling mass of horses, dogs, and men surrounded him.

He raised his voice above the panic. "Find the archer."

Aonghas and Domnall peeled off, riding low in the saddle as they streaked in the direction of the arrow's origin.

A lone figure broke from the shelter of a low copse and ran.

Fist in the air, Domnall bellowed a battle cry and gave chase, Aonghas sharp on his heels.

"Alive," William yelled after them. "I want him alive."

* * *

Battered, bruised and near terrified out of his simple mind, the poacher trembled at William's feet.

Aonghas and Domnall had delivered the man breathing, but had availed themselves of the opportunity to teach a little hard justice along the way.

"I did not mean it, my lord." Saliva dribbled down the poacher's chin, mingling with the blood from his split lip. "I did not see you until I had loosed."

"You aim like a woman." Domnall drove the point home with a boot in the ribs.

"Cease." William winced as the poacher gave a harsh grunt and curled into a protective ball.

"He shot you," Domnall, face red with outrage, yelled at him.

"Aye." William thumped the big brute in the chest. "And we will never discover why if you beat him to death."

Domnall loomed over the cowering man, fists clenched.

"Who are you?" William crouched beside the man.

"Caomh, my lord. I was aiming for the hart. I swear it."

The hart had long since disappeared into the craggy outcrops.

"You realize this is Tarnwych land?" William took pity on the sniveling cur and handed him his water skin.

The man eyed the offering warily.

"Take it." Domnall cuffed him. "And be grateful it is not the end of his lordship's sword."

"Aye, thank you, Domnall." William admired loyalty as much as the next man, but if Domnall continued in this manner, Caomh might very well die of fright. "Drink."

Caomh took the skin as if it were made of vipers, raised it to his lips and sipped, his gaze not leaving William. "It was just one hart. We have not seen the like for many a year."

"But it were not yours." Domnall loomed closer.

"I think I have this, Domnall." William motioned the younger man back. "Take your brothers and sweep the area. Make sure there are no more unpleasant surprises lurking hereabout."

"I am alone," said Caomh.

"So you say." Domnall spat and spun back to his horse.

William waited until the pounding of hooves moved away from them. "Now, perhaps you can tell me why you were poaching on my land."

"We be hungry...my lord." Anger flashed in Caomh's eyes, and he lowered them to the water skin and sipped again. "I just wanted the one. For my family."

"There are easier ways." William rested his elbows on his bent knees, attempting to look harmless. "You could come to Tarnwych and plead your case."

Caomh smeared a trickle of blood across his cheek. "Do not be nobody at Tarnwych what hears. Now that Dunstan is dead."

William raised his brow. "I believe I reside at Tarnwych, and my hearing is excellent."

Caomh kept his head down.

"Begging your pardon, Sir William." Rufus slunk closer, still not one to seek out William's attention. "I know this man. We were raised in the village together."

"And?" William would never make a soldier of Rufus until the man ceased his doglike servility.

"I know him to be honest." Rufus shifted, coloring to his ruddy hairline. "Leastways he used to be. But that is not what I wanted to say."

"As I have pointed out, moments ago"—William pinned Rufus with a stare—"my hearing is excellent, and thanks to an arrow, sharper than usual."

"The villagers." William did not think Rufus could flush more, but the man went clay-red. "They used to come to Tarnwych, in the past. Dunstan always dealt with them. He did not like them to speak to anyone but him. Sister Julianna and Dunstan had a sort of agreement. As long as they stayed clear of each other, all was well."

"Ah." The truth struck him clear as a bell. "And Dunstan took the opportunity to take care of himself?"

"Aye, my lord. And those he favored." He gave Rufus credit for standing his ground.

"Before I render judgment, Caomh, I want to see this family."

* * *

"God's Bones." Aonghas whistled through his teeth.

William was glad someone had the words, because they escaped him. Appalled came closest to what raged through him. "I am afraid God is nowhere in this."

He dismounted and tossed the reins to Cedric.

Caomh slid to the ground from where he rode with Rufus.

"Caomh?" A woman appeared in the crooked doorway to the hovel. With her dead eyes and sunken cheeks, he could not guess her age, but hopelessness and fear trailed her.

"Mags, meet Sir William." Caomh moved to her side and stood beside her, bristling like a broody mastiff.

"Aye, but what be he doing here?" Mags paled and dipped into a curtsy. Her threadbare skirts revealed bare feet. "Begging your pardon, my lord."

"Nay, Mistress Margaret." William took it all in. The bare, cracked yard, the skin covered windows, the gaping holes in the thatch. Most of all he could not drag his eyes from the three emaciated children huddled in their mother's skirts. "It is I who must beg your pardon."

Empty beast pens sagged to one side of the dwelling.

"Are there many like this?" he asked Rufus.

"Aye, my lord." Rufus's face wore grim resignation. "Most of the village fare no better."

"Dear God." Untilled earth, choked beneath weeds and nettles stretched out behind the cottage. By now, the soil should have been turned to rest for winter, ready for planting with the thaw.

The children's pinched, chapped faces would follow him to the grave. The rags they wore barely covered their stick limbs.

"How long has it been thus?"

"Many a year, Sir William." Rufus took position beside him. "There is more, if you care to see it."

"I must see it." William's breakfast soured and churned in his gut. He would not suffer a beast to live in such conditions. "How long since these fields were planted?"

"Planted?" Mags gave a bitter laugh, crossing her arms. "What shall we plant, your lordship? Acorns?"

Caomh tugged his wife back to his side. "Whist, Mags."

"Did Tarnwych not send you seed?" William already had the answer and he barely heard Mags's reply.

"Dunstan sold the seed." Rufus cleared his throat. "He sent just enough of the harvest to the keep to make sure Gord did not ask too many questions, and sold the rest."

"Gord said nothing?"

Rufus stared over his shoulder. "Gord sent his reports to Sister Julianna."

Dunstan and Sister, a perfect pairing that rendered the bailiff impotent. He had seen Gord's frustration that first day in the kitchens. With no reason to trust him, still Gord had tried to tell him that the keep larders remained all but bare because the villagers had nothing to spare. They had not even enough for themselves. Mags would lose one if not all her children before winter turned to spring.

In the months following his wedding, he and Gord had built a solid relationship, but William had reeled from one problem to the next. Putting out the fire in the barn, only to have a new one spring up in the henhouse. Alice, Sister Sunshine, even his own family had conspired to keep his eye from where it should have rested all along.

By God, this stopped now. "Cedric!"

"Aye, my lord."

"Ride hard for Tarnwych. I want Gord here as fast as you can get him. I do not care what he is doing."

"Aye, my lord." Cedric wheeled his horse and cantered away.

William motioned Rufus. "Let me see the rest of it."

It got worse in the village nearby. Oldsters, too ill and starved to rise from their matts. Children with hollow eyes and sunken bellies. Women wearing that dull resignation that comes from seeing your children's deaths looming irrevocably closer. And men, beaten by life and loss, unable to lift their heads and call themselves men.

"Pick a group of men," he said to Rufus. "Find out what the villagers need the most, and get it here. Get Mistress Ivy here to see what she can do."

"Aye, my lord." Rufus's eyes glistened and he turned his head away. "I will see it done."

"Everything, Rufus. Clothing, linens, food, implements, whatever they need. If you must chop firewood for them, do it."

"Aye, my lord."

"And when Gord gets here, have him make a list of repairs. I want it by sundown."

"Aye, my lord."

"Donnchadh."

"My lord?"

"Ride for The Crags. Tell your father how matters lie here, and see what help he can offer."

"Aye." Donnchadh scuffed the earth with his boot. "Only, I am as likely to return with more of my brothers."

"Every sodding one of them, if that is what it takes." William leaped onto Paladin's back. "I am going to find out how matters came to this sorry state."

Anger drove William back to Tarnwych. Each strike of Paladin's hooves on the ground driving his fury higher. A lord of a demesne had a responsibility to his people. They paid his taxes and fed the keep, and in exchange he provided his protection and his aid. Not all lords honored their duty, but for him to have become one of those lords made him want to empty his belly.

Attuned to William's mood, Paladin outstripped the other riders and arrived in the bailey in a shower of mud and sod.

Sir Arthur had raised his sons to honor their duty, shoulder their responsibilities. In one morning, William had become the sort of scavenging cur who fed off his people. Some part of his brain warned his anger lay with Sister Julianna, but she nestled safe in the convent now.

Amidst her ladies, Alice sat in a pool of wintery sunlight that burnished her hair to flame. The very picture of a chatelaine at her sewing, laughing and chatting with the keep women.

Whilst less than a mile hence, babes would not see their next birthing day.

She looked up as he strode forward, his heels ringing on the flags. Her smile of welcome died, replaced by a wary expression.

"Leave us."

Women snatched their sewing and scattered.

"William?" She rose, her embroidery clutched in one hand.

Here she sat, warm, fed and sheltered. He shoved his hands behind his back before he shook her. "Are you enjoying your morning, my lady?"

"Aye." Alice held up her scrap of fabric. "We were doing some mending, and sewing some...Did the hunt not go well?"

"It went well. Until a poacher nearly split my head in half with his arrow."

She stepped toward him, concern creasing her face. Her embroidery fluttered to the ground. "Are you hurt?"

"Step back, my lady." He did not trust the control he had on his anger. "I am well enough. At least I was well until I discovered why the poacher had fired on me."

"William, I do not understand."

"That may be." He clasped his hands together, battling to control the fury writhing within. "Ask me why the poacher fired at me."

Her chin came up, a tiny gesture of defiance he wanted to stamp out. "I do not like this game, William."

"I do not care, my lady. Ask me why." He stepped toward her and she backed up. Good. At least she had a God-given sense of self-preservation.

"Why did the poacher fire at you?" Her throat worked as she swallowed.

He frightened her. She needed a fright to shake her out of her life-long slumber. "He was starving." His boots touched her bliaut hemline. "Along with his wife and children, and every other soul in the village."

Alice averted her gaze and frowned. "Surely not. We send supplies from the castle through the harsh months."

"Do we?" Her innocence made him even angrier. How much

of her life did she spend closing her eyes to what happened about her? She was not a child anymore. As a grown woman she had duties, and she sat here and embroidered silly green swirls on white linen. "When was the last time you went to the village?"

"Sister did not—"

"When, Alice?"

She rubbed her hands on her bliaut. "A long time."

"Weeks?"

"Aye."

"Months?"

Her pretty face crinkled in confusion. "I do not—"

"Years?"

"Not years." Up came that defiant chin again. "I was last there..." Her eyes widened to sparkling green gems. Her shoulders slumped. "Surely not years."

"Years." William drove his point home. "You have not been there in years. Yet you have been chatelaine at Tarnwych since your marriage to William."

"I was not really chatelaine." She held her hands out to him in silent appeal for understanding.

He had none for her. She did not deserve his compassion whilst her people died of disease and hunger. Her complacency sickened him. "Nay, you were not chatelaine at all. It was too easy to let that wicked nun take charge of your life and the lives of everyone around you. You lived in your own private world, Alice, whilst your people"—he gripped her shoulders—"your people, not hers, suffered. They still suffer."

Tears turned her eyes brighter green. "I did not know."

"You know now." He dropped his grip. "What are you going to do about it?"

"What would you have me do? I know nothing of—"

"I would have you grow up, Alice. Become a woman I can respect."

She flinched as if struck, and tears glistened in her eyes. "What if I cannot become the woman you want me to?"

"Then, my lady, you are someone to whom I cannot be husband."

* * *

The churchyard was the worst. Alice went from grave to grave, some no better than a crude, wood-fashioned cross.

So many graves, scattered over the winter-brown grass like pockmarks.

Earth mounded beside the gaping maw of a fresh grave. Another soul to add to her guilt tally.

"My lady, we should return to the keep." Seamus trailed after her.

"Not yet."

After a lonely night she had risen early this morning and asked Seamus to bring her to the village. From hovel to hovel they had gone until Alice felt she would be sick.

William's anger made horrible sense in the face of the aching poverty all about her. She had left her people to die awful, painful deaths.

Work crews teamed like ants over three village dwellings. William already making his presence felt. Cart after cart rolled into the village from the castle, bringing barrels of dried meats and fruits, bales of linen, sacks of wheat and barley, and stacks of farming implements.

The villagers huddled in small groups and watched as if they had lost the will to take part in their resurrection. Everywhere she went the women's hostile stares tracked her. Faces that spoke of tragedies almost past bearing.

Alice met each stare, and pressed into her memory the knowledge of their suffering, the lashes her soul must bear for her apathy.

"Lady Alice?" An emaciated priest strode across the churchyard toward her. "I am Father Joseph."

Up in Tarnwych, Father Mark cowered in silence, whilst this

man bore the weight of his deathwatch on his stooped shoulders.

"So many." Alice motioned the crosses.

"Aye." Father Joseph folded his hands before him. "Last winter was especially harsh. Many fell ill and some who did survive the contagion succumbed during the summer."

"I had no idea." Pitiful and inadequate, she could not even look him in the eye.

"Aye." Father Joseph picked up a handful of earth and dribbled it through his fingers. "I tried to send messages to Father Mark, but..." He shrugged. "At least you are doing something now."

"It will not help these people."

"Nay." Father Joseph crossed himself. "They are with God now, and their suffering is eased. It is the living to whom we must turn our eyes."

"You have Sir William to thank for this." Alice motioned the increased activity about the village. "He saw in an instant what I have been blind to for years."

"God bless him." Father Joseph's voice choked with emotion, and he cleared his throat. "And God bless you, my lady. We cannot fix the past. We can only go forward."

If only it were that easy. Alice nodded and waved Seamus closer. "I am ready to return now."

"My lady." Father Joseph touched her arm. "I have found life rarely falls into clear paths of good and evil or right and wrong. We are human, and we live our lives in the gray area betwixt these things."

His words made no sense to Alice. All that she saw about her came from the evil of neglect and ignorance. There were none of Father Joseph's gray areas here. She nodded and led Seamus back to where he had tied their cart.

Back at Tarnwych she hunted down the one person who could help her.

Beatrice sat in the hall with Richard, Mathew, and Adam playing a game of stones beside her.

"Lady Beatrice. Could I speak with you?"

Beatrice stiffened, and her face tightened in anger. "I have spoken with William earlier this morning."

"Aye." She deserved all the anger Beatrice and William heaped on her head. "I need to ask you to help me with something."

Rising, Beatrice dusted off her skirts. "I do not know that I am inclined to help you, Lady Alice."

"Teach me how to be a chatelaine."

Beatrice stilled and stared at her. "What did you say?"

"I know what William must have told you. I only now returned from the village and have seen it for myself. Whatever he said cannot convey the horror of what goes on there. I cannot fix my past mistakes." She had Father Joseph to thank for that one. "But I can make sure I do not make them again."

"Let us walk." Beatrice motioned Martha to watch the children. She waited until they had moved far enough away for privacy. "How is it that you do not know how to care for a keep? My mother taught Faye and I from the time we were little."

"I was raised by Sister Julianna, and I do not believe she had any experience to pass on."

Beatrice toyed with the end of her flaxen braid. She stopped before a casement overlooking the moors. "I suppose not."

"I am not excusing what has happened." Alice swallowed past the dryness in her throat. "I want to learn."

"You know, Alice, I keep trying not to like you." With a sigh, Beatrice looked at her. "First there was you not wanting to allow us into Tarnwych, then the thing with Mathew, and now this. I look at all these actions and my head condemns you as a cold, miserable bitch."

Put before her like that, Alice could see how Beatrice would think thus, still...

"But here is my problem, Alice." Beatrice took her hand and led her to the casement seat. Drawing Alice beside her, she said, "I do like you, Alice. You are funny and sweet, and despite your dull dresses and that God-awful wimple, there is a sparkle to you that I want to draw closer to. I know William sees it, and I have struggled not to see it since I arrived here."

It sounded better than a cold, miserable bitch. "I have not worn the wimple for a while now."

"You see." Beatrice squeezed her hand. "That is exactly what I am talking about. You try. And here you are begging me for help when you know I am wroth with you."

Not begging, precisely. "Will you help me?"

"Aye, Alice." Beatrice patted her knee. "Why do you not tell me how much you know of a chatelaine's duties, and we can go from there."

Beatrice listened. It did not take long and when Alice fell silent she wanted to crawl beneath the casement seat and hide.

"Well." Beatrice dusted her hands and rose. "It seems we have a lot of ground to cover." She winked at Alice. "And I do like a quest."

* * *

Tapers guttered in their sockets as night gave way to first blush of morning. William rubbed his tired eyes and turned them back to Gord's list.

The list staggered him, and Gord kept adding to it. He had brought much wealth to Tarnwych, but not enough for this. The list spoke of years of neglect. Some of it went back to when Sir Ivo had charge of Tarnwych demesne. As much as he would relish doing so, he could not lay all of this at Sister Julianna's feet. Or Alice's.

He had stayed away from her throughout the night, his anger rising and falling in dizzying waves as he unpacked the bundle of wrongness at the heart of Tarnwych.

Aonghas might not agree to assist them, or perhaps might not be able to. It would mean another harsh winter for the villagers. He would wait for Donnchadh to return and maybe send to Calder for Gregory and Faye's aid. It stuck in his craw, but what was his damnable pride compared to the villager's lives?

Beatrice slid into place on the bench beside him. "Have you been at this all night?"

"Aye." He took a long draught of wine, but it tasted sour in his mouth and he grimaced.

"Hmm." Beatrice bent and examined Gord's list. She traced the parchment edge with her finger. "I spoke with Alice yesterday."

"Did you?" God spare him one of Beatrice's self-righteous harangues at Alice this morn. She could say nothing that he had not already voiced, in his head, at least.

"She came to me to help her understand the duties of chatelaine."

"A little late, is it not?" Women knew these things. They were taught from girlhood.

"You know, William, you are a horse's ass."

"Eh?"

"She told me what you said to her." Beatrice tossed her head.

Anger had him on his feet. "She has been telling tales of what should stay between us."

"Oh, sit down." Beatrice yanked his tunic sleeve. "She was defending you when she told me."

"Defending me?" He took his seat, feeling a bit like a horse's ass.

"Aye, I was telling her you had no right to say such things to her, and she was saying you were well within your rights."

"No right." He sprang to his feet again before he boxed his sister's ears. "Did you see that village? Did you?"

"Shut your cake hole." Beatrice stood and stuck her face closer. "She should have taken care of her people. I know that. But you are forgetting how she was raised. You want to be angry with someone and you have picked Alice."

"She deserves it."

"Nay, she does not." Beatrice rapped his forehead with her

knuckles. "You and I, we grew up with Mother and Father working as a team to keep their people cared for. Mother came from a well-run keep and she had Nurse with her to give her guidance. Who has guided Alice? That horrible old woman."

He wanted to tell Beatrice she was wrong, but she was not, and he threw himself back on the bench.

"And another thing." Always another thing with Beatrice. "Do you see Father constantly telling Mother what is wrong with her or what she needs to do better? Or Garrett carping on at me like I do not meet his expectations? I know without doubt you have never seen Gregory pointing out Faye's inadequacies. And do you know why?"

As much as he suspected he wouldn't want to know why, he knew she'd tell him anyway. "Enlighten me."

"Because they accept us for who and what we are. They do not love us for what we could be with a little help from them, but accept and love what we are."

"I do not love Alice."

"Then you are an even bigger horse's ass, because there is a lot about Alice to love."

* * *

William would wager his sword arm Beatrice accompanied him to the village the next day to vex him further. Barely lucid on a couple of hours of snatched sleep in the last couple of days, his patience with his younger sister wore thin.

Two days of Alice floating around the keep like a regretful ghost and Bea giving him meaningful looks had him ready to lop heads off.

The activity in the village eased his ruffled feathers. Tarnwych crews made slow but steady progress with the dwellings. Beneath a blustery wind, village men had taken up tools to hurry the process along. The icy bite of snow hung in the air, and roiled in the clouds above them. If they could get some of the hovels weather-tight, he would rest easier tonight.

Father Joseph stood on a roof crossbeam, his robe tucked into his belt, and called orders to the village men. The man went some way to restoring his faith in the clergy. For every Sister Julianna, a Father Joseph kept the good side of the scales balanced with the bad.

Beatrice dismounted and kept pace with him as he approached the nearest work area. "You have done well here."

The words filled him with a warm glow. "My thanks."

"Of course, none of us would have expected such of you." She huddled deeper into her furs.

And there went the glow, tossed into the stiff wind and carried away. Cursing himself as he said it, he still needed to know. "And why not?"

Beatrice laughed. "Come now, William. This is hardly your sort of thing."

"Caring for people?" He cared. He had always cared. At Anglesea he took his duties seriously, had built more than his fair share of barns, and harvested alongside the villagers.

"Taking things seriously." Beatrice tucked her hand into his arm. "Assuming responsibility for those around you. Normally you wait for Roger to lead, and you follow."

"That is not true." William disengaged his arm. Roger did not lead him anywhere but straight into their father's disapproval.

Beatrice gaped at him. "Do not be wroth, William. It was not meant to offend."

"Well, it does offend." He strode away from her. He took his responsibilities seriously. He did. He always assumed the mantle of duty and took control of a situation. All right, when Bea had done her crazy London jaunt, he had made the decision to ride for home. Nay, Father had made that decision. All right then, Faye. When young Simon went missing. He had given Faye the knife. After Faye had decided to pursue her son.

Damn sisters. Always pointing out a man's faults and rubbing his nose in it. "We have all changed."

"Indeed, we have." Beatrice pinched his arm. "Some of us for the better."

"Riders coming!" The call came from Father Joseph.

Work stopped and men turned toward the fast-moving party coming across the moors.

William pulled his sword free. Most of his men were armed only with lathes and hammers, but the riders would not find them untrained. He had done that. Let Beatrice remark on that. "Can you see who it is?"

Father Joseph shaded his eyes and squinted. "Aonghas the Red," he said. "And he brings a large party with him."

William released his sword. Wily as a fox, but Aonghas would not make war with his sons on the opposing side. William motioned the work crews. "Get back to work."

Aonghas slowed his horse as he entered the village. "William."

"Aonghas."

Aonghas turned in his saddle and took a long, slow look all about him. "Well, this is a sorry sight."

As much as it galled William to admit it, Aonghas had a valid point. "Aye."

"I knew Dunstan and that blasted nun were up to no good." Aonghas dismounted and swaggered to him. "Word reached me over the years of how matters lay here."

"It was not your land to do aught about it."

"True." Aonghas's step lost some of its jaunty twitch. "But up here, we care for our own, and we do not take the meat from another man's table."

Not an apology for Aonghas's poaching but near enough, and William nodded.

"Which is why I offer you my help." Aonghas toed aside a piece of rotting lumber thrown there by the work crew.

"What did you bring me?"

"Strong backs." Aonghas clapped him on the shoulder. For

such a small man, he packed a wallop decent enough to send William forward a step. "Found a few of those lying about my hall growing fat and thought I would bring them over."

The rest of Aonghas's party had dismounted and stood beside their horses. Some of them bore a strong resemblance to their sire.

Donnchadh stood to the side, his fist around the collar of a filthy, gangly boy. William felt sure he had seen the lad before.

"More sons?" William raised his brow at Aonghas. In truth, Aonghas's boys had proved somewhat of a blessing. Loud, a bit unmannerly, and inclined to question orders, but they had grown into good fighters and did not quibble with picking up the axe when work needed doing. Aonghas had raised them well. "I will take them. They can stay once the village is repaired."

Aonghas's shoulders drooped. "Now, William, you take all the sport out of it when you roll over like a thirty-year-old virgin."

Beatrice snorted a laugh from behind him.

Aonghas glanced behind at Beatrice, stilled, and leered. "And who might this be?"

"Aonghas," William said through gritted teeth. "May I present my sister, Lady Beatrice."

"Ah." Aonghas strutted past him and bowed low to Beatrice. "A pretty name for the prettiest flower in all of the kingdom."

"My married sister."

Aonghas rubbed his belly. "Happily married?"

"Aye."

"A blow indeed." Aonghas raised Beatrice's hand to his lips. "But if that should change, my lady, know that you have a true heart at your pretty feet up here in the north."

Beatrice giggled. Giggled!

William took savage satisfaction in picturing what Garrett would do to Aonghas if he were here.

"And how many women is that heart promised to?" Beatrice had his measure.

"A small detail." Aonghas placed Bea's hand upon his arm.

"Now, if you are Beatrice, then I have a lad with me who claims you will be happy to see him."

"Newt?" Beatrice peered at the lad still in Donnchadh's clutches. "Is that you?"

The gutter snipe Beatrice had befriended on her trip to London. Come to think on it, the lad had played a role in Faye's adventure as well. "What is he doing here?"

"Let me go." Newt wrenched at Donnchadh's hold. The bigger man opened his hand and Newt's struggles sent him staggering forward. "Fine welcome Newt gets for coming all this way on a deed of mercy."

"You must have grown two feet." Beatrice looked the boy up and down with a maternal air. "You are near my height."

Newt adjusted his filthy tunic. "Same thing as Lady Faye said, and then she gave me new raiment."

Newt's tunic and braies hardly qualified as "raiment," but someone had educated the lad. "You saw Faye? Is she well?"

"Aye." Newt pressed his shoulders back. "Has a new baby and all."

"Oh." Beatrice clapped her hands in delight. "What did she have?"

"A baby." Newt pulled a face at her.

"Boy or girl?" That expression Newt pulled made a man itch to cuff him.

"Girl." Newt hawked and spat. "They plan to name her Elizabeth, Bess for short. Only they are waiting for people to get better at Anglesea."

"I wish I could see her." Beatrice's teary whisper tugged at William's heart. The distance between them and family yawned at times like this.

"I came up here with news." Newt puffed out his chest. "I was sent by that rude old Nurse woman to tell you Lady Mary is recovered."

Beatrice gave a cry of delight and hugged Newt.

William would never hug the smelly scoundrel, but the news he brought sweetened his day. His mother would grow stronger.

"Nurse said to tell you not to come home yet, though. She wants to be sure the outbreak is over. Said she would send for you when it was safe."

"Any news of Tom?"

Newt dropped his gaze to the floor. "He still ails."

Age had not improved the lad's looks any. His ears still stuck out the side of his head, and his ratty features now wore a smattering of blemishes. He would grow tall, though, with those hammers sticking out his sleeves and the big trenchers at the end of his legs.

Beatrice nodded, her face saddened again. "I will tell Ivy. Thank you, Newt. You were kind to come all this way and tell us."

Newt looked alarmed. "It were not kind. You and your family owe me a sack load of favors that you cannot very well deliver if the lot of you are dead."

Chapter Twenty-Three

Alice caressed the velvet. Such beautiful fabrics, and she had no notion how to fashion them. Perhaps a woman in a gown made of these fabrics would not feel like such a dull, brown wren. Her husband might even think her pretty. Beatrice had suggested—if Beatrice's broad statements could be called suggestions—that perhaps a chatelaine should dress the part.

From where she lounged on Alice's bed, Beatrice propped herself onto her elbows. "Now that was a big sigh."

"Are you certain it is right, given what is happening in the village, for me to float around dressed as a queen?"

"Alice." Beatrice sat up with a groan. "We have been over this. You are the head of this demesne, and as such your appearance is noted. Besides, how will any of the village women benefit from you not wearing those silks?" She patted her hair into order. "Indeed, it might be considered wasteful letting them molder in that chest."

Beatrice had an answer for everything. Her reasoning sometimes needed a little growing accustomed to, but she had no lack of opinions.

"William does not walk about in sacking." Beatrice sniffed

and rearranged the pillows behind her back. "He is a lord. He looks like a lord and he behaves like one. It would only be wrong if you dressed yourself sumptuously and refused to provide for Tarnwych folk. As that is being addressed..." Beatrice shrugged.

"I think you are wise to consider your people." Crouched beside her, Ivy squeezed Alice's shoulder. "It speaks well of your compassion. But I do agree with Beatrice."

"Let us make it so my brother barely knows you when he returns." With a smirk Beatrice rolled to her feet. "We shall knock him down a peg or two."

"I do not think we will manage that." No matter how lovely the fabric, she did not aim quite so high. Still, to have him look at her for the tiniest of moments...

"Why not?" Beatrice dipped into the chest and pulled forth a swathe of midnight-blue velvet. "He deserves it for disappearing like this with no word of what he is about. You need to curb him of that habit, Alice."

Aye, but she would have to get him to speak with her first. William had kept his distance since he had harangued her in the hall. Her logic argued he was busy and working hard to prepare the village for the onset of winter. This morning they had woken to frozen ground covered in a light dusting of snow. Her heart doubted.

The velvet brushed soft and luxurious beneath her fingers.

"This will look perfect with your hair." Ivy draped the fabric over her shoulder.

"See what it does for her complexion." On a happy laugh, Beatrice turned her toward the looking metal.

Alice pulled a face at her reflection. She looked like a short, plain woman with a beautiful shawl.

"I think someone is having some difficulty." Over her head, Beatrice winked at Ivy. "Perhaps we should help her and show her."

"I think you could be right." Ivy smiled, though her eyes bore sad shadows. "It needs to fit close to her body."

On a nod, Beatrice spread the velvet taut over Alice's breasts and hips. "We definitely need to show off these."

Alice's face burned as they discussed her. "I do not know how to make a dress."

"What?" Both women gaped at her.

"Aye, you do." Ivy adjusted the lay of the velvet at her waist. "I saw you at your embroidery in the hall."

"I can embroider." Yet another shortcoming to confess. "Sister had me help with the altar cloth, but Martha sewed all my other things."

"That explains it." Beatrice laid Alice's braid against the velvet. "Martha is a sweet woman, but she should be kept away from a needle and thread. Just what did Sister teach you?"

"Um…I can pray. And deliver penance. Also supplicate myself for hours on end."

Beatrice cupped her shoulders and stared at Alice's reflection over her shoulder. "I am sure you can. We will make you a new bliaut together, and Ivy and I will show you." She pulled a face. "Only be sure to listen closely to Ivy, because I am not that skilled."

Ivy chuckled. "True enough. Now, what have we in that chest for a new chemise?"

* * *

Alice had three bliauts to choose from. Three! The sapphire velvet, a yellow samite, and a green silk. Also, Ivy and Beatrice had insisted on making her another four daytime bliauts, in wools so soft they felt near as wondrous as silk. It had taken them four days to create this bounty.

She also had a new chemise made of silk. Who had ever heard of such a thing? Sinfully soft, the silk caressed her skin, all over. A woman in silk could imagine all kinds of wicked games. A woman in silk could have more courage than a woman in coarse linen. Brave enough to win her husband back.

Beatrice said she had wiles. Alice peered at her reflection in the looking metal. The silk clung to the taut peak of her breasts and created interesting shadows at the apex of her thighs. Perhaps she did at that.

She went back to the bed and studied her choices. Definitely, the blue with its lustrous sheen that clung to her curves. Curves, her newest discovery. She had them, and she liked them.

Alice slipped the blue velvet on.

"Alice?" Ivy knocked at the door. "May I come in?"

"Aye."

Ivy poked her head around the door. "Ah, I was hoping you would choose that one. Now turn about and I will fasten your laces."

"Is it not too fine for a simple keep dinner?"

"Nay." Ivy turned her about. "And William rode in a little earlier."

"William?" Alice's belly tightened. What would he think of her new dress? Would he even look at her or continue looking past her?

Ivy nodded and smiled her sadness-tinged smile. "There is no better time to show off your new finery."

Alice sucked in a breath as Ivy applied herself to the laces. For a tiny woman, she had remarkable strength. "Do you think he will like it?"

"Nay, nay, nay." Beatrice sashayed into the chamber, looking regal in garnet-red. "That is not the question you should be asking." She put her hands on her hips. "You should be asking how much he will like it."

Ivy giggled. "Indeed! Will he lose the power of speech, or will he scoop you up and carry you away?"

"Argh!" Beatrice made a retching noise. "William is my brother, just...ergh!"

Ivy fetched the gold and sapphire girdle and clasped it about Alice's hips. Then she and Beatrice stood back and surveyed Alice with smug smiles.

"Perfect." Beatrice clapped her hands. "I came here to stop you from slinking into the hall like a thief." She rested her hand on Alice's shoulder. "You have made your amends, Alice, done the best you could to fix what was broken. No more timid Alice waiting for approval. Aye?"

"Perhaps." Beatrice frowned and Alice laughed. "Aye."

"That is better." Beatrice looped her hand through Alice's arms. "Come along. Let us make our entrance."

* * *

Nothing. Alice jabbed her knife into a slice of meat. No reaction, not a flicker, not a wince, nothing. William had stridden into the hall, bowed to her, and taken his seat. Now he sat beside her guzzling wine and shoving meat in his face.

Not that William ever did anything so inelegant as guzzling or shoving, but he paid no attention to her.

Beatrice glared at the back of William's head and jabbed her eating dagger into her meat.

"Did you have a successful trip?" Wherever he had disappeared to this time.

"In part." William gave her a polite smile, which Alice wanted to slap off his face. His smile went past a person as if she did not exist. "I will speak to you about it. Later."

"I paid a visit to the village today."

"Indeed."

"Aye. They are making good progress."

"Good."

There perished her final attempt at conversation. If he did not wish to speak with her, he could rot in his silence.

"I think I will retire." Alice rose and William rose with her.

"I will see you there later." He assisted her over the bench. "I will wash my travel dirt away first."

"Shall I call for your bath?"

"Nay, I will use the bathing room in the barracks."

In her chamber, Alice ripped the girdle from her hips. Only the knowledge of how hard Ivy and Beatrice had worked on her bliaut gentled her hand. For how long did William intend to punish her with his silence? She had tried to right her wrongs. Everything he asked of her, she did. He did not care for her wimple—no more wimple. He wanted her to ride, and Alice rode. Had she not made every effort with Mathew and her fear? Aye, she had lived her life in a sort of half-sleep, but she tried to wake. She had even agreed to Sister returning to the convent.

The stupid laces proved hard to reach, no matter how far she bent her arms back.

Naive of her to think a pretty dress would soothe his ire. For one magical moment, she had thought he would see the dress for what it represented, an effort on her part to do better. Be a better chatelaine and wife. Every day she visited the village and made sure his instructions were carried out. In William's absence, Gord had come to her with problems as they arose. Assisted by Beatrice's experience, she had solved them, too. Not waited for William's return.

She may as well have had Gord write him a list and set it before him.

The tight bliaut arms prevented her from raising her arms and attacking the laces from above, and she slumped onto the bed. She would have to wait here for someone to assist her. Or she could find Ivy and have a group grumble whilst she did.

As Alice reached the door, it opened.

Hair still wet from his bath, chemise draped over his shoulder, William entered.

It was not fair that his naked chest should stop her in her tracks and render her speechless. His absence from their bed had nagged at her.

"Are you going somewhere?" Clearly, he had no trouble forming words.

"I was going to get Ivy's assistance. To unlace me."

"Here." He spun her about. "I can unlace you."

"Nay I—"

"Alice." His deft fingers got to work. "How much do you know of Sister Julianna's life before she came here?"

He wanted to speak of Sister, now? They had no end of other topics to choose from. First off, the screaming pit of silence between them. "Not much. She never spoke of it."

"Did she ever mention a child?"

"Child?" Alice turned and stared at him.

He spun her about again. "I am not done unlacing. Aye, a child."

"Nay."

"And there was never a child with you and Sister Julianna at Yarborough?"

"What are you asking?"

"Done." William slid the bliaut from her shoulders. The warm caress of his calloused palms on her shoulders sent shivers snaking through Alice. Just one innocent touch from William and her knees turned to pudding.

He stilled. Then, his fingers slid over the neck opening of her chemise. "Alice?"

"Aye." The deep, throaty throb of his voice brought her skin to prickling life.

"Did I tell you what a pretty dress this is?"

"Nay, you did not."

He pressed closer to her back, heat coming off him and wrapping about her. "You looked lovely in it, but I am afraid I am going to have to remove it from you now."

"I did not think you had noticed." A mortifying note of peevishness entered her voice.

"I noticed." William stroked the line of her shoulders and slid his fingers into the hair at her nape. "The moment I walked into the hall. How boorish of me not to have said something sooner."

"I thought much the same."

He chuckled, a low sound vibrating from his chest through her back. "I also noticed the silk sleeves of your chemise beneath. I spent a long time wondering how it would look without the bliaut."

"You might have said something."

"You are wroth with me." He kissed the sensitive spot beneath her ear.

"Na—" William insisted that in this chamber they should have truth between them. And so she would give him truth. "Aye, I am wroth. I have tried to do as you asked since you came to Tarnwych. Tried to be the sort of wife you desired."

He nibbled at her ear. "Aye, you have. And I thank you for it."

Well, that was better. "Did you really like my dress?"

"Very much." He eased the bliaut down and pushed it from her hips. "I liked it very much."

Velvet sighed to the floor, and Alice leaned back the tiniest bit closer to the furnace of William.

He gripped her hips. "I am a terrible husband, am I not?"

"Maybe not terrible." Silk slid beneath his hands as he stroked it over her hips. "Just inattentive. And you have been so angry with me."

"Strangely, I seem to have forgotten why I was wroth." Wicked hands eased up her belly, on a slow trail toward her breasts. Silk caressed her jutting nipples, hardening them further.

"You were wroth because I…"

He cupped her breasts, the silk no barrier for the heat of his hands. "I do not want to talk about that now, Alice." He thumbed her aching nipples and she arched into his hands. It seemed far too many days since he had placed his hands on her. "There will be plenty of time for talk. After."

"William." She had something she needed to say, something she had thought much on, if he would stop caressing her she could order her thoughts. "I know you do not wish to talk, but I do."

"Later."

"Nay. Now."

He kissed down her neck to her shoulder.

Her thoughts grew muddled and she forced them into order. "You cannot correct me like a child in the hall and then expect a woman in your bedchamber."

He tensed, and his hands dropped from her breasts. "Are you telling me nay?"

"I am saying I need to be your wife throughout the keep. Speak to me, William, tell me when something angers you or you feel I have been remiss in my duties. I may have led a strange life, but I am not short on understanding."

He laughed softly. "I did insist on you speaking your mind."

"Aye, you did."

"In this, you are right. I was angry about the villagers, and I took that out on you. For this, and for the other times I have treated you without respect, I beg your pardon."

"I accept your apology." She didn't mean for him to stop the kissing altogether, and she tugged his head closer. "May I now say that your mouth would be better employed elsewhere, my lord?"

"Here." He chuckled, and nipped her shoulder.

"Aye." His mouth had magical properties, the way it seared her skin and made her ache for him.

"And here." His hands returned to her breasts "How about here?"

"Aye." Alice turned in his arms, every inch of her strung tighter than a bow.

His mouth tormented her, wet and warm through the chemise. The fabric clung to her where he sucked. He raised his head. "As pretty as it looks, it will also have to go."

Grabbing fistfuls of her chemise, he pulled it over her head. "Alice." His blue gaze devoured her. "There is no bliaut lovely enough to rival this."

Alice stood still for his study. His hot gaze made her feel alive. Impatiently she loosened the chord and his braies slid to the floor. His rod stood proud and full for her.

"Did you miss me, Alice?" He slid his hand between her legs.

His fingers parted her wet folds and penetrated her where she ached the worst. "I see that you did."

"Aye." She opened her thighs, needing what he offered and more.

"I missed you, too." He thumbed the spot that made her moan and grab for his shoulders. "Let me show you how much."

"Please." Alice moved with the rhythm of his hand. So close, completion hovered near and drove her hips forward. He worked his hand across her woman's flesh, skilled and deadly. He stroked her higher and higher, attuned to the motions she made.

"And that was before you wore a beautiful dress, and your hair unbound."

She had trouble concentrating on his words. "You do not like the dress."

"I like the dress fine." He clasped her nape and dragged her mouth to his. "But I like you better. You have no need to dress up for me, Alice. You enter a room and make me hard with wanting you."

His words drove her over the edge, and she shattered on a loud cry.

He swallowed her sounds in a kiss. Devastating and hungry, it swept through her. In his kiss lay the truth of his wanting, and Alice melted into it.

"Let me love you, Alice."

"Aye." *Love me, William. Love me with all that you are.*

Chapter Twenty-Four

"I guess the dress appealed to William." Ivy chortled and gave Alice a nudge.

Good Lord, could the entire keep see how long and hard she and William had loved last night?

"If her glowing cheeks did not tell the story, the noise that kept me up certainly did." Beatrice shuddered and dug her spoon into her pottage. "I am fond of you, Alice, and I love my brother, but I think it is time for us all to go home." She added more honey to her bowl. "Or for you and William to keep your voices down."

Ivy bumped Beatrice's shoulder. "You are merely out of sorts because you miss that handsome husband of yours."

"True enough." Beatrice sighed as she stirred. "How much longer do you think it will be before we can go home?"

Ivy's face grew shadowed. "I am not sure."

"My lady." Seamus beckoned her from the doorway to the bailey. "Lady Alice, might I have a quick word?"

Alice rose and followed the boy out the hall, keenly aware of Beatrice and Ivy watching her. "What is it, Seamus?"

Seamus examined the passage before he slid further into the

shadows and motioned her to follow. "She said I must only speak to you, my lady. To be sure you were alone."

"She?"

He ducked his head. "I would not have done it, except she said she would call down God's vengeance on my head."

A nasty feeling wriggled through Alice.

"And she is a Holy Sister, my lady. I reckon if anyone can call God down on you, she can."

Gripping Seamus by the arm, Alice forced his frightened babble to a halt. "Slow down, Seamus, and tell me from the beginning."

Seamus took a deep breath. "I was on the moor, my lady, checking the snares for rabbits. I always do that because my brothers say I am not old enough to go on the hunt."

"And then what happened?"

"Well, you know where the trees grow a little thicker, by the tarn?" Seamus wiped his palms on his tunic.

"Aye?"

"It is the best place for snares, because the rabbits think they are safe from foxes in the thicket."

"Aye, Seamus." She needed patience. Screaming at Seamus to get on with it would only frighten him more. Her mind whirled. As much as she knew to her core that it was Sister Julianna, her brain tried to reason the dread away. Sister bided safe with the nuns at St. Stephen's.

He leaned closer to her. "She came upon me so sudden, I did not see her at first."

"Who came upon you?"

"Sister Julianna, Lady Alice. And at first I thought it could not be her, that she was some sort of haunt, because I saw her leave that day with the others."

She had left with the others. Alice had stood in the bailey and watched her go, waved her on her way. Sister had sat in the cart beside the Prioress and never turned as they cleared the gate. Surely, the Prioress would have sent word if she were missing?

"She is in the woods?"

"Aye, my lady. Upstream a ways, there is an old shepherd's croft and she has taken shelter there." Seamus's eyes widened. "She said I had to come and find you. I was to tell you to bring food."

* * *

Alice rummaged through the quiet larder, cursing her stupidity.

Beside the banked kitchen hearth, Cook and Walter slept bathed in the ruddy glow of the coals. Soft snores rose from their bundled forms. She slipped into the kitchen with ease, waiting and half-wishing with every step for someone to hail her and stop her.

The wise course would be to tell William. It would only go badly for her if she did not and he discovered what she planned. She'd had her mind made up to tell him after dinner. Then William had arrived in their chamber in a sportive mood, and conversation had fled from her thoughts.

Cook left a few provisions out for nightly kitchen raids.

Alice snatched a couple of loaves of bread, a wheel of cheese, and some winter apples and stuffed them into her sack. Going to Sister like a thief had to be one of the stupidest things she had ever done. But she did it anyway. Because she felt some lingering loyalty for the woman who had raised her? Partly, but more because she wanted to make this go away without William having to involve himself.

Wonderful peace lay between them now. Her courses had still not come, and the growing conviction she carried their child made this time sweeter. Perhaps if she could see Sister, speak with her, she could make her see reason. If Sister went away, and without notice, perhaps Alice could avoid the nastiness that followed Sister.

From the stores beside the larder, she pulled an old blanket and pushed it into her sack. A couple of tapers followed, and a flint. Who knew what she would find when she reached Sister.

Through the kitchen door, she crept into the still inner bailey. Cold night air stole her breath. On the walls, the sentry's torches flickered as they moved. Before William, the walls had stayed dark. Some part of her still hoped one of the guards might see her and call out. Then she could shut her nagging conscience up and return to her bed, knowing she had failed.

Then she would tell William.

Alice clung to the walls as she made her way around the bailey to the gate leading to the outer bailey. From the stables, horses whiskered and stamped. Low voices murmured to each other from the barracks. She inched past and into the outer bailey.

William would be so angry. She had made him angry so many times in their short marriage. His last accusation nestled in her breast with the sting of truth. Too often she had turned her head and let others take charge. Not this night. She would assume responsibility for Sister.

Alice stopped, her hand on the latch for the postern gate. Once she went through that gate, she set her course.

Out there, in the dark and the cold, Sister waited, and she had only recently recovered from her illness.

Nay, she would go to her. Persuade her to return to Tarnwych and in the morning they could send for the Prioress. Or better yet, take Sister to St. Stephen's and make sure she stayed put this time.

Oiled hinges opened the postern gate onto the moor.

By night, dark shadows made secret shapes on the moor, and she tripped over something and fell on the icy ground. Her sack slipped from her hand and rolled away. Alice scrabbled after it and stayed crouched low to the ground.

William had trained the sentries well, but the moon hid behind heavy-laden snow clouds.

As she moved through the dark, her eyes grew surer and she quickened her pace. The dark shape to her left must be the rocks she could see from her casement.

The furs William had given her kept the worst chill off her body, but yesterday's small snowfall seeped through her boots and chilled her feet. Sister risked freezing to death if she sheltered close to the tarn. Wind came off the water there with a dagger-sharp cut of ice.

Surely, the river lay close now. Distances confused her in the dark, and Alice took a moment to find her place. There, thick and hulking, rose the towers of Tarnwych. She went the right way.

Water whispered to her long before the thin glitter of the river in the moonlight peeped between the trees. Turning left, she followed its course upstream. As she moved closer to the water, the chill deepened, and Alice huddled into her furs. Sister had left with nothing more than her wool cloak. Alice should have thought to bring another.

"There you are." A scream caught in Alice's throat as a thin form appeared out of the dark.

"Sister?"

"Aye." Sister gripped her arm and tugged. "Come. I have been waiting outside for you."

"I came as soon as I could." Fool she for coming at all.

"I prayed for you." Sister ducked around the ghostly tree trunks. "I prayed you would see the truth and come to me. God has answered my prayers."

Alice felt sure God had very little to do with this. "I came to take you back to the keep with me."

"Whist, Alice." Sister's fingers dug into her wrist. Her breath made clouds in the air about her head. "Do not be stupid and come along. Anyone could be out here. They are looking for me, you know? I can feel them. They bring their dogs with them."

"St. Stephen's keeps hunting hounds?"

"I did not see them, but I know they are there."

Limned by the sparse moonlight, the hut came into view between the trees.

With a loud creak, the door opened and Sister pulled her inside. "Did you bring tapers?"

"Aye."

"Light them."

Alice's hands shook with cold, and it took several strikes to raise a spark. In the taper's dim light, the hovel looked long since deserted. Leaves and branches littered the floor from where one part of the roof had collapsed. The walls did little to ward off the cold.

"You should light a fire." Alice's teeth chattered, and she rubbed her hands together for warmth.

"I cannot light a fire." Sister turned to her. "They will see it. They hunt me."

Her first good look at Sister shocked Alice speechless. Hair matted and snarled, writhed about her head like a nest of vipers. Her face appeared gaunter beneath the layers of grime. She still wore her habit, but it was torn in places and soiled. Sister's eyes shocked Alice the most. Alice could not drag her stare away. If not completely mad, Sister teetered close to the edge of the abyss. Her gaze darted about, burning fever-bright.

"I brought food." Alice held up her sack.

Sister scuttled forward and snatched it from her. Like an animal, she squatted on the floor and opened the sack.

"Sister, you must come back with me. You cannot live like this."

"Nay." Sister scrabbled through the sack. "If I go back with you they will send me to that place."

"St. Stephen's." Alice crouched beside her.

Sister tore into the bread with her teeth. "It is filled with whores and adulterers."

"It is an Abbey, Sister, surely not."

"You know nothing." Sister huddled over her bread. "You know nothing about those places and the sin behind their walls. But I know." She took more mouthfuls of bread. "I know." Crumbs sprayed from her mouth, and Alice inched away from her. "Because I know their secrets, they have to kill me."

There did not seem any point in carrying the conversation

further down that road. "I promise William will not send you back to St. Stephen's." But clearly Sister needed to go somewhere. The creature in front of her had drifted beyond reason. It hurt to see her thus.

"William." Sister cackled and grabbed the wheel of cheese. Digging her dirt-encrusted fingers through the rind, she pulled out a handful. "William the fornicator. He took my Alice." She looked up, her gaze sharp. "He turned my Alice against me with his lewd ways, and his stiff man's rod."

Alice had never heard Sister refer to...that. She scuttled further away from Sister, wanting to put distance between herself and the addled stranger spitting cheese from her venom-thinned lips.

"He sticks it in her, again and again and again. Spills his seed and sin deep inside her until she is rotten from it. Rotten and stinking of him and the devil."

Alice needed to leave here. She rose. Coming here tonight had been a worse mistake than she had first thought. Reason would not prevail here. The creature cackling through her meal in the hut was not Sister. Not the Sister she had known, anyway.

Had the nuns coming to take her back driven her mad, or had it lain inside her, coiled and waiting to appear? Flashes of incidents tumbled through Alice's mind. Rages that would shake Tarnwych for days. Not often, but vicious enough to send everyone running. Days spent on her knees in the chapel as Sister ranted Bible verses at her and implored her to repent.

Dear God. Sister had not grown mad. She had always been mad.

Sister stood and stalked Alice. "What are you doing?"

"I must return to the keep. They will note my absence."

"You lie." Sister closed on her.

Alice sprang back. The hut rattled as her back jammed into the wall. "Nay, Sister. I must return but I will be back." With William and an army if that was what she needed.

"You want them to kill me."

"Nay, Sister. I would never want that."

Kill.

The hut shimmered and dipped about Alice and she lost her bearings. Beneath her nails, the wood wall provided her only anchor.

Kill him. Sister screamed in her mind. Clear as if it happened right now. *Kill the abomination before he soils my Alice.*

Alice's head spun, she could not draw a decent breath.

The boy. The one like Mathew, but not Mathew. A different boy. A boy who had lived at Yarborough. *Play, Alice, play.* Then gone.

Vanished into a deep hole in her memory, but now his face rose clear as day and stared at her through his heavy-lidded eyes. *Kill him!*

So much blood. Warm and sticky, it clung to her hair and her face. Blood, red and thick, as it pooled around the boy's head. His eyes, open and staring, and even then she had known he was dead. Like the rabbits that lay on the kitchen table before Cook skinned them.

Sour bile stung Alice's mouth.

Sister watched her, head cocked as if she saw what Alice saw. "Come back soon, and we will make a plan to escape."

"Aye, Sister." Alice's hand shook on the latch. Flinging open the door, she fell into the night.

Dear God, what had she remembered?

Mind whirling, Alice stumbled to the keep. Rocks and low vegetation caught her feet and tangled them. The door had opened in her mind and she could not shut it, did not want to shut it as the images blasted her.

The boy had lived with Sister at Yarborough. Then one day he had disappeared and left a gaping hole in her memory. Strange, quiet, and existing on the outskirts of keep life, he had intrigued her and frightened her. Sister told her never to go near him.

Evil.

Abomination.

Until that day she had, and they had played for hours until it went tragically wrong. She could not have been more than three when it happened. He had held her above the water in a game her childish mind could not grasp. Her screams had brought the castle folk running, and then...Sister shrieking for the boy to die, and her father's sword, raised in one deadly flash.

"My lady?" A gate guard stepped into her path. "Are you ill, my lady?"

She shook her head. But she was ill, sick to her stomach.

The quiet bailey mocked the storm within her. Her frozen fingers fumbled on the door latch. Heavy wood doors resisted her attempt to push them open and Alice shoved her full weight into them. Warm air rushed from the hall hearths, and her extremities prickled and sparked as they thawed.

"Alice?" Beatrice wove into view. Face creased in a frown, she looked at Alice and then beyond her to the still-open door. "Have you been out?"

"Aye." Rusty as if forced from the depths of her, Alice managed a reply.

"But where can you have been?"

William. Alice needed to get to William. In his arms she might find peace. "Moors."

"Why would you go to the moors? In the middle of the night?"

She stumbled past Beatrice to the stairs. "I needed air."

"But..."

Alice took the stairs at a run. Her legs shook but William, and respite, lay in her bed, and she wished she could fly to him. She had to tell him all of it. Sister was quite mad, and she had been for all the years Alice had grown up with her. Sister had set her thoughts, molded Alice's opinions, and made her believe the fevered lies of a lunatic. All these years, lies and mistruths cloaked one within the other—until William came and brought light into the shadows.

She slid into their chamber and removed her old bliaut.

William had warmed the bed. He murmured and wrapped his arms around her.

Tears filled her eyes and snaked onto the pillow. Safe.

* * *

Alice woke with her belly heaving. She barely made it to the basin before her stomach repelled its entire contents.

"Alice?" William's groggy voice filled with concern.

Alice waved her hand to reassure him, and lost the battle again.

"Are you ill?"

Nay, she always vomited for the pleasure of it. Dear God, she had no words, not a one for how wretched she felt. Her stomach clenched, and there she went again.

"Sweeting." William rushed to her side as another spasm wrenched through her. "Shall I fetch Ivy?"

Alice shook her head. She did not want him near her in her soiled state. She must smell appalling.

William smoothed her hair back and held it in a bunch at her nape. "God's teeth." His voice sounded weak. "I've seen men after days in a war camp do better than this."

"William?"

"Aye?"

"Please be quiet."

"Aye, sweeting." Long, soothing strokes ran from her nape to her waist. "Cedric!"

His bellow made her jump, which reminded her stomach it had not settled. At this rate she would lose all her innards. Had yesterday's meat been spoiled?

William appeared a touch green.

The door crashed open and Cedric rushed in. "Aye, my lord."

"Get Mistress Ivy. Tell her my lady is ill."

"Lady Alice is ill?"

He frowned at her, concern in his eyes.

Then Alice faced the noxious mess in the basin again. Death take her now. Her legs sagged, and William caught her about the waist.

"There now." He leaned her against his chest and dipped a washcloth in the water ewer. "Ivy will find what ails you."

She pressed her face into the heavenly cool of the cloth. "You should not see me thus."

"Really?" William stroked the cloth over her forehead and cheek. "And when should I see you? When you are gowned and perfumed and ready to go a-Maying?"

How anyone could make her laugh at this time, she knew not, but she did.

"I am sure there will be many days when you will see me squalling like a wounded bull over a stubbed toe."

Alice rested her forehead against his strong chest. "I feel horrible."

"Never mind, sweeting." He bent and picked her up.

Alice's stomach mounted a protest and she screeched, "William."

He dropped her smartly to her feet and stepped back.

When she was done, he helped her back to the bed with an arm about her waist.

Ivy followed her discreet knock into the chamber. "Cedric said Alice was ill."

"Aye." William pushed a hand through his hair. "She has been going at it like a camp follower."

She lay down. Her stomach felt more settled. "I am sure I am fine."

"See to her." William's hair stood about his head.

"I will." Ivy pushed him toward the door. "Now, out you go. Have a bath brought up. I am sure she will feel a lot better after she smells better."

Ivy asked a few questions and listened to Alice's responses with her quiet, cool air. "You have not told William yet, have you?"

For a nasty moment she thought Ivy referred to Sister. She must tell William as soon as her stomach settled. Sister could not remain in the woods, a danger to herself and anybody who stumbled upon her. Then it hit her what Ivy meant. "About the…" Alice waved over her belly.

"Aye, about that."

And her morning's illness nearly made her laugh. "Is the sickness because of the baby?"

"I would wager so." Ivy sat on the edge of the bed, hands folded in her lap. "You have no fever or any other ailments to go with it. If I am right, you should feel much better shortly."

"Then this is normal for a woman carrying?" You could not live in a keep and not see what happened to other women in her condition.

Ivy shrugged. "Nurse would know better, but I believe most women experience some of this."

Alice touched her belly beneath the covers. If it meant she carried William's child, she would gladly bear the upset stomach. Well, perhaps not gladly, but she would bear it.

"Could you take any food? I have heard it helps."

The mere thought rippled through her on an uneasy shudder. "Nay."

"Perhaps later then. I will steep some root ginger for you to drink, and perhaps an apple."

"Ivy?" Alice clenched her teeth.

"Aye."

"Could you stop speaking of things I must swallow?"

Ivy rose and smoothed the covers about Alice. "You need to tell him, Alice. I have known William for a little while, but I know he does not like secrets."

Alice nodded. Fatigue swept over her. "I will tell him after I have rested."

"Good."

William entered, followed by an entourage bearing her bath.

Alice did not feel up to a bath, but William cajoled her into it.

With tear-bringing gentleness, he stripped her and placed her in the warm water. He even washed and braided her hair for her before putting her back to bed. All the while he spoke as he worked. Snippets of his life, his various boyhood illnesses and injuries.

Alice's jaw cracked on a mighty yawn as she sank into the bed's softness.

"Sleep, Alice." William kissed her forehead. "I will be right here when you wake."

When next Alice woke, fat, lazy snowflakes drifted outside the casement. New snow had a magical quality about it, in the way it quieted everything about it.

She sat up slowly, testing her stomach's willingness. William must have left.

She felt refreshed from her sleep. Indeed, she not only felt well, but hungry enough to devour an entire suckling pig. Quickly she dressed in one of her old bliauts. She welcomed the demise of the mud brown fabric. Soon Ivy and Beatrice would have her new bliauts ready for her. Perhaps just in time to let the seams out again.

Sister! It struck her midway down the stairs. Sister huddled beside the tarn in the deepening snow. Hurrying now, she went in search of William.

Beatrice, Ivy, and the boys clustered about the hall hearth. Little Adam made a great game of tangling himself in yarn skeins as his mother, and Ivy sewed.

"Feeling better?" Beatrice smirked at her.

Ivy stayed bent over her sewing.

"Ivy told you."

"Told me what?" At feigning innocent, Beatrice had no talent. She must have thought so too, because she scrunched her nose and laughed. "Aye, she did. William will be delighted when you tell him." She pointed at Alice. "And you are going to tell him soon, are you not, dear Alice?"

"Where is William?" She expected to see him when she woke.

"He had to leave." Beatrice rescued her sewing from Adam's grasping fingers. "The men reported some strange activity near the tarn this morning."

"Tarn?" It burst from her on a near shriek.

Beatrice and Ivy stared at her.

She might tell them, but then they would speak with William, and she wanted him to hear it from her first. She did not fancy the retelling of her night's foolishness second hand. "The tarn can be dangerous. I hope a village child did not wander too close."

Beatrice jabbed her needle into the cloth. "I am sure it is nothing."

"Could you eat?" Ivy folded her sewing and rose.

"Aye." She could eat her way through a barracks worth of food.

Beatrice chuckled. "I am exactly so when I carry. Losing my belly one moment and hungry the next. Fortunately, for most of us, it passes off before long."

Alice touched Adam's soft curls by her knee. "I would like it to be me who tells William."

Beatrice laid her hand on her heart. "Your secret is safe."

Ivy snorted and raised her eyebrow at Beatrice. "Only if she tells him soon."

"She will tell him." Beatrice shushed Ivy with her hand. "A woman needs to find her own time and words to do such a thing."

"There you are." William strode into the hall, his handsome face ruddy with cold. His smile was warm and intimate. No sign of having encountered aught untoward.

"Did you find anything?" Beatrice voiced the question Alice dared not ask.

"Nay, nothing." William pressed his cold face against Alice and kissed her cheek. "You look much better."

"I feel much better." Relief added extra warmth to her smile.

"There were signs that somebody has used the old crofter's hut recently, but they were gone when we got there. Probably some poor soul taking respite from their travels." He chafed his hands and held them out to the blaze. "It is cold out there," he said. "Cedric! Wine!"

"Aye, my lord."

"And warm it, Cedric."

"Aye, my lord."

Cedric's boots clumped on the floor, followed by a loud clatter. "Beg your pardon, my lord."

"He improves."

"You are rather cheerful today." Beatrice cocked her head and studied her brother.

"Indeed, I am." William bestowed a soft, sweet smile on Alice before warming his back at the fire. "I find the cold most bracing."

"That is not what you said when you arrived here." Alice still giggled at William stomping around their bedchamber grousing about the cold.

"Indeed." He winked. "That was before I discovered what a warm welcome Tarnwych really offers."

"Dear God, William." Beatrice clapped her hands over her ears. "You will upset my stomach if you continue."

* * *

Alice preceded William to their bedchamber to change for the evening meal. From the twinkle in his eyes, she could look forward to returning very late to table.

He shut the door behind them and braced his back against it. Fine perspiration gleamed on his forehead. Despite William's eagerness for bed sport, they must speak. The secrets between them would fester like an old wound, and she wanted them gone before she shared her good news. "William, there is something I must tell you."

A sort of pained grimace crossed his face. He leaned his head against the door and a wicked smile took its place. His voice grew heavy with lust. "I do not want to talk now, Alice."

"I can see that." Her blood warmed. "Unfortunately there is something I must tell you, and you will not be pleased."

Scowling, William took a shaky breath.

"It is not that bad." Perhaps she should forget the idea of speaking and adopt William's plan. "Well, it is bad, but not as bad…"

He leaned forward, shoulders to knees.

"William, are you well?"

"My head…spinning, aching."

"Sit a moment." Alice hurried to him and propped her shoulder beneath his arm.

William attempted a few steps on his own, stopped, and leaned into her. His tunic was soaked through with perspiration, his face pale.

"William?"

"Water." He worked his tongue in his mouth as if parched.

This could not be right. "Do you need to be ill?"

"Aye." William clenched his jaw as she helped him onto the bed.

She brought the basin to him.

"Get Ivy."

"Cedric!"

"My lady?" Cedric made his usual clumsy entrance. He glanced at William, stilled and stared. "Is Sir William ill now?"

"Aye." Could it be that her morning's ailment had not been a result of being gravid? Could it be the same ailment that beset Anglesea?

William groaned and grabbed the basin.

Alice could not suppress her flinch as he lost the contents of his stomach.

Cedric paled and scrambled out of the room.

The basin dropped from William's hands, spewing vomit and pottery shards across the floor. "My hands." William peered up, his eyes wild and unfocussed, his breath coming in slow, shallow rasps. Sweat poured down his face. "There is no strength in my hands."

Alice sidestepped the mess and ran to him. She pressed him back onto the bed.

Ivy entered at a run. "What is it?" She leaned over William. Her long delicate fingers pressed into the pulse at his neck.

"Is it what I had?" Alice did not remember sweating like William did, or losing control of her limbs.

"Nay." Ivy shook her head as she examined William. Her face grew still and grave.

He knifed his legs into his belly and yelled.

"William." Ivy grabbed his face and held it firmly. "Listen to me, William. Does your stomach hurt?"

"He was sick." Alice indicated the mess on the floor.

Cedric hovered in the doorway, retching as his horrified gaze locked on the befouled floor.

"Get some buckets and rags."

Cedric pressed his hand to his mouth.

Alice raised her voice. "Cedric!"

He blinked at her.

"We need to clean this up so we can attend Sir William."

Cedric backed out of the room, hit the doorjamb, and froze.

"Go, Cedric."

Ivy murmured to William as she pressed gently on his belly. She glanced at Alice, the concern on her face setting light to Alice's simmering worry. "What did he eat?"

Her stupid mind refused to function. She had not seen William all day. "I do not know. He was out and he came in not long ago."

"Get somebody who will know. I need to know what he ate and drank today."

"What is it, Ivy?"

William jerked onto his side and was violently ill.

"It cannot be." Ivy pressed him down again.

William thrashed out, and Ivy ducked his arm just in time.

"What is it?" Alice wanted to grab Ivy and make her look at her, but Ivy's entire being stayed intent on William.

"Help me strip him," Ivy said.

Glad of something to do, Alice wrestled William out of his boots and chausses.

Constant thrashing from William made the task doubly hard. His dazed eyes locked on something only he saw.

"Ivy!" Alice yelled the other woman's name in a desperate plea. "Tell me what ails him."

Ivy looked up at her, her face deathly pale. "William has been poisoned."

Alice shook her head. "Nay."

"Aye, Alice." Ivy ran the washcloth over William's soaked chest. "I have never seen it before, but all his symptoms suggest black nightshade."

"Nay." Every child knew not to touch the deadly black nightshade berries from the day they could understand. Routinely, Gord had the plant searched for, pulled up, and burned. The berries, the flowers, they were unmistakable. "It could not be. There are none here."

"Alice." Ivy gripped her arms. "I know what I am seeing. William has been poisoned, and deliberately. He would never eat the berries, mistaking them for something else. I saw him take Adam and Richard out at Anglesea and show them the plant and warn them."

"Dear God." Alice's legs crumpled and she grabbed the bedpost for support.

"Aye." Ivy hurried to the door. "I am going to find some vinegar. We will attempt to purge him. You stay with him and make sure he does not harm himself."

"Legs." William writhed on the bed. "They cut off my legs."

"The purge will work, will it not?" Alice took William's arm and held it. "He will be fine once you get the poison out of him."

"I do not know." Ivy slumped in the doorway. "I need to know how much he took and when he took it."

Cedric appeared with two cleaning women.

Ivy drew her shoulders back and marched from the chamber.

"Find me Aonghas." Alice caught Cedric by the arm. "Or anyone else who went scouting with William."

"Alice." William knifed into a tight ball.

"I am here, William." She pressed her hand to his forehead. It was clammy and blazing hot.

He stilled and turned his dead stare in her direction. "Alice."

"Aye, William."

He calmed enough for her to straighten his legs and get him to lie back.

"You must be still."

"They cut off my legs, Alice."

"Nay, William."

He turned his head and stared at her.

"Your legs are right here. I can see them, and touch them."

With a sigh, William closed his eyes. He lay deathly still, his chest rising and falling too slowly.

"The boy said you were looking for me." Aonghas panted as if he had run all the way. "He said it was desperate."

"Ivy says…" The words caught in her throat as if by uttering them she made them real. She could not collapse like this. William needed her. "She says Sir William has been poisoned. Nightshade. We need to know what he ate and drank today."

Aonghas gaped at her. He raised his hands and dropped them again. "Ate? Took no food. My lord said better scouting on a sharp belly."

Could Ivy be wrong? If William had not eaten aught—

"His water skin." Aonghas smacked the door.

"Find it." Hope crashed to the floor.

Aonghas left at a run.

"What is amiss?" Beatrice entered, chuckling. "Aonghas near plowed into me. Are that boy's braies on fire?" She moved deeper into the chamber and her smile vanished. "William."

"He is ill." Alice grabbed Beatrice's hands and clung. "Ivy says he has been poisoned."

"Nay." Beatrice squeezed Alice's fingers. "Who would poison William?"

Dear God, the room swayed about Alice. Who indeed hated William enough to do this?

"Aye." Grim-faced, Ivy bustled through the door. "You two, hold him. He will not want to swallow this. And get some buckets and washcloths ready. This will not be pretty."

If the poison did not kill William, the purge might finish the task. Time and movement blurred into one endless, nightmarish blur.

Alice lost count of the sheeting she stripped from beneath William, the washcloths she and Beatrice used as William expelled the poison from his body.

Agonized screams ripped from him as he convulsed and flailed.

It took hours, with Beatrice and Ivy beside her, working alongside her.

Finally, he stilled and drifted into a restless sleep.

"He is strong." Alice wiped her brow as she stood frowning over William. Damp tendrils of hair stuck to Ivy's face. Her dress bore the stains of William's hard battle against the nightshade. "We have done all we can and it is up to him now."

Beatrice collapsed onto a rug by the hearth. If anything, she looked worse than Ivy. The beautiful gown she had worn for dinner was ripped in places from holding William.

"My lady?" Domnall the older tapped on the doorframe. "Is he...?"

"He must fight the poison now." Alice's voice seemed to come from some part of her that still clung to sanity. "What is it?"

"Aonghas has all the men who scouted with Sir William rounded up in the hall. We added a few malcontents to the bunch. What should we do with them?"

"Find out who did this to him." Beatrice rose from the

hearthrug like a soiled, avenging angel. "Break every one of them until you know who tried to kill my brother."

Domnall nodded, his expression fierce and unbending.

"Wait," Alice called before he left. "I might know who did this."

Domnall jerked his head back. "Tell us, my lady."

Alice sagged against the wall at her back. As they battled for William, she had chained her bitter certainty deep within her and kept it there. "The crofter's hut. The one by the tarn. I know who was in there."

"Alice?" Beatrice staggered toward her.

"Sister Julianna." Alice dared not look at Beatrice. She had lied to Beatrice, and William now paid the price of her deceit and foolishness. "She escaped from the Nunnery. She is quite mad and she would have been more than capable of doing this."

William's uneven rasps of breath sounded loud in the deathly hush about her.

"You knew she was there?" An eerie calm inhabited Beatrice. "The night you came in so late, you came from that awful woman."

"Aye." Alice stood in the condemnation of Domnall's gaze. She had done this to William, as surely as if she had administered the poison. "I thought I could persuade her to return with me and we could send her back to St. Stephen's."

Beatrice's blow caught her across the cheek, so powerful it smashed her head back into the wall.

"You knew." Beatrice hit her again. "Were you in league with her?"

"Nay, Beatrice." Ivy stepped between them. So tiny Beatrice's looming rage dwarfed her. "Alice would not have done that."

"She lied to me." Tears ran down Beatrice's cheeks. "She lied to me and she may have cost my brother his life."

"William is not dead yet." Ivy cupped Beatrice's face in her palms. "And he will not die. Not as long as there is strength in me and in him."

"She killed him." Great sobs wracked Beatrice. "She killed my brother."

"Stop it." Ivy shook Beatrice's head. "She would not kill him because she loves him. And you know already that she bears his child."

Beatrice drew herself up, pushing Ivy's hands away and stared at Alice. "For that reason, and no other, I will not kill you."

* * *

"She does not mean it." Domnall patted Alice's shoulder as he led her down the stairs. "It is her grief and worry that speak for her."

Beatrice would not allow Alice to remain in the sick chamber. Her shouts upset William, and Alice had left. William needed his strength for the battle to come. "Aye, I know that, but if I had told William about Sister when Seamus first brought me the message, none of this would be happening."

"Seamus knew?" Domnall's bellow echoed off the walls. "I will strip an inch of the little turd's hide."

"Nay." Alice squeezed Domnall's arm. They had enough to contend with without the brothers fighting. "It was not his fault. He is young, and Sister put the fear of God into him. I know of what I speak. She did the same to me for years."

Men packed the hall in an eerie silence. Some sat, most stood, tense and alert. Heads spun their way.

"Sir William?" Aonghas rose from his place at the nearest bench.

"Fights for his life." Alice had no words of comfort for him.

Nuns sat amongst the men, their black lifeless habits like doom portents amongst the men. Nuns? Alice knew she stared, but exhaustion and nagging worry bogged her thinking.

The Prioress pushed between two men. "We arrived just before Compline. We brought you the news that Sister Julianna escaped from us." She took Alice's hands in hers. "I hear you have already discovered so."

"I believe she poisoned Sir William."

A low murmur from the men greeted her words.

"Not these. Wager my life." Aonghas gestured to the gathered men. Amongst the men were a number of bruises, black eyes and split lips. "Made sure."

"We need to find her," Alice said.

Men surged to their feet, eagerness to take action pulsing from their taut posture.

Dubhghall stepped forward. "We will tear Tarnwych apart if we must."

"Do it." This she could do. Later, when it would not upset William, she would brave Beatrice again, but for now she needed to do something.

As men streamed from the hall, Sister Margaret stood with her. "I brought a larger party with me this time. Most of my sisters hold prayer vigil for Sir William. Others will join in the search."

The hall spun about Alice and she dropped onto a hearth chair. She could not afford weakness. William needed her to stay strong and do what must be done. Thus far, as a wife, she had been a dismal failure.

Sister Margaret sat across from her. "You must eat, Lady Alice."

Alice's stomach roiled. "I cannot."

"Change at least. Your appearance will increase the speculation and fear throughout the keep."

The prioress was right, and Alice nodded. "My clothes are all in my bedchamber, and I cannot go in there."

Sister Margaret fixed a keen stare on her. "And why is that, Lady Alice?"

How to explain what she had done? Under Sister Margaret's fox-stare she had only one course. "I knew Sister Julianna was here, and I did not tell anyone."

Sister Margaret rearranged her skirts about her knees.

"And now William has been poisoned, and we are certain it

was Sister Julianna. Lady Beatrice blames me for William being so ill and will not allow me near him."

"I see." Sister Margaret adjusted her crucifix. "It was certainly foolish not to say something about Sister Julianna being back as soon as you knew."

William's poisoning weighed on her until she could barely sit straight. "It is my fault he might—" That tiny word that she could not utter. It meant a life forever empty of William's smile, the twinkle in his clear-sky eyes, his arms about her, the resonant murmur of his rich voice.

"No tears, Lady Alice." Sister Margaret offered her a handkerchief. "The time has not yet come for tears. This is the time for firm resolve and strong prayers."

Alice did her best to stem the flow of tears, but she did not feel resolved. She wanted to crawl into a corner and weep the pain out.

"But I have a more pressing matter to discuss with you." Sister Margaret frowned at her crucifix. "Whilst you were above, I did some thinking. I spoke to a couple of those who have been here for as long as you have."

"There is nothing more pressing than William. For me."

Sister Margaret snorted. "And yet here you sit, too frightened to brave your sister by marriage and take your rightful place by your man's side."

Alice jerked in her seat. If nothing else, Sister had stemmed her tears, and replaced them with a strong urge to smack the woman about her wimpled ear. What did a nun know of these matters?

Raising her brow, Sister Margaret chuckled. "Aye, you did not like that, did you?"

"Our hot words were upsetting William. That is why I left."

"Ah." Sister Margaret smiled.

The smile irked Alice further. "It is. He needs his rest."

"He needs his wife." She flapped her hand. "But whilst you are finding your courage, tell me of your other husbands."

"Eh?"

"Sir William came to see me a few days ere. We spoke of Sister. We believe she used his departure to escape." Sister Margaret leaned forwards. "Amongst other things, we spoke of your husbands. The ones who came before William. They all met with an early death, did they not?"

"Aye?" Alice's nape prickled a warning. "The first William died with his friend. They drowned." It had been a tragic accident. "John slipped in the rain and fell from the castle walls." Unease grew with each word she said.

"Is it possible he was not alone on the battlements?"

"Aye." As sure footed as any knight, John walked the battlements nightly. "Steven died from a summer chill."

"Who nursed him?"

"Sister Julianna." Her stomach roiled. Please let them be reaching the wrong conclusion.

"She is quite mad you know," Sister Margaret said.

And dangerous. Perhaps deadly. "Aye."

* * *

Grasping her courage, Alice opened the door to her bedchamber.

William lay on his back, pale and vulnerable. Her William, so vital and yet struck down and battling for each breath he took.

"You are not welcome here." Fierce, loyal, a bitch protecting her pup, Beatrice rose from her place by the fire.

Beatrice loved her brother, but then, so did Alice. "I do not require your welcome. That is my husband who lies there, and my place is beside him."

Beatrice placed herself between Alice and the bed. "It is because of you he clings to life."

"Nay." Aye, she should have said something about Sister, but she hadn't poisoned William. "I did not feed him nightshade. I might have prevented this by speaking sooner, but none of that changes the fact that he is my man. I vowed to love him and honor him, in front of God, you, and the rest of Tarnwych. And that is what I intend to do."

"Love him?" Beatrice tossed her head with harsh laugh. "You do not love William. You tolerate him. We have all seen it."

William needed her more. Alice shrugged. "He is my everything."

"Leave it, Bea." Ivy brought a basin of water to Alice. "I was about to bathe him in cool water, but if you are here, Beatrice and I can get some air, and maybe something to eat."

Beatrice jammed her hands on her hips. "I am not leaving her alone with him."

"Aye, you are." Ivy hooked her arm through Beatrice's. "She is his wife. You are his sister. She wins."

Alice approached William. His body and face, so beloved to her, yet lacking the vital essence that drew her to him. Her hands trembled and water slopped onto her gown. On a table by the bed, she set the basin.

"William?" She stroked his clammy cheek, just beginning to prickle with new growth. Such a fine, beautiful man, her William. Strong and noble, all that her girlish heart had dreamed a knight should be. "It is Alice."

He murmured and pressed his face to her hand. Even knowing she might have imagined it, the gesture gave Alice hope.

She dipped the cloth into the tepid water and wrung it out. "I am going to bathe you now." It did not seem right to not speak with him. "Ivy says it helps keep your fever down." She ran the cloth over his forehead and neck. Pushing the covers lower, she moved to his chest. "Ivy says the poison is mostly out now, and you must fight the lingering effects."

If he were able, William might laugh and tell her Ivy always had a lot to say about everything. Or cup her face and tell her not to worry. But William lay like a helpless babe. William could not die. He must not die.

Tears trickled onto her cheeks. The harder Alice tried to stop them, the faster they came. Sister Margaret had rebuked her tears, but they would not stop.

"Stay with me, William." She pressed her palm to his chest. Like a faint bringer of hope, his heart thumped beneath her touch. "Stay with me, and I will do better. Be better." She dipped the cloth in the water and brought it back to him. "I do not know why I did not tell you Sister was hereabouts, but I thought I could spare you. This once, I wanted to deal with her."

William thrashed his head. His eyes opened, glazed and uncertain.

"William?"

With a moan he shut them again.

"I am so sorry." She might not have given him the poison, but she had brought this on him. "If you stay with me, I will make it better." And if he left, she would never have the chance to tell him all that lurked in her heart. Perhaps some part of William could hear her, and understand her words. "I love you," she whispered. "I might have loved you from the moment you entered Tarnwych." She scrubbed fresh tears from her cheeks and sniffed. "I loved you then because you were the most beautiful man I had ever seen. You still are, for all you are so pale. I thought you would despise me for being plain, but you made me feel pretty. You have never once looked at me as if I was lacking."

Nay, caught in the blue beam of William's gaze Alice had felt like the only woman in the world. The one he had chosen. "I can be a better wife. I know I can. If only you will give me the chance."

William sighed in his sleep.

Alice moved the basin away and perched on the bed. In this bed, she had discovered what it was to be a woman. Under William's care she had learned not to fear and dread that part of her marriage. Here he had freed her.

Moving carefully so as not to disturb him, Alice crawled onto the bed beside him. The need to touch him overwhelmed her, and she lay on her side and pressed her forehead to his still arm. "Stay with me, William. With me and our baby."

* * *

A hard shake dragged her out of the warm dark.

"Wake up, Alice." Beatrice stood by the bed, her face cold and drawn. "You fell asleep."

Perhaps she should apologize for that, too, but Alice sat up and rubbed her tired, gritty eyes. "I wanted to be near him."

For an instant, Beatrice's face softened before it grew hard again. "I hope you did not disturb him."

Alice whirled to check on William. There appeared to be no change, but he had rested quietly beside her.

"Anyway." Beatrice folded her arms across her chest. "I came to get you because there is someone here to see William. When I told him William could not come, he insisted on speaking with you."

"Who is it?"

Beatrice stalked out of the chamber.

"I will stay here until you return." Ivy spoke from by the hearth. "Do not mind Beatrice. She does not mean half the things she says."

Alice eased the crick in her neck. "Then she should not say them."

"Aye, now you sound like Garrett." Ivy stood and stretched her back. "But you are needed downstairs. The poacher is here, the one who shot William, and he will not leave until he has spoken to you."

* * *

The air in the hall oozed tension. Alice entered quietly and could read nothing in the faces of those present.

Aonghas stood with the Domnalls, all three of them. Between

them cowered a wiry man of medium height, his new clothes still stiff.

"My lady?" The man approached her, kneading his hat. "I am Caomh. I am the one who shot Sir William."

"It was an accident, I hear." If guilt brought the man here, why could Beatrice not have dealt with him? Perhaps because Beatrice did not feel inclined to help her in any manner at this point.

"That is just it, my lady." Caomh put a healthy distance between himself and Aonghas's sons. "It were not an accident."

Domnall younger growled and lunged for the man. "Bow, you cur, before our lady."

"Let him speak." Domnall senior cuffed him.

Caomh took a few more steps away and executed a wobbly bow.

Domnall senior strode beside Alice. Legs braced, chest thrust out, he silently dared anybody to come near her. "You wanted to tell Lady Alice what you know, and after I heard it, I agreed, but I do not trust you. Take one step closer and your wife will be a widow."

Caomh leaped back and into middle Domnall.

"Get on with it." Middle Domnall shoved him.

"I shot him apurpose." Caomh spoke in a breathy rush. "That nun, the one you are all looking for, she gave me food to do it."

Middle Domnall grabbed him by the collar and shook him like a rat. "You murderous little churl. I will have your head for this."

"Put him down." Alice needed to hear the rest of the truth, however unwelcome. "Sister Julianna gave you food to kill William?"

"Aye, my lady." Domnall's grip on his tunic made his voice rasp. His toes scrabbled for grip on the floor. "I would not have done it, my lady. Only Mags had just lost the little one, and the others had nothing to fill their bellies. I could not ask her to lose another child."

Would she have done any different for this child of hers? Nay. Alice touched her belly. "Why are you telling me this?"

"We heard about what happened to Sir William." Caomh coughed against Domnall's tightening hold. "And he has been good to us, has Sir William. Mags urged me to come. She said you need to know what that nun is up to." The last words barely escaped the constriction of his tunic.

"Put him down." All her earlier suspicions crashed about her in an exhausting wave. Before her conversation with Sister Margaret, she might have thought Caomh lied. But the man had no reason to lie. "Has Sister Julianna been located?"

"Not yet, my lady." Aonghas shifted his feet.

"Gresby found signs that somebody other than him and his boys had been in the stables. He thinks she slept there the night before we went out with Sir William." Older Domnall stuck his hands in his belt. "And there's more, my lady. That time Sir William fell off his horse, it were not an accident either. She put a splinter in his saddle. One of Gresby's lads found it while he were cleaning the tack."

"Find her." Alice let her harsh gaze sweep all the men standing about the hall. "And Caomh must help you do it. None of us are safe until she is found."

Chapter Twenty-Five

William breathed in water and came awake choking.

Beatrice loomed over him, smiling. "You are awake."

"Are you trying to drown me?"

Beatrice frowned at the washcloth in her hand. "I was bathing your fevered brow."

"Try not to." He felt like a herd of bullocks had trampled him. "Where is Alice?"

Beatrice hovered, her cloth dripping water onto the bed. "About."

Alice had been curled up beside him, wrapped about his arm like a child, and now she was gone. Had he imagined her here? The blasted soup in his brain would not clear enough for him to think. "I need her."

"We will send for her."

Beatrice made a terrible liar, always had. "I want her, Bea."

He was weaker than a newborn foal, and the dark claimed him again.

* * *

Alice made another mark on the maps Gord had brought her. Tarnwych demesne stretched out on parchment on the table before her. So much land, she had not realized, and so many places for Sister to hide.

Beatrice guarded William's door like a dragon. Alice's skirmishes with the other woman left her bruised, but she braced for another one soon. After she had given the men their instructions for the search, she planned to spend the rest of her morning with William.

Domnall prodded the map with his large, square finger. "There is only this area left to search. We have found no recent signs of her in the keep, but there have been traces of someone hard by. Bedamned woman moves like a wraith."

All through the long early morning hours they had searched. Rare glimpses, lingering signs of Sister's passage, but nothing more.

Young Will had been combing the area with the keep hounds. Dark shadows underlined his eyes, and he swayed.

"Find your pallet, Will." She gave the boy an encouraging smile.

He pushed an unruly lock of hair out of his eyes. "I am well, my lady. I will give the dogs a little rest, they eat now, and we will get back to it."

"Rest, boy." Aonghas glowered at him. "Grand job, but useless if not rested."

Will's lip quivered and he dropped his head. Despite the look of mature resolve on his face, he was just a boy. "I want to find her."

"We all want to find her." Alice leaned across the table and tousled his hair. "And we will find her, but you are dead on your feet."

"Sir William would not rest." Up came Will's chin, determination back on his face.

"Of course he would." Weary and disheveled like the rest of them, Beatrice entered the hall. "William knows a battle is rarely won in a day. A warrior needs to know when to retreat and nurture his strength."

Will absorbed her words with a thoughtful nod. "The dogs could do with a sleep."

"There you are." Beatrice clasped his shoulder. "Know when those you command need to regain their strength before they join the fray."

When this was over, Alice dearly hoped she could repair the rift between them. Beatrice made a fierce ally and a wonderful friend. She made a formidable enemy. "Is there something amiss with William?"

"Nay." Beatrice folded her arms across her chest. "He woke."

Alice staggered under the strength of emotion that surged through her. William awake must mean William on the mend.

"Grand." Aonghas managed the words she could not.

"He is still very weak." Beatrice crossed her arms. She kept her eyes averted. "He asked me to fetch you."

Alice left the hall at a run. Aonghas could take care of managing the men. She had far more important things to do.

In the bedchamber, Ivy sat beside William. Her quiet smile confirmed the news.

Alice braced against the doorjamb to stop her knees from crumbling. "He awoke?"

"Aye." Ivy tidied around William, putting rags back in the basin. "It seems the worst is over."

"He will...?"

Tears swam in Ivy's eyes. "Aye, he will live."

Alice met her gaze, her eyes misted, and they shared their silent communion of profound joy.

Ivy broke the contact and moved her things away from the bed. "He will be very weak for a while yet. We will have to keep him as quiet as we can, but he will live."

"I can do that." Alice walked to the bed and climbed up beside him. His color had improved, and his breathing seemed to come easier. She could do anything now that she knew William would live with her to see it done.

"He asked for you." Ivy cocked her head at William. "You should stay until he next wakes."

"Aye." Nothing would move her from his side until she could look into his face again and see her William there.

"Send Cedric for me if you need me." Ivy opened the door.

"Could you make sure people know?" Alice's voice shook and she cleared her throat. "About William."

"Aye." Ivy shut the door behind her.

Alice eased onto her side beside William. His chest rose and fell in wondrous, deep, steady breaths. His skin was cool to her touch and she pressed her cheek against his shoulder. Emotion gathered and grew like a flaming ball behind her breasts. She had no tears, no shouts of joy, nothing except this burning need to touch him.

William stirred. "Alice?"

"Aye."

"There you are." His fingers twined with hers, and he closed his eyes.

Ivy checked back in after noon prayers and left a bowl of broth to stay warm beside the fire. "When he next wakes, see if you can get him to eat. He has nothing in him, and he will need food to regain his strength."

William woke a short while later. He pulled a face when Alice fetched the broth.

"You have to take it." Alice brandished the spoon close to his mouth.

"I am not a babe." William took the spoon from her, but it slipped out of his hands and soiled the bedlinen. "Damn!"

Alice picked it up. "Shall we try again?"

His eyes met hers and promised a touch of retribution when he could. "Feed me, woman."

Alice cajoled him into a fair portion of the bowl. Restive, she fiddled about the room. With William awake, emotion prickled beneath her skin and she could not settle. She stripped the broth-stained linens and replaced them. Added more wood to the fire. Even picked up a cloth and dusted the furniture.

All the while, his steady gaze tracked her about the room. "Alice?"

"Do you require aught else? I could go and find Ivy and ask what else you may eat, if you like?"

"Alice?"

"I believe you should sleep some more. If you can, that is."

"Alice?"

"Or perhaps you want to dress?"

"Cease, Alice." His voice carried a heavy trace of weariness. "You are making me dizzy with your bustling about." He patted the bed beside him. "Come here and stay with me."

"Indeed." Alice climbed up beside him. The moment pressed heavy on her shoulders.

He clasped her fingers and gave a weak tug. "Closer. That bloody broth has worn me out, and I need to rest. But after, Alice, you can tell me what has you jumping around the room, and why I am no stronger than a puff of smoke."

Which was exactly the reason she bustled about in the first place. "I will."

He closed his eyes, and soon drifted into a peaceful sleep. Beyond the casement, winter mocked his efforts in a driving snow that pattered against the glass. Alice let the drift and swirl lull her.

Truth must out, because Beatrice's anger brought one thing clear before her. Lies, evasions, half-truths had beset her marriage from the start. God had given her another chance to do things right with William, and she would use it.

The door opened and Beatrice crept in. "Is he asleep?"

"Aye." She did not care how much Beatrice glowered at her, she was staying right here. Her rightful place. Except, Beatrice looked a little furtive as she slid deeper into the room. Alice sat up.

"I am glad that he is sleeping." Beatrice seemed fascinated by the drape of her girdle.

"Aye, he needs his rest."

"Aye." Smoothing her dress, Beatrice sighed. "I have been speaking with Ivy. Indeed, Ivy did most of the speaking, and I had to listen."

"Oh?"

"She...Ivy that is, thinks that I have been...harsh with you." Beatrice stared out the window at the snow. "Needlessly harsh."

"Do you think that?"

"Alice." Beatrice lowered her voice and glanced at her. "This would be a lot easier if you did not keep asking questions."

Alice snapped her mouth shut. She agreed with Ivy but had not the stones to say as much.

"William is my brother," Beatrice said. "And we are a close family, so when his life was threatened, it made me want to..." She made a slashing motion with her hand. "Do something to fix it, make it right."

She envied the loving bond between siblings. How could she be angry with Beatrice when they shared a love for the same man? Had they switched places, she could not say she would have done differently.

"It was unfair to blame you for what that awful woman did." A fierce expression twisted Beatrice's features. "I have to tell you if I see her, things will not go well for her."

"As with me." Beatrice would have to wait her turn, because Alice had a whole lifetime of Sister's malice to address.

"William said you were loyal." She nodded at her brother. "And I can understand that, perhaps even respect it. I still believe you were wrong not to tell us about the escape, but I was wrong to try to bar you from William."

"I did not allow you to do so for long."

"Indeed." Beatrice rolled her eyes. "But I made a hard time harder for you, and for that I am sorry."

She could not have hoped for more. Blinding light shone through the angry clouds of dissent between them. "As am I sorry for not telling you about Sister. I knew that night I should not have gone to her, but I felt I owed it."

Beatrice snorted.

"Not just to her but to all of you. There has been so much trouble with Sister. Just this once, I wanted to make it go away without dragging everyone else into my battle."

"We are family now." Beatrice stepped closer. "We face our battles together, and that makes us stronger."

Family. The word chimed sweet as a prayer bell through Alice. People united by bonds strong enough to weather any storm.

Beatrice sat on the bed near her. "Can we be friends again?"

"Aye." She would truly like that. "Or we could be sisters. If you like."

Tears glistened in Beatrice's eyes. She grabbed Alice into a hard hug and held her. "Sisters it is."

"But no more slapping me." Alice's voice was muffled in Beatrice's shoulder.

Beatrice shook them both with her laughter. "Agreed."

"And I do love William," Alice said. "I love him more than you can know."

"Have you told him?"

"Nay. I plan to do so once he wakes."

Beatrice pulled away. "I think you just did."

Alice whirled.

William lay on his side, his eyes fixed on her with a soft light. "I think it is time for you to go, Bea."

"You could be right." Beatrice rose and shook her skirts out. "But I shall be back later to torment you with more of my nursing.

William groaned and grimaced. "Spare me that. But we will talk later."

Beatrice walked to the door.

"And Sweet Bea?" William stopped her. "We will also speak later of you barring my wife from my chamber. And the slapping."

Heart thundering, Alice faced William.

"You love me then?" He raised a dark brow.

"Aye." Sick nerves twisted her belly. "I feel you must know, but I understand that you do not share the same tender regard."

"You do, do you?" William smirked. "And why would I not love you?"

Had the nightshade rotted his head? "You are the peacock."

"Eh?"

"The peacock. You are the peacock, and I"—she pressed a finger to her chest—"am the dull brown wren."

"A peacock?" William laughed. "I am not sure I want that shared around the barracks." His face grew serious. "And as for the being a dull brown wren...Alice." Her name uttered thus by William touched her like a caress.

He grew pensive as he twined his fingers with hers. "My Alice is never a dull-brown wren. She is fire and joy and sweetness. She fills my life to overflowing and holds my heart in her tiny, little hands." He kissed first one hand and then the other. "She is my help mate, my lover, my comfort, and my friend. That she loves me makes me the most fortunate man in all the kingdom. And that I love her..." He shrugged. "It was inevitable."

"William." His illness must have scrambled his brains because William could not love her. He could not say those wonderful things about her and mean them. "You do not have to tell me this because you heard me say I love you. You are very kind."

"Kind?" William chuckled. He tugged her to lie beside him. "Nay, Alice. I am conceited, arrogant, judgmental, and ill-tempered. All of which you have seen in abundance. But I do love you, Alice, and I vow to do better." A gentle kiss pressed to her forehead. "I heard you the day when you crawled in beside me. I, too, will do better. I will make you a better husband."

"You could not have heard me." Alice tried to think what else she had said that day.

"I did not remember when I first woke, but it is all coming

back to me." He groaned and closed his eyes. "God knows, I have little else to do but sleep and think."

"Perhaps you will not love me when I tell you my part in your poisoning."

"I already know your part," he said. "You should have told me she was about, but you already know that."

"Did Beatrice tell you?"

"Aye." William pressed his forehead to hers. "It is past, Alice. We need to move forward. Which reminds me, are you ever going to tell me about our babe?"

"Beatrice did not—"

"Nay, she did not tell me." He placed his palm on her belly. "I know this body like I know my own. I have two sisters, a mother, and Nurse, who do not spare me the details of their women's trials. I suspected a little while ago, but when you were so ill, I grew sure."

"You never said." Clearly he could also keep the truth hidden.

"I wanted you to tell me. Why did you not?"

This was a little trickier to explain. Nay, it really wasn't—she had bared so much of herself to him already. "I thought you might leave my bed if you knew the task was accomplished."

"Why in the name of God would I do that?" He jerked his head back. "I enjoy being in your bed and intend to stay there for the rest of my life. And Alice?"

"Aye."

"I will give you as many babies as it is safe for you to bear." His eyes gleamed wicked. "Only perhaps not right this minute."

"There is more you should know." Alice snuggled closer. "I wish to tell you all of it."

Alice spoke first of the days before William arrived at Tarn-wych and all that led to her meeting Sister beside the tarn that night.

Then she went further back, sharing her suspicions about her dead husbands with him.

Once she spoke of her dream, the mist surrounding the

memory cleared. Sister had brought a son with her to Yarborough. A boy born like Mathew, but unlike Mathew, Sister's child had no loving family to shield him. He had existed as a shadowy figure in Alice's life. Without even a name, he had flit around the edges of life in the busy keep. Until the day he had seen her playing by the lake that fronted Yarborough. Sister had stepped away for a moment. Alice no longer recalled why Sister went, only that she had been alone when the boy had found her. Their game had grown more boisterous. Strong for his age, the boy had grabbed a very young Alice and swung her over the water. Sister had returned in time to see what she thought was the boy trying to drown Alice. Her screams had brought the keep knights running, and the boy had been struck down. With chaos, screaming, and death surrounding her, Alice had huddled in a pool of the boy's blood until a knight carried her back to the keep.

By the time she finished, they were both wrung out. William tightened his arms about Alice.

Safe and loved.

Chapter Twenty-Six

Alice woke to the prickly sensation of being watched. Opening her eyes seemed too much to ask of someone beside a peacefully resting William.

"Alice," Sister said.

Alice froze. She opened her eyes.

Sister stood on William's side the bed, her hair snarled and her habit filthy and torn. Unholy fire burned in her eyes as she stared at William. Light from the casement glimmered on the dagger blade Sister held. The sort of dagger used for hunting, large and sharp and deadly.

Alice scrabbled off her side of the bed. In his weakened state William would not be able to fend her off. "What are you doing, Sister?"

"The sinner." Sister waved the dagger at William. "He must be cut from the flock."

Alice edged closer to Sister. "Nay, Sister, he is my husband."

"Ah, Alice." Tears sprung into Sister's eyes. "Look what has become of you that you would defend such evil."

"Perhaps you are right, Sister. We should sit before the hearth and discuss it."

"The time for discussion is passed." Sister adjusted her grip on the dagger. "The Lord has shown my path, and I must be obedient."

"Nay." If she could get between Sister and William. "Let us pray first."

Sister blinked. "Pray?"

"Aye."

William stirred and flung himself onto his back.

Sister's gaze snapped back to him.

The linens had fallen, baring his chest.

"Nay." Sister shook her head, waggling the dagger at Alice. "I see what you are doing. You mean to trick me into praying with you. You seek to turn me from my purpose."

"Alice?" William opened his eyes.

Sister shrieked and raised the dagger.

Alice seized the chamber pot and shattered it over Sister's head.

Sister dropped like a stone. Blood trickled into the noxious mess surrounding her.

William peered over the edge of the bed. "Dear God."

Alice grabbed the bedpost and dry heaved.

The door flew open and Cedric barreled through. On his heels came middle Domnall and Seamus. As one, they looked to Alice, William, and then Sister.

"You hit her with the chamber pot?" Domnall clapped a hand over his mouth.

"It was the nearest thing." Alice collapsed on the end of the bed. The smell alone brought her to her knees.

Seamus snorted and turned his back, shoulders shaking.

Domnall's eyes twinkled, whilst poor Cedric tried to choke back his laughter.

William glanced at Alice and then back to Sister. "Not the most heroic ending."

* * *

Alice managed to keep William confined to their bed for another two days. By the third day she could either let him rise or bash him over the head for being the worst invalid in the kingdom.

Over the two days, Tarnwych slowly settled after the excitement. Sister had come to her senses before the laughter in their chamber had stopped. The Prioress had waited only long enough to clean Sister up before they left for St. Stephen's. A large armed guard escorted them. William had insisted on clemency. Sister was an ill woman. The death of her child had left scars that had festered over the years. Beatrice had been all for stringing Sister from the nearest tree. But that was Beatrice for you.

William agreed to go no further than the hall on his first outing. Fortunately, the weather aided their cause. Deep snow fell all around Tarnwych, and it would be days before it cleared enough for William to venture out.

He sat before a roaring hearth fire, peevishly insisting that Beatrice, Ivy, and Alice keep him company.

Alice replaced the blanket on William's lap.

He huffed and pushed it to the ground. "God's teeth, woman! I am not in my dotage."

She had tried. Alice left the blanket where it lay and took the seat beside him.

"You look like death." Beatrice picked at the knot in her yarn.

Ivy took it from her. "He is well enough if he does not overdo it."

The hall doors flew open on a gust of wind and snow. Two fur-mounded lumps staggered in with it and barred the door behind them.

William rose, his hand moving to his waist. But Alice had instructed Cedric to hide his sword, and the lad had done a fine job of it. "Blast."

"Sweet Mother of God." The nearest lump stomped his feet, showering the floor with melting snow. "Is it always so cold this far north?"

Beatrice shot to her feet. Her embroidery dropped to the floor and she stepped on it, her stare fixed on the man.

From the furs a tall, dark-haired man emerged. He dropped them to the ground with a grunt of distaste. "Sweet Bea." A smile lit his handsome, carved features. "I have fought my way through the depths of winter to find you." He opened his arms. "The least you can do is get your pretty ass over here."

"Garrett." William winked at Alice.

Beatrice pelted across the hall and straight into Garrett's arms.

At their feet, Adam bounced on his bottom, waving his little arms in the air and yelling, "Da!"

Richard trotted to his parents and flung his arms around their knees.

Garrett released his wife and swung his oldest son into his arms. "I swear, Richard, you have grown a hundred feet since I saw you last."

"This is my Garrett." Beatrice tucked herself beneath his arm as they turned and walked toward Alice and William.

"I am glad to meet you, Lady Alice." Garrett gave her a grin that set Alice's heart aflutter. Not as handsome as her William, but the man had a roguish charm she would have to be entombed not to appreciate. He turned to William with a sniff. "Are you an old woman now?"

William squared his shoulders. "Then that would make you the sorry sod about to have the piss beaten out of him by an old woman."

"I am all a-quiver." Garrett sent William an evil grin and snatched Adam. "Shall Da rearrange your uncle's pretty face?"

Adam chortled and bobbed in his father's arms.

"I like his face just as it is." Alice stepped between the two men. She suspected Garrett jested but she took no chances with her man. She had grown rather partial to his pretty face.

Ivy made a choking noise, and all heads swung her way.

She was so pale, Alice moved swiftly into a catching position.

Ivy's attention stayed fixed on the second figure, her hand clasped to her throat.

"Aye." Garrett nodded at the man placing his furs carefully on a table. Flaxen haired and broader than Garrett, he looked drawn, as if recently ill. "He insisted on coming."

"Tom." Ivy took a step forward.

"Tom!" Beatrice broke into a run.

Garrett grabbed her about her waist.

"It is Tom." Beatrice slapped at his arms.

"Aye." Garrett jerked his head toward Ivy. "And he is not here for you."

Ivy took another few steps.

Tom waited by the door, his hungry gaze locked on the tiny woman. "I have been a trifle laid up."

"I heard." Ivy reached Tom and stopped before him.

He towered above her.

"Are they just going to stand there?" Beatrice twisted her hand in Garrett's tunic.

"Hush, sweeting." Garrett tucked her against his side. "Let them be."

Ivy drew back her fist and punched Tom in the shoulder. "You scared me." Ivy hit him again. "Do not ever scare me like that again."

"Ivy." Tom caught her fist in his huge paw. "I could never leave you."

"Oh, that is very good." Beatrice sighed and gave a happy smile. "He is learning."

Tom swept Ivy into his arms and kissed her.

William chuckled and turned to give the couple their privacy. "He is learning rather fast."

With a snort, Garrett turned away as well. "It took the silly sod long enough."

"Aye." William resumed his seat and pulled Alice onto his lap. "Some men take a while to see what is right before them."

* * *

Books in the Sir Arthur's Legacy series include **Sweet Bea** and **My Lady Faye,** which come before **Conquering William**. All can be read standalone, but reading them in order gives you extra insight into the characters. Next sibling to find their happily-ever-after is oldest brother, and heir, Roger, in **Defying Roger** (previously published as Roger's Bride)

* * *

A battle for the heart.

As oldest son and heir, Roger of Anglesea must marry and do so advantageously. It is his duty. But his tough warrior exterior hides the heart of a true romantic. Deep down, he longs for the love and companionship shared by his parents and newly married siblings.

Strong-willed and fiery, Kathryn of Mandeville is an "unnatural" lady. She wants nothing more than her independence and to follow in the footsteps of the Viking shield maidens of old. Once her sister, Matty, is wed, Kathryn is free to follow her chosen path.

When Matty flees her arranged marriage to Roger, however, their respective plans are routed. Kathryn proposes an alliance. She will help Roger find Matty, and Roger will keep her beloved sister safe from their cruel father. As the hunt for Matty takes an unexpected turn, a fiery mutual attraction flares, and Kathryn and Roger quickly discover they are fighting a battle within—one for the heart—and one that draws them ever closer.

* * *

Read Defying Roger

* * *

Chapter 1

Roger wanted to jab his dagger into his eye. He despised failure, hated it, yet judging by his intended bride's reaction to his courtship performance, he and failure now shared a bed. Love and war, with a clear plan, a man could manage one in much the same manner as the other. Hadn't a lifetime under the guiding hand of Sir Arthur of Anglesea set this lesson into Roger's marrow?

Except, Roger's courtship had veered from the battle plan.

Lady Mathilda had accepted his flowers with her sweet, lovely smile and even moved her skirts to make place for him beside her. Since then, his plan had moved from disarray into rout. Lady Mathilda should be sighing by now, at least peeping at him from beneath thick dark lashes. He'd watched William turn a woman sweet a hundred times.

In her haste to put distance between them, she inched her

curvy hips down the bench, almost tipping onto her pert ass. She pressed a fluttering hand to her throat. "Five sons, Sir Roger?"

"Aye." He softened his tone. A woman would not enjoy being bellowed at like a man-at-arms. "My mother had four, and the two girls. I wager we could do better." He gave her a tiny nudge. "Aye?"

Agape, Lady Mathilda shook her head. Her nut-brown hair made a silky swish on the bench.

Too abrupt? Perhaps. He should have refrained from the nudge for certain, but desperation crept through him with each passing moment. "Of course, that is if you are willing, my lady."

Gentle, his mother had urged. Woo her with sweet words and smiles.

Roger smiled.

About the Author

Sarah Edwards is also published under the name Sarah Hegger

Born British and raised in South Africa, Sarah Hegger suffers from an incurable case of wanderlust. Her match? A hot Canadian engineer, whose marriage proposal she accepted six short weeks after they first met. Together they've made homes in seven different cities across three different continents (and back again once or twice). If only it made her multilingual, but the best she can manage is idiosyncratic English, fluent Afrikaans, conversant Russian, pigeon Portuguese, even worse Zulu and enough French to get herself into trouble.

Mimicking her globe trotting adventures, Sarah's career path began as a gainfully employed actress, drifted into public relations, settled a moment in advertising, and eventually took root in the fertile soil of her first love, writing. She also moonlights as a wife and mother. She currently lives in Ottawa, Canada, filling her empty nest with fur babies. Part footloose buccaneer, part quixotic observer of life, Sarah's restless heart is most content when reading or writing books.

Hegger's utterly delightful first Ghost Falls contemporary is what other romance novels want to grow up to be." – Publisher's Weekly, Best Books of 2017

"The very talented Hegger kicks off an enjoyable new series set in the small Utah town of Ghost Falls. This charming and fun-filled book has everything from passion and humor to betrayal and revenge." –
Jill M Smith, RT Books Reviews 2017 – Contemporary Love and Laughter Nominee

Becoming Bella
"Hegger excels at depicting familial relationships and friendships of all kinds, including purely platonic friendships between women and men. Tears, laughter, and a dollop of suspense make a memorable story that readers will want to revisit time and again."
Publisher's Weekly, Starred Review

"...you have a terrific new romance that Hegger fans are going to love. Don't miss out!"
Jill M. Smith – RT Book Reviews

Blatantly Blythe
"Ms. Hegger has delivered another captivating read for this series in this book that was packed with emotion..." Bec, Bookmagic Review, Harlequin Junkie, HJ Recommends.

Nobody's Fool
"Hegger offers a breath of fresh air in the romance genre." – Terri Dukes, RT Book Reviews

Nobody's Princess
"Hegger continues to live up to her rapidly growing reputation for breathing fresh air into the romance genre." – Terri Dukes, RT Book Reviews

"I have read the entire Willow Park Series. I have loved each of the books ... Nobody's Princess is my favorite of all time." Harlequin Junkie, Top Pick

321

Also by Sarah Edwards

Sarah Edwards also writes as Sarah Hegger

Sports Romance
Ottawa Titans Series
Roughing

Contemporary Romance
Passing Through Series
Drove All Night
Ticket To Ride
Walk On By

Ghost Falls Series
Positively Pippa
Becoming Bella
Blatantly Blythe
Loving Laura

Willow Park Romances
Nobody's Angel
Nobody's Fool
Nobody's Princess

Medieval Romance
Sir Arthur's Legacy Series
Sweet Bea

My Lady Faye

Conquering William

Defying Roger

Henry's Honor

Love & War Series

The Marriage Parley

The Betrothal Melee

Western Historical Romance

The Soiled Dove Series

Sugar Ellie

Standalone

The Bride Gift

Bad Wolfe On The Rise

Wild Honey